King Satin's Realm

The Legend of Draconis

The Legend Unfolds

in

Book I

Janet Taylor-Perry

Semi-finalist, 2014 Faulkner Wisdom Competition

King Satin's Realm

The Legend of Draconis

The Legend Unfolds

in

Book I

ISBN-13:
978-1530286959

ISBN-10:
1530286956

Other Books by Janet Taylor-Perry

The Raiford Chronicles:

Lucky Thirteen
http://amzn.to/1ld8grm
Heartless
http://amzn.to/1iWuYmP
Broken
http://goo.gl/6YTwyz
Whatever It Takes
http://goo.gl/1eLv66

Dedication

This book is dedicated to my five children, Matthew, Nathan, Mary Catherine, Caleb, and Samuel, whose vivid imaginations personified our precious pets, Satin, P.C., Lightning, and Kiki.

𝕯isclaimer

𝕬ll   people, places, and incidents in the following story come from my imagination, if inspired by real-life incidents. This is my labor of love and the first novel I ever penned. This novel is labeled as fantasty, but it is not intended for young children. It deals with some dark issues that some might find disturbing.

𝕬cknowledgements

𝕬 million thank-you's to my family and loved ones for their continued support and encouragement.

I can never express enough appreciation for my beta readers: Christopher Stowe, Rob Finney, Rebecca Vaughn, Randall Krzak, and Megan Fox.

Lottie Brent Boggan, you are the best editor and my dearest friend, and much love to my proofreaders—Mary Catherine Perry and Rob Finney.

Nidia Hernadez and Sarai Storment, how can I tell you how much your work with the Spanish translations means to me? Nidia, I also must acknowledge you as a beta reader times three.

Betty Brock, I owe you a great debt for all the research you did to help me identify curare.

For my small group from Mississippi Writers Guild— Christopher Stowe, Dorian Randall, and Elizabeth McKinley, mucho gracias for all the feedback on this book. You stuck with me for over a year to complete this task.

To The Red Dog Writers, Judy, Lottie, Lydia, Carlene, Vivian, Edrie, Joyce, much obliged for your continued encouragement.

Thanks to the Mississippi Gulf Coast Writers for your support and to the promoters of Celebrate Literacy.

And all my friends and critics from thenextbigwriter.com/, much obliged for all the terrific help while this novel was being workshopped. There are too many of you to name individually, so I dare not list anyone for fear of omitting one of you.

A shout-out to my fans and readers of *The Raiford Chronicles*. Your votes made this happen.

Last, kudos to Christopher Chambers, once again, for his awesome cover work. If you'd like to use his expertise, contact him at cchambers@juroddesigns.com.

Introduction

For most of us, at least one pet comes into our lives that we love with our whole hearts, a pet that becomes more than just an animal to care for, more than just a companion, more than just a warm body to snuggle up with—they become another human to us. Such a pet was Satin.

Satin was fifteen pounds of satiny, glossy black cat. For years my children and I joked and even role-played that Satin was not a cat, but a panther. Further still, we often pretended that he was actually a human that some witch had transformed into a panther, who became king of not only the panthers, but his entire realm.

Of course, if Satin were human, then all our other pets had to be human, too. Thus, were born many of the characters in this book.

A Sonnet for Satin
By Janet Taylor-Perry

If there was magic in Frosty's old hat,
Then there was enchantment in my sweet pet.
It came in the form of a small black cat,
The dearest creature that I ever met.

His name was Satin for the smoothest fur.
His love was the unconditional kind.
His magic could be heard in his soft purr.
He was the best pet I will ever find.

But, oh, what sadness in my heart was wrought,
When the magic left creating dark space!
Never a battle with him had I fought,
And nothing his sweetness can e'er replace.

    The magic drew his final ragged breath,
    Leaving an emptiness in me in death.

Do this now, my son, and deliver thyself, when thou art come into the hand of thy friend; go, humble thyself, and make sure thy friend.

Proverbs 6:3

Contents

Part Three
Witch Hunt

Part Four
New Lives for Old

Prologue

"'**Tis** there. It does not matter whether you can see it. 'Tis there! I have been there, lived there. I know what is real." His green eyes snapping with authority, the stately, refined older gentleman engaged in a heated debate with the captain of *The Typhoon*.

"Sir, there is nothing there," argued the captain. "It's obvious. I'm turning this ship around. I am taking my crew home."

"I'm staying," declared the older man.

"Staying where, sir?"

"On Draconis. I supplied a dinghy. Leave it with me, and I shall get there by myself."

The captain objected, "Sir, that would be suicide."

"So be it. I shall be home."

"Sir, I cannot allow it."

With his eyebrow arched in correction, the gentleman said, "Captain, you have no say in the matter. I have paid you a great deal of money to bring me here. Return home and live a good life. I'm home, and here will I stay."

Unable to dissuade the man, the crew lowered the gentleman in a rowboat, supplied with a week's provisions. The man carefully stowed his bags, a large painting, and a brass urn, which he caressed lovingly and whispered, "The time has come, my love, when Draconis is no longer visible to the eyes of ordinary men. I can only pray when they are gone, I might once again be viewed as an exceptional man. If not, I know we are within a day of Isla Linda. We have sailed through the fog. I shall die where we began."

Just as the sun set, the billowing sails of *The Typhoon* disappeared over the horizon. The gentleman in the boat, called in a clear, loud voice, "Smoke, I need you. Come and fetch me, if you will be so kind."

On an island visible only to the eyes of exceptional men, a gossamer gray dragon lifted his head from the nap he had been taking. He heard a voice he had not heard in more than forty years, yet he must have been dreaming. He laid his head back down. *No! There it is again.*

He soared from his cave, leaving his mate staring at dust swirling in his wake like mist rising over the ocean. He flew with all his energy toward the sound of the voice. He spotted a small boat with a lone figure. The figure waved to him.

I can smell him. It is! It is he! He is home!

The voluminous creature snatched the boat into his talons. His spirit rejoiced.

My human is home!

Part One

Longing

1
𝕬𝖎𝖉𝖆𝖓'𝖘 𝕯𝖎𝖑𝖊𝖒𝖒𝖆

𝕬𝖎𝖉𝖆𝖓 O'Rourke was miserable. At seventeen, his world was gone. Nothing would ever be the same.

The words of comfort the vicar offered did little to heal the boy's broken spirit. A cat yowled outside as the back door of the church creaked and a stooped old man entered. Aidan paid little attention to the old fellow, but the meowing sounded like lament, long and pitiful. It caused his skin to prickle with goosebumps. He released a sad sigh.

The distraught young giant, standing well over six feet, followed the closed casket to the graveside. He caught his breath in gasps as it was lowered. Mechanically, he threw the first shovel of dirt to cover his mother.

The iron gate into the cemetery squeaked as he pushed it open to leave. He looked back to see the same old man shoveling the rest of the dirt. *Must be the caretaker, but he looks familiar.* Aidan furrowed his brow.

The man dropped into the hole a moment. Aidan thought he heard, "As I suspected. Aye, indeed." Then a white cat, its tail swishing fiercely, perched on the mounded dirt yet to be shoveled back into the open grave. The old man hoisted himself out and rubbed the cat's head. "P.C. without a doubt."

"Strange," Aidan mumbled to himself.

It seemed the entire village of Stonebridge offered him condolences, but nothing comforted him. His mother was gone. He wandered aimlessly home, his mind filled with a million thoughts. He sank in dejection onto the porch stoop. His emerald eyes glistened with moisture as he suppressed a flow of tears. "What do I do?" He dropped his face into his hands and mumbled, "I am alone, so alone."

Brushing a lion's mane of golden curls back with both hands, he stared across the landscape of bluffs covered in lush greenery. He looked toward the small church and the graveyard beyond. His heart ached with sorrow at the loss of his mother. He closed his eyes and remembered, breathing her name aloud. "Priscilla Cecelia O'Rourke. Even yer name sounded loike a song. Oh, Mam, why did ya leave me? Two days ago, ya were fine. Ya were not ill. Ya simply went to sleep and never awoke."

He could hear her talking as she baked bread to take to the other widows of the town. It was her nature to give. Recalling the smells and the way she moved, he understood why the villagers called her a sprite. She was tiny with amber irises, like a cat's. Though she smiled, the light did not reach her eyes. He remembered asking, "Mam, why aire ya so forlorn?"

She patted his cheek, leaving a bit of flour. "Me fire died with Duncan, but ya keep the embers alive. Ya have yer father's eyes. When I look into them, I see Duncan."

Aidan cocked his head to the side. "When I look into yer eyes I see meself."

Priscilla laughed with a sound like a gentle, gurgling brook. "That, me son, is because the eyes aire windows to the soul. Ya see yerself for ya aire me soul," she replied.

Aidan stretched his long legs in front of him as he sat on the narrow stone step-up into the only home he had ever known. He was tall, as Priscilla had said Duncan was. He had almost outgrown the wool breeches his mother had sewn for him only months before. His doublet stretched tight across his chest. He sighed. "If I am yer soul, am I loike ya? Ya were so kind and giving, but always a little sad." He felt his mother's melancholy as he thought. He smiled at the memory of her. She had reminded him of sunshine, but with a brooding, aching soul, like a sunny day with a storm cloud on the horizon.

He turned his head to the door of the home she had made. "Ya saw Duncan when ya looked at me. The only similarities to me father aire me eyes and size. I never knew him even if ya did talk aboot him all the time, aboot how he took me to sea on short trips."

Aidan considered the stories he had heard about his father, a sea captain. When Aidan was a baby, Duncan embarked on a voyage to discover the mythical land of Draconis where it was rumored men and dragons lived together in harmony. A fierce storm severely damaged his ship, and he and most of his crew were lost forever. Only one member of his party survived to tell the tale, and everyone knew old Diggory was insane.

The aging sailor returned bearing a story so strange and bizarre it could not be believed. He ranted about an island where animals talked, and he swore his ship's crew had not been lost at sea, but had been changed into talking animals by an evil sorceress and left on the enchanted island. When nobody would take him seriously, he became a recluse and lived on the outskirts of the village, although Aidan had seen him from time to time at the livery or at the market. Most people shunned the old man. Aidan, too, had been afraid of him.

Aidan laughed. "Me father believed in dragons. Mayhap, he was as crazy as old Diggory." He flexed and relaxed his fists causing his muscles to ripple as he pondered the possibility. *Why would a man in his roight mind desert his family for such a dream? Could it have been the lure of riches and glory? Had he hoped to give us a better life?*

Aidan stood and looked into the house. It smelled like his mother, like lavender in the spring. That once sweet fragrance now turned his stomach with the agony of longing. He stepped inside. The emptiness seeped into his pores.

He walked to the fireplace and stared at the painting of his father over the mantle. It had been an extravagant gift from some earl with whom Duncan had found favor. He wore his finest naval uniform, silver glistening in the creases of the black doublet. His raven-black hair gleamed. His piercing green eyes pulled Aidan. As he leaned closer, a voice whispered to him, "Destiny." For a brief moment, Aidan saw a pearly-white dragon. He shook himself, but he had come to a decision, ending his dilemma. He bumped the mantle with the palms of big, strong hands to solidify his choice.

With no plans for the future, nowhere to go, and no one to care for him and the love of the sea in his blood, Aidan began to wonder about the story. *What if 'tis true? What if me father is somewhere on some bewitched island?* With much resolve and purpose, Aidan packed his meager belongings. He decided to go in search of the enchanted island and, perhaps, his father. He could think of only one person who might give him some answers. He garnered his nerve and went to talk to the town fool.

2
Crazp Old Diggorp

Walking toward the dilapidated hut through the litter-strewn yard, Aidan had to summon all the courage he could find. He had always been afraid of crazy old Diggory, the only surviving member of his father's crew. Seeing coils of rope, fishing nets, and pikes did not put him at ease. The wind blew bits of garbage against his feet, and it seemed the breeze once again, whispered, "Destiny." The vision of a white dragon flashed across Aidan's mind once more. He blew out a breath, feeling disconcerted.

As Aidan approached, the stooped old man thrust the door open and shrieked, "Who are ye, and what do ye want? Canna ye young heathens leave me in peace?"

Aidan stopped in his tracks. He was taken aback by the appearance of this frail old soul. He appeared to be bent almost double with a hump on his back. He was swarthy and completely bald; his chin was covered in a scraggly mixture of auburn and gray, and he leaned on a cane carved from a knotted piece of wood. Aidan remembered someone much bigger and more intimidating. *Can this really be the same Diggory? That's the old man from the cemetery.*

Aidan cleared his throat, but he still seemed to croak when he spoke. "I am Aidan O'Rourke, Duncan's son. I only wish to talk with ya."

Diggory's eyes squinted, and he motioned for Aidan to come closer. "I canna see ye from this distance. Me eyes be ol'," he growled.

Aidan crossed the yard to be close to Diggory. The youth held his breath and his head drooped. The ancient mariner reached out a big, rough, gnarled hand to lift the boy's chin. "Me eyes be fine, so let me see yers. Aye," whispered Diggory with the gentleness of a dove. "'Tis ye almost grown to a man. Ye 'ave yer father's eyes and size, but the rest of ye be yer wee precious mother. God rest 'er soul." He squinted again. "Ah, ye 'ave 'is ears, even that little pointy thing. Just loike Duncan and yer grandfather."

"Me grandfather?" Aidan asked.

"Aye." Diggory nodded. "Come in, me boy, to me 'umble abode. Will ye 'ave a bit o' soup with me?"

Aidan took in the dimly lit, sparsely furnished hut as he stood in the doorway. It was only one room with a bed in the far corner. At the foot of the bed sat a large worn seaman's chest with a rusty lock holding it shut. On the bed lay a gorgeous white Persian cat. *The cat was at the cemetery too.* Aidan shook his head, thinking perhaps this was all a dream.

There was a table and two ladder-back chairs in the middle of the room and a stone fireplace against the back wall with a small, but surprisingly well-stocked cupboard, as seen through its mesh doors, to the right of the fireplace. In the near corner next to a trap door that led to a root cellar, a little insulated box could be seen. Aidan looked over his shoulder. The woodpile was just outside the door. The aroma of the soup, which bubbled over the fire, brought water to his mouth. His stomach rumbled loudly as he had not eaten during the two days since his mother died.

"Aye, I'd love a bowl," replied Aidan, warming to the withered old sailor.

Ushering the lad inside, Diggory served supper. He spooned a small amount of soup into a little silver bowl and set it on the floor for the cat that was now circling his ankles. "She be a stray loike us. Wandered up two days ago. I call the wee sweet mite P.C. 'cause all cats think they be privileged characters. P.C. be short for Privileged Character. Nobody be alookin' for 'er, so methinks she done come to keep ol' Diggory company." The cat encircled Aidan's ankles and mewed. Aidan patted her on the head, and P.C. purred loudly.

"She be alikin' ye, lad."

"She is beautiful," Aidan replied pensively. *That purr was strange. It sounded almost loike me mother's laugh.*

As they sat down to fish soup, barley bread, applesauce, and buttermilk, Aidan ventured, "Were you at me mother's funeral?"

"Aye. I owed it to Duncan."

"Will ya tell me aboot me father?"

A three-toothed smile broke across Diggory's face and a light gleamed in his faded blue eyes. "Aye, me boy, aye, when the time be roight; but for now, ye tell me aboot ye, and I shall tell ye aboot me. So, when I tell ye aboot me dear friend, ye won't think ol' Diggory a fool."

"'Tis not much to tell ya aboot meself," replied Aidan shyly.

"Nonsense!" Diggory snorted. "Ye be aturnin' the heads of every lass in the village. Stonebridge be not so big that ol' Diggory canna see and hear the goins-on. Ye be a mite popular with young and old, lad and lass. I been awatchin' ye all yer life. I promised yer father I would."

"Then it would seem ya know a great deal aboot me. Tell me aboot ya. The townspeople think ya aire crazy. The little children aire frightened of ya. Even I was afraid when I was a youngster."

"And now that ye be all grown up and met ol' Diggory yer fears be allayed," teased Diggory.

"I know not. Ya seem harmless, even likeable."

Diggory laughed aloud. "Ye be much loike yer father. He said almost the same thing twenty years ago."

Aidan sighed.

With a touch to Aidan's hair, Diggory said, "Ye be safe and home now, me boy. Ol' Diggory be spared all these years to take care o' ye. Tonoight ye sleep on a pad. On the morrow, we be afetchin' yer bed and aputtin' it near mine. We be arentin' yer place out. Ain't no reason to try to keep up two places. Yer daddy wudda wanted it that way."

Weary from the pressures of the day, Aidan began to sob. The old man leaned around the corner of the table and hugged the boy, tenderly patting his head. He cooed in a soothing voice, "It be all roight to mourn yer mam. There be no shame in that. Ye be a wee bairn yet."

Overwrought, Aidan released all his pent-up tensions in the embrace of a man he hardly knew, yet felt drawn to. A third time, the word, "Destiny," played through the boy's thoughts as a white dragon flashed in his mind's eye. The scent of sweet spices, tobacco, and whiskey burned into his memory as Diggory—*Not crazy, just odd.*

That night Aidan slept peacefully with a feeling he belonged to somebody, but he awoke with the burning desire to know the truth.

Over a breakfast of porridge, rye bread, peaches and cream, and strong, hot tea, Diggory reminded Aidan, "Patience, me boy. Ye must prepare yerself to hear some 'ard things. Be patient. In due time, ol' Diggory will tell ye all. But know this: Duncan was me friend. He was a gentle giant, never araisin' his voice in anger."

That day, they rented the O'Rourke cottage to the new town doctor, Drake Fitzpatrick, who had returned to his hometown from Dublin, and Aidan moved in with the man known as the town fool.

Upon their return to Diggory's cottage, the old man retrieved a bow and arrows from behind a loose board. Aidan caught sight of a number of other weapons and pointed, his mouth agape.

"There be robbers aboot," Diggory said. "Best to 'ide valuables." He went into the root cellar and returned with two items. "Wash and dice these whilst I find meat."

Aidan did as Diggory requested, and soon heard loud quacking and the *whoosh-thump* of an arrow finding its mark.

That night they ate roasted duck, cottage fries, a dish Diggory made using a strange root Aidan had never tasted, and honey-glazed carrots. Then, they settled into a time of getting to know each other with Aidan daily nagging to hear about his father.

3
𝕹𝖊𝖜 𝕱𝖗𝖎𝖊𝖓𝖉𝖘𝖍𝖎𝖕𝖘

𝕾𝖙𝖔𝖓𝖊𝖇𝖗𝖎𝖉𝖌𝖊, a small unimportant fishing village, was fortunate in many ways. At a time when Ireland strongly resisted Tudor rule and education was still private, the Stonebridge area was lucky to feel relative peace. The Murphy brothers and Ian Gilhooley, land barons, had long since been re-granted their titles by the monarchy to manage the village of Stonebridge. They were also blessed since several former Catholic priests had remained behind. In an unusual move, one of the priests opened his home to tutor the boys of Stonebridge for a price. Aidan had sat under the man's tutelage for a number of years. This was the final year the old priest would teach him. Only a few other boys had enough income to afford the old man's instruction. The new doctor's son, Colin, joined to make a group of eight.

Diggory Danaher insisted Aidan finish his last year of school; thus, life took on a new routine with Diggory's saying, "Ol' Diggory be just an ol' salty dog with seawater in his veins; me friend's son's gonna be a great man," and Aidan's constantly questioning Diggory about his father with only, "Be patient, me boy," for an answer.

P.C. immediately started sleeping on Aidan's bed, prompting Diggory to tease, "First ye steal me heart. Now, ye be astealin' me companion. Peradventure it be better she belong to ye. Ye be more apt to be around longer to care for her."

In the afternoons Aidan would come home and make repairs to the little house. He filled in missing mortar, washed the stone until it gleamed white, and put on new thatch. Although he lived simply, Diggory seemed to have an endless supply of money. After a few shillings and some days of work, Diggory's tiny one-room shack was almost unrecognizable. After the house repairs, Aidan turned his attentions to the yard, and in no time he had several shrubs and flowerbeds planted, in addition to the vegetables Diggory grew. The place was becoming a home.

On Saturdays Aidan played Gaelic caid. The sport seemed more like a group of crazy men with a ball, as two teams from different villages pounded one another from a starting point half way between and attempted to get the ball into the opposing village's border. Diggory had never missed watching a game, but now he followed along with the other spectators while he proudly watched "his boy" play. The townspeople now looked at Diggory with new respect; after all, he had taken in his old friend's orphaned son. There must be some good in him even if he were crazy.

On Sundays they went to worship at the little Anglican village church. Often Aidan served as an altar boy. Last Sunday the Dowager Gilhooley, who only associated with the most elite in the community and was by far the wealthiest citizen in Stonebridge, asked Diggory and Aidan to Sunday dinner.

There were other changes taking place in Aidan's life. The biggest went by the name of Caitlin Fitzpatrick, the new doctor's daughter. Tall and statuesque, she had vivid azure eyes, an ivory complexion, and a few freckles on her nose. Her most distinctive features were her flaming red hair, which flowed over her shoulders and down her back like lava when unbraided and unpinned, and a temper that matched her hair. Of late, it seemed as if she went everywhere Aidan went.

The days passed in ease. The only problem in Aidan's life, other than being impatient to hear about his father, was Colin Fitzpatrick, Caitlin's twin brother. With the exception of his being male and her being female they were identical. He had the same blue eyes and the same fire-red hair.

Another difference was that while Caitlin's complexion could be described as ivory, Colin's skin tone was pale; and when he became angry his face burned as red as his hair. He was often angry with Aidan. Colin was of the opinion Aidan was not good enough for his sister. He frequently referred to Aidan contemptuously as the "winsome waif" or the "unblemished urchin."

After an exceptionally trying afternoon football practice for the upcoming rivalry with Wyckeville and dealing with Colin's taunts, Aidan returned home to find a note on the table. It read:

Do your assignments. Supper be in the oven. Will be back later.

Diggory.

This was the first time Diggory had not been home to greet Aidan with his snaggletoothed grin. Aidan reached inside the earthen oven attached to the fireplace where embers smouldered and retrieved a pewter plate. He devoured supper of hot roast beef; new potatoes, which is what Diggory called the unusual vegetable he often cooked and grew in his personal garden behind his cottage; steamed squash; rye bread with strawberry jam; and fresh milk that someone left on Diggory's stoop every other day.

After the meal, Aidan was at a loss regarding what to do. He finished his writing and tried to read a book the old priest had given him, but he found it hard to concentrate. It was getting dark early now, so he could not do outside work. He began to wonder what Diggory kept secreted in the trunk at the foot of his bed. After a time, his curiosity got the best of him. He took the filet knife from the kitchen block and tried to pick the old rusty lock. He was becoming frustrated with the stubborn lock when he heard stamping on the porch. He started and dropped the knife, which clattered to the floor and slid under Diggory's bed. He plopped onto his bed and pretended to read just as Diggory entered.

"Where have ya been?" Aidan queried. "Do ya know what time 'tis?"

"A gent's entitled to a wee bit o' privacy. I 'ad an engagement." The old man looked over his shoulder and gazed at the moon. "It be somewhere after nine, I would guess."

Aidan sat bolt upright. "A rendezvous? With a lady?" His eyes big with curiosity he asked, "Who?"

"Now, 'twould be me own business." Diggory tapped his chest.

"Is it a secret?"

"No, jest not common knowledge yet."

"But I'm not common knowledge. I'm family. Roight?"

"Aye, that ye be."

Eagerness to hear some news rolling from his voice, Aidan begged, "Then tell me."

"Lizzie."

The boy's blond brows with a hint of brown knitted in confusion. "Lizzie?"

"Miss Elizabeth Gilhooley." The words were uttered with an air of pride and affection.

"The Dowager Gilhooley! You had a rendezvous with that old crow!"

"Watch yer tongue, lad." Diggory's voice took on a tone of chastisement. "That old crow be a moighty fine lady. She was once a lovely maiden. We spent a great deal of time together in our youth, but 'er father didna approve of me sort. A sailor weren't good enough for his daughter. The mean old codger. He done be abreathin' smoke in Hell now."

"Oh, I understand." Aidan grinned. "She was your beloved, and ya couldna be together. Now ya can. I think this is wonderful! Tell me all aboot her."

"Another time. It be bedtime now. But perhaps we can step oot with ye and that bonnie redhead sometime," Diggory teased as he blew out the lights and slipped into bed.

"What?"

"Good noight, Aidan."

The last day of the month of October dawned cold and damp. It wasn't a good day for the game between Stonebridge and their archrival, the neighboring village of Wyckeville. As much as he loved caid, Aidan hated falling in the freezing mud, and no matter how hard he tried to keep his feet, he knew someone would invariably take him out with a slide tackle. He did chuckle to himself at the thought of Colin Fitzpatrick constantly hitting the cold, hard ground.

There was a big dance planned for that evening, especially for those who did not in any way hold to what the church deemed the pagan practice of the Feast of Samhain, the celebration of the Celtic New Year. Hopefully it would be a victory dance. Though the town itself was more affluent than Stonebridge, the team from Wyckeville was not half as fast or strong. Moreover, Caitlin had told her brother to jump in the lake and agreed to be Aidan's companion. Aidan loved seeing the steam coming from Colin's ears. *If he weren't so ill-tempered, he could be a comrade.* Aidan sighed for deep within he wished that were the case.

Diggory strengthened Aidan against the odds with a hearty breakfast of barley cakes smothered in butter and honey, crisp bacon, scrambled eggs, and coffee, another delicacy Diggory had discovered during his voyages. After that meal and the encouraging conversation, Aidan felt he could take on the world and "Colin the Colon," as Aidan had dubbed him. He grinned at using the information Colin had shared from his father's books with the students to find a name for Colin.

Aidan was the second to arrive at the field. His archrival was already there and doing sit-ups in the mud. *Well, he is a teammate, so for the duration of the game we shan't spar. There will be time for that at the dance.* Aidan grimaced as he realized it could be a real possibility.

As the game got under way, the rain moved in. It was a hard-fought battle with bruised ribs, cracked lips, black eyes, and broken noses, but the Stonebridge boys emerged victorious as Aidan stretched his full body length to place the ball within Wyckeville's border. Aidan was glad he was unusually tall and that the game was over. He looked forward to a hot bath, some warm, mulled cider, and the dance. "I am sure if me face looks as badly as it feels, Dr. Fitzpatrick will keep an extra eye on me," he confided in Diggory as they walked a number of miles back home. "The good physician and his wife are to be chaperones at the dance." He sighed. "I only hope Colin will somehow disappear before nightfall."

Sporting a shiner and his Sunday best, Aidan called for Caitlin promptly at seven o'clock. Unluckily, Colin and his date for the evening, Mary Kate Murphy, were there, too; and Dr. Fitzpatrick insisted all of them walk together to the dance. At least Colin was on his best behavior with his folks around.

The ball was uneventful until it came time to announce the dance's favorite couple, a Stonebridge tradition. The couple would dance a slow dance alone before the crowd joined them in a jig. When the mayor announced, "Aidan O'Rourke and Caitlin Fitzpatrick have been voted favorite couple," Colin completely lost self-control, despite the fact his parents were present.

"That dirty street urchin willna dance with me sister and put his filthy hands anywhere on her!" he bellowed. He grabbed Aidan by the front of his doublet and threw him to the ground.

"Colin!" his family shouted in unison.

Aidan stood slowly and held his hand out to Caitlin. At the gesture, Colin punched him in the face, causing blood to trickle from his lip. Aidan, with slow deliberation, wiped the blood away with his hand and clenched his fists as he glowered at Colin.

Through gritted teeth, Aidan muttered, "I have had enough of yer condescending, holier-than-thou manner. Ya have insulted me. Ya have embarrassed yer family. Ya have made a fool of yerself and proven that ya aire no gentleman. 'Tis time somebody taught ya a lesson. Let us take this outside the townhall."

Caitlin grabbed Aidan's arm as the lads started for the door. "Wait!"

Aidan glared at her and spoke firmly but gently. "Let go. This is a matter of honor and must be settled now."

She nodded her assent and released his arm.

The crowd followed them out the door, abuzz with chatter and someone already taking bets on the outcome. Once outside, both boys removed their doublets and left them with their girlfriends. Aidan looked squarely at Colin and spoke with authority. "In a few months we shall both turn eighteen and finish our education. At that time our culture will consider us to be on the final path to adulthood. Hopefully, we will be men of honor. Tonoight I foight for me honor and the roight to court yer sister. Seeing as how yer father does not object to me, if I win this battle, ya will no longer oppose me. Is that understood?"

"And if I win?" Colin smirked with cockiness.

"Ya will have the satisfaction of knowing ya oot boxed me, but only yer father has the roight to forbid me to court Caitlin."

"Ya will say I am the better man?"

"I will."

Unknown to Aidan, Diggory and Elizabeth Gilhooley had joined the crowd. "We should stop this," Elizabeth whispered.

"No," replied Diggory. "Aidan must foight 'is own battles, but I do 'ope 'e wins. That upstart Fitzpatrick could be a strong ally in spite of 'is manner."

"Yes, but who has taught Aidan to foight?" Elizabeth sounded worried.

Diggory chuckled. "'Tis in 'is blood. There be more to 'im than the 'uman eye can behold."

The boys squared off. Colin had already drawn first blood. Aidan led with a straight jab, landed precisely on Colin's nose. Blood seeped into Colin's mustache. Colin countered with a rounded punch to Aidan's jaw. Aidan went for Colin's midsection followed with an uppercut. After several minutes, both boys were battered and bruised, but Colin lay on the ground, gasping for air.

"Get up!" Aidan spat along with a glob of bloody mucus.

"I canna. 'Tis over. Ya win." sputtered Colin. "I hope ya know what a spitfire ye're getting. Ya may want to do this all over again and lose on purpose someday. I warn ya she is a handful. She has a mind of her own, but I love her. Ya'd better take care of her, or we *will* do this again."

"Fair enough." Aidan offered Colin his hand. Colin took it, and Aidan helped him to his feet. The two shook hands.

"This be good. This be very good, Lizzie," whispered Diggory.

"Aye," Elizabeth agreed as they made their way through the crowd.

Diggory made his presence known. "Aidan, me boy, it be time to go 'ome and get cleaned up."

"I agree," replied Aidan. He turned to Caitlin. "Go home with yer family." He brought her hand to his lips and then held it close to his heart for a brief moment. "I shall talk to ya on the morrow."

"Aidan, go 'ome and soak in the washtub. I shall be there after I escort Lizzie 'ome," Diggory said.

Aidan nodded and hobbled home.

The Fitzpatricks turned to go. As soon as they were out of the crowds' sight, Colin felt another blow to his gut as Caitlin walloped him with a limb. "Ya prig! I trow ya got what was comin' to ya!"

"Caitlin! Act loike a lady!" Mrs. Fitzpatrick ordered, and they walked the rest of the way in silence.

Diggory came home to find Aidan soaking in cold water.

"It hurts everywhere," moaned Aidan.

"I be sure it does, me boy. 'Urry and get dressed. It be time ye 'eard aboot yer daddy."

4

𝕯𝖚𝖓𝖈𝖆𝖓

𝕬𝖘 soon as Aidan, dressed in his nightshirt, joined him, Diggory began his story.

"I met Duncan twenty years ago during a voyage when I was first mate for Cap'n Murphy. Yer friend, Mary Kate, be his granddaughter. Loike ya, Duncan was a big strappin' man, a head taller than most o' the crew. He was quiet and only spoke when it was necessary or privately to 'is friends. But 'e was not one to be tested. 'E could clear a room of foightin' men in minutes, without a single blow atouchin's 'im. 'E didna stand for brawlin' among 'is crew..."

Diggory's voice took on an ethereal quality. Aidan felt transported to another time and place.

"We were atransportin' flax to Molinia where we were to purchase salt to bring 'ome. 'Twas a long and grueling voyage. It took us nigh on a year to complete the trip. Cap'n Murphy was a 'ard man to please and really quite incompetent, but yer daddy needed the work. Duncan took the job with Cap'n Murphy 'cause Murphy 'ad at one time been a military man 'isself and quite a sailor, but in 'is later years, 'is mind 'ad begun to drift. Bein' a lieutenant fresh from the navy, 'aving a wife and daughter to support, and not truly knowing the cap'n's condition, Duncan came aboard with 'igh 'opes. This was 'is first voyage on a commercial ship..."

"Daughter?" Aidan interrupted.

"Aye, daughter. She was yer sister, Anna. Be quiet and listen. Ye will understand soon enough."

"But me mother never mentioned that I ever had a sister."

"Mayhap 'twas just too 'ard for 'er to talk aboot. Alosin' Duncan and 'er baby girl was mor'n she could bear. Now, quiet. Pay attention." Diggory scowled and went on.

"Duncan 'ad served in the navy for six years. 'E was used to giving orders, but taking orders from a fool grated on 'is nerves. 'E took the job so 'e could save enough money to buy 'is own ship. Things went from bad to worse when Cap'n Murphy made the wrong call during a gale and sent us off course by two months..."

The gale raged. Diggory shouted orders, "Secure that jib!" He coiled rope as he bellowed over the storm.

Diggory barely heard Duncan's yell. "Diggory! Move!" Some barrels came loose as the ship pitched and rolled over Diggory's leg. He uttered a gut-wrenching cry.

Duncan knelt beside his friend. "God-a-mercy, man! Can ya move? I'll help ya below."

Duncan maneuvered the injured man to his quarters. He examined the leg, which was already swollen and blue. Diggory moaned in agony. "'Tis broken," Duncan informed and splinted the injury.

The storm settled and Duncan fashioned a crutch for the first mate, but mobility remained nearly impossible. Some days later, Duncan entered Diggory's quarters. "Captain Murphy is burning up with fever. Ya have to take over."

Diggory shook his head. "I canna. Me leg has rendered me unable to take command. I canna stand or walk. Ya will have to do it, Duncan."

Reluctantly, the gentle-spirited man took control of the ship and the crew. His size garnered immediate respect, but his compassion and understanding deepened it. Without more incidents, the ship returned safely home two weeks later.

Captain Murphy, weak from illness, stood at the ship's rail, and Diggory hobbled to his side. Duncan stood with them. "Something is greatly amiss," he observed. He pointed out plumes of smoke in a number of areas.

Realizing the ship had returned, Priscilla O'Rourke raced to the wharf. Seeing his wife, Duncan leapt over the side of the ship and met her in a full run. He gathered her to him; she buried her face in his chest and wept.

"Priscilla, what has happened?"

"While ya were at sea, The Plague swept through Stonebridge. Many a folk, including"—She gulped—"Anna and the captain's wife, died."

"No! Not me wee girl." Duncan groaned, devastated to learn his child was gone. "We tried for so long." His heart broken, he cried with his wife.

Late in the evening, they visited Anna's grave and shared their grief. Closer to the front of the cemetery, Murphy wailed in despair. His twin sons sought to console him, but he stormed away, countenance dark.

Two days later, he jumped off the cliff to the rocks below at Porpoise Point. The letter he left said he blamed himself for not being home when his beloved died. The letter went on to say, "Knowing my sons hate the sea, I bequeath my ship to the one person I deem capable of running it, Duncan O'Rourke."

The twins raged against the document, but Ligon Murphy, as a barrister, acquiesced to his father's request though he voiced his doubt that his father had been of sound mind.

Duncan started his business with wanderlust although he did not make long voyages for fear of leaving Priscilla. He mended the old caravel Captain Murphy had acquired as payment for a debt and named her *The Sea Bird*. He scoffed at the superstition that renaming the ship would bring bad luck. He made a decent living running trade missions, but he confided to his wife, "I'll never get rich without taking riskier expeditions. 'Tis all roight. I love ya too much to chance it."

A year after his return, Duncan entered the pub in jubilation. Seeing Diggory, Duncan ordered two pints and joined his old friend. Diggory asked, "What's made ya so happy?"

"I have a son." Duncan glowed with pride. "Aidan Duncan O'Rourke." The two men clinked tankards and drank down the ale in celebration.

Even with the baby still in swaddling clothes, Duncan took him to sea on little trips just around the point. Priscilla warned, "Ye're gonna get him addicted to sailing."

He simply replied, "He is me boy. He was born loving the sea. 'Tis in his blood."

One bright spring day, Michael Flannery from Wyckeville came to the pub where Duncan was having a pint with Diggory and a few other fellows. Michael was spinning a whopper of a yarn about some far-off place where dragons and men were friends and gold lay in plain sight on the ground. Diggory and Duncan laughed heartily, thinking he had drunk a pint too many.

The next day, Ligon Murphy and his twin brother, Logan, knocked on Duncan's door. They made Duncan an offer he was hard-pressed to refuse. Their deal was to back an expedition to search for this mythical land and to split the booty that might be found fifty-fifty. He laughed at them and asked, "Aire ya crazy to believe Michael

Flannery's tale? There is no way I will go on a wild goose chase."

After a good deal of haggling, Priscilla spoke up. "Come back on the morrow. Give Duncan and me a chance to talk."

The brothers left and Priscilla said, "Ya know ya want to go."

"I canna leave ya and Aidan."

"We shall be fine. If ya doona follow yer dream, ya will be miserable."

"I couldna bear losin' another child. Ya canna be serious."

She stroked his raven black hair. "I am quite serious."

"When ya touch me loike that, I would do anthing ya ask."

Duncan scooped his petite wife into his arms and carried her to bed. Snuggled later, he caressed the scars near each of her shoulder blades. "Ya must hold some magic sway over me. Mayhap this is where angel wings once grew."

"Stop a moment," Aidan interrupted. "How do ya know so many personal things aboot me mam and da?"

"Duncan confided many a thing to me." Diggory narrowed his eyes and continued.

Priscilla talked Duncan into following his spirit's desire. When the Murphy brothers returned he laid out his requirements. "I will agree to take on the voyage if ya agree to care for me family if anything happens to me, if ya set aside an annuity fund for me crew and their families if anything should happen to them, and if ya give me total control over choosing the crew."

In way of explanation Diggory said, "That be why I 'ave an income. Logan Murphy kept his end o' the bargain. That also be why ye and yer momma was cared for." The old man dipped his head as he explained.

"So, the crew selection began. Duncan asked me to come on as 'is first mate, and we began in earnest to build a reliable, competent crew..."

Ligon Murphy insisted on being part of the crew. He argued with Duncan, "After all, 'tis me money financing this endeavor."

"But 'tis me ship," Duncan said with a scowl.

"Only because me own da thought more of ya."

"Is that what has ya so riled against me? Ya doona even sail."

"I coulda paid ya to be me captain."

"Ah." Duncan smiled with a misty eye. "'Tis greed that plagues ya. Yet, ya agree to equal shares when in actuality me share will be larger if I be hellbent on cheatin' me crew."

"'Tis not greed. 'Tis not feelin' a father's love."

"Aye. I can understand that. I never knew me da."

"Ye're a good man, Duncan. I need yer allegiance if I am to finance this voyage, and one of us must go. Logan has a wife. I doona. It falls me lot to journey with ya."

Duncan agreed with great reluctance.

As captain, he chose his crew carefully. Carter O'Day came aboard as steward. Patrick O'Leary was the cook; young Connor Donohue, fresh from medical school, signed on as ship's doctor; and a young orphan boy, Seamus O'Donnell, who lived by his wits on the streets, signed up as cabin boy. There were various and sundry men from the neighboring villages needing work, so Duncan, with his kind heart, took on many of the hearty, more responsible fellows. It took several months to put together a crew that pleased Duncan. He would accept no slackers.

The gleam in Diggory's eyes made Aidan smile. He could feel the genuine affection the old man had for his father.

With the crew and supplies ready, Duncan spent one last quiet evening with his family. Once they put Aidan to bed, Duncan and Priscilla cuddled up with hot cider and talked about what they would do with their fortune. They fell asleep on the rug before the fire and dreamed beautiful dreams. Duncan awoke once, his slumber disturbed by a vivid dream—a dream of a white dragon.

"A *white* dragon?" Aidan interrupted.
"Aye," is all Diggory responded before shushing Aidan again.

The dream gave Duncan a sense of urgency, yet confidence. He kissed Priscilla's head as she slept and nestled closer to her, drifting back to peaceful slumber.
The sunrise dawned crystal clear. The sea was glassy calm, almost too still. All the families came to the wharf to see *The Sea Bird* off.

"Yer momma never shed a tear as she waved good-bye, but kept 'er pearly white teeth ashinin' in the sun loike a beacon to show Duncan the way 'ome.
"Things went real smooth for a while..."

Duncan walked among the men. Spirits were high, and the weather was marvelous. A good steady breeze made use of the oars unnecessary for almost two weeks. Then, a vicious gale blew up. As much a part of the crew as anyone else, Duncan barked orders. "Batten down the hatches!" They struggled against sloshing rain, powerful winds, and overwhelming surges for nearly three days. Many of the nonseafaring men turned green and almost tossed their innards, especially Ligon.

Diggory chuckled at the memory.

"Finally, that she-devil of a storm blew 'erself oot, and we caught our breath with thanks that nobody was 'urt or lost..."

They sailed on for four months, stopping at every little out-of-the-way island they passed. Most of them were uninhabited by humans or had small settlements with a few colonists or natives. They took on some new supplies and a few men at the last island, and then they sailed on for two months with no sight of land. The crew started to get antsy.

Around midnight the ship encountered a deep fog, which made breathing hard. The spotter in the crow's nest started hollering. "Land ho!" Before they knew what happened, the ship struck boulders protruding from the shallow waters and ran aground. When morning dawned Captain O'Rourke assessed the damage. They were stuck. It would take quite a while to repair the destruction.

There were plenty of trees to cut and use for wood, but not much else that they saw. Some curious little creatures—a lizard, a tortoise, several gulls—crept closer to the campfire every night. After about two weeks, the little animals ate right out of the men's hands.

Diggory held his hand out as he talked; P.C. gave it a good lick.

"It took nearly four weeks to mend the ship. Yer daddy called the little island Isla Linda, meanin' Purty Island. The island was so purty we 'ated to leave, but we got under way again beneath a 'eavy-laden sky. Some of the fellas protested 'cause they in truth loiked that little island. So, the cap'n made a deal with 'em. 'E told 'em that after the voyage, he would bring 'em and their families back to settle there if they wanted to come. That seemed to pacify the whiners..."

About three hours out the rains started again, and the men seemed nervous, whispering among themselves. It did not amount to much more than a little thunderclap. It rained hard, which made it difficult to see; but within a day the sun broke through, and they had smooth sailing for several days. Sighs of relief were audible.

A week later near twilight they spotted land. Duncan ordered that they drop anchor until morning. "I want to be able to see and not run aground again," he told the men. Next day, they came into view of the most gorgeous, lush island any of them had ever seen. They sailed into a deep blue bay with a natural harbor. This place was a paradise.

Diggory seemed lost in his memories as he relayed the story. His voice continued the quality of another world.

"We could 'ear the call of all kinds o' animals, but we couldna see a one. The cap'n took the crew ashore, aleavin' only three of the less experienced boys on ship. 'E left young Seamus in charge of the small contingency. We made camp a good way into the 'eart of the island. We threw

together some limbs and leaves for shelter. Duncan could sense that this place was worth explorin'..."

Next morning, they broke into five teams. One small team had to stay in camp. It was made up of Ligon Murphy, Patrick O'Leary, and Connor Donohue. Carter O'Day took a team northward. Michael Flannery took a team southward. Duncan led a group toward the east, and Diggory took a group west. After a week all the teams reached the beach again and they all returned to camp with their reports within two weeks.

As Diggory spoke of direction, he pointed as if showing the way.

The reports were all similar. They gave a lay of the land. The north was rugged terrain. It came to a mountain range with snow-covered peaks. "There appears to be many caves in the mountains. There aire natural springs and numerous streams filled with fish. The far side of the range drops off to the sea and jagged rocks. The cliffs appear to have fifty or more clefts," Carter reported. "I couldna tell the depth of each cleft because the face of the cliff is so sheer. The waves crash dangerously on that side of the island." Carter's team reported hearing all manner of animals, but never spotted a living thing.

Michael Flannery's team said the same about the animals toward the south. He relayed, "The landscape is different in that direction. This area comes oot on the bay where we are moored. There's a long beach with sparkling white sand. Coconut palms grow all along the way. There be other edible vegetation, too."

To the east there was a vast forest that held various fruit-bearing and nut-bearing trees. There was a deep, clear lake fed by the mountain streams. Duncan talked as if he had seen a piece of Heaven. "There are fallen trees filled with honeybees. The forest thins oot after two days of hard walking and slowly becomes grassland that borders the beach." As in the other two directions, Duncan's team heard many animals, but they had not seen a single one, save for the fish in the lake.

"My group 'ad not traveled far," Diggory said to Aidan. *"After going through a lightly wooded area the first day, we came upon a vast desert. We could see many blooming cactus plants and through the spyglass we could see an oasis, but we were not prepared to travel over the desert. We also 'eard the noise of animals without ever seein' one..."*

Through the spyglass the oasis looked inviting. Duncan said to his men, "'Tis beautiful. We shall resupply and go. Ligon, Carter, Connor, and Diggory, ya aire with me. The rest of ya, return to the ship and wait. Seamus is still in charge. Doona question me decision. The lad has strong character. Michael, ya will be his second."

After the first night in the desert, the men finally saw an animal. A snake slithered through the sagebrush. It stopped and looked at the men. The snake laughed. The men looked at one another, but each shook his head feeling he must have imagined hearing a snake laugh. The next day they saw a hawk soaring overhead. Connor said, "The hawk was calling oot, 'Stay away!'"

"'Tis ludicrous," said Duncan. "Did ya eat something to cause ya to hallucinate?" They kept going.

The next morning the hawk was perched on a cactus above Duncan's head. It swooped down and landed decidedly on his shoulder.

"We were shocked that a wild animal would do such a thing. But what 'appened next shocked us even more."

Diggory took a deep breath and got himself a drink of water.

Aidan jumped to his feet and dogged the old man's steps. "Diggory, doona stop now. What happened?"

Diggory sat down with crackling bones and a grunt.

5
Admonitions and Temptations

"When we awoke the next morning and saw that bird asittin' there astarin' at us, to be sure we was quite shook."

Diggory continued his revelation.

Duncan jumped a yard away from the bird. Then, he thought better of his actions and said that it was just curious.

"Ha, ha, ha," cackled the hawk. "Don't be foolish, man," it said. "I've come to warn you. Do *not* go anywhere near that oasis. You'll be very sorry if you do. You'll be like me." Then it soared away.

For several minutes the men sat there looking at one another in astonishment. Nobody knew what to say. Finally, the doctor ventured, "Did that hawk in truth just speak to us?" All nodded.

Duncan came alive. "This must be the place! If that hawk can talk, it can tell us where to go and what to do. We must find the hawk and talk to it some more."

"But it flew back the other way," whined Murphy at the inconvenience.

"I know, but we must discover what it knows," explained Duncan.

Murphy grumbled, "Mayhap we should ignore it and go on."

"We canna ignore a thing loike a talking hawk!" rebuked Dr. Donohue. "'Twasn't a parrot."

"If ya recall, a snake laughed at us the other day," Carter O'Day reminded the group.

"We were all awonderin' if this could be real, or if we were imaginin' it. In our 'earts we knew 'twas real. 'Ow could we all see and 'ear the same thing if 'twas imaginary? We fell silent for a while. Then, Duncan spoke up and decided we were gonna follow the 'awk," Diggory told the boy listening in rapt attention.

While they were packing up, the crewmen had another visitor. A huge rattlesnake slithered into camp.

"A what?" interrupted Aidan.
"A serpent with rattles on its tail. Ye'll 'ear aboot some animals ya've never seen."

Not being used to snakes of any kind, Murphy pulled out his pistol and took aim. Nothing happened when he pulled the trigger. "Heh, heh, heh," chuckled the serpent. "I shall tell you those weapons will not work here. No harm can come to us animals from humans with any kind of weapon not found here."
The men stood wide-eyed, mouths agape as another animal spoke to them.
"You can't take that hawk seriously," the snake went on. "He's jealous since he's not welcome at the oasis. He has caused us much trouble. You, however, are welcome to visit. We have a queen that adores visitors. She sends you an invitation to join her for supper tomorrow evening. 'Twill take you another day to journey to her paradise. I shall take your reply to her."
"Did one of you laugh at us the other day?" Carter asked timidly.
"Aye. 'Twas Colby. He got mad because the queen wouldn't let him have his way. Now he is chums with Hank Hawke. Beware those two."

"Ya sound reasonable. Peradventure, we shall join yer queen for supper." Duncan took command of the conversation. "Can ya guarantee our safety? We aire on a quest. Mayhap, we can get some answers at the oasis."

"Excellent. I shall tell her to expect you." With that the snake coiled up and disappeared, leaving behind a strange, cloying smell that all the men breathed deeply.

Duncan knitted his brow with a hint of unease at the lack of answer from the serpent, but shook off the feeling.

They started toward the oasis. All at once, Hank Hawke swooped in and screeched, "Are you *all* crazy fools? Did I not warn you to go back?"

"We aire going to see the queen," Duncan informed him.

"Queen! Queen! She is *not* a queen, my good man! She's a wicked witch. Do you not comprehend the seriousness of the situation?"

Duncan asked, "What aire ya talking aboot? I understand we aire witnessing a bunch of talking animals. Believe me, 'tis strange to us."

"You idiot! Animals don't talk. Do you not see I'm not in truth a hawk? I was once a man like you. If you go to that woman, you'll end up like me."

"Verily, this is too much," Duncan replied. "The serpent warned us aboot ya. He said ya were jealous and ya were unwelcome at the oasis. He told us yer serpent friend was put oot with the queen, too."

"Lies! I tell you be on your guard. If I cannot dissuade you from going, at least be careful." He flew away in a huff.

The men traveled for a few hours before they stopped for a break. As they sat down to get a drink of water, a jackrabbit popped out of his burrow.

"How now, travelers?" he quipped. "I'm Jackson O'Hara. Most folks call me Jack. Hmmm," he said, looking toward the oasis and back toward the camp. "I reckon you're heading to the pretty spot over yonder. 'Tis a real bad idea. There's a hag there you don't want to meet. She'll do bad things to you if you stir her ire. Look at me. Alack, I used to be a traveling performer."

"Methinks the hawk sent you," said Duncan.

"Nay. Haven't seen him in days, but if he warned you, you should listen."

"He's right, good sir," came a squeaky little voice. "Jack won't steer you wrong, and neither will Hank. I wish I had listened."

The voice was coming from a tarantula.

Aidan interrupted the story again. "Tarantula?"

"'Uge, 'airy spider," Diggory answered curtly, held up his hands to form a circle the size of a plate, scowled, and went on.

Jack piped up, "Let me introduce you to this little lady. Gents, meet Legs, I mean, Leslie Malone."

The men chorused, "Hail."

"How now? Do you not love my name?" she said sarcastically. "Alas, I was a danseuse at court. The old hag does have a sense of humor. My performance displeased her."

All these varying opinions began to bother the travelers, but they were too far from camp to go back through the desert. They had no choice but to go on to the oasis, if only to resupply and return to ship.

They made camp that night, but nobody had much appetite. They toyed with their food when they had another visitor. A coyote wandered up to the fire and sat down.

Aidan huffed again. Diggory cocked an eyebrow, and then smiled. "A coyote is loike a wolf, but smaller."

Aidan grinned and nodded.

The coyote looked around and spoke. "Good evening. That smells delicious. Have you any to spare? I'm famished."

They spooned him some onto a plate, and he wolfed it down. He licked his chops and said, "Many good thanks. I didn't mean to interrupt your supper, good sirs. Her Majesty was concerned about your progress. She sent me to inquire of you. I'm to spend the night in your camp and come back with you tomorrow. 'Twill be very pleasant to sleep by your fire tonight. I pray you have no objections to this arrangement. It has been quite a while since the queen had new visitors, and she's extremely excited."

They had no choice but to comply with this creature's request. Duncan bowed his head in deference since the creature had been sent by a queen.

The men slept fitfully. The coyote was already awake when they woke. "We should away," he said. "This is going to be an exceptionally hot day. I do hate traveling by day, but duty calls. Queen Quazel bids you come. I forgot to introduce myself last night. I'm Carl Covington, professor of anthropology. Trust me, you have nothing to fear in our little heaven."

Diggory sighed. "We felt better, although gettin' assurance from a serpent and a wolf's cousin made us a little uneasy. Why 'adn't Queen Quazel sent us a beautiful, respected animal?

Nevertheless, we 'astily ate breakfast, packed up, and followed our furry friend. We noticed Hank flying at a 'ealthy distance..."

As Duncan's men neared the oasis, they stopped to take in their surroundings. They smelled crystal water, tropical flowers, and all forms of savory eats. They heard hundreds of different animals, and the temperature grew cooler.

Upon arrival Duncan noted the whole island of beauty was fenced with iron spikes, and there was a massive black horse standing just inside a gate. He gestured to Diggory to take heed. He later learned that gate was the only way in or out.

The horse shouted as they approached, "Halt! Who goes there?"

"'Tis Carl and the visitors, imbecile! Whom did you think 'twould be?" Carl snarled.

"Oh, welcome," stammered the horse. "I'm Jean Noir, guardian of these premises. Enter."

Duncan stopped briefly and patted the horse's nose. "I pray that does not offend ya. I have always loved the way the nose of a horse feels."

"Quite the contrary. It feels good to have some human contact." Then, the horse whispered something to Duncan.

"I doona think so," Duncan replied.

"I pray so," Jean stated flatly.

6
𝔓𝔞𝔯𝔞𝔡𝔦𝔰𝔢

"**What** did the horse say?" Aidan shouted when Diggory made as if to stand.

Diggory yawned. "Old Diggory be agettin' tired, me boy. Let us get a wee bit o' rest and continue in the morning."

"What! You canna stop now! I shan't be able to sleep a wink," protested Aidan. In the end, Diggory's wisdom won, and they went to bed in the early hours just before dawn.

Aidan awoke to the smell of sausage; another dish Diggory made using the strange, but versatile potato; barley cakes with fresh honey, including the comb; coffee, and fresh milk from some unknown source.

Diggory chuckled as Aidan stumbled to the table. "For someone who wasna able to sleep a wink, ye in truth wasted 'alf a day."

Aidan asked, "How late is it?

"Nigh on to midday."

"Zounds! Why did you not wake me?"

"It be quite all roight, lad. I 'ave only been up aboot an hour meself. Ye 'ad a rough day and a long noight. Ye needed the rest."

"Gramercy," Aidan said humbly.

"The way the rain be acomin' down today, we shouldna be bothered with no unwanted guests, so we can continue with me tale whenever ye be ready," Diggory said as he served Aidan a plate and sat down to his own.

"Fire away. I am all ears," replied Aidan enthusiastically, touching his ear and feeling the small protrusion Diggory had said Duncan also had. *And my grandfather.*

"Indeed." Diggory laughed and ate a few bites before beginning the story again.

"We arrived and met Jean Noir, the big black horse who guarded the gate..."

Just as Diggory spoke, there was pounding at the door. "What the devil?" Diggory grumbled. "Who be idiotic enough to come oot in this downpour?"

"I could venture to guess," said Aidan with half a smirk on his bruised face. "It could be somebody stubborn rather than stupid," he continued as he got up and limped to open the door.

"I was roight," Aidan said over his shoulder to Diggory as he held the door open. "Will ya come in from the storm, milady?"

Caitlin Fitzpatrick, wearing a bright blue cape over blue and white layers of skirts and boots, stepped into the little home. "Good morrow, or should I say afternoon?" she said cheerily. "Ya look terrible, Aidan. Do ya feel as bad as ya look? Hail and be well met, Mr. Danaher."

"Lass, ye shouldna come oot in this weather. The lad will recuperate nicely."

"Diggory is roight. I hurt all over, but I shall be fine. How is Colin?"

"Worse than ya. He did not even get up this morning. Mam and Sarah had to serve him breakfast in bed. Alackaday, he got what he deserved, so I have very little sympathy for him. Ya, on the other hand, I worry aboot," Caitlin said, smiling at Aidan. "Aire ya not goin' to ask me to sit down?"

"Where?" asked Aidan. "We only have two chairs, and we were just aboot to have something to eat."

Taking off her cape and hanging it on the hook by the door and pulling off her boots she said decidedly, "Oh, I shall just sit on the bed." She plopped down, picked up P.C., and started rubbing her head. The cat purred loudly.

Aidan and Diggory looked at each other questioningly. "It be up to ye, son," Diggory said with a snigger, "but ye'll 'ave to tell 'er sooner or later."

"Very well," sighed Aidan. He turned to the stubborn redhead. "Caitlin, Diggory has been telling me what happened to me father. Since yer family is new to the area, ya probably have not heard much aboot Diggory. His story is strange to say the least, but if ya laugh or make fun once, I will take ya home straightaway. Ya may stay and listen under those conditions. Understood?"

"On my troth," Caitlin replied, wide-eyed. "This must be good."

"Fine," said Diggory. "Let us finish our repast, and I shall begin."

The two men finished their meal. Then, Diggory said, "Aidan, ye and Caitlin wash the dishes, and I shall set us up for some storytellin'."

While the two young people cleaned, the old man scrounged up some cushions and blankets. "Why so many?" Aidan queried as he dried his hands.

"I 'ave a funny feeling," Diggory replied with a shrug of his humped shoulders.

Just as Diggory stoked the fire, there was another knock at the door. "Uh-huh," Diggory murmured. Then, he joked, "I be clairvoyant!"

"What now?" Aidan said with irritation in his voice. He opened the door. "Miss Gilhooley! Colin! Mary Kate!"

"Invite 'em in, lad. We may as well make this a party. Pop oot some teacakes, Aidan. Sit down, one and all." Diggory rumbled a hearty laugh at the look of consternation on his young charge's face.

Aidan balked a moment in front of Colin. "Why aire ya in truth here?"

Colin quirked an eyebrow. "I thought we made our peace yesterday. Mary Kate came to check on me and we met Miss Gilhooley on the way. I asked Mary Kate to accompany me with the hope that ya and I moight begin anew." He shrugged and made as if to back out the door. "But if ya doona care to try…"

"No!" Aidan said too hastily. *Oh, I hope we can be friends yet.* He tried to smile and pressed a hand to his cracked lip. "Caitlin said ya were still abed. I was just surprised to see ya. Please, stay."

"Good then." Colin offered his hand, and Aidan shook it.

In a short time there were teacakes and hot cider. Aidan laid down the ground rules for listening to Diggory's tale. Then they were ready for Diggory's yarn. Gathered around the fire, the youths lounged on the pillows while the elders sat in the chairs. Diggory began again.

"Suffice to say Duncan O'Rourke and 'is crew 'ad traveled for some months. They reached the legendary land of Draconis where men and dragons were friends and animals talked, though nary a dragon 'ad they seen. Nor any sight o' gold. Many o' the animals they met said they were not animals a'tall, but 'umans who 'ad been bewitched. Many o' them also warned the party traveling to the oasis not to go there. One member of the party was Ligon, yer uncle, Mary Kate. Needless to say, curiosity got the best of us and we went to the oasis. 'Tis where we will begin…"

As the group walked through the gate, it shut with a clang. They could not believe their eyes. There were brightly colored, highly fragrant flowers everywhere.

Peacocks strutted to and fro. Tigers, lions, and leopards lounged in great hammocks.

Monkeys swung from vines overhead. All these animals and many more carried on conversations all around the men. They stood with their eyes wide, mouths agape. None could find words to speak for their bewilderment.

All manner of food covered tables around them. There were grapes as big as plums, melons so sweet they dripped sugar, and honey cakes that melted in their mouths. Several apes offered the men these delicacies and more. There was nectar wine so potent they were intoxicated from the mere smell. Duncan pressed the heel of his hand to his temple after the first sip. "Beware, mates. This brew is strong," he warned.

Just from the scent, Diggory's eyes blurred and he burped. "I never encountered anything loike this," he whispered to Duncan. "Mayhap 'tis a witch's concoction."

Duncan shushed him with a finger to his lips.

Then, the apes showed each of the party to his own lavishly furnished abode. The dwellings were only one room with a large tub and basin for washing and a recessed area where water trickled when a valve was turned, as well as a private chamber pot, but they were so elegant they had nothing to compare with them. They were far more fabulous than the finest inn even the wealthy Ligon Murphy had used. All bathed and promptly fell asleep on the luxurious beds.

After a few hours, a white ape knocked at their doors and told them the queen's personal bodyguard wanted an audience with them. He presented the party with robes of the finest silk to wear during their stay.

Diggory sighed, "I 'ad never felt anything so pleasant against me skin."

He rubbed his arms at the memory.

The group gathered under a huge palm and was once again served a truly fabulous feast. As they enjoyed themselves immensely, they were interrupted by a deep, throaty sound. They turned to see the most enormous bear that ever existed. He stood on his hind legs and must have been twelve feet tall.

"Good even, gentlemen. Allow me to introduce myself. I'm Orson Bruin, Her Majesty's personal protector, at your service. Queen Quazel bids me make her apologies to you since she's unable to join you this eve. She suffers from a particularly excruciating malady." He placed a paw against his head. "She often gets exceedingly painful headaches, and she has been severely afflicted this day. She hopes to be able to join you on the morrow. Until then, at least for this evening, I'm your host. Prithee, before we begin our evening, tell me something about yourselves."

Because he was the leader, Duncan began. "I am Duncan O'Rourke from Stonebridge, Ireland. I am captain of our ship, *The Sea Bird*. We have been sailing for quite a while to get here. I am a former military man; I served in our navy for six years and retired as a lieutenant. I left me wife months ago, and I must confess I am becoming dreadfully homesick."

"'Tis a pleasure to meet you, Captain O'Rourke. Queen Quazel will be greatly pleased with a gentleman of your stature and background." Turning to Ligon, he said, "And you, sir, are?"

"I am Ligon Murphy, attorney at law. I have a twin brother at home. We aire the backers for this expedition."

"Wealth and power. Her Majesty will find those two things desirable." Then, he turned to Carter O'Day and gave him a quizzical look, drooping one eye almost closed.

Carter never was comfortable with an interrogation. When he was a boy he had stuttered, and all the other children had laughed at him. He was most greatly afflicted when he was in trouble. At Orson's gaze he began to stammer. "M-m-m-me? I-I-I-I am just a fisherman on an adventure with an old friend."

Then, Orson turned to Diggory. "And just what are you?" he asked in a most condescending tone.

Diggory confided to his captive audience, "I must confess I was 'ighly offended at 'is way of thinking, so when I replied I tried to sound very self-confident. The truth is, I was ashakin' in me boots.

"I replied, 'Me name is Diggory Danaher. I am the first mate of our most worthy vessel. I 'ave been a seafarin' man all me life, and I am proud to say I am a friend and confidant of Captain Duncan O'Rourke.' Children, know no truer words were ever spoken..."

Orson grunted, obviously unimpressed. He turned his attentions to young Connor Donohue. "What position, fair child, do you serve with this motley crew?" Fair child was an apt description of the doctor. He was handsome and young.

"I am no child, sir. I am Dr. Connor Donohue, physician by trade; and I, perchance, can be of some use to your queen. I may have some medicines that can relieve her headaches. An' it please you, take me to her?"

"Aye. Aye," Orson said thoughtfully. "I like you. You're most definitely stronger than you appear. Queen Quazel will be most pleased."

Turning toward the rest of the men, Orson continued, "Good gentles, pray pardon us. I shall return momentarily. I wish to take the doctor to the queen. Come, Dr. Donohue. Let us be off."

"Let me get me bag," said Connor with excitement, and off he ran to his quarters. He returned shortly, and the two disappeared.

After they left, the others looked at one another. Diggory finally spoke, "Is it just me, or was that strange? I felt loike I was bein' measured for a coffin."

"'Twas most disconcerting," Duncan whispered. "Good sirs, I am beginning to think that mayhap we should have listened to Hank Hawke. This place seems too good to be real."

For a while they walked around the general area deep in thought. Diggory went to Duncan and said quietly, "Duncan, old chap, why did ya only mention yer wife and not little Aidan?"

"I know not exactly, but I felt uncomfortable letting a bear know I had a baby. Keep quiet aboot Aidan; and if anything happens to me, promise me that ya will watch after him."

"On my honor, me friend. Ya know I would guard either of ya with me life."

"I know," he said, clapping Diggory on the shoulder.

At that point, their conversation came abruptly to a halt as they saw Orson approaching. "Gentlemen, let me show you around our little paradise. Dr. Donohue is with Queen Quazel. I do hope he has something that can aid her. She can be most ill-tempered when these headaches persist. Alack, enough of that." He motioned with his paw for Duncan and his men to follow him. "Shall we?"

They walked for hours with Orson. He showed them everything except the silk and satin tents where Queen

Quazel rested. Everywhere they went were all sorts of exotic animals as well as some common critters. All of these animals carried on various conversations.

The foliage was unbelievable. Vividly colored frangipani blossomed, and all over the fence ran ivy and fragrant climbing roses with blooms as big as plates. Throughout the oasis, arbors burst with wisteria, roses, and honeysuckle. The aroma was exhilarating.

The food was incomparable. The sweets were the sweetest, the sours the most sour, and the salty had to be chased with sweet and water. The flavors were intense and thrilling. This place was truly the Garden of Eden.

Connor rejoined his friends about halfway through the tour. He reported Queen Quazel was experiencing relief and had fallen asleep. He was enamored with the queen, as could been seen in his heavy breathing and round, wide eyes. He described her as breathtaking.

Finally, Orson took the visitors back to their quarters. They retired for the night. Unable to sleep, Diggory knocked on Duncan's door.

He answered still dressed. "Come in, Diggory. I see ya couldna sleep either. Methinks we should have a courtesy visit with Queen Quazel and, then, away from here as soon as possible."

"Agreed, Captain. This place is loike the Garden of Eden, and we know what happened there. Temptation will be strong here. Some of us may not be able to resist it. Young Connor, a prime example."

"Roight. And I disloiked not seeing any other exit to this place except past that giant steed."

"By the way, what did he say to ya when we came in?"

"'Twas strange. He asked me if I was the one who had been prophesied. I told him I didna think so, and he said he prayed so. If this place is so wonderful, why do so many of its inhabitants seem to want oot?"

"We went to sleep that noight with a lot on our minds," Diggory said, refilling his mug with cider and continued his discourse.

7
Queen Quazel

The next day dawned just as brightly as the day before. Every day the men spent there was clear and sunny. It never rained, and the temperature stayed steady and pleasant.

They dined together on a scrumptious breakfast of scones and melon. Before they had finished eating, Orson appeared with a message from the queen. "Her Majesty wishes to thank Dr. Donohue for his attentions and medicines. She is feeling quite well this morrow and desires you join her for a picnic in the meadow at high noon. She is most eager to meet the rest of you. You will find the proper attire in your rooms. I shall return promptly at half past eleven to guide you to your destination." With his proclamation, Orson turned and left the men to their own designs until dinner.

Duncan called a meeting in his chamber. Before they met the queen, he wanted to know all he could about her. "Connor, tell us what ya learned aboot our hostess last night."

"She is exquisite, refined, and gracious. She is absolutely gorgeous. Her voice reminds me of a lark's tune. She is the most fabulous woman I have ever met." His eyes seemed to lose focus, and he spoke as if hypnotized.

"In truth?" Duncan said, an eyebrow arched. "Orson seems to stand in awe, if not terror, of her. The other animals seem only to speak her name in whispers unless 'tis in a command performance to sing her accolades. Aire ya sure ya found nothing unusual aboot her?"

"No, sir, with the exception of her rare beauty and the fact that she has six fingers and toes on each hand and foot."

I have been accused of having devil blood. Duncan rubbed the small protrusion on his ear as he thought. *The nice comments were that I am Elven. All superstition, but still...Six fingers and toes?* He cleared his throat. "The ancients believed this to be a sign of witchcraft." He took a deep breath. "What aboot her character?"

"She does command authority and respect. She seemed in control of her emotions although she was suffering excruciating pain last even. Despite her agony, she still managed to be warm and welcoming."

"Well, much thanks, Connor. Mayhap my apprehension is unfounded. Has anyone else had foreboding aboot this place or its inhabitants?"

Diggory said to those assembled at his home, "I could tell Duncan was concerned, but we 'ad already 'ad our conversation the night before. 'E knew exactly what I thought..."

Carter spoke up, "I doona loike the fact that we canna leave except past that brooding stallion. He gives me worry."

"I doona loike the fact that there is only one way in or oot either," agreed Duncan, "but I doona think Jean Noir is a problem. On the contrary, I think he could prove an ally should we need one. Anybody else?"

After a long pause, Ligon cleared his throat. "Peradventure, this is silly, but is this place too perfect? Many of the creatures have called it 'Paradise' or 'Heaven'. I doona think I have died yet, and the *goddess* of this place seems a bit elusive. And, mates, I have never pictured St.

Peter as a mammoth black stallion or the Angel Gabriel as an enormous bear. Methinks the cost of this paradise may be too high."

After a bit more discussion and a great deal of dissension from Connor, it was agreed that they would have a perfunctory visit with Queen Quazel; but they planned to leave the next day.

They returned to their quarters to get properly dressed for a picnic with a queen. Each found white linen breeches and doublets with sleeves inlaid with silk, crisply starched white cotton shirts, white shoes, silk stockings, and wide-brimmed white straw hats. Everyone had a different color inlay in his doublet, and the band on each man's hat and stockings matched the inlay in the doublet. Duncan's was green; Ligon's was gold; Carter's was red; Connor's was royal blue; and Diggory's was black. Meeting outside to wait for Orson, they looked at one another and burst into peals of laughter.

Diggory began to chuckle at the memory.

"I couldna 'elp meself when I blurted, 'Are we suppose to be peacocks, or does Queen Quazel want us to be court jesters?"

"'Neither,' came a snarling response behind us. Orson 'ad arrived. "Er Majesty likes well-dressed, well-groomed, well-mannered gentlemen.' 'E leveled a gaze at me that let me know I was none of these things. 'E continued without pause. 'Let us depart, gentlemen.'

"I must confess, I 'ave never worn more comfortable clothing..."

Duncan's party followed with minimal conversation. They arrived in a clearing that would have made a nice size park. Most of Queen Quazel's entourage was already there, and a bountiful feast was spread before them on silver, gold, and white satin blankets. Many of the foods none of the men had ever tasted.

Diggory took a moment and said, "Tis where I discovered wonderful potatoes..."

"Trust me," Orson assured, "none of the meats we have come from talking animals."

A trumpet blast shattered the festive air, and Orson announced in a booming voice, "Ladies and gentlemen and subjects all, Her Royal Highness, Queen Quazel, ruler of the Zone of Perfection and rightful heir to all the land of Draconis. Bow before her presence in humility and awe!"

The men removed their hats and took a knee, showing her the homage of her title and custom; but none felt comfortable bowing before this unknown entity.

Preceding the queen came two snow-white apes with golden coronets to announce her entrance. Upon another blast from the horns, Queen Quazel arrived through an opening in the trees. She was mounted on a shimmering white unicorn that had a gold and silver entwined horn. It was a magnificent beast. A number of courtiers followed the queen. Some rolled out a plush white carpet for her to step upon. Others helped her dismount. All backed away from her bent double. Even the powerful Orson fell to all fours with his head lowered.

Queen Quazel was a ravishing creature. Although everything surrounding her was glimmering gold, sparkling silver, glittering white, or dazzlingly colorful, Queen Quazel wore a long flowing garment of black silk, unlike anything the men had ever seen. She had a creamy white complexion, as if the sun had never touched her skin. Her tresses were as raven black as her apparel and flowed loose and unbraided from a widow's peak at her forehead to her waist. Her hair was perfectly straight; her eyes, endless black pools, absorbing everything in their path. They were fringed in long fluttering, ebony lashes and highlighted with thin arched, coal-black brows. Her lips were scarlet and her long slender fingers were tipped in crimson. She stood regally, tall and voluptuous. The neckline of her bodice plunged deeply, revealing the tops of an ivory bosom. She was a temptress.

She spoke with the voice of a siren. Laughing, she bid, "Rise, subjects and honored guests. Feast and enjoy yourselves. Let the merrymaking begin!"

After one crisp clap of her hands, everyone stood and the clamor began. She held her hand out directly to Duncan. "Captain O'Rourke, prithee come forward and bring your comrades."

Duncan took the queen's proffered hand and kissed it. "'Tis most enchanting to meet ya, Yer Highness," he said with reverence.

"Let's not be so formal," she gurgled. "I'm sure we shall be fast friends. Call me Quazel, and I shall call you Duncan."

"As ya wish," whispered Duncan still enthralled with the vision before him. "Let me introduce ya to me friends. Ya have already met Dr. Connor Donohue."

"Aye," replied the queen. "I owe you a tremendous debt of gratitude, Dr. Donohue, or Connor, as we agreed last even."

Connor took her hand and kissed it. "Quazel, 'tis a pleasure to see ya feeling so well. My services are yers to command."

"Oh, you sweet man," she flirted openly. She removed her hand and turned for the next introduction.

Duncan obliged. "This is Mr. Ligon Murphy, our benefactor for this journey."

Ligon, too, kissed her hand. "Yer Majesty," he said with a click of his heels. "I am truly honored."

"Nonsense. Call me Quazel. I should very much like to discuss some legality with you at a future time. I may be in need of your counsel."

"I am yers to command."

"Yer Maj... Quazel, this is me old and dear friend, Carter O'Day," Duncan said gaining the queen's attention.

Carter took her hand and kissed it. "Yer Majesty," is all he said.

"Aye, aye. The fisherman." She waved a dismissive hand and turned for a final introduction.

Last, Duncan turned to Diggory. "I have saved the best for last. This is me roight arm, practically an extension of meself. Let me introduce me first mate, Mr. Diggory Danaher."

As Diggory told the story, his expression changed from one of nostalgic to nauseated. He said, "I kissed 'er 'and. 'Twas cold and bitter to the taste." He pushed his tongue out as if trying to get rid of the unpleasant reminder. "The only words I could manage were, "'Queen Quazel, I am speechless.'

"'Mr. Danaher, 'tis a pleasure to meet you, I'm sure,' she said, but her lips turned down in an expression of scorn.

"She turned abruptly from me.

"'Shall we feast, gentlemen? Eat, drink and be merry.' 'Twas a command..."

All through the afternoon, Queen Quazel ignored all the men except Duncan. She clung to his arm and weaved fingers in his hair. Her lips were often against his cheek and ear. Connor was peeved at her lack of attention, and muttered to himself, "He's married."

As evening approached, Quazel prepared to leave. She announced that Captain O'Rourke and she would be dining alone that evening. Diggory was uneasy about that. This woman had a power that lured men, even strong, sensible men like Duncan. Diggory sent up a silent prayer for his friend's protection against her charms.

All the way back to their quarters, Connor and Ligon sang the queen's praises and talked about how becoming and charming she was. Connor sulked that he was not dining with her. Carter and Diggory walked back from them.

"I trust her not," Carter said bluntly.

"Me either," Diggory replied. "She is up to something. I am worried aboot Duncan this eve. What if he falls prey to her wiles loike Connor did?"

"He will not. He has an everlasting love guarding his heart," Carter said with confidence. Then, they walked on in silence.

Meanwhile, Queen Quazel served intoxicating nectar wine and wore a tantalizing and sensuous perfume. A yellowish powder pervaded the room, making the candles flicker hypnotically.

"Your eyes are a most unusual shade of green, Duncan, almost like emeralds. They're beautiful," whispered Quazel.

"Gramercy," Duncan acknowledged groggily, feeling the effects of the wine.

"You must be weary and lonely after such a long journey," the queen breathed while she removed Duncan's doublet and unlaced his shirt to reveal his firm, muscled chest sparsely sprinkled with inky hair. "Let me soothe away some of those tensions." She began to rub Duncan's temples, neck, and shoulders.

"That feels so good," sighed Duncan, relaxing to her touch. He closed his eyes.

"I know," she purred as she softly brushed her lips to his.

Duncan licked his lips in anticipation, beguiled and lost under her spell. Quazel circled Duncan, slowly, gently brushing her fingertips across his bare chest, kneading the small patch of hair dead center and running one nail along his thinly bearded jawline.

"Priscilla," Duncan murmured.

All at once, there was a breathless cry outside the queen's tent. "Your Majesty! Your Majesty! 'Tis Carl! I have urgent news!"

"What do you want?" Quazel shrieked, her plans foiled. The spell was broken. The shimmering air around Duncan disappeared.

"Hank Hawke just flew over the Zone of Perfection. You gave command to let you know if he came," said Carl, fear evident in his voice.

"Fie me!" raged Queen Quazel. "We must find out what that scoundrel is up to." She turned to Duncan and in a sugary voice said, "Duncan, I beg pardon. We must continue our conversation another time." She ran from the tent after placing a kiss on his lips. "I trust you can find your way back to your quarters."

"Of course," Duncan replied to her back. A few minutes later he roused a little. He felt as if he were dreaming. Disoriented, he returned to his quarters very late, and Diggory waited for him.

Diggory stood and stretched his legs. Impatiently, Caitlin urged, "Mr. Danaher, what did you say to Duncan?"

Diggory cracked his neck and continued.

8
The Prophecy

*"**I** suppose I sounded loike a stern father because I jumped Duncan the second 'e walked in the door. 'Where 'ave ye been? What 'appened? Prithee, tell me ye didna succumb to that wench's charms.'*

"'I doona roightly remember,' Duncan said, shocked back to reality. "'Everything is blurry. Let me think. I vaguely remember drinking wine. Oh, give me some coffee or water or something to get me oot of this fog!'"

Duncan took a cold shower in a cubicle from which water from the waterfall flowed and drank a cup of strong Turkish coffee. He turned deathly pale. "God-a-mercy! Diggory, what have I done? I remember Quazel's voice being seductive. She massaged me neck and shoulders. She started to undress me and to touch me. She kissed me! Her lips!" He licked his lips with a grimace on his face. "Oh, my lips taste so bitter.

"Diggory!" Duncan shouted as he grabbed his friend's shoulders. "God save me! Tell me I did not betray Priscilla! I couldna live with meself." Duncan buried his face in his hands and wept like a baby.

He caught a deep shaking breath. Then he mumbled, "Nay," and turned toward Diggory. "I remember. That coyote came to the door. He was hollering something aboot the hawk flying over. Quazel took off loike a bat oot of Hell."

Just at that moment someone pounded on Duncan's door. "Open up quick, man. Let me in." The voice sounded panicky. They opened the door to see Jean Noir standing there. He kicked the door shut as he darted inside.

"If Quazel saw me here, she would turn me into a seahorse or a newt. Hank sent me. We must talk, Duncan. You must know the prophecy. Your very life could be in danger." He said all this in one breath.

"Slow down, Jean." Duncan was back in control of his faculties. "What aire ya talking aboot? Take a deep breath and go slowly." He turned to Diggory. "Get Jean some water."

Diggory wiggled past the massive horse since Jean's presence in the sleeping chamber took quite a bit of space. He caught water in the hand basin from the trickling cascade. Jean gulped his water and then started again.

"We all know she almost got you tonight. Don't look so taken aback. We've all been there in one way or another. She has a knack for finding your deepest desire and preying upon your need. Thanks to Hank's quick intervention, you didn't stay in her clutches long enough to yield."

"Duncan, listen to the man." Diggory said, thinking of Jean as a man, not a beast.

"Relax. I am listening. Jean what do ya mean: 'Turn ya into a seahorse'?"

"Duncan, all of us talking animals were once human. I know you met Jack and Leslie. What they told you was true. Hank was our constable. Orson was a linguistics professor and had a beautiful baritone voice. I was a simple farmer. My betrothed, Isabella LeBlanc, ran the best tavern in town. She was turned into a white mare. Luckily, she escaped to the mountains. All of us angered Quazel at some point, and paid for it. Now, we're not human. She'll do the same thing to you and your entire crew if you aren't the one prophesied, or if you miss your calling and stir her ire in any way. She is *not* a tolerant person." He shook his mane and nickered softly.

Duncan looked stunned, mouth slightly agape. "Aire ya saying Queen Quazel is a sorceress? Did she change all of you?"

"Aye, man! I know you're not slow-witted," Jean said in frustration.

"What?" Duncan and Diggory said in unison.

Undaunted, Jean continued, "Her ship wrecked here some years ago. We took her in and cared for her. She said she'd been falsely accused of witchcraft, of practicing black magic. She'd been banished from her country and had not been welcome in any other place.

"What you heard about Draconis is true. The dragons and we men were once friends. We lived together in harmony. Our children played together. I vouchsafe one of the human children's greatest pleasures was to soar over Draconis on the back of a dragon friend.

"Then, the dragon babies began to disappear. We humans were accused. Hank began an investigation. He found Quazel eating a baby dragon."

"Stop! Wait a moment!" Aidan shouted. "Eating a dragon? How could a human do such a thing? Aren't those creatures strong and practically indestructible?"

Diggory sighed. "Quazel is more than a 'uman. Even dragons are susceptible to poison and magic. And babies, 'atchlings, aire not much bigger than a large dog."

"Very well. Please, continue."

"Jean was speaking," Diggory went on...

"When Hank tried to arrest her, he immediately changed into the hawk you met.

"Quazel went mad! Within weeks, almost every human was an animal and all the dragons were dead."

"Stop!" Aidan yelled again, both hands raised over his head. "Not *all*! Surely not all." His voice broke at the thought. "She somehow poisoned *all* of them?" He shook his head. "But I…"

"Ya what?" Colin asked, his own eyes wide.

"If I say, ya all will think me mad too." He thought back to the vision of the white dragon as he heard the word, "Destiny," on the wind.

"Then 'old yer peace," Diggory grunted and scowled at his young charge. "That is if ya wanna finish the story today."

Aidan nodded.

Diggory rolled his head around on his shoulders, and the creaking of his old bones resounded before he went on.

Duncan's face contorted in a disgusted look. "Ya mean she managed to kill all dragons—enormous beasts with scales loike armor?"

"She somehow got a poison into their blood. The shrieking as they withered to dust haunts me to this day." Jean's entire body shook. "Only one human escaped into the mountains. Quazel couldn't go after him because she couldn't abide the cold. Peradventure because she came straight from the fires of Hell itself, and her long-distance spells failed when they met ice.

"So, if you be not the prophesied one, run as fast as possible to the mountains and find our wizard. His name is Alexander. He'll help get you away from this island. Go home!"

Duncan shook his head and rubbed the aching muscles of his neck. "I am just a man. How do I know anything of yer prophecies? What makes ya think I might be the one ya aire expecting?" said Duncan with discomfiture.

"You fit the description of the one that the prophet, Nathan, foretold. Let me start at the beginning.

"I've already told you that once dragons and men lived together peacefully here. This place also had other enchanted beasts such as unicorns and mermaids. 'Twas a wondrous and magical land.

"There came a prophet a hundred years ago. He told us that our tranquility would be shattered by, *'One as dark as night, yet as light as day; as weak as thread, yet as strong as iron; as sweet as honey, yet as bitter as gall.'* We in truth didn't know what to expect. We had no idea he could've meant a woman with ebony hair and ivory skin. One who was physically weak, but mentally strong, who seemed to be kind, but seethed with bitterness and rage.

"Nathan went on to say that one would come some day that could defeat the evil one. *'A man will come from far away. He will have eyes of emerald and tower over those under him. He will be accompanied by one of fiery hue and nature that will stand by him to the death.'*

"Duncan, you're a giant of a man. You have green eyes, and you came from far away. Diggory, you have the fiery hue."

Rubbing his hand across his bald head, Diggory explained to those listening to the tale, "At that time I 'ad a mop of red hair..."

"'Tis obvious that you would stand by Duncan, even unto death. What would you think if you were we? What do you think Quazel thinks? She knows the prophecy, too."

Duncan said, "Jean, I can see yer reasoning, but let me ask ya another question. Why have not the animals annihilated one another? I have seen natural enemies frolic together. If Quazel is so evil, why have ya not killed one another?"

"Ah, aye. I shall tell you. I told you our wizard, Alexander, escaped. He was unable to undo Quazel's spell, but he cast a protection on us. His protection was that natural enemies would live in harmony and do no harm upon natural instinct. They might fight upon human instinct; but, for example, Hank Hawke can't prey upon Jack O'Hara. Do you understand?"

"What aboot natural animals?" Diggory interrupted, his eyebrows drawn into a tight V.

Jean bobbed his head. "Well, yes, Hank can hunt naturally occurring rabbits and such, and Jack, must be wary of the real birds of prey."

"How do ya know the difference?"

"Alexander's doing as well. You can't smell the differences as you are in human form, but we can since he cast that spell as well. He was just too late to keep the dragons from breathing the poison in the air. Quazel acted fast for she knew he'd confront her. And now, Duncan, we all are concerned for your safety as well as our future. I told you the day we met that I prayed you're the one prophesied. I do so hope it's true."

"Aye, but, oh, Jean, I doona feel special." Duncan ran his hand through his charcoal locks. "How can I possibly be yer deliverer? I hesitated to make this voyage. I didna want to leave me family. The last time I left Priscilla, our daughter died. I doona think I could bear it if something happened to me family this time. If I am not the one ya have been looking for, I could only make matters worse or leave me family widowed and orphaned."

"Orphaned?" questioned Jean, dropping long horse lashes over dark brown eyes. "Don't let Quazel know you have a child. She's capable of casting spells over long distances. I don't know how far her evil can reach. I do know they can't penetrate icy regions."

"Well a day!" Duncan gasped. "I shall be extra careful. Ya aire the only one from here who knows. I can trust you to keep it secret, aye?"

"Indeed. I shall go to my grave before I let that witch know anything. Furthermore, I shall fight by your side, my friend, to the end. You have my word of honor."

"I am sure I do, Jean. I am sure I do."

It was apparent that Duncan was exhausted as he yawned widely behind his hand and took a deep breath. He had endured quite an ordeal with Quazel, and Jean's words weighed heavily on his mind and heart.

"Jean," Diggory said, placing a protective hand on his friend's shoulder, "Duncan needs some rest. This has been a hard night."

"Aye, of course. Let me see if the way is clear." The transition to look out would have been comical if the situation were not so grave. Jean stumbled and stepped on Diggory's feet with many apologies. When Jean turned back from the door, Duncan was already asleep.

Diggory continued, "Before ya go, tell me whom else can we trust if we need to contact ya?"

"Do *not* trust your misguided young doctor. The Empress of Darkness has already poisoned his impressionable mind. His heart is pure, but 'tis not worth the risk to try to save him right now. Some of the animals, especially the apes, in truth believe Quazel has created a paradise here. 'Tis better not to trust any of them. You can trust Orson."

"Orson!" Diggory snapped. "Surely ya jest. I know he hates me even if he moight admire Duncan."

"Don't let his demeanor fool you. 'Tis meant to deceive Quazel. He's an ally. You can also trust Eunice if you can get close to her. Eunice would love to run Quazel through with her horn, but Quazel keeps her unicorn closely guarded. Eunice is a real unicorn. She isn't a transformed human. Eunice is Quazel's slave. That witch has done evil things to her." The mammoth horse shivered again. "I can't talk about that, but she's the last of her kind.

"I must away now. 'Tis almost daybreak, and I must be at my post at sunup. Take care, my friend, and take special care of that one." He indicated Duncan with his head. Then he was gone.

Diggory grabbed a blanket and a pillow and caught a few hours of restless sleep on Duncan's floor. Early the following morning, they heard banging next door. Duncan shot out of bed. Diggory cracked the door to see Orson knocking on Connor's door. "Queen Quazel has awakened with a splitting headache. She wishes you to bring some of your magic powders to comfort her."

Connor left in a great hurry. Orson grunted after him, "Young fool." He had no idea Duncan and Diggory were watching him through the cracked door. When he turned toward Duncan's room, they shut the door quickly.

Diggory stowed the blanket and pillow under Duncan's bed and set about making some coffee. Duncan answered the door with a cheery smile on his face. "Good morrow, Orson. What can we do for ya this fine day?"

Orson barged in and slammed the door with a thrust of his massive back leg. "You can stop pretending! You know why I've come. I can't abide being under that monster's thumb another day! I think you're the savior that was promised. You fit all the criteria. 'Tis time you faced the truth. No matter how reluctant you might feel, you *are* the one!

"I'm here to offer you my assistance. The old hag trusts me. I can get close to her. Tell me what you want me to do, and I shall do it."

"Wait, Orson," said Duncan, his very practical side showing. "You must realize all this prophecy rhetoric was thrown at me last eve. I have not had time to consider the possibilities yet.

"I know that ya and Jean and Hank think I am the one ya have been expecting. Doona ya think I need to believe it, too? Verily, 'tis hard for me to think I could be responsible for something of such magnitude. Ya have suffered for years. This is brand new and foreign to me."

Duncan's military thinking took over. "Moreover, if I am yer *deliverer* we canna jump into a war with a witch blindly. We must plan our strategy. We must know our enemy."

"Aye, you're right. You just don't understand what 'tis like. When you look at me, you see something formidable. I see a baffoon. I feel like a circus bear, jumping at Quazel's every command. 'Tis humiliating!" With that outburst, the towering ursine slumped on the floor.

"I know ya must be miserable," Duncan consoled Orson while stroking his warm fur. "Let me investigate the situation. If I am the one, surely I shall know somehow."

Diggory stood again and hobbled to the door of his hut to peek outside. All those present began to mumble among themselves. He turned back. "It be agettin' late. The rain be still asloshin'. Let us eat a bite. We 'ave some 'am and bread and apples. Will you lasses make a bite o' supper?"

Caitlin and Mary Kate found the food items and sliced thick chunks of meat. Elizabeth joined them saying, "Let us add some of this fine cheese." She cubed that and buttered some of the bread.

Aidan got up and helped by filling mugs with fresh water. Colin groaned as he tried to get up. Aidan waved off his assistance with a faint smile.

After a hastily prepared meal, eaten in an even bigger hurry, Diggory once again related past events.

9
𝕽𝖊𝖇𝖊𝖑𝖆𝖙𝖎𝖔𝖓𝖘

*"**The** day passed without event," Diggory explained. "Connor spent the day with the queen. 'E gave 'er a strong sleeping powder because 'er 'eadache was severe. The fact that she was sedated worked to Duncan's advantage..."*

Just after dark, Orson and Jean came to Duncan's door. They wanted him to meet somebody. Stopping to get Diggory, the four of them went around the fence perimeter until they got to a heavily wooded area. Four iridescent luna moths went before them, lighting their way.

Here the temperature was much cooler. Standing on the outside of the fence was a distinguished looking gentleman, illuminated by a soft glow from fireflies in a jar. He was covered from head to foot in a black monk's robe. An imposing figure, he stood almost as tall as Duncan, but much slimmer. He threw back his hood and cowl to reveal short salt-and-pepper hair and a thin, closely clipped graying beard. His eyes were as green as Duncan's, but even more intense with the wisdom that comes with age and experience. They looked so much alike that he could have been Duncan in thirty years or Duncan could have been him thirty years earlier.

Duncan gasped at the vision. "Who aire ya?"

The older man smiled, and a light gleamed in his eyes. "Be well met, son," he said tenderly. "I wondered when you'd come. You've become a fine man, full of character and integrity. I'm well pleased. Your mother did a fabulous job. How is she?"

"Dead. Who the devil aire ya?" Duncan answered curtly.

"I'm so sorry." The man choked a sob. "Genevieve was a wonderful woman. I'm grieved by her loss."

"What do ya know of me mother? Who aire ya?" Duncan became agitated, clenching his fists. Diggory placed a reassuring hand on his shoulder.

"'Tis good you have such a loyal friend. You'll need him in the years to come," said the mysterious man.

"Oot upon it! Stop talking in riddles. Who aire ya, and what do ya want with me? Answer me!" Duncan demanded grasping the bars between them.

"Your mother was the former Genevieve Brady of Willow Hollow. She was the magistrate's daughter, a statuesque beauty with golden ringlets for hair and violet eyes. She married the wrong man, a man the rest of the community distrusted. Consequently, they moved to Stonebridge to start afresh.

"In this realm I'm Alexander, a wizard. Twenty-seven years ago in Stonebridge I was known as Alex O'Rourke."

"'Tis impossible!" Duncan turned away, and then back to face the man. "Me father died before I was born. He went on a mission and died from a fever aboard ship."

"So, that is the story they told." Alexander stroked his beard in thought. "Aye, I went on a voyage because the people of Stonebridge and Willow Hollow forced me to leave. They feared me because I had special powers. No one had had such abilities for centuries. I never returned because the ship's crew left me here." He waved his hand to indicate Draconis. "They blamed me for the bad luck they experienced on the voyage."

"Ya canna be me father. Ya canna," Duncan said in a voice strangled by tears. He was near hysterics.

"You're welcome to ask Michael Flannery. He was the cabin boy on the ship. How do you think he knew about this place?"

"No," was the almost inaudible reply.

"Ask Diggory." Alexander looked at Duncan's friend with a glare that bored a hole in Diggory's soul and continued. "He was a young man just starting his livelihood in the village. In your heart you know I speak the truth."

Eyes brimming with tears, Duncan looked imploringly at Diggory.

Diggory told him all he remembered. "Duncan, I remember many of the leaders thinking yer father was a warlock. We young ones just wanted him to tell our fortunes. I knew he left, but I didna know why. When he did not return, we all thought he was dead."

"Diggory, ya canna believe him," Duncan said choking back tears.

"Duncan, look at him. Ya aire his spitting image. Aye, I believe him."

"Son," said Alexander beseechingly, "I never wanted to leave. I tried several times to get back, but I always was forced back here. I couldn't understand why I kept being forced back to this island.

"Then, I met the prophet, Nathan, just before he died. He told me that someday my son would come to me. Then, he told me the prophecy. For a moment I thought he was talking about me. I fit his description, except for my partner." He shook his head. "I didn't have a partner. Nathan told me I'd dwell in the mountains and guard the young there, but *that* is another story. He assured me I would help to keep this land from being completely destroyed. He told me my descendant would emancipate those whom the evil one would afflict. He wanted me to find his scrolls he had hidden in the mountains to understand how to defeat the sorceress. He died before he could tell me where they were, but I have searched from the day he died.

"Duncan, you *are* my son. You must be the one who has come to free these people. You have everything Nathan prophesied, including Diggory. You must be the one. I don't have the scrolls yet, but we are looking for them so you can know your course of action. Sometimes I fear Quazel has found them and destroyed them." He breathed deeply. "I don't have time to convince you further right now. Her spies are everywhere, though she, herself, would never venture here for the coolness of the place. If they should overhear or see us, the consequences could be your life. I shan't risk that." He turned as if to go.

"Father," whispered Duncan.

Alexander turned back, a smile on his face.

Duncan asked, "How can this be?" Both men were overcome with emotion. They clung to each other through the bars, unable to speak for a while.

After a time, they released their embrace. Alexander confided, "I can't stay here. There are those whom I must protect. Search your heart, Duncan. You will find the answer. I'll continue to search for the scrolls, as I have for years. If you need me, Hank will get me. Know that I love you. I've *always* loved you from the day your mother told me we were expecting a baby. A part of me has been missing all these years, just as a part of you is missing even now." He held up a hand when Duncan started to speak. "No. No one has divulged your secret. I'm a wizard. I know things. Listen to me. You and your mother were always in my heart, just as those you love are in your heart.

"You must be careful. Quazel is pure evil. She's not all she seems. I've seen her true identity. I'm sure when you see her for what in truth she is, you'll know what to do. Take care, heart of my heart." Alexander kissed Duncan's forehead and held him for another moment before he vanished into the night.

Duncan stayed in his room for the next two days. Orson told the queen Duncan was not well. By the second day, Quazel grew impatient. She wanted Connor to examine Duncan. Orson told her it was the new, rich, spicy food that disagreed with Duncan's stomach and that he was recovering.

The third day, Duncan took Diggory by the shoulders. "'Tis time to take action." He sent Quazel a note requesting a private picnic by the brook. He met her there and began his charade.

As he held her hand he enticed, "I pray thee, be patient with me. Remember me heart has belonged to one woman for a long time, but 'twas before I met ya. I have never known anyone loike ya. I want to get to know ya better, but let us court slowly. I am a gentleman, and I want to court ya properly."

Diggory looked around at the enthralled faces.

"Quazel bought 'is ploy loike a fish swallowing bait. She was in love with 'im as much as pure evil can love anything other than itself..."

They had outings after that—dinner, tea, picnics, evening strolls, tennis matches, unicorn rides. Duncan always made sure they were together on his terms, never alone on hers.

While they were out, Orson and Diggory searched for anything they could use against Quazel. On one occasion, they found a spell book and an amulet, which they sent to

Alexander. Another time they discovered gemstones buried around Quazel's tent. They dug them up and sent them to Alexander. There were seven different ones.

"What kind?" Caitlin asked.
Diggory gave her an indulgent smile. "I'll tell ye soon."

Then, after an evening stroll, Quazel entreated Duncan to come into her tent. She pouted, "You don't love me or trust me. If you did, you wouldn't be reluctant to be alone with me." She lifted her hand and spoke behind its cover. "Connor isn't afraid to come in here."

"I doona want ya spending time alone with Connor." He pretended to be jealous and turned his lips down in a pout. "Quazel, ya must choose. Do ya want me, or is it Connor?"

"There is no choice, my beloved. Connor is a child, a plaything. I want you. Nothing would make me happier than to have you reign by my side." She latched her fingers around Duncan's neck and kissed him passionately. "Come in, Duncan," she breathed against his neck. "Prove your love to me." She pulled him into her lair and kissed him again.

He felt pulled into a void, a roaring sound as a giant waterfall in his ears. The air grew warmer, more humid, yet his breath formed ice crystals when he spoke. What Duncan saw in that moment chilled him to the bone. He tried to maintain his composure as he looked into the glowing red eyes of a withered pasty face, the head covered in scraggly, black, matted hair. The hands were long and bony and tipped with razor sharp claws. The voice sounded like the squawk of a crow. Quazel was not a ravishing beauty. She was an old crone.

Duncan pried her hands from his neck. He knew he was trembling. He whispered, "Quazel, ya make me heart faint. I tremble with desire, but I need a little more time. Good noight, me love." He kissed her fingertips and backed out the door.

Looking around, he caught his breath in sharp puffs. There were no beautiful palms, no vibrant flowers. There were only burned trees, rotting stumps, weeds, brambles. His silk robe became burlap. This whole place was an illusion.

Duncan ran all the way back to where his entourage was quartered, stopping only once to vomit. The farther he ran from Quazel's tent, the more the beauty returned. By the time he got to Diggory's quarters, the illusion was completely restored. He burst through the door. "Diggory, I saw her," he panted. "Me father," he gasped for air. "I need me father."

He drafted a note to Alexander. Diggory gave it to Jean who summoned Hank.

The old sailor beheld his captive audience. Caitlin squeezed Aidan's hand, her eyes wide while Aidan breathed in short gasps.

Diggory nodded toward the boy. "That be exactly 'ow yer father sounded."

Mary Kate buried her face in Colin's shoulder as he stroked her hair in comfort and listened without comment.

Elizabeth leaned forward in her chair. "Go on," she encouraged.

10
𝕻urgatory

𝕯iggory grinned his toothless grin, feeling some vindication for all those who had doubted his story as the expressions on the faces before him indicated belief.

"'Twas amazing how fast Alexander could travel. He was there within hours. We met in the same place as before…"

"How now? What's wrong?" Alexander shouted on his way up to the fence.

"I saw her, Father. That hideous thing must be killed. How can I do it? Is there some kind of protective spell ya can cast to guarantee the safety of anyone who helps me? Orson and Jean aire terrified of being turned into an even lesser being than they aire now."

"Done. Years ago."

"What aboot me men? What can ya do to keep them safe?"

Alexander's face went ashen. Duncan said, "Father, why such a long face? What has happened?"

Alexander narrowed his eyes to slits toward Jean. "You have *not* told him."

"Nay. I was afraid of his reaction." Jean hung his head. "I'm sorry."

"What should I be told?" Duncan bit out. "I am not a child, and I am not stupid. What has become of me crew? Obviously, something has happened. What has Quazel done?"

"Duncan, they were all changed the minute you entered the gates of Purgatory," Alexander told him with closed eyes and a long, slow head shake. "I have them in the mountains with me, but they're all animals. I'm so sorry."

Duncan fisted his hands. "Father, if Quazel dies, will all the animals be restored to personhood?"

"Aye, but don't be rash. Let me finish reading Quazel's book. We've also unearthed Nathan's scrolls"—He gave one delighted hand clap—"only yesterday. Give me time to finish reading them. They may offer us more clues about how to defeat her."

"Father, I fear we aire running oot of time. I doona know how much longer I can fool her, especially now that I have seen her for what she in sooth is. I am not a play actor. I am a sailor, and I am not afraid to admit to ya she scares the daylights oot of me. I suppose I am also getting impatient. This has been going on for *months*. I want to go home. I miss Priscilla and Aidan so much. Ya must know how I feel."

"I do, son," empathized Alexander, and he embraced his son the best he could through the iron bars. "Give me another week to read. Remember"—He placed his index finger to his lips—"don't talk about your family here. Mayhap soon you'll be with me in the mountains, and you can tell me all about them. Perchance I can even go home with you," he finished, the longing heavy in his voice.

"I shall hold on to those dreams. Contact me as soon as possible. I shall try to be patient." Duncan tried to sound confident and plastered a smile on his face.

They bade each other farewell and went to bed.

Quazel arrived early the next day. She came prepared for a day of picnicking at the brook. The only attendant she brought with her was Eunice. With great reluctance, Duncan rode off with her.

Quick of thought, he hit on a plan to keep Quazel busy for a few days. While he had his head on her lap, he looked up at her with his dazzling smile and said, "Quazel, me birthday is in one week." He rose up on his elbow and stroked her cheek. "I want a feast, a big party. Invite everybody. I want a big cake. Place one candle for each of my years on the cake. I've decided to make a new tradition—a wish upon the lit candles as they are blown out. I want music and dancing and laughing. I want a celebration. Doesna that sound loike amusement?" he said with the eagerness of a child. "What say ya? An' it please ya," he cajoled.

Quazel laughed and declared, "I shall start planning it today! And I can assure your wishes will come true."

"Marry!" Duncan feigned enthusiasm. He grabbed her hand and pulled her to her feet. "Let us go for a swim!"

Quazel shrank from him. "I don't know how. I just sit on the bank and watch the swimmers."

Duncan got a glint in his emerald eyes. "I shall teach ya. Come hither." He pulled her toward the water that gurgled clear and clean over smooth stones.

"Fie!" she screamed, jerking her hand free. "I don't want to go into the water."

"Verily, I shall not let go of ya," Duncan pleaded. *I shan't let go. I'll drown you like the rat ya aire.*

"'Tis too cold. If you persist with this, I shall away." She waved her hand toward Eunice. "I don't like the water," she asserted with apparent trepidation.

Duncan thought for a moment and shrugged his shoulders. "Have it yer way, but I am taking a dip." He took off his clothes slowly, one piece at a time and dropped them at Quazel's feet. Then, he walked to the water's edge. He turned toward her and said with a wink, "Last chance."

Quazel sat on the shore and hugged her knees to her. "'Tis quite all right. I shall watch from here."

Duncan took his swim. He told Diggory later, "I needed to wash away the feel of her."

They returned relatively early. Quazel departed to plan Duncan's birthday festivity. He told his friend about their morning. "Diggory, she is afraid of the water, and there be more to it than not being able to swim. As many times as she has tried to lure me into her boudoir, she wouldna swim naked with me. The temptation of the one thing she has been after ever since the first day we met wouldna even get her to let go of her fear of the water. Mayhap water can hurt her in some way."

Duncan sent Alexander a note about his suspicions. He failed to notice a wasp buzzing above the doorway to his quarters.

Time passed. The party was to be the next day. They still had not heard from Alexander. Finally, a note arrived. It said:

Duncan, I think water must burn her. When we found her on the beach, she had burns on much of her body. None of her spells use water.

That confirmed Duncan's suspicions about the water.

At daybreak on the day of the party, Orson came to the door with a grave countenance. Quazel had planned an all-day affair beginning with breakfast. It was clear that Orson was disturbed.

"Is something amiss, my friend?" Duncan asked.

"I know not. Have you noticed any unusual creatures around?"

Duncan shook his head.

Orson sighed. "Duncan, be not alarmed," he started. "There's a jackass in Carter's bed and an iguana in Ligon's bed. Connor's with Quazel. He's laughing like a fool."

"I shall kill her with me bare hands!" Duncan stormed. It was all Orson and Diggory could do to restrain the furious captain. Diggory had never seen his friend so angry.

By the time they dressed, Carter and Ligon had disappeared. When they got to the clearing for breakfast, Duncan asked Connor, "Where aire Carter and Ligon?"

Quazel lied, "They asked to return to the ship yesterday. I sent Carl to take them back."

Quazel was surrounded by apes most of the day. Diggory whispered to Duncan, "She must suspect something. She's guarding herself closely."

Duncan went to talk to Eunice where she stood near a laden honeysuckle vine. "Don't eat the cake," Eunice warned. "The frosting is made with nectar wine. You know what that does to you. Feel in my mane. There's a note from Alexander."

Duncan motioned for Diggory. They moved carefully to hide behind the cats' hammocks. The note read:

Son, get out of there! You cannot do this alone. There is more to the prophecy. Away now!

"'Tis too late," breathed Duncan as Quazel called him. He cocked his head to the side, seeing a red wasp fly away from Quazel's ear. "Damn!" he muttered and pointed out the bug to Diggory who breathed out a long sigh.

"I saw a wasp at me door. Why did the thought not occur to me that it could be a spy?" He looked at his first mate, his mouth in a tight line. "Diggory, if I say anything the least bit confrontational, climb on Jean and go to my father. Remember yer promise to me."

"If I go, I will certainly return for ya," Diggory promised. They clasped hands around their wrists. Then, Duncan moved toward Quazel.

"Aye, dear, what do ya want?"

"'Tis time to blow out your candles and make a wish." Duncan closed his eyes. Visions of Priscilla and Aidan floated across his mind. *I am so sorry. I have failed ya. I love ya with all me heart.*

He blew.

Diggory surveyed the listeners. He lowered his voice a bit. "Jean and I were on the fringes watchin' and listenin'. Orson and Eunice 'ad disappeared.

"'What did ye wish for?' inquired Quazel.

"Duncan looked sharply at 'er. 'E never blinked. 'E never flinched. 'I wished all these people would be returned to their original form and would see ya as ya in truth aire.'

"The former did not 'appen, but the latter did. There was screamin' and runnin' as everyone saw exactly what Duncan 'ad seen a little over a week before.

"Jean and I did as we were told. On our way to the gate we could 'ear Quazel, 'Before I deal with you, arrogant one, see what your foolishness has cost.'

"We could see from the gate as Quazel turned her wrath toward a trembling Connor Donohue. 'Oh, fair child, I almost regret this, but your commander must be punished:

**'Always laughing and foolish,
Some even think you ghoulish.'**

"With a pop and many painful screeches, Connor was a hyena.

"'*No!' cried Duncan. Quazel turned just as Duncan lunged at her with the 'uge knife from 'is birthday cake. She sidestepped 'is strike, and Duncan sprawled on the ground from the force of 'is thrust. Quazel cackled.*

"*I suddenly realized Jean 'ad sprouted wings. We were flying. 'Get Duncan,' I begged. Jean started to turn just as we 'eard Quazel's next words:*

> **'Big and black you will be seen**
> **With one identifiable trait, eyes of green.**
> **My death for you, a change will not affect;**
> **For you only one thing will correct;**
> **To restore you my death will not be dear.**
> **Only from the eyes of one you love without bound,**
> **a tear.'**

"*I saw all this from 'igh above. I watched as Duncan fell to the ground, writhing in agony as 'is body contorted and 'e screamed sounds worse than a woman in childbirth. I saw a 'umongous panther swipe a paw across Quazel's face. Blood spurted everywhere, and the panther screamed, 'Diggory, ya have yer orders! Obey them!' 'Twas the last time I saw Duncan. I doona know 'ow many black panthers aire on that island. I saw at least twenty. 'Twas seventeen years ago. I be sure 'e is with Alexander. Alexander swore 'e would find 'is son. I know 'e would die trying.*

"*Quazel was not dead. I 'eard 'er wail, 'Where is that fool?' Then, I 'eard another incantation begin:*

'A beast of burden you have always been...'

"*I 'eard nothin' else as we flew into the clouds, but all of a sudden I felt a searing pain in me back, and a 'uge 'ump popped up. I still 'ave the 'ump as ya can see. I suppose she was trying to turn me into a camel. 'Tis a good thing she did not think aboot a Bactrian camel, or I would 'ave two 'umps,"* Diggory added with a sardonic grin.

"I also began talkin' loike a buffoon once I left the island. I didna always sound so ridiculous. Now, no matter how 'ard I try, the words come oot wrong." He waved a hand. *"Enough of that tangent.*

"Jean must 'ave flown into an ice cloud, so Quazel's spell was incomplete. I am still 'uman, just ludicrous to see or 'ear. Jean and I flew to Alexander. 'E was devastated. 'E kept saying. 'Why did 'e not listen to me? I told 'im to leave.'

"Before Alexander sent me 'ome, 'e told me the rest of the prophecy. There was more than the people could remember. Only part of it 'ad been passed down. Alexander read the scrolls. It went loike this:

> ***From a land far away one and one and one will come. With eyes of emerald they will tower over those under them. Though one may be beaten, two can stand strong; but a three-strand cord is not easily broken. The victor will strike from the left, decisively and without warning. By his side will stand those of fiery hue and temperament even unto the call of death. In the power of seven there is unbeatable strength to defeat evil—emerald, diamond, ruby, sapphire, topaz, opal, onyx. More powerful still: love that knows no end.***

"I 'ave it written down.

"I know ye all loikely think I be crazy, but I 'ave some things to show ye." Diggory hobbled to the old trunk and took a key from around his neck.

"The knife didna work very well, did it, Aidan?"

"Pardon?" Aidan tried to deny his actions.

Diggory laughed. "I found the filet knife under me bed. Ye shoulda jest asked. Course I woulda told ye the time wasna roight. Now it be roight." He clicked the key in the lock and said, "Foilsigh rúnda." The trunk popped open. He turned to the group, "Alexander enchanted the lock. Only this key and those words can open it."

Diggory pulled a smaller box from among a burlap robe, a collection of peacock feathers, and several large scales. He sat back down and opened it carefully. He pulled out a golden amulet with Sanskrit writing on it.

"This be for ye, Aidan. It be the amulet me and Orson dug up. Yer grandfather sent it to ye. Ye may need to wear it someday." Diggory handed the amulet to Aidan, and Aidan turned it over in his hands. "We 'ave no clue what it says."

Next, Diggory opened a small velvet pouch and dumped out seven gems: one emerald, one diamond, one ruby, one sapphire, one topaz, one opal, one onyx. "These be the stones we dug up from around Quazel's tent. We be purty sure they 'ave somethin' to do with the power of seven. Seven stones moight indicate seven people. Which seven?" He shrugged.

Last, Diggory pulled out the written words of the prophecy. Everybody passed it around and read it.

Caitlin spoke her mind. "Mr. Danaher, first, what is a panther?"

"Ah, child. It be a large wild cat. 'Ave ya seen drawings of tigers?"

She nodded. Diggory smiled his gummy grin. "Similar, but all black."

Caitlin asked, "Do ya think when the prophecy says 'one and one and one' that means three? Does that mean three men from the same place, all tall and with green eyes? Could that mean Alexander, Duncan, and"—She paused— "Aidan? Aidan is Alexander's descendant. Nathan told Alexander his descendant would come to liberate the people. The prophecy also talks aboot the strength of a three-strand cord."

With a hand to the younger woman's shoulder, Lizzie questioned, "Caitlin, child, do ya believe Diggory's story?"

"Oh, aye," Caitlin affirmed with hearty head nodding.

"Diggory," Lizzie said, putting her hand on the man's hand, "she believes ya."

"Does anyone 'ere think I be batty?" Diggory asked.

After an awkward pause, Colin spoke up. "Sir, if I believe ya, I think everybody believes ya; and, sir, I believe ya."

"Aidan," Diggory said softly, "what think ya?"

Aidan looked up with tears on his cheeks. "Do ya have anything that belonged to me father?"

Diggory went back to the trunk and lifted the burlap robe. "Only a silk robe," chuckled the old man.

He handed the cloth to Aidan.

11
𝔇ecisions

𝔄idan donned the tattered piece of burlap with the care he would have given silk. It fit as if it had been made for him. The storm having subsided, Aidan slipped quietly out the door. Caitlin started after him.

"Leave him be, Sis." Colin restrained her, a hand on her wrist. "He needs to be alone. If he wanted ya with him, he woulda asked. Doona worry. He will come to ya in time."

"Colin be roight, lass," confirmed Diggory. "The boy's 'umours be in a fragile state. Give 'im time to gain control." Diggory patted Caitlin's hand.

Then, Diggory turned to Colin. "Lad, it be late, and the storm be over. Why do ye not escort the ladies 'ome? I be worn oot meself."

"Of course, sir. We have stayed far too late. We shall check on ya and Aidan on the morrow. God keep ya." Colin left with Mary Kate on one arm and Elizabeth on the other. Caitlin trailed behind.

As soon as the visitors were out of sight, Diggory grabbed his cane and went in search of Aidan. Diggory knew Aidan was hanging dangerously on the precipice of adulthood, still a boy struggling to be a man and a man still clinging to boyhood. What he did with the information he had received during the last two days would affect many people. If he rejected his calling, Draconis would remain cursed forever. If he accepted his destiny, there would be much planning to do.

Diggory finally found Aidan at the livery. He was in a stall rubbing the nose of a big black horse with strange markings on his back. He looked up and saw Diggory.

"When I was a wee lad, I would see ya in here grooming this horse, and I would hear ya talking to him. I thought ya were sentimental and lonely or mayhap a little crazy, but 'tis Jean Noir, is it not?" He touched the long lines. "And this is where his wings sprouted."

"Aye, lad, but the wings were only that one time, a spell from Alexander."

Aidan continued to stroke the horse. "Be well met. I am Aidan O'Rourke. I believe ya know me father and me grandfather, Duncan and Alexander. I am honored to meet someone with so much courage, spirit, and endurance."

"Aidan, he canna talk here. The farther we sailed from Draconis, the less he could speak until he appears merely a horse. He can still understand, though. I be sure Jean be pleased to meet ye too. What say ye, old friend?"

Jean pawed the ground, whinnied, and nodded.

"Aidan, it be late. We all need some rest. Let us away home. We can talk as we walk. Fare thee well, Jean."

Jean responded with a neigh.

Diggory and Aidan left the livery with the older man's hand on the younger one's shoulder. They walked along in thought for a while. Finally, Aidan broke the silence, "Diggory, was Caitlin roight? Is the three-strand cord all of us O'Rourke men together? Am I supposed to go to Draconis?"

"I think all those questions can be answered, 'Aye.' Before I left Draconis, Alexander read and reread the scrolls 'e found. Everything indicates that the power of the three of ye can somehow undo the 'arm Quazel caused. We know if she dies the curse will be lifted, but she must be killed by a man.

"Alexander 'as become an old man by now. 'E wouldna 'ave the strength to defeat 'er. Moreover, 'e must protect the children.

"Duncan be not 'uman roight now. In his present state, 'e canna kill Quazel. Part of the curse be that those she changed canna mortally 'arm her.

"Ye be so young. Ye be smart and strong, but ye also be innocent." Diggory shook his head, eyes closed, and breathed a weighty sigh.

"That thing be evil, Aidan, pure evil. She changed an entire land and tried to exterminate a whole race. 'Twill take the special strengths and gifts from each of ye to defeat this woman. Ye must work together. Aye, Aidan. To be sure, the three of ye together will not be easily defeated."

"What aboot the power of seven? What does that mean?"

"Verily, I doona know. Mayhap Alexander knows by now. We do know the stones allowed Quazel to 'ide her true nature. When they were gone, Duncan saw the fiend she in truth be."

"Diggory, what aboot the part that speaks aboot love that knows no end? Do ya have any idea what that means?"

"I always thought 'twas talking aboot Duncan and Priscilla. Now, I know not. Me boy, mayhap it be ye and Caitlin," Diggory said halfheartedly.

"Mayhap." Aidan brightened.

"Lad, what be ye asayin'?" Diggory was taken aback by Aidan's response. He stopped walking and stepped back a pace.

"Doona sound so astounded!" laughed Aidan. "I am almost grown. Me father was married when he was eighteen."

"Aidan, Duncan 'ad only a mother and came to manhood oot o' necessity. Priscilla...no one knows a thing aboot 'er life afore Duncan rescued 'er—not even yer mother 'ad any memories, save 'er name."

A voice came to Diggory. "'Tis time. Do not fight it."

Aidan's words brought the old man back to the moment. "I do love Caitlin. I think ya already knew that. I plan to marry her. Believe me, she feels the same. I need only to speak to her father."

"Aidan, I figured the two of ye would eventually wed, but do ye think the time be roight for such a major decision?"

"Think aboot this, Diggory: Whom do ya know that has a fierier hue and temperament than Caitlin? Who would stand by me side through thick and thin? She fits the prophecy."

"She be a woman!"

"So is Quazel."

"Colin fits the prophecy, too."

The voice came to Diggory again. "Stop fighting. This is the prophecy."

Hands clenching and unclenching Diggory took a sharp breath. *I shan't even tell Aidan I be a'earin' voices in me 'ead.*

"Surely ya jest. He hates me."

"Nay, lad. Ye 'ave won his respect."

"Respect? Mayhap, but not his love. When I marry Caitlin, he will be me brother-in-law. I can only hope that someday he will love me loike a brother."

"'Ow do ye feel aboot 'im, Aidan?"

"He could be me best friend, if he would get over the animosity he has aboot Caitlin and me."

"I think 'e 'as, but we 'ave time to make those decisions. Ye will go nowhere and do nothing until ye finish school."

"We can make plans and get things ready."

"Forsooth, but roight now the only plan I 'ave is to get some sleep."

"Agreed," concluded Aidan as they arrived home. He yawned widely.

The next day dawned clear and clean. After church, Elizabeth invited all the previous night's participants to her home for dinner. The young people eagerly accepted. None of them except Aidan had ever been inside her mansion on the banks of Cypress Creek.

When they arrived, the cook set about preparing a delightful dinner of minced pie, fruit, and egg custard. As they ate, Elizabeth remarked, "I had forgotten how much young men can eat, Diggory. We must remember to furnish plenty of supplies when Aidan goes to Draconis."

It seemed everyone present stopped chewing or drinking immediately, and all eyes turned toward the dowager.

Aidan broke the silence. "What do ya mean, Lady Gilhooley?"

"You may call me Elizabeth. What I mean is simply that when ya go to Draconis, I intend to finance yer voyage. I know it will be some months yet, but we must begin preparations now. An endeavor of this magnitude doesna take place overnight."

Aidan eyed Diggory, wide-eyed. Diggory saw the look and answered, "Doona look at me, lad. I be as baffled as ye. Lizzie, ye 'ave some explainin' to do."

"Ya men can be so slow sometimes. 'Tis when it becomes incumbent upon us women to take charge." She laid her fork down and rolled her eyes.

"We all know the question is not *if* Aidan goes, but when. If we insooth believe the things Diggory told us, 'tis inevitable. Someone must finance the trip. The only other person in this community with anything at stake or the funds to do so would be Logan Murphy. I pray ya aire not offended when I say this, Mary Kate, but I doona think he would be willing to put oot that kind of money again. Moreover, he thinks Diggory is just an old fool who lost his mind because he lost his whole crew. He thinks Diggory made up the story of Draconis because he couldna cope with reality. Besides, Logan himself has let go of most reality these days, probably because he blames himself for the fate of *The Sea Bird* and her crew."

She placed her linen napkin on the table. "I have more money than I could spend in three lifetimes. I shall finance this voyage. I have much at stake besides money. I want the honor of a man I have loved all me life restored. I doona care if he speaks poorly, or if he looks strangely. I care aboot his heart. Diggory is the same man he was when we loved each other when I was eighteen. We were forced apart then. 'Twill not happen again. Aidan, my only request of ya is that ya bring him home.

"I am not foolish, man," Elizabeth continued, as she looked Diggory in the eye. "I know ya will go with the boy. Ya promised Duncan ya would come back for him. Ya aire honor bound.

"Aidan, ya must face the fact 'tis yer destiny to go to this strange, enchanted land. The rest of ya must decide what yer roles will be in this adventure. I am positive ya all have one. I know what mine is, yer financier."

Destiny ran through Aidan's mind, and he again envisioned a white dragon, and just like the other times as quickly as the shadowy vision came, it faded. He shook himself back to the moment. "Verily, I must go," Aidan affirmed. "I have a covenant with Diggory to finish school first. 'Twould be foolish to leave on a voyage in the dead of winter anyway. Spring will be soon enough. There aire a few other things I must take care of before I leave." Aidan smiled at Caitlin as he took her hand and kissed it.

"Me too," put in Colin.

"What do ya mean, Colin?" Aidan asked.

"I have a few things to take care of before I go."

"Why would ya embark on such a dangerous undertaking with me?"

"Doona be silly, Aidan. I think we have put our differences behind us. 'Tis obvious ya will loikely be part of me family someday. Me family sticks together. Voila! I am your redheaded, bad-tempered chum. Ya aire stuck with me."

"I am going, too," declared Caitlin.

"Uh, no," chided Colin. "This trip will be no place for a woman."

"We shall see," defied Caitlin. Then, she pointed a finger at Aidan. "Doona ya say a word. Ya know I am stubborn, and mayhap I have a worse temper than Colin."

"Amen," chimed Mary Kate.

Colin asked in surprise, "What did ya say?"

"Pay me no attention. I am just a little mouse taking all this in," replied Mary Kate with a coy smile.

All this dumbfounded Diggory. He never knew Elizabeth could be so forceful. He must have been sitting there with his tongue hanging out for Elizabeth turned to him and said, "What is the matter, dear? Cat got yer tongue?"

P.C. crossed his mind and he scowled. "I doona know what to say. I be flabbergasted."

"'Tis not a problem," quipped Elizabeth. "I have everything under control. 'Tis plain we have a few details to work out, but I think we have the beginnings of a crew at this table. Do we have a ship?"

"*The Sea Bird* be in dry dock," confirmed Diggory.

"Good. Over these winter months ya lads and lasses can whip her into running order. Aidan, methinks ya should be ready to sail by early summer. Let us make that our working plan."

"Aye, ma'am," submitted Aidan. Then, the conversation turned to other things

The young people left about mid-afternoon. Colin took Mary Kate home while Aidan walked Caitlin home. They strolled quietly holding hands for a while before they stopped on the small covered bridge over the creek. Built of

irregular stones, which gave the village its name, it was a peaceful, romantic spot.

As they leaned against the rail, Aidan brushed a stray wisp of hair from Caitlin's face. He could not help thinking she was beautiful and vivacious. He caressed her cheek with his fingertip and tipped her chin upward. He softly and gently kissed her. Then, he pulled her to him and kissed her forcefully. Caitlin responded in kind, passionately returning Aidan's affections. After that he held her in his arms and tenderly stroked her collarbone. He whispered, "I had not intended to move this swiftly. I wanted more time to be together without any pressing decisions."

He lovingly pulled back from her. He cupped her face in his hands and looked deeply into her eyes. Aidan was so overwhelmed with the intensity of the moment it took him a few seconds to speak. The silence between them was riveting.

He found his voice and composed his thoughts. "Caitlin, ya know I love ya more than I ever thought I could possibly love anyone. Ya take me breath away and fill me senses. I doona know what is going to happen in me life over the next few months, but I do know me life without ya would be empty. Ya aire heart of me heart, life of me life. Ya are me reason for breathing, and I will love ya until the day I die. So, in spite of all me shortcomings, if ya will have me, I want ya to be me wife. Will ya marry me?"

Caitlin ran her hands up and along Aidan's muscled arms finally finding his curls and entangling her fingers in his hair. "Ya know I will," she answered as she pulled his face to hers and kissed him with all the passion in her soul.

After a few more moments in each other's arms, they slowly began to walk toward the Fitzpatrick home hand in hand. Aidan's voice quivered when he next spoke. "I suppose I should speak to yer father today."

She giggled quietly and squeezed his hand. "He willna bite ya. I promise. He loikes ya."

Aidan took heart and they quickened their pace. He now felt an urgency to complete this mission.

They came up the one step, and Caitlin burst through the doorway. "Da! Mam!" she called.

Dr. Fitzpatrick came in from the kitchen with a cup of tea. "Good den, children. Would ya loike some tea? Miss Thames just brewed a pot in the kitchen with Martha."

"I shall get it," volunteered Caitlin, and she joined her mother and their housekeeper in the kitchen, leaving Aidan alone with her father. The young suitor suddenly felt an unidentifiable terror.

"Come on in, Aidan, and sit down. I in truth am harmless. I doona bite, not very hard anyway," Dr. Fitzpatrick teased.

Aidan swallowed and replied, "Ya might grow fangs after I talk with ya."

"I doubt it. Sit down. I am listening."

"Aye, sir. Well, uh. I, um."

"Aidan, the easiest thing to do is just say it quickly. Get it over with. It should mayhap go something loike this, 'Dr. Fitzpatrick, sir, I am in love with yer daughter. I would loike to marry her with yer permission.' Doona be a coward. It took me six weeks to work up the nerve to ask for Martha's hand."

"How did ya know?" Aidan asked in amazement.

"I recognize the look of terror. Colin has been having the same symptoms. I caught him practicing in the looking glass. And after ya thoroughly whipped Colin's arse the other night, I calculated 'twas a matter of time. So, say what ya have to say."

"I do love Caitlin very much, and she loves me. I would loike yer permission to marry her, but there is much more ya should know."

"She and Colin told us aboot Draconis." He drank a quick sip of tea. "Ya and she are very young, but something in me spirit tells me this is roight. Martha and I talked, and we agreed to allow ya to wed, when ya asked. I know ya will be going in search of yer father. I would go if 'twere me father. Colin already has permission to accompany ya. Ya, lad, aire a fine young man. I would be honored to have ya for a son-in-law. I do wish ya had a couple of years to court." He took a long gulp of his tea and sighed. "Ya have me blessing, but, loike Colin warned ya, ya may come back six months after the wedding and ask me to take her back. She is willful and headstrong, and she can throw one whale of a fit. Then, me answer will be, 'Ya made yer bed; lie in it. Ya're stuck with her. She is not me responsibility any more. She is all yers.'"

The two men burst into laughter just as Caitlin and Mrs. Fitzpatrick brought the tea.

"What is the mirth?" asked Caitlin.

"Mother"—Dr. Fitzpatrick motioned for Mrs. Fitzpatrick to sit on his knee—"This young man wants to marry our little hellion. What say ya?"

Mrs. Fitzpatrick chortled. "God bless ya, son. More power to ya."

"Mam! Da!" exclaimed Caitlin, her face bright red.

Everyone laughed uproariously. Then Dr. Fitzpatrick became serious. "Come here, children." Dr. Fitzpatrick joined the two young people's hands. "Me little girl is me pride and joy. Ya have our blessing. Aidan, take care of her and guard her with yer life. Caitlin, give this man the honor and respect due him. If ya do this thing, ya will no longer be two, but one: one in thought, one in spirit, one in body. Always work together, even when ya foight; for ya *will* foight. As much as ya will be one, there still will be two natures. The key is to talk and to forgive and to love no matter what occurs."

Dr. Fitzpatrick kissed his daughter's cheek and gave Aidan a bear hug. "Welcome to the family," he said as he clasped Aidan's hand firmly.

Mrs. Fitzpatrick piped up, "There aire a few conditions. One, both ya and Colin will finish school this spring. Two, Caitlin will *not* go on this upcoming trip."

"Agreed," said Aidan.

"Now, wait a moment," began Caitlin.

"I said, 'agreed,'" Aidan reaffirmed with assertiveness.

Caitlin said nothing else, but she set her lips firmly. This battle was far from over.

Just at that second Colin burst through the door. "Mr. Murphy said 'aye!' Can ya believe it?"

Drake lifted an eyebrow. "He gave you no argument?"

Colin shrugged. "In truth, I am not sure he understood the question, but Mrs. Murphy agreed, although reluctantly. She said, 'I knew this day would come. So be it.'"

The doctor nodded. "There is more at work here than mere man can understand."

"Dr. Fitzpatrick," said Mrs. Fitzpatrick formally, "mayhap we shall have a double wedding."

12
Plans

During the long cold winter months Aidan, Diggory, and Colin kept busy in the few hours of daylight after school, putting *The Sea Bird* into shape. There were a lot of barnacles to scrape, boards to replace, and accommodations to make. The sails had to be replaced along with most of the rigging. The ship suffered from years of neglect. The new captain also added small compartments to be used as quarters. Aidan suggested a change of name so Quazel wouldn't recognize the ship. Diggory cringed at the idea, saying, "Duncan done changed it once, an' it brought nothin' but bad luck."

Aidan laughed. "I doona believe that nonsense." As P.C. rubbed against his legs, Aidan shot over his shoulder to the other two, "Let us call her *The Privileged Character*." Thus, the ship had a new name, despite Diggory's misgivings.

Diggory watched the two former enemies grow inseparable. Their bond really did become one of being brothers. They often talked of their futures with the women they had chosen. On one such occasion, Aidan sought counsel. "Colin, I have been thinking. Do ya think we should wed before we sail for Draconis? What if something should happen and we should leave two young women behind to become widows, or, God forbid, children to be fatherless?"

"I have pondered this as well. Mary Kate says she would rather have a few weeks of happiness than a lifetime of regrets. I canna leave her without making her truly mine. Ya should talk to Caitlin aboot yer concerns, but I guarantee her reaction will be stronger than Mary Kate's." He began a deep belly-laugh. "Ya know her temper. I wouldna be surprised if she lashed ya to the church pew until the wedding."

"Yer sister is smarter than ya think. She might see the sense in waiting."

"Who said love was smart? Ya have as much chance of making me believe she will be sensible as ya do of making me believe ya can swim all the way to Draconis beginning roight now."

"Oh, ye of little faith," chided Aidan.

"Nay, oh, he who knows his sister," countered Colin.

Dr. Drake Fitzpatrick often joined the men in their preparations, especially when his house was filled with "women and wedding plans." The girls regularly gathered there to discuss ideas. Aidan asked his opinion on the matter.

"Ya aire welcome to try that suggestion. I see the wisdom in it, but I can also guarantee the futility of yer argument with that strong-willed redhead."

Aidan's stubbornness rivaled Caitlin's. He decided to broach the subject on a day she visited the ship.

"Aidan, if ya aire getting cold feet, just say so," Caitlin said near tears.

"'Tis not it, honey. I love ya. I fear I moight not come back just loike me father and grandfather. I doona want to be the cause of another woman alone or another child fatherless. I know how that feels." He placed a hand over his heart. "It hurts."

"I promise yer fears are unfounded. 'Tis not going to happen." Caitlin went behind Aidan and hugged him under his arms. Then she came back around him nibbling on her index fingernail. "Besides, if I am not yer wife when *The Privileged Character* sails, who can assure I shall be here when ya get back? Ya aire not the only handsome man around," she added with an impish grin.

"What do ya mean by that? Has someone made advances toward ya?" Aidan's green eyes flashed with jealousy. "I shall kill him. Who is it?"

"Relax, dearest. I was only trying to provoke ya," defended Caitlin. She realized she had poked a sore spot and that Aidan might have a temper to match her own. "Aidan, I love only ya. 'Twould break me heart if ya left without making me yer wife." Caitlin entwined her fingers in Aidan's curls the way she enjoyed doing and kissed him fiercely.

Relenting, he knew he had lost the battle. He longed to take her with him, but he had made a promise. He gathered Caitlin in his arms and swung her around. "Ya win, me little spitfire. I would never break yer heart."

The women spent their spare time making wedding plans and keeping secrets. At least, Caitlin, Mary Kate, and Elizabeth kept secrets.

The ladies spent most of their time in the Murphy house. Diana Murphy had a hard time leaving her home since Logan Murphy had become an invalid. Each year his brother was missing, he had blamed himself more and more until he finally made himself ill. Diana feared he might become as distraught as his father had. So, the actual wedding preparations took place in the Murphy home.

There were times when Mary Kate was sure her father had no idea he had given her permission to marry someone headed for Draconis. Perhaps he did not even realize he had given her permission to wed at all, but the plans went on with her mother's full knowledge and approval.

Caitlin and Mary Kate met the seamstress who would sew their dresses. The girls decided to wear matching gowns. The dress they agreed upon was made from soft clinging white linen. Sleeves beneath a front and back panel of heavy brocade flowed from a square-necked, tightly fitted bodice in royal blue. The picture was completed with the accent of a silver tiara. In the dresses,

Mary Kate resembled a fairy while Caitlin looked like a slim statuesque wood elf. The mothers and Elizabeth thought the girls were visions of loveliness

During all these wedding plans, Caitlin and Mary Kate had a brainstorm. "Lizzie, why do ya not ask Diggory to marry ya and let us make this a triple wedding?" Mary Kate voiced their thoughts

"Pardon? I ask *him*?"

Caitlin urged, "If ya wait for him, it might never happen."

Lizzie admitted, "Ya do have a valid point."

That afternoon Elizabeth made a trek to the ship. "Diggory, we need talk for a few minutes. Can ya spare a little time to walk with me?"

"Forsooth." Diggory came right away. He thought something must be seriously wrong. "What is the matter, love?"

Elizabeth put her hands on her hips. "I can see I am going to have to be the one in charge again. I swear, Diggory Danaher, ya must be dense."

"What 'ave I done to rile ye so?"

"Nothing. 'Tis the point. Ya have not asked for me hand in marriage. These children aire to wed and ya aire just going to let me wither away waiting for ya. So, now, what say ya? Are ya going to marry me or not?"

"Lizzie!"

"Well? I am waiting for an answer."

"I am supposed to ask ye to marry me."

"Why?"

"'Tis the way it be done."

"If I wait for ya, we shall both be cold in our graves. Do ya love me, Diggory?"

"Ye know I do. I always 'ave."

"Then what is the hesitation? Let us marry. Let us do it tonoight. Ya can move into the house with me, and then Aidan will have someplace to take Caitlin."

"Woman, I wish ye had been this independent years ago."

"So do I. What is the answer?"

"Aye."

All work halted, and Elizabeth went home and put on her prettiest rose-colored silk and linen dress. Diggory donned his Sunday finest. All their friends met at the church. The two lovers who should have been wed years before finally joined their lives.

There were three birthdays to celebrate during the spring. Mary Kate's birthday came in the summer. Aidan had a quiet celebration with Elizabeth, Diggory, Caitlin, Colin, Mary Kate, and Dr. and Mrs. Fitzpatrick. He was not the flamboyant type, and a small intimate celebration was all he desired. The Fitzpatricks, on the other hand, threw a feast to celebrate their twins' turning eighteen. Caitlin reveled in the attention, but would have traded every moment of the party for one minute alone with Aidan.

The priest who taught a few boys had the desire to show off his prize pupils, so the young people were involved in planning a fabulous commencement festivity for Aidan and Colin. They decided to have the merrymaking on Swan Island, half a mile into the ocean. They decorated with lanterns, streamers, and brightly colored quilts to sit on. There was a buffet and kegs of ale. The young people danced and celebrated late into the night before they were ferried back to their own villages to await the long anticipated graduation the next day.

Graduation day brought great excitement that had to be tempered for the old priest insisted on a solemn ceremony where he announced the two boys' completion of study. Caitlin pouted that only the boys were allowed this honor. Her father had always taught her at home while Mary Kate's family had provided her with a private tutor.

After the ceremony, Diggory and Elizabeth Danaher had a quiet dinner for their young folks and their families at their home. They had a sumptuous feast of roast duck, vegetables, hot rye bread, plum pudding, and a stout port. Diggory made a toast in his awkward, but sweet manner: "To four lights that dawned in an ol' man's life. May yer lives be filled with 'appiness, stability, and realized dreams."

The ladies began frantic last-minute preparations for a gala wedding three weeks hence. Meanwhile, the men continued to make ready for the impending voyage. Aidan, Diggory, and Colin seriously began to consider a crew manifest. Diggory was the first to suggest, "Lads, if I may be so bold, I think it be best that only we three go. Of course, we must take Jean with us. I promised to get 'im 'ome." P.C. mewed at Diggory's feet. "Aye, me sweet little mite, ye may go along to catch the mice." The cat purred happily.

Colin questioned, "Just we three? Can we handle the ship?"

Diggory assured, "Aye. Remember when I returned to Stonebridge, I was by meself except for Jean."

Aidan agreed, "I think Diggory is roight. The fewer people who go, the fewer who will be endangered. Moreover, Quazel may not see three men as much of a threat. Mayhap I should disguise me eyes somehow. She might see the green eyes as a threat. And ya, Colin, perchance ya should dye yer hair or wear a wig."

"Mayhap I shall shave me head after me wedding," challenged Colin with a hearty laugh.

It was decided. The three of them would make up the crew. The ship was ready to sail.

Aidan decided to bring the ladies aboard and sail around Porpoise Point, back to Swan Island for a picnic, and finally back to port. He called it a test run to be sure everything was working. The day went splendidly.

Upon their return to dock, Diggory and Elizabeth went home to order supplies. Colin and Mary Kate debarked and started home. Colin called over his shoulder, "Aire ya two coming?"

Caitlin answered, "No, I want to stay aboard a while. I shall see ya at home." She waved good-bye.

Caitlin bounded back to the helm where Aidan worked shirtless making certain all items were in place. "I sent Colin and Mary Kate on alone. I thought they and *we* could use a little private time. All this planning makes one irritable and tired." She wove her fingers into Aidan's hair, and he encircled her with his arms.

"Ya aire naughty," Aidan teased.

"Aye, and ya love it," she bantered back.

"Ya aire correct, milady. The truth is that I love ya." He kissed Caitlin first on the forehead, and then the nose. His lips found hers and he smothered her with his mouth. He moved to her neck and throat. Caitlin moved her hands over Aidan's back and arms caressing him sensuously as he kissed her. Aidan pushed Caitlin from him with some force and gasped, "Pretty lady, I must take ya home at once, or I shall be forced to plunge into the icy waters to keep us from temptation." He kissed her hungrily once again and murmured in her ear, "Three weeks. Only three more weeks, and I shan't stop. I love ya so much."

Caitlin breathed back, "'Tis too long."

Grabbing his shirt, he took her by the hand. They walked languidly toward home, in no hurry for a perfect day to end.

Three weeks passed quickly for the parents who were about to give their children over to adulthood and another home, but moved at a snail's pace for the anxious and eager young people. The weeks were filled with bridal fetes and a stag party to which two disguised girls sneaked.

"They had better not have some gypsy dancer there, or I shall be forced to pull all of her hair out," threatened Caitlin.

"Leave her eyes for me to claw out," said Mary Kate.

Caitlin looked down at her delicate friend. "I canna imagine yer hurting a fly."

"Ya have never seen me pushed to me limit. If some half-naked woman is dancing for Colin, ya will be in for a big surprise."

All the spies found were a lot of men drinking ale and telling anecdotes about their friends who were about to meet their doom. Caitlin and Mary Kate left quickly, feeling ashamed.

The long awaited day arrived dull and overcast. Caitlin pouted. Mary Kate said, "'Tis supposed to be good luck if it rains on yer wedding day."

Caitlin responded, "Mayhap a little shower, but this looks loike a downpour."

Sure enough it poured buckets for about an hour, but then the sun broke through and even gave the wedding parties a brilliant rainbow as a gift.

Stonebridge talked about this wedding for years to come. The pretty petite daughter of the richest man in town married the hot-tempered son of the compassionate doctor; and the equally fiery twin daughter of the doctor married the orphaned son of Priscilla and Duncan O'Rourke, the son who had been taken in by a blithering idiot turned laird of the manor. The combinations were mind-boggling.

The wedding was beautiful with fresh flowers and candlelight even if it was a bit unconventional. Elizabeth sat in for his mother. Diggory's white cat wandered in and jumped onto Elizabeth's lap. Dr. Fitzpatrick gave both girls away, one on each arm since Logan Murphy was unable to escort his daughter. He sat passively in his place on the family pew and watched the ceremony. After Dr. Fitzpatrick gave the girls away, the guys stood as bestmen for each other. The two girls took turns serving as each other's maid of honor. It was a strange and unforgettable wedding.

After the reception, which was held at the Murphy home, Colin and Mary Kate Fitzpatrick left for a honeymoon at O'Shaughnesy's End, a lavish inn where they planned to enjoy the accommodations, the cuisine, the hot springs, and each other, for they knew their time together would be short.

Aidan and Caitlin O'Rourke sailed off to parts unknown aboard *The Privileged Character*. Their plans were totally secret.

Aidan dropped anchor just beyond the horizon. Alone aboard their ship, he took his new wife in his arms and kissed her ravenously. "Mistress O'Rourke, have I told ya how beautiful ya aire and how much I love ya today?"

Caitlin slipped from his grip and held him at arms' length. "Nay, but hold that thought. I shall be roight back."

It took all his restraint not to follow her. Caitlin returned in a few minutes. What Aidan beheld was worth the wait. The vision standing before him wore a soft peach gauze chemise. She walked to him, removed his doublet, and slipped his shirt over his head. She ran her fingertips down his chest. Then, she kissed him from his navel upward until her mouth found his. The two locked in passion. Aidan tenderly removed one strap of the gown and then the next. He kissed her lips, her neck, her shoulders, her throat. She leaned her head back for him to go farther.

"I doona have to stop any more," he murmured, and the two fell onto the soft down quilt-covered bed.

Part Two

Quest for a Lost Father

13
Bon Voyage

The next month passed far too quickly for everyone. The appointed day for departure approached rapidly. *The Privileged Character* was well stocked, but Elizabeth ordered more dried fruit, preserved meats, salt, barley flour, sugar and coffee. She also ordered extra blankets, pillows, and medicines. She placed them in an empty compartment near the stern of the ship

Diggory said, "Do ye think ye ordered enough supplies, Lizzie? How much do ye think three men can eat?"

Elizabeth snapped, "Better safe than sorry. Ya never know what might happen. Ya could pick up more crewmembers along the way. Duncan did. Besides, all the new things I ordered will not spoil. If ya doona need them on the way to Draconis, ya can use them on the return voyage. Ya will have a lot of men to bring home." She started to cry.

Diggory hugged her gently. "Now, now. It be all roight. The stress be agettin' to ye, too, precious."

"Diggory, I have lost ya twice. Promise ya will come back to me. I doona want to grow old alone."

"Doona ye worry yer sweet head none aboot me. I be tough as nails."

Caitlin came up with bread, meat, fruit, cheese, and ale for the men. "What is going on here? Looks loike dawdling on the job to me," she joked with her two friends as she came aboard before she saw Elizabeth crying.

"Lizzie, is everything all roight?" she asked, genuinely concerned.

"Aye, dear," said Elizabeth, drying her eyes. "Just a foolish woman having doubts." She gave the young bride a hug and whispered in her ear, "Everything is set."

Aidan and Colin came swinging down from the rigging. Colin called, "Do I smell food? Aidan, is it edible?" Colin teased his sister.

Caitlin punched him in the arm as he reached for a piece of chicken. "For that comment ya may not get anything to eat," she laughed. "I have ya know, Mam and Miss Thames taught me well." She stuck her tongue out at her brother.

The night before the men were to leave, the families gathered at Cypress Manor, the Gilhooley family estate where Elizabeth and Diggory lived. They had a quiet supper of venison stew, pears, barley bread, strawberry short cake, and buttermilk. Then, they spent a time praying for the safety and wisdom of those leaving and retired early to their homes.

That night Aidan held Caitlin close and moaned, "How can I leave ya? Ya aire heart of me heart, life of me life. Ya aire me reason for breathing, and I will love ya until the day I die."

Caitlin put a finger to Aidan's lips and shushed him. "Shh. Remember what I told ya. Ya will not leave me behind, never to return. I will be with ya wherever ya go in here"—She put her hand over his heart—"and here." She touched his temples. "I will never leave ya, and I will forever hold ya in me heart. I will pray for ya every day, and ya will know I am one with ya."

"What did I do to deserve ya?" Aidan smiled, comforted by her words.

"Ya did that. Ya flashed those pearly whites at me and melted me. From that moment I was clay in yer hands."

"Clay!" scoffed Aidan. "Ya aire more loike quartz or marble that I have to form with a chisel. Trust me, lady, ya aire not easily molded."

"I would be boring if I bent to yer every whim. I never intend to bore ya."

"I can believe that. Ya definitely keep me on me toes."

"I'faith! I love to dance!" Caitlin giggled and kissed Aidan on his soft, sensitive lips. They lay awake until the wee hours of the morning and finally fell asleep from sheer exhaustion.

The morning dawned clear and warm with strong gusts coming from the right direction. Aidan sprang to life as the first streaks of sunlight drifted through the window. It was a perfect day for beginning a journey. Caitlin stirred and reached for her husband. She sat upright, startled from her rest. "Aidan!"

"I am here at the window."

"Is it time already?"

"Almost. Let us breakfast. What would you loike?"

"I am not hungry. I think I shall be sick if I eat a bite."

"I understand. How aboot some coffee?"

"That sounds good."

Aidan scooped some coveted sugar and cocoa into the coffee because it was Caitlin's favorite. He wanted her to have pleasant memories of their last few hours. She came to the table with a box in her hand. "'Tis for ya. Every ship's captain needs one."

Aidan opened the gift to find a golden pocket watch. It was cumbersome, and he knew he would leave it on the table in his quarters rather than wear it dangling from its chain. Inside the cover over the face was a wedding portrait a friend had hastily sketched. On the cover was inscribed, "Heart of my heart, life of my life: May time fly until we are together again. Always and forever, Caitlin."

"'Tis exquisite," choked Aidan.

They drank coffee in silence. Neither of them had an appetite.

Caitlin took Aidan's hand. "I am not going to the wharf to see the ship off."

"E'en so?" Aidan said, a pout etching his face.

"Darling, I want my last memory of ya to be here with me, not waving good-bye. Prithee, understand. I canna bear to watch ya leave. I shall be fine if I can only think of ya going to the ship. I shall deal with the rest later."

"If that is what ya want."

"'Tis. When ya leave, I am going to Mary Kate. She is not going to the dock either. She is not as strong as I am. I am afraid she will fall apart. We will have to be strength for each other. We will have Elizabeth, too. Perchance we will be another strong three-strand cord."

Aidan held Caitlin as long as possible before he had to go. He kissed her and started down the lane. He looked back. The door was closed. Caitlin refused to watch him go.

As soon as he went around the bend, Caitlin ran as fast as she could to her sister-in-law. Colin was just coming through the gate of the Murphy home. He hugged his sister. "Take care of me wife. She is not as strong as ya. She is inside sobbing."

"I will. Colin, I love ya. I pray thee be careful. Watch Aidan's back."

"'Tis done. I love ya, too, Sis," he said, and he was gone.

Caitlin went in. "Mary Kate, aire ya ready? Let us away." The two women took off at breakneck speed.

Aidan and Colin met at the Danaher home. Elizabeth and Diggory were ready to go. "So, one of our ladies is actually seeing us off," commented Aidan.

"Not exactly," said Diggory.

"No," confirmed Elizabeth. "I am going to the wharf to get P.C. settled into the hold. Then I am going to find the girls. I think they need me more today than any of ya.

Diggory and I have already said our good-byes. So, doona look for me in the crowd. I shan't be there."

Dr. and Mrs. Fitzpatrick were at the dock. They had come to support their son and son-in-law in their endeavor. "Where aire the girls?" they inquired.

Colin said, "They refused to come down. They aire at the Murphy house. Caitlin was coming in as I left. Mam, perchance ya can check on them later."

"Ya know I will," responded Mrs. Fitzpatrick.

Elizabeth stowed P.C. and came back on deck. She settled Jean in a cabin they had prepared for him. She hugged the two young men and kissed her husband. "I shall see ya soon. I love ya." Then she disappeared.

Diggory and Colin set about casting the lines while Aidan steered them out of port. It took almost an hour to get underway, but soon they were clear and headed for the open sea. Aidan kept scanning the docks.

"What aire ya looking for, mate?" asked Colin.

"I was hoping Caitlin would change her mind."

Colin placed his hand on his new brother's shoulder. "Me too." The dock remained bare except for the two parents waving good-bye until they could no longer see the ship. Then Drake and Martha Fitzpatrick turned to go. Drake gave one more glance toward the ocean, sensing something was just a bit off.

"Let us look in on the girls," suggested Martha.

Drake chuckled.

Aidan, Diggory, and Colin sailed along calmly. Diggory gave Jean some hay. Then, he opened the hold and called P.C. She mewed all the way up the ladder. Diggory picked her up and rubbed her under her chin. She purred loudly. "That be me girl. It be your job to catch any mice or rats that might be on board. We doona want 'em agettin'

into our stores." He put P.C. down and she began to make herself at home. "That's roight. Ye be good luck on this voyage, no matter if ye be white. Ye must come with us."

Later, as the sun cast crimson, magenta, and violet streaks across the sky, Colin presented an evening repast. "I beg pardon that I am not a gourmet chef, but 'tis edible, good sirs. I tasted it, and I lived." Realizing they had not eaten all day, they were starving. They dined on baked cod fish, barley cakes, cinnamon apples, and fresh milk that Elizabeth had placed in a small, insulated box. The milk would be gone in a few days, so they savored every swallow. P.C. had milk and fish. She seemed content.

Aidan played with the cat and said, "If we feed ya this well, ya moight forget to catch the rats."

The men agreed to take turns on the night shift. As they worked out their schedule for a few weeks, there was a noise in the hold. They started. Diggory assured, "'Twas somethin' P.C. got off balance while she was down there, and it finally tipped over."

They strained their ears for a while, but the night was deafeningly quiet. Colin said, "In this stillness we could take care of the rats ourselves because we could hear their every footstep. We had better get used to it soon, or we shall scare ourselves to death at every little creak."

"True," Aidan agreed. "So, whenever we aire alone on the night shift, let us whistle or sing or recite poetry. Just make some noise."

The days on the ship were long and hard. The nights were stretched and eerie, but the three men tried to keep one another's spirits high.

After two weeks at sea, P.C. began to behave strangely. She would stand at the edge of the hold and yowl as if she were in pain. Aidan, growing irritable with the incessant noise, shouted from the helm, "Diggory, what is wrong with that cat? Is she dying?"

Colin laughed. "It sounds as if she be in heat. Sorry, girl. Ya willna find a mate oot here."

She turned and hissed at Colin.

Aidan laughed. "Maybe she brought a friend with her."

Thinking, *Oh, she'll find 'er mate*, Diggory followed P.C. to the hold. She refused to go down the ladder, but just yowled. The seasoned sailor peered into the darkness, but could see nothing. "Colin, lad," Diggory called, "bring me pistol and a lantern."

Colin and Diggory made their way down the ladder into the hold. What they saw there put the fear of God into them. The two men backed out of the hold quietly. Diggory closed and locked the hatch. They looked at each other in terror, both shaking their heads.

Without a word, they walked to the helm. "Aidan, lad, we need yer 'elp. P.C. done be found three of the biggest rats I ever seen. There be no way she can kill 'em. Drop anchor, get yer pistol, and come with us," Diggory said mysteriously. "The anchor will only slow our speed at this depth, but we need ye."

Aidan wrinkled his brow in confusion, but he did as Diggory had asked.

The men made their way to the hold. Diggory unlatched the hatch and put his finger to his lips. Aidan had no idea what he was about to find as they sneaked down the ladder.

Aidan screamed at the top of his lungs, "What in hell aire ya doing here?"

14
𝔖mooth 𝔖ailing

𝔈lí𝔷abeth Danaher, Mary Kate Fitzpatrick, and Caitlin O'Rourke sat around a makeshift table playing cards with straw as markers. When Aidan bellowed, Caitlin screamed and jumped to her feet, upsetting the table and its contents. Mary Kate and Elizabeth stood and backed against the wall. They had not heard the men come into the hold.

Caitlin looked at Aidan. She had never seen him so angry, not even when he had fought with Colin. Aidan stomped to the cowering woman and grabbed her hand. "Come with me." He escorted her at a fast clip to his cabin. Slamming the door, he leaned against it and rubbed his hands down his face. "What kind of hare-brained scheme do ya think this is? Have ya absolutely lost yer mind?"

Caitlin opened her mouth to answer, but Aidan cut her off. "Doona speak," he yelled while pointing his finger at her. "Doona say a word." Aidan paced. "I am so angry that I could in truth hurt ya roight now. Yer actions have caused me to be a liar. Ya have behaved in such a way that I have dishonored my word to yer mother. How could ya?"

"Aidan…"

"Verily, I said, 'do *not* speak!'" He held his hand up as a shield. "If I take ya home, ya will have cost us an entire month. Woman!" Aidan was so angry he was at a loss for words. He clenched and unclenched his fists and jaw as one, and then stormed from the room and locked the door behind him. "I canna talk to ya roight this moment," he yelled through the door.

Caitlin ran to the door, but she was locked in. She pounded the wood and screamed, "Aidan, open this door! Let me out!" Her words fell on deaf ears. Aidan got the ship under way.

Aidan was not the only one who was upset. Colin simply gave Mary Kate the come-hither gesture with his finger. She followed sullenly all the way to his cabin. He closed the door softly. Mary Kate started, "I thought ya would be the one shouting, not Aidan." She lowered her eyes and would not look him in the eyes.

"I am too angry to scream. How could someone as sensible as ya be lured into Caitlin's folly? Doona try to tell me this was yer idea. Some actress I married. Were any of those tears ya shed as I was leaving real?"

"I am sorry," Mary Kate sniffled. Tears flowed down her cheeks.

"Oh, doona start that. How can I know if they aire genuine?"

Mary Kate began to cry harder.

Colin moaned, "Ya know I canna take that. Stop it."

She covered her face with her hands and sobbed, falling on the bed in a heap. Her shoulders shook with the force of her weeping.

Colin threaded his fingers through his hair and sighed. "Mary Kate, stop crying. Ya aire breaking me heart. I pray thee, doona cry." Colin crossed the room and sat beside his distraught wife on the bed. He stroked her loose brown curls. "Love, stop that. Everything will work oot for the best. Stop crying."

Mary Kate took deep gasps of air. Colin lifted her into his arms. "Shh. Stop crying, I beg ya. Ya aire tearing me heart out."

Mary Kate wrapped her arms around Colin and laid her head on his chest. "I am so sorry," she whispered, "that I upset ya, but I am not going back. Caitlin is roight. We aire supposed to be with ya. Ya need us. Where aire ya going to find seven people on an island of animals? Ya must convince Aidan to take us with ya. I shan't leave ya. I shan't." She started to cry again.

"Shh. I shan't ask ya to leave. Ya may stay," Colin soothed. "Even if Aidan takes Caitlin home or puts her oot on the next place we come to, ya may stay."

"Oh, Colin, I love ya so much. I will never leave ya or ever let ya leave me again."

Mary Kate relaxed and fell asleep. Colin gently laid her head on the pillow and crept from the room.

During this time, Diggory stood with his arms folded across his chest glaring at Elizabeth. "I knew that little dickens would manage to follow Aidan. I just didna know she would bring ye along. How did she hoodwink ye into this escapade?"

"Nobody hoodwinked me, Diggory Danaher. I have planned this voyage from the noight ya told Aidan aboot Duncan. When I found Caitlin was not included in the party, I set aboot to find a way to get her where she belongs. Admittedly, I came along as an afterthought, but I shall not lose ya again to anyone or anything, even if that means I must help kill the monster ya seek. So, doona stand there and be cross with me." Elizabeth stomped her foot and her eyes flashed fire. She was ready for a fight. "I did the roight thing, and ya know it."

"Aye, ye did. I be very proud of ye. Ye showed real spirit and ingenuity. Come 'ere and give me a 'ug," Diggory said with a smirk.

She sailed across the room and into Diggory's outstretched arms.

Diggory chuckled. "Ye couldna done this alone. Who 'elped?"

"Jean and P.C., of course."

"I can see 'ow Jean could help, but P.C. be a cat." *Or mayhap, not.*

"She didna give away our secret until I whispered to her."

"Ah."

Elizabeth encouraged, "Ya must convince Aidan. Alackaday! By my troth he was furious." She put a hand to her throat. "I didna know he had it in him to get so angry."

"Doona worry aboot the lad. 'E will come around."

Near midnight Colin went to the helm. "'Tis me turn on the night shift."

Aidan replied stiffly, "I shall take yer turn." He jutted his chin out.

"Aidan, mayhap ya should go to yer quarters. Everything in there might be broken by now."

"Then, I shall change cabins. Caitlin can sleep in her mess."

"How long aire ya gonna be angry with her?"

"I know not. The rest of me life."

"Aidan, ya love her."

"'Tis beside the point." He pounded the wooden wheel with the heel of his hand. "She defied me. She defied her parents. She did exactly what she wanted to do with little or no regard for anyone else. I should have known something was up when she gave up the battle so easily. Sneaky, conniving..." He gusted a growl. "If I go to her this angry, I might do something I would regret."

"'Tis up to ya, but ya aire gonna to have to face her sooner or later."

"I know. I am just so mad." He fisted his hands.

"By the way, she has not had supper."

"Let her suffer tonoight. Mayhap on the morrow she will be remorseful."

"I wouldna wager on it. Alas, ya need some sleep. Take another cabin, but get some rest. I shall take over here."

"Ya aire roight. I shall see ya anon."

Aidan grabbed some blankets and a pillow from the hold. "Ah!" he roared. *Elizabeth helped all along—all these extra supplies.* He went to an empty cabin to try to get some rest but tossed and turned all night. He dozed now and then, but the blasted blanket smelled like Caitlin. Just before dawn, he uttered an expletive and went to his own cabin.

As Aidan opened the door, his shaving mug almost hit him in the head.

"Who do ya think ya aire?" came a shriek from the darkness.

When he closed the door, he had to bat Caitlin's shoe away from his face.

"That is it!" shouted Aidan. Marching across the room, he could hear Colin singing loudly off key at the helm.

Aidan took Caitlin by the shoulders and glared at her. "Stop."

She kicked him in the shin.

"Caitlin, settle down."

Caitlin stopped struggling. "How could ya lock me in this little dark room? I would rather ya had stayed and screamed at me. I never thought ya could be so cruel."

"Caitlin, ya lied to me. Do ya know how much that hurt?" He let go of her and placed a fist over his heart.

"I didna. I just didna tell ya quite everything."

"Caitlin," Aidan said, exasperated. He turned in a complete circle. "Doona split hairs. Ya deceived me."

"No, I did *not*." She snapped her hands to her hips. "I told ya that ya wouldna leave me alone, never to return. I told ya I would always be with ya."

"Caitlin!" Aidan raised his voice again. He stepped away from his wife and walked back to the door, punching the wood. "Not only did ya deceive me, but ya also dragged Mary Kate into your scheme." He leaned his forehead against the door. "And Elizabeth."

"Alack! I...I tricked ya, but what choice did I have? Yer bloody honor would never have allowed ya to take me with ya after ya told Mam ya wouldna. It didna take much to convince Mary Kate to come along. She thought 'twas a splendid plan." She smirked to his back and then waved a finger in a tick-tock motion. "As for Elizabeth, ya can stop roight there, sir. 'Twas *her* idea."

He whirled around. "Caitlin Fitzpatrick O'Rourke, canna ya admit that ya were wrong."

"I was *not* wrong and would do it again." She folded her arms across her chest. "If ya turn this ship around, I shall hire one and follow ya. If ya try to put me off on the next little atoll and send me back, I shall swim after ya if I must." She tapped her shoed foot and set her jaw in a tight clench.

"Caitlin, ya aire spoiled, and...and..." Aidan took hold of her by the shoulders again. The staring match ended when Caitlin's blue eyes welled with tears.

Aidan sank onto the bed and pulled his wife beside him, putting a protective arm around her. "I am sorry I got so angry. I was terrified when I saw ya. Doona ya know I would die if anything happened to ya? I wouldna want to live without ya."

"I feel the same way, Aidan. I never woulda lied to ya if I coulda thought of any other way to get here. I *am* sorry. Prithee, forgive me. Doona make me go back. Do ya remember the verses Father O'Malley read at our wedding? Let me remind ya. They were the words Ruth spoke to Naomi:

"Entreat me not to leave thee, or return from following after thee: for wither thou goest, I will go; and where thou lodgest I will lodge: thy people shall be my people, and thy God my God; where thou diest, I will die, and there will I be buried: the Lord do so to me, and more also, if ought but death part thee and me.

"'Tis my plea to ya now." Both sat quietly for a long time before Aidan pulled Caitlin into an embrace.

He kissed her forcefully. "Aye. I have no destiny without ya. Ya aire me fiery helpmate. I would be lost without ya."

Topside, Diggory was taking over the helm. Colin headed toward the cabin area.

"Doona knock on Aidan's door," warned Diggory. "Quarter hour ago they were yellin' at each other. All be quiet now. They may 'ave killed each other. If a stench comes from under the door in a few days, we shall open it. Until then, leave 'em be."

Colin saluted Diggory in acknowledgement and went to Mary Kate.

15
𝔑ew 𝔆rewmembers

𝔚hen Colin got to his cabin, Mary Kate wasn't there. He finally found her at the stern of the ship, retching over the rail. Instantly worried, he asked, "What is the matter? Aire ya seasick?"

She moaned, "I know not. I have been aboard for two weeks, and I have not been sick before. Mayhap what I ate for supper disagreed with me."

"Go lie down. I shall get ya some tea. Mayhap 'twill help."

The tea did not help, and for the next several days, Mary Kate vomited into early afternoon before she could function.

Aidan and Caitlin emerged from their cabin. The battle was over, and Caitlin was staying. When Caitlin saw how sick Mary Kate was, she ran to her with genuine concern. "Look at us. I thought Aidan would kill me, and ya look loike death warmed over. Did we make the roight decision?"

They looked at each other and answered in unison, "Aye."

After two weeks of Mary Kate's illness, Colin became truly alarmed. He confided in his best friend, "Aidan, I am in truth worried. Mary Kate canna eat. She has lost weight. She cries all the time. She doesna want me to touch her. I think she needs a physician. I wish Da were here."

Elizabeth overheard the conversation and laughed aloud.

"What is the mirth, Lizzie?" Colin wanted to know.

"I beg pardon, lads. I didna mean to eavesdrop. Colin, how long have ya and Mary Kate been married?"

"Two months."

"Have ya consummated yer marriage?"

Colin blushed to the roots of his hair, his face burning as bright red as his hair. "What did ya say?"

"Ya heard me. Answer the question."

"Aye, of course we have."

"Lad, have ya considered the possibility she might be with child?"

"What?"

"Ya aire going to have a wee one."

"Huh?"

"Colin, Mary Kate is pregnant," Elizabeth diagnosed, shaking her head at the time it took for him to understand.

Colin looked wide-eyed at Aidan. "Do ya think?" he questioned.

"'Tis logical, mate. Congratulations," Aidan concluded and slapped Colin on the back.

Colin jumped from where he sat and ran to his cabin. He found Mary Kate curled up on the bed with a cool cloth on her head. He sat down on the bed.

"Love."

"Colin, doona make the bed move. I shall vomit all over ya."

"Mary Kate, aire ya expecting? Elizabeth thinks ya aire with child."

"I doona know, and I doona care," Mary Kate answered irritably. Then, her eyes popped wide open, and she sat up smiling from ear to ear. "'Tis it. 'Tis why I have been so sick. We aire having a baby. Colin, is it not wonderful?"

Colin looked stricken rather than overjoyed. As red as his face had been, it now blanched pasty white. He replied, "'Tis scary."

Mary Kate started to cry, "Ya aire not happy. Ya doona want a baby."

Colin gathered the woman in his arms. "'Tis not it. I am scared. We aire on the open sea in the middle of nowhere going to do battle with a dark witch on an island filled with talking animals in order to free a land and rescue loved ones. I am absolutely terrified."

Mary Kate giggled. "Relax, Colin. I shall be in great hands. Before yer family came to Stonebridge, Lizzie and Priscilla O'Rourke delivered most of the babies born there, and I doona think yer father has delivered many if any since he came. Women have had babies for thousands of years under much worse conditions. I just wish I could stop vomiting." She ran to the washbasin.

The next day Aidan called a crew meeting. "I figure since we now have six crewmembers, we should redo the scheduling. Ladies, since ya insist on being here, ya must work. I have posted a list of chores. Everyone will take turns at the helm. During the next week, ladies, ya will learn to steer this craft. Mary Kate, seeing as you plan to provide us with a seventh crewmember, I have assigned ya lighter duties." Aidan winked at the dainty young woman.

"When ya feel better, Colin can teach ya to steer. Forsooth, I am very happy for ya. Everybody, get busy!"

Confused, Caitlin and Diggory looked at Mary Kate. Caitlin chimed in, "Is there something we should know?"

Colin took Mary Kate's hand, "We aire having a baby. There! The cat is oot of the bag."

P.C. mewed as if she had known all along, and the women began to chatter as the men went about their duties. After a few more weeks, everyone, including Mary Kate, had learned to pilot the ship. They took turns for the late shift by couples. This made the long hours after midnight pass more easily.

Jean was brought on deck everyday. He helped, too, by pulling heavy objects that had to be moved. As they worked, Aidan asked Diggory, "When do ya think Jean will regain his voice?"

"Not yet. We be too far from Draconis. Aidan, we be making slow progress. With such a small crew, 'twill probably take over a year to get to Draconis. For sanity's sake we will need to stop at some of the islands along the way. Aboot two days away there be a small island village. Let us put into port for a time. We can get some fresh fruit and milk."

"That sounds wise," agreed Aidan.

The Privileged Character stopped at Ichthys Isle, so called because it was shaped like a fish. Ichthys Isle was a small fishing village. The dark skinned inhabitants welcomed the visitors and furnished them with the supplies they needed. They spent several weeks in rooms above the only pub in town. The first night, they had a pint and relaxed for the evening. Mary Kate ate three bowls of cabbage soup and drank milk until she thought she would explode.

The next morning Colin took Mary Kate to visit the local wise woman and received a good report. The day before they left the island, Colin insisted Mary Kate visit the midwife again; Diggory and Elizabeth strolled along the beach; and Aidan and Caitlin went to pick blueberries at the suggestion of the proprietress of the pub. They ate as they picked.

Aidan joked, "Caitlin, ya aire eating more berries than ya aire picking."

"They aire delicious."

"Save some for the rest of us."

The next thing Aidan knew, he was being pelted with overly ripe blueberries. "Zounds! Ya little imp!" he stammered and went in pursuit of his assailant. Caitlin ran, squealing. When Aidan caught her, he proceeded to mash a handful of blueberries all over her face. They laughed until their sides ached. When they returned to the village to board the ship, they looked like two naughty children.

The small crew thanked the villagers for their hospitality and got underway once again. Once on board, Caitlin sought her friend.

"What did the old mother say?"

"We aire fine, just as Lizzie said. The baby should be born in midwinter. I bought some cloth and thread to make baby clothes and yarn to knit. Ya will help me, aye?"

"Of course, I will, ya ninny." Caitlin hugged Mary Kate affectionately.

That night in bed, Caitlin said to Aidan, "I want a baby."

"That sounds good," concurred Aidan as he nibbled Caitlin's neck. "At least we can have fun trying."

"I am serious," pouted Caitlin as she punched Aidan softly in the stomach.

"So am I," chuckled Aidan, tackling Caitlin.

Life aboard ship took on a monotonous routine. There was very little excitement. Mary Kate began to look pregnant, and Caitlin began to fret because she was not pregnant. Elizabeth kept a wary eye on both girls.

Sailing was smooth for several months with only an occasional rainstorm. Just before the first of the New Year, the winds died. The water grew ominously still. The men had to row the ship to make any headway. This went on for nearly two weeks. Aidan complained, "At this pace 'twill take us *two* years to get to Draconis. I wish the wind would pick up."

From the crow's nest came a warning. "Be careful what ya wish for. There aire threatening clouds on the horizon." It was Elizabeth.

Diggory scolded her. "What be ye adoin' up there? Come down afore ye get hurt."

"Somebody had to come up here to look around. Mary Kate is steering. Caitlin is helping to row. Who was left?"

"Send P.C. up there and let her meow if she sees trouble."

"Diggory, she's a cat."

"She be a smart cat." *If she be a cat a'tall.* "I recollect her acatchin' three great big rats."

"No, she didna," retorted Elizabeth. "P.C. knew we were down there the whole time. She chose that time to let the cat oot of the bag." Elizabeth laughed merrily.

Just then, lightning flashed. "No need to worry, dear. I am coming down." Elizabeth scampered down, dressed in breeches and a loose linen shirt just like the men. Everybody else scurried to pull in sails and rigging and to batten down the hatches. Aidan sent everyone below deck into the hold. One hellacious gale blew their way.

Aidan tried to pilot the ship in the storm. It was all he could do to fight the hurricane-force winds, the pelting rain, and the gargantuan waves. Numerous times he was knocked from his feet and had to grasp the wheel with great effort to keep from being swept overboard.

In the midst of the tempest, Caitlin started to go on deck. Diggory restrained her. "Nay, lass. I shan't let ye go oot there."

"Aidan canna do this alone. I must help him."

"Nay, sweet girl. I best be agoin'. I know more what to do. Colin, lad, come if we call ye."

Diggory came out just in time to pull Aidan to safety. "Doona try to foight against the force! Go with her, lad!"

"'Twill throw us off course!"

"Better off course than dead! We can get back on course!" Diggory looked around him as he thought: *If there be a course. We shoulda been there by now. We seem to be going in circles. Some force must be at work to keep us away. But which one and why? Be it good or evil?*

It took the strength of both men to hold the helm steady. During the next two hours, the ship pitched fiercely. Diggory cried out in pain. In the blinding rain, Aidan could not see his friend.

"Diggory what is wrong?" he shouted over the howling wind.

"I think I broke me 'and! Call Colin, boy! I canna 'elp ye 'old 'er steady!"

Aidan hollered as loudly as he could. His voice died on the wind. He struggled to hold the helm and his dear comrade. "Colin!" he screamed urgently.

Down below, the occupants were tossed about like rag dolls. Colin harkened to a voice on the wind. "They aire calling me," he shouted and started to the deck.

"'Tis just the wind," groaned Mary Kate as she grabbed Elizabeth's hand.

"No, 'tis Aidan." Colin disappeared in a gush of water.

Once on deck Colin grappled with the wheel. He roared above the wind, "I can hold her. Get Diggory to a cabin." Aidan clutched Diggory's arm and dragged him to the nearest compartment. Diggory dropped onto the bed.

"I be fine, boy. Colin needs ye more. Go!"

Aidan fought his way back to Colin, and the two young men continued to wrestle the bluster.

Meanwhile, in the hold, Mary Kate screamed. She was still clutching Elizabeth's hand. Elizabeth realized they were standing in a puddle.

"Did that much rain get in here when Colin opened the hatch?" mused Elizabeth.

"No!" Mary Kate screamed again. "Me Water broke!"

16
Secrets

Mary Kate mauled Elizabeth's hand and let out a sob. "Not now. 'Tis too early."

Elizabeth comforted her, "When the baby says 'tis time, 'tis time." Then, she turned to Caitlin.

"Caitlin, get some blankets and towels. Then, see if ya can get to the galley and boil some water."

Caitlin hurried back with blankets, towels, and some pillows. They made a bed for Mary Kate, and then Caitlin started to the galley. It took all her might to push the hatch open against the raging storm. She had to hug the wall of the ship to get to the galley. She arrived to find it in total disarray, cooking utensils strewn all over the floor. Caitlin tripped over a mug and fell against the table. Blood oozed from her head. She snatched a dishtowel and pressed against her forehead to stop the bleeding.

Using one hand, she dipped a pot of water and set it to boil. She sat for a moment, feeling dizzy from the fall. When the water began to boil, she was faced with the task of getting it to the hold. She thought aloud, "Oh, God, how am I going to get this to Lizzie? I pray Thee, help me."

Cautiously, she opened the door. The rain still pounded the vessel, but the wind had subsided somewhat. Carrying the huge stewpot full of scalding water, Caitlin walked awkwardly toward the hold. Colin caught a glimpse of her through the deluge. "Aidan." He indicated for Aidan to follow his eyes.

Aidan hollered, "Caitlin, what aire ya doing?"

She paused briefly and flung over her shoulder, "Delivering a baby." Then, she hurried to the hold.

Still battling the roar of the storm, Colin said, "What did she say?"

"I think she said she was delivering a baby," Aidan strained over the howls.

With ashen face, Colin said, "That canna be. 'Tis too soon."

"Try not to worry." Aidan attempted to comfort his brother-in law. "Lizzie is taking care of Mary Kate and the baby. Colin, stay focused with me. We must keep this ship afloat." Colin nodded, and the two men held fast.

Caitlin descended the ladder to the hold. Spilling some of the water on herself, she let out a wail. Elizabeth ran to steady the pot, and together they wrangled it to a secure spot. "Aire ya burned?" questioned Lizzie.

"I am all roight," lied Caitlin, ignoring the searing pain on her legs. She lit several more lanterns to give Elizabeth enough light. That is when Elizabeth saw the gash in her forehead.

"Lass, ya aire bleeding. Sit down and let me look at that." Mary Kate screamed loudly again. Elizabeth snapped at the girl, "Mary Kate, take a deep breath and breathe the way I told ya. I must see to Caitlin for a minute."

"It hurts," wailed Mary Kate.

"I know it does, but 'twill be over soon," consoled Elizabeth while she dug in a trunk of medical supplies.

"I shall be fine," insisted Caitlin. "Take care of Mary Kate."

"Nonsense, girl," scolded Elizabeth. She bathed Caitlin's face. "'Tis not very big, but this will hurt."

"I am tough." Caitlin smiled wanly.

Within minutes, Elizabeth had put three stitches near Caitlin's hairline. Caitlin gripped the side of the barrel on which she sat. She ground her teeth, but she never uttered a sound. When Elizabeth was done, she bragged, "Ya aire a tough sailor. Well done." Meanwhile, Mary Kate was screaming again.

For six more hours as the ship pitched, Mary Kate screamed and groaned periodically. Finally, Colin, dripping wet, descended the ladder. It was still raining in sheets, but the wind had lulled. He went to his wife and looked at Elizabeth, "Is she all roight?"

"She is having a hard time, Colin. She is so tiny, and the baby is large. 'Tis going to be a long noight."

Just then Mary Kate let out another moan. She clutched Colin's hand so hard he winced. She glared at him through matted hair and drops of sweat and screamed vehemently. "Ya bastard! 'Tis yer fault! I hate ya!" Colin took a step back, bewildered that such anger could come from his gentle Mary Kate.

When the contraction subsided she lay back and cried, "Colin where aire ya? I need ya."

"Lizzie?" Colin said, his face contorted in confusion.

Lizzie assured him, "When 'tis all over, neither of ya will remember a single vicious comment that came from Mary Kate's lips. 'Tis normal for a woman in labor to hate her husband momentarily. 'Tis the pain."

Mary Kate screamed a sharp cry that was different from the ones she had been uttering. Elizabeth sprang into action. She examined Mary Kate and turned to Colin.

"Lad, ya need to go topside now. Caitlin and I have work to do."

"But I want to stay with Mary Kate."

"Colin, go! Now!" Elizabeth practically pushed Colin up the ladder. "None of ya open that hatch unless we call for ya. Do ya understand?" He nodded his assent and closed the hatch.

"Caitlin, this is bad. The baby is breech and very large. If I doona get that baby turned, we could lose both of them," said Elizabeth, worry etching her brow. "Ya try to comfort Mary Kate. What I am doing down here will hurt loike hell."

Mary Kate wailed and dug her nails into Caitlin's hand. She pled desperately, "Lizzie, doona let me baby die." Then, she collapsed briefly.

Caitlin had tears on her cheeks when she looked at Elizabeth. "Is she going to die, Lizzie?"

"I know not, child."

"Does it always hurt so badly?"

"Not always this badly, but it hurts. I remember when I had my baby..." Elizabeth's thought trailed into silence.

"Yer baby? Elizabeth, I didna know you had a child," Caitlin questioned.

Elizabeth looked at Caitlin. "Caitlin, dearest, what I say to ya can go no further than yer heart. Nobody knows, not even Diggory."

Caitlin nodded. "I promise."

"Ya know that me father disapproved of Diggory. Father thought his background was 'unsuitable,' and he was too old for me, being fifteen years me senior, though Father was thirty years older than me mother. Father thought that Diggory was too old to have never married, so there must have been something queer aboot him. Father forbade me to see him, but we loved each other so much that I would often sneak oot to be with him. We planned to elope. Not long before he left for Draconis, we met at Porpoise Point. On that occasion, one thing led to another. Well, ya know what happened. I conceived, and before I could tell Diggory, me father sent me away to the old abbey to have the baby. I know 'twas a little girl, but I never saw her. I was told she was adopted by a very well-to-do family. After I recovered from the delivery, Father sent me away to a convent in France. He didna want anyone to suspect what had in truth happened." She snorted and clenched her jaw in anger. "'Twould have tarnished the family's reputation. He said my wicked mother had already put blight on the family name and he wouldna allow me to add to it. He had her put away when I was very young. He told me she was mentally deranged and he feared for my well-being. By the time I got back to Stonebridge, Diggory had sailed for Draconis." She stifled her own sob. "I have never found the courage to tell him he has a child he can never see. I think 'twould break his heart."

"Lizzie, when was yer child born?"

"Late summer. She would be a few months younger than ya."

"Lizzie, did ya know Diana Murphy was barren?"

"No. She has Mary Kate."

"Mary Kate is adopted. The Murphys were told a wayward girl in the village had given birth, and her baby girl needed a home. The orphanage in the old abbey brought the little girl to their home, and they instantly fell in love with her. 'Twas late summer. Lizzie, how many 'wayward' girls could there have been in Stonebridge? I think ya aire looking at yer daughter."

"Help me turn her. My baby had a strawberry birthmark on her back. I saw that when they slapped her buttocks. 'Twas all I saw before they scurried her away."

Right in the middle of Mary Kate's back was an almost perfectly shaped strawberry birthmark.

"Oh, God!" gasped Elizabeth.

Mary Kate suddenly came to and screamed again.

Elizabeth went to work again. "Caitlin, I canna get the baby to turn. I am losing both of them."

"Is there nothing ya can do?"

"Aye, there is, but 'tis unconventional."

"Do it!"

"Caitlin, whatever ya see in here must never leave this room. Do ya understand? Ya canna even tell Aidan. That means keeping secrets from yer husband. Can ya live with that? I canna do the procedure alone. I need yer help, but I also need yer silence."

"I shan't say a word. I swear it. This is yer daughter. Do whatever ya must."

"Aye, I must. There is a small wooden bowl in that chest in the corner. Get it." Elizabeth pried the lid off a barrel and mumbled, "I never wanted to open this."

Inside were all sorts of vials and herbs. Elizabeth removed a strange looking black leaf and a vial of clear liquid. She crushed the plant in the bowl and poured a few drops of the liquid on top. The concoction began to smoke. Then, Elizabeth took a branch of hyssop and painted a cross at the bottom of Mary Kate's belly.

All the while Mary Kate groaned and writhed in agony. Caitlin sat in wide-eyed wonder and whispered, "Lizzie, is this black magic?"

Elizabeth snapped, "Not black magic, child. *Never* black magic. Now be quiet and hold her hands down. Doona let her move."

In bewilderment, Caitlin lay across Mary Kate to keep her still. Elizabeth said, "Elfringo et prodo spiritus," and then took a strange looking blade from the barrel. She used the instrument to cut along the lines she had drawn. There was a spurt of blood. Mary Kate's abdomen was wide open. Elizabeth reached in and pulled out a whopping baby boy. He instantly started to bawl. She snipped the cord with shears, wrapped him in clean towels, and laid him on a blanket.

Caitlin screamed, "Elizabeth, 'tis another one. 'Tis much smaller. Come quick."

"No wonder I couldna get the baby to turn. I never knew which foot I was grabbing." She pulled out a tiny little girl that was not breathing. Elizabeth had to slap her bottom several times before she gave a weak cry. Elizabeth wrapped her, too, in clean towels and laid her by her brother.

"Now comes the hard part," said Elizabeth gravely. She removed the afterbirth and cleaned the incision she had made. Elizabeth closed the area with thread, leaving a cross-shaped scar. Then, she ran her finger over the incision and said more words Caitlin did not understand. "Sacrificum per amor, occludo et medicor." It looked almost as if nothing had happened, except for a pink puffy cross. Elizabeth looked at Caitlin and said, "Alas, many physicians do this procedure, but the mother invariably dies. Most midwives think 'tis barbaric and evil to use the items I did, but 'tis a life-saving procedure they could learn and perform with surgical instruments and sutures if they would let go of their archaic ideas. Then, I wouldna be branded a criminal for what I just did. The only drawback to what I have done is Mary Kate will never be able to have another child, but she has two. She has been blessed. If no infection sets in, she will be fine." She looked at the twins. "Some say a child taken is not born of woman and might be Satan's spawn."

Caitlin shook her head. "Untrue."

Lizzie smiled. "I think 'tis time to let Colin know he has a son and a daughter. Peradventure, the man has pulled all his hair oot by now."

When Caitlin opened the hatch there was only light rain falling, but Colin sat by the hatch huddled in a blanket and drenched despite the oiled seal-skin slicker he wore. Aidan was piloting the ship after having set Diggory's hand. Diggory slept.

"Colin." Caitlin touched her brother's arm lovingly. "Come down and meet yer children. Ya have twins, a boy and a girl, just loike us." She smiled warmly.

Colin leapt down the ladder. "How is Mary Kate?"

"Sleeping. Let her rest," responded Elizabeth as she handed him two bundles. "Ya have yer work ahead of ya."

Colin beamed. "Aire they all roight?"

"Aye, they aire fine and healthy. They need names. We canna call them Boy and Girl Fitzpatrick."

"No. We had decided to call a boy Declan or a girl Morgan. Well a day!" He chuckled. "We get to use both names."

"Good choices," said Lizzie. "Colin, let Caitlin put the little ones in the barrel beds we made for them. I need to talk to ya."

"Is something wrong?"

"Yea and nay. Mary Kate and the babies will be fine, but things did not go well during the delivery. There is a good chance she will not be able to have any more babies. I am sorry. I did all I could do."

"Ya saved them all, Lizzie. I am eternally grateful."

Thus, Declan and Morgan Fitzpatrick came into the lives of the crew of *The Privileged Character*.

Caitlin took Elizabeth to the side. "Elizabeth, I want to see Aidan glow the way Colin did when he held his babies. We have been trying and trying, and I am not with child yet. Is there anything ya can do to help us? I pray thee."

Elizabeth softly laid a hand on Caitlin's belly. She said one almost inaudible word and looked at Caitlin. "The key is to keep trying."

Caitlin smiled an exhausted smile and mumbled, "Gramercy." She started to leave, but turned back. "Lizzie," she whispered. "I think ya should tell Diggory the truth aboot Mary Kate. He deserves to know. Ya should tell the other thing, too. I shan't say anything. 'Tis yer responsibility, but I know deceiving the man ya love can hurt him more than the truth. I love ya, Lizzie. We all do, but Diggory adores ya. 'Tis nothing that will make us stop loving ya. We aire not yer father. Do the roight thing." She hugged Elizabeth and went to get some sleep.

17
𝔗𝔯𝔲𝔱𝔥𝔰

𝔚𝔥𝔢𝔫 Caitlin returned to her cabin, she found Aidan fast asleep. He was exhausted from the ordeal of the day. She tried to undress quietly, but when she removed her under garments, they were stuck to the burns she had received from the boiling water. She let out a shriek that made Aidan jump straight from bed. "Out upon it! What has happened now?"

"'Tis nothing. Go back to sleep." She tried to hide her pain, but her voice was thin.

"Ya did not cry oot loike that for no reason." Aidan got up and lit a lantern. He saw Caitlin's legs. "That needs some ointment. I shall be roight back." Aidan stumbled out the door to the hold for the medical supplies.

He paused only momentarily to look at his niece and nephew and quickly explained the situation to Colin who sent him back to Caitlin immediately. Aidan found her sitting in a chair, slumped over the low bureau. She cried softly onto her folded arms.

"There, now," Aidan said tenderly while he stroked Caitlin's hair. "This horrendous day is over. Everyone is safe. Let me rub this ointment on yer legs. Ya will feel much better."

Caitlin wiped her eye. "I feel silly and selfish."

"Why?"

"Because I was wishing I was the one below holding a newborn baby. I was thinking of only meself. After all we went through today, how could I be so heartless?"

"Oh, honey, 'tis all roight." Aidan took Caitlin's hand and led her to the bed. He blew out the lantern and cradled his wife in his arms. "Insooth, it took me mother and father years to have their first child, or so she said. I thought she meant me, since I didna know aboot me sister at the time. Mayhap 'tis a family thing on me side. Give it some more time. Marry! I doona mind practicing; but, forsooth, I am too tired to practice this eve." he concluded with a sigh.

"Me too," yawned Caitlin. "Just hold me." They fell asleep.

Colin sat by Mary Kate's bed until she awoke. Her eyes darted around the room as she opened them. "My baby," she said in agitation.

Colin caressed her head. "Good morrow, beautiful," he greeted her. "Ya mean babies."

"What?"

"We have two of them. Mam Fitzpatrick, let me introduce ya to yer firstborn, Declan Quentin Fitzpatrick." He laid their son in her left arm. "Now, Mam, let me introduce our little surprise, Morgan Celeste Fitzpatrick." He laid their daughter in her right arm.

"Oh, Colin. They aire perfect. Look at the little toes."

"They aire perfect. Just loike their mother."

"I am not perfect. I think I said some ugly things to ya earlier. I beg pardon."

"'Tis nothing to regret. I can never understand what ya went through. Whatever ya may have said came from the pain ya were experiencing. Only, tell me ya doona hate me."

"Hate ya? Impossible. I love ya more than me own life. I must. Look what I did." She looked down at her children.

"I love ya, too. Doona ever scare me again loike ya did today. Lizzie said she almost lost ya."

"I told ya I'd be in good hands with Elizabeth."

Declan began to cry. "Mam, methinks he is hungry and there is nothing I can do aboot it," Colin said.

Mary Kate laughed softly and began nursing her son. Colin watched and swelled with pride at the sight of his family. Mary Kate had to wake Morgan to get her to eat. After she was done, Colin carried her to their cabin. He placed the babies in the half barrels turned into cradles on the far side of the room. He kissed Mary Kate on the head and breathed, "Sleep, me love."

Diggory was steering the ship when Elizabeth took him bread and meat. She touched his shoulder. "How is the hand?"

"It hurts, but I can steer in these calm waters. I am only concerned that we aire not there yet. It seems though we aire sailing, we aire going nowhere. We are running low on supplies. We might need to dip into the extras ya placed in the 'old. The storm caused great damage, but at least it refilled the water barrels with fresh water." He sighed. "How be everybody else?"

"Just fine. Mainly tired. Just loike ya."

"I be fine. I slept for a while after Aidan set me hand. The boy did a fine job, too."

"Verily, ya love him, aye?"

"Aye."

"How would ya loike a child of yer own?"

Diggory's eyes twinkled and his lips twitched with mirth. "Lizzie, I think we be a little too old for that."

"Diggory, drop anchor for the night. I need to talk to ya. 'Tis important."

Diggory could see that Elizabeth was deeply troubled. He did as she requested. Though the anchor did not reach the ocean bottom, it slowed the vessel considerably. It would list without incident. They went to their cabin. Before they could even sit down, Diggory asked, "Lizzie, what be wrong? Be ye ahavin' a late-life surprise?"

Ironically, she chuckled, "No. I wish, but, no."

"Then, what be it?"

Elizabeth took a deep breath and said calmly and distinctly, "Diggory, we have a daughter aboard this very ship."

"What?" Diggory responded in amazement. Elizabeth told him the whole story. When she was done, Diggory sat in total silence.

"Diggory, say something, prithee."

Misty blue eyes looked at Elizabeth. "I doona know what to say. I be hurt; I be angry; I be happy. I feel mixed up inside." He moved his hands as if juggling. "For fifteen years, I 'ave been back in Stonebridge. For ten years that old reprobate of a father of yers 'as been dead. Ye 'ave lived up in that mansion almost loike a 'ermit for years. Until Priscilla died, ye wouldna even look me way when we passed on the street."

She interrupted, "I thought ya and Priscilla..."

He lifted a hand to cut her off saying, "Then, loike a whirlwind ye blew back into me life. Ye know me 'eart 'as never belonged to anyone else."

Elizabeth dropped her eyes to stare at the wood planks of the floor.

Diggory went on. "I was willin' to die ol' and alone rather than betray me love for ye. Now ye throw this bit o' news at me. Ye 'ave 'ad fifteen years to tell me, and ye waited. Even if ye didna know it be Mary Kate 'erself, ye coulda told me I was a father. Ye coulda told me I made one beautiful thing in me life. All I ever thought I might do roight was to rescue me old friend, and, so far, I 'ave not done a good job o' that. Lizzie, ye shoulda told me." Tears streamed down Diggory's cheeks.

Elizabeth sobbed. She pleaded with Diggory, "I pray thee, doona hate me. I couldna bear that."

"I doona hate ye, woman. It be much worse than that."

"Oh, God's me," choked Elizabeth.

"I love ye. That be why it 'urts so much. I love ye."

Elizabeth ran to Diggory. She dropped to her knees and put her head on his lap. "Can ya ever forgive me for keeping this from ya?"

Diggory lifted her chin. "Aye, Lizzie. That be what love be aboot." The two old lovers held on to each other for quite a time. Then, Diggory looked deeply into Elizabeth's eyes. "I see in yer eyes there be other things ye need to tell me, but ye be too afraid. Tell me in yer time, but know I will love ye no matter what ye might 'ave done or what ye might do. Ye aire me 'eart and soul. The question before us now is what to do aboot Mary Kate. Do we tell her the truth, and if so, when?"

During the next few days, the topic of conversation was always the two new crewmembers. Whom did they look like? What kind of personalities were they developing? Even in the midst of all the necessary repairs from the storm damage, the babies were discussed.

All the talk about the babies upset Caitlin, but she kept her thoughts to herself. She did not even talk to Elizabeth anymore. She just went about her chores quietly. Then, she would go to her cabin to rest or read. One afternoon, Aidan found her in the cabin crying. "Caitlin, what is wrong?"

"I didna hear ya come in." She rubbed her hand across her red eyes. "Nothing. I am all roight."

"Doona lie to me."

"Aidan, I am melancholy. 'Tis the same thing as always. I am trying to deal with me feelings, but sometimes I get sad."

Aidan snuggled up beside Caitlin and whispered in her ear, "Do ya want to practice making a baby?"

"Now?"

"Why not?"

"'Tis the middle of the afternoon," said Caitlin, shocked at Aidan's unconventional suggestion.

"God save me!" He placed a hand over his heart. "How daring!"

"Stop mocking me."

Aidan looked seriously into the eyes of the woman he loved and asked, "Does God need darkness to create a baby?"

"No."

"Then make love to me." Aidan kissed Caitlin with desire.

Caitlin took on a new attitude toward her niece and nephew. She began to dote on them, spending as much time as possible with them. Six weeks later, Caitlin, Mary Kate, Elizabeth, and the babies lounged on deck. It was a beautiful sunny day. Morgan began to cry. "I shall get her," said Caitlin sprightly. She jumped up, stood still a moment, and fainted. Elizabeth was beside her in a flash. "Get Aidan," she instructed Mary Kate.

Aidan bounded up. He carried Caitlin to their cabin while Elizabeth went for medical supplies. When Elizabeth got to the cabin, Aidan was bathing Caitlin's face in cool water. She was coming around.

"What happened?" he asked.

"I know not. I was lightheaded when I stood. I am in good health now." She stood to prove her point.

"If ya insist," said Aidan, still concerned. "Lizzie, keep an eye on her."

"Aye, aye, captain," Elizabeth joked and wiggled her eyebrows at Caitlin. Aidan went back to repairing the fishing nets.

"I vouchsafe I am fine," protested Caitlin.

"I am sure ya aire. Ya doona have a fever. Do ya feel sick in any other way?"

"No. I was only dizzy. Let us away to the deck. 'Tis such a lovely day. I doona wanna spoil it."

"E'en so, but let me know if ya feel faint again."

The next day while Elizabeth and Caitlin served dinner, Caitlin lifted a pitcher of water to bring to the table. When she turned, she paused. The pewter pitcher hit the ground with a clatter. She had fainted again.

"Lizzie," Aidan said in alarm. "Something must be wrong." He carried Caitlin to their cabin. Elizabeth followed.

"Aidan, wait outside," Elizabeth ordered.

"I will not," Aidan defied her.

Elizabeth shot Aidan a reproachful look.

"I am not going anywhere until I know Caitlin is all roight," he maintained.

"Fie. Stay. Ya can help me undress her."

They undressed Caitlin and laid her back on the pillow. She came around.

"I fainted again, aye?" she questioned.

"Aye, ya did, and this time we aire going to check ya oot whether ya loike it or not," stated Elizabeth with authority.

Elizabeth checked her pulse. She listened to her breathing. Elizabeth felt Caitlin's breasts.

"Ouch! That hurt." Caitlin winced.

"Hmmm," mumbled Elizabeth.

"What?" said Aidan.

"Shh," scolded Elizabeth.

She pushed on Caitlin's abdomen.

"Ouch!"

"Hmmm."

"What?" demanded Aidan.

"Aidan, prithee wait outside. I would loike to do the rest of this examination in private. It embarrasses me to perform some of these elements in front of a man."

Sufficiently chastised, Aidan went outside and closed the door without another comment.

Elizabeth finished examining Caitlin, and Caitlin dressed. Elizabeth called Aidan back into the room.

"What is the matter, Elizabeth?" he demanded to know.

"Nothing is the matter that time will not cure," said Elizabeth with a twinkle in her eyes. "'Twill take aboot seven and a half months."

Aidan and Caitlin looked at each other.

"Caitlin is with child," Elizabeth pronounced. "I shall leave ya two alone, but I shall remind ya next time afternoon delight can work miracles," she teased as she left.

Caitlin squealed in glee and bounced on the bed like a mischievous child. Aidan swung her around the room. They were ecstatic.

"Peradventure we should always make babies in the afternoon," he said, beaming.

"Whenever ya want," she replied and kissed him with joy.

Caitlin continued her fainting spells for about a month. Then, everything returned to normal, except that she was always hungry. She saw Elizabeth for an examination on a regular basis. She got very large.

"Lizzie, do ya think 'tis twins?" she inquired.

"If 'tis not, girl, ya should name him Goliath."

During one visit, Caitlin asked Elizabeth, "Have ya told Diggory aboot Mary Kate?"

"Aye, child."

"What aboot the other thing?"

"No, child."

"Why?"

"Discovering he had a child was hard enough. Discovering his wife dabbles in witchcraft is another thing. The only witch he has ever had experience with was Quazel. What would he think of me?"

"He would think more of ya if ya tell him than he will if he finds oot some other way."

"I know, child. I am still working up the courage to tell him."

"Would it help if someone went with ya?"

"I know not."

"Think upon it."

"I will."

Slipping into her dressing gown, Caitlin asked, "What aboot Mary Kate? When are ya going to tell her the truth?"

"Oh, Caitlin, 'twould upset her whole life. She loves Diana Murphy. She is the only mother Mary Kate has ever known."

"Lizzie, Mary Kate grew up miserable. She lived in a house where her mother was constantly unhappy and her father had lost his sense. She took care of herself with the help of the household servants. Colin is the only one who put her first. She deserves to know her real mother loved her even when she didna know who she was. She needs that. I think it would make her feel worthwhile and important.

"Mary Kate has often told me how ya would do nice things for her when she was a little girl. She told me how ya would pin flowers in her hair and jump rope with her. She has told me how she would come to yer house for tea parties in the garden. She has often said when she was very young she would wish ya were her mother."

Elizabeth said wistfully, "She was always such a sweet little thing. When the other children would tell tales aboot me and put dead rats on me doorstep, she would get so angry. She would stomp her little foot and tell them to go away and leave 'Lady Elizabeth' alone. Many of the other children thought I was a witch because from the time I came home from the convent until me father died I wore black. When me father died, I started wearing colors again. 'Twas rumored I killed him. Mary Kate defended me."

"Lizzie," Caitlin said, taking the older woman's hand, "in good sooth there has always been a bond between ya. Tell her the truth."

Caitlin left, but being the headstrong, willful person she was, she took matters into her own hands. She went to talk to Diggory. It was his turn to make supper, so he was in the galley.

"Be well met, Diggory," she said merrily as she headed for the biscuit jar.

"Can ye not wait an hour, lass?" he teased her.

"No. I am starving now."

"Do ye want a cup o' tea to go with it?"

"'Twould be nice. Ya have one, too. I'd loike to talk to ya."

He chuckled. "If we doona spot land soon, tea and biscuits might be all there is left to eat." Diggory sat down with two cups of tea. "What be on yer mind, Caitlin?"

"I doona know if Aidan has said anything to ya yet, but we want ya to be this baby's godfather. I think ya would make a great father. Ya aire warm and loving. Ya aire full of fun, but ya aire also firm when ya have to be."

"I would love to be yer baby's godfather, but what in truth be on yer mind?"

"I know aboot Mary Kate. Elizabeth let it slip that she had had a child during the delivery. We deduced it had to be Mary Kate. I think she should know who her parents aire. Ya should tell her. In truth, I have said what was on me mind."

"Ye usually do. This time I 'appen to agree with ye. Secrets can be damaging."

"Good. I am going now." She stood to leave.

"Caitlin, do ye know Lizzie's other secret?"

"I canna talk to ya aboot that. I am sorry, Diggory." Then, she waddled toward the door. "Diggory, how much longer 'til Draconis?"

"In truth, I know not. We shoulda been there by now."

"Did the storm throw us off course?"

"There is no course." He rubbed his hands on his breeches. "Only a general direction."

Caitlin cocked an eyebrow. "A secret?"

"Aye." The old sailor gave a discreet nod. "And a leap of faith."

That night Aidan could not sleep because he was being kicked in the back by little feet. He finally slept only to awaken to find Caitlin asleep in the rocking chair that he had made for her. He woke her and told her to go back to bed. "I have some things on me mind and this baby was kicking so hard I couldna sleep," she grumbled.

"Ya only have aboot six weeks left. Then, ya can get some rest," said Aidan sleepily.

"Surely ya jest. Then I shan't sleep because somebody will be hungry or wet or stinky," she countered, patting her protruding belly affectionately.

"I shall change the baby, but I canna feed him."

"Him? Who said 'twas a boy?"

"Her. I care not. Caitlin, 'tis too early to be awake," complained Aidan.

"Pray pardon? Who woke whom?"

"I shoulda known better. Would ya loike something from the galley? I shall raid the cupboard for ya. I know there are some wonderfully sweet raisins hiding in the back left corner."

"No. I am not hungry," she said snuggling up next to Aidan.

"'Tis a change."

"'Twas mean," she retaliated, punching his arm. "I am beginning to think this bed is not big enough for the three of us."

"I had it first."

"Aidan Duncan O'Rourke!"

"Turn the other way."

"What?"

"Turn over."

Caitlin turned her back to Aidan. He put his arm over her, spooned against her, kissed her on the neck, and said, "I love ya. Go to sleep."

The next morning at breakfast, Diggory took Caitlin to the side. "Ye and Aidan aire 'aving supper in yer cabin tonight, and ye are tending the young ones."

"We aire?" Caitlin said momentarily confused.

"Ye aire," Diggory said with a stern look at Caitlin.

"Oh, aye, we aire," Caitlin acknowledged with a knowing grin.

That evening Mary Kate and Colin had supper with Diggory and Elizabeth. They ate charred sea bass, not by choice, but because Elizabeth was so nervous that she burned the first one. Diggory pitched in to finish preparing the meal so they, "Wouldna starve afore morning."

After supper, over a glass of whiskey, which Diggory kept hidden for special occasions, Elizabeth spoke timidly. "Mary Kate, Diggory and I have something we must tell ya. We doona want to upset ya or hurt ya in any way, but we feel ya must know the truth."

Mary Kate jumped from her seat and ran to Elizabeth. She knelt at Elizabeth's feet and began breathlessly, "Aire ya in truth going to talk to me aboot what I overheard while I was in labor? Ya didna think that I could hear ya, but I heard what ya told Caitlin. Aire ya, indeed, me mother? Aire ya me father?" she added as she turned her gaze toward Diggory.

The only response Elizabeth could muster was to pull the girl into her arms and shed tears into her hair. Elizabeth finally found her voice. "They took ya away from me. I never even got to hold ya. I barely saw ya for a moment. I didna know Diana and Logan had adopted a child. I thought she had a baby while I was away. I never wanted to give ya up. If I had known where ya were, if I had known who ya were, I doona know what I would have done. Oh, child, can ya ever forgive me?"

"There is nothing to forgive," consoled Mary Kate through her own tears. "I always wondered why I loiked ya so much, why I felt close to ya. I thought 'twas because ya showed me the attention I craved. Now, I know somehow through all the lies and secrets we were connected.

"There were times when me mother, Diana, would be so sad she would forget to tuck me in at night. I would lie awake and wait for someone to kiss me and tell me she loved me. At those times, I would try to imagine what me other mother looked loike. Sometimes I couldna see anything. Sometimes 'twould be yer face. I would think *if Elizabeth were me mother, she wouldna forget to tuck me in and kiss me good night.* Then, I would pretend ya came in the door and kissed me and tucked the covers in tightly. Ya would say 'I love ya, Wee One,' the way ya always called me when we talked.

"Oh, I am so glad ya finally want to talk to me. I was so afraid I was a disappointment to ya. Mayhap ya were not proud of who I had become." Mary Kate gushed all the feelings and thoughts she had kept bottled inside.

"Not proud? I am very proud of ya. I was afraid ya would hate me for letting ya go."

"And *ya*," Mary Kate turned her attention to Diggory. "Ya, the crazy man, the town fool. Oh, I am so sorry. I was afraid of ya. Ya talked to animals. Ya told fantastic, scary tales. Sometimes I would watch ya from behind the wisteria arbor. I wanted to see if the animals talked back to ya. I thought to meself, *Mayhap he is lonely because the people are so mean to him.* I concluded ya were harmless at the very least, especially after the day ya caught me when I fell oot of the big elm tree. Of course Diana came screaming for ya to put her baby down without any gratitude for yer having kept me from harm."

Diggory asked shyly, "Mary Kate, aire ye the one who left all those baskets of good things on me doorstep?"

"Aye. I thought I owed ya something for saving me life. I couldna think of anything else I could do. I knew me mother, Diana, would never miss a few berries or a loaf of bread."

"That was the most precious thing anyone ever did for me. That little kindness brightened me life."

"Oh, what do I call ya two? I have always called Diana and Logan Mother and Father. What do I call ya?"

"Whatever feels roight to ye, wee lass." Diggory smiled.

"Oh, I doona know. Colin, what do ya think?"

Everyone looked at Colin who had been observing the whole ado. He suddenly roared with laughter. "Who, me? Am I in truth here? Do ya want me opinion? I thought I was a spectator, a fly on the wall. Mary Kate, ya have not said that many words at one time since I have known ya. I never knew ya could be such a magpie."

Everyone looked around and realized how absurd they must have appeared. It really was funny.

"Oh." Mary Kate blushed. "Indeed, I want yer opinion."

"Well, I think Diggory is roight. Do what feels comfortable."

"Aye, well," mused Mary Kate. "Mother and Father are so formal and stiff."

Elizabeth interjected, "Ya doona have to make a decision roight this minute."

"Oh, but I do," argued Mary Kate. "It has been long enough as 'tis. How do ya feel aboot Momma and Papa and Nana and Pap for the grandchildren?"

"Zounds! Diggory, we have grandchildren." Elizabeth gasped as the realization of the truth finally hit her full blast.

During this time, Aidan and Caitlin were getting a taste of parenthood.

Caitlin griped, "When will these two ever get quiet? They have been fed and changed. Why will they not sleep?"

Aidan calmly picked up Declan and sat in the rocking chair. "Hand me Morgan."

Caitlin placed Morgan in Aidan's other arm. He began to rock gently and to sing softly. In a few minutes, both babies were sound asleep.

Caitlin just stared at the sight. She whispered, "I never knew ya had such a beautiful voice."

As they placed the babies in makeshift beds, Aidan said quietly, "I am glad I had an appreciative audience and the song had the desired effect."

While they ate their supper, Caitlin said, "Aidan, ya had better sit back and relax. I have a story to tell ya." She told him all about Mary Kate, Elizabeth, and Diggory.

18
Life and Death Choices

𝕬 few weeks later, the ship sailed into a deep fog. Diggory closed his eyes at the familiar feeling. The weather grew tempestuous. Some days the rain came in sheets. Other days the wind gusted to gale force. Sometimes the sun peaked precariously through the blue-black clouds. The crew stayed alert to the ever-changing weather.

One morning when Aidan took Jean some breakfast, he was met with a surprise. "Good morrow, Aidan. Be well met this gloomy morn. Nasty weather we're having."

"Jean, ya spoke!"

"Aye. We must be getting close to home."

"By yer leave, Jean. I must talk to Diggory."

"Of course, of course."

Aidan arrived breathlessly at the helm. "Diggory, how far are we from Draconis? Jean spoke to me this morning."

"Aboot a month. I knew when we went through the fog bank. If the weather holds, Caitlin may have yer little one on the island."

"A month. Lord, grant the weather holds. I pray Thee, help me find me father, and take care of Caitlin."

Aidan became increasingly anxious with each passing day. Every time a raindrop fell or the wind blew hard, he held his breath. A week passed, and the weather still threatened, but did not change. At supper one evening, Aidan looked around at Caitlin, Mary Kate, Morgan, and Declan. "Peradventure 'twould be a good idea for ya ladies and the children to stay on board when we get to Draconis. It could be extremely dangerous there."

"Not on yer life," differed Caitlin, and the other ladies concurred. "If we need protection, we will find yer grandfather. He is already protecting some children in the mountains. Doona attempt an argument. Ya will not win the battle."

"Fie. Have it yer way."

"I usually do," Caitlin said blithely as she bent over to kiss Aidan's cheek. "Ouch."

Aidan sprang to his feet. "Aire you having contractions?"

"No. Someone kicked me in the ribs."

Around midnight Colin pounded on Aidan's cabin. Aidan stumbled to the door. "What is it?"

"'Tis blowing up a bluster oot here. It looks loike we might need all the hands we can get."

Aidan threw on his clothes. Caitlin was getting dressed, too. Aidan turned to her and said firmly, "'All hands' does not mean ya. Stay here. Ya aire in no condition to battle a storm. I mean it, Caitlin. Doona come on deck or I will tie ya to yer rocking chair."

"Ya would *not*," she began defiantly.

"I would."

Caitlin caught her side and submitted. "I think I shall stay here. Better yet, mayhap I should go to Lizzie's cabin. Prithee take me there before ya go on deck?"

"Is something wrong?"

She nodded her head yes, and then shook it no. Then, she shrugged her shoulders. As she finished dressing, she clutched her side again.

"I think I am having contractions," she confessed as the three of them walked to Elizabeth's cabin. "Why do babies loike to be born in storms?" she asked as Elizabeth opened the door.

"Many babies do come when a storm arises. We shall be fine."

"Call me if ya need me. I know from experience that ya will take good care of Caitlin," said Aidan.

"As if she were me own," assured Elizabeth.

A fierce gust hit Aidan as he came on deck. The rain was just beginning.

"I have never seen it this stormy so close to Draconis. As long as I was there before, I never saw anything loike this," declared Diggory clearly and distinctly.

"Mayhap 'twas an illusion, too."

His hump lifted toward his shoulders. "Mayhap."

"Diggory, did I just hear ya use correct grammar all the way through two sentences?" questioned Colin.

"I told ya I didna always sound loike a blithering idiot. 'Twas part of Quazel's curse on me. We aire in Draconian waters. Remember that Jean is speaking again."

"Yer hump is still there," Colin observed.

"Methinks I shall have it until the wicked witch is dead," said Diggory scornfully.

All through their conversation, the men were tying down sails and securing any number of loose items. The ship began to pitch to and fro. "The good thing aboot the storm is that 'tis blowing toward Draconis," hollered Diggory.

"Diggory, can ya steer us with the storm?" asked Aidan.

"Aye, aye, Captain."

Colin and Aidan finished securing sails and rigging before they went to the helm. Diggory was holding the ship steady.

Colin urged Aidan, "I shall stay with Diggory. Look in on Caitlin."

"Gramercy. Come and get me if ya need me."

"I will. Now away."

Caitlin had hit true labor. Aidan walked in during a contraction. Caitlin was not screaming. She was puffing and holding Mary Kate's hand. She relaxed. "Good," said Mary Kate and Elizabeth together.

"Now we wait for the next one," comforted Elizabeth.

"Look who is here," said Mary Kate. "Be careful what ya say. Ya may be apologizing on the morrow."

Aidan stayed for a while with Caitlin. He held her hand and cooled her face. He breathed through contractions with her until he almost hyperventilated.

Elizabeth suggested, "Let Caitlin breathe. Ya talk her through."

Aidan nodded with embarrassment.

Colin knocked at the door. He came in briefly. "How now, Sis?"

"Great. I have not called Aidan a bad name yet, although I am thinking of some for meself roight now. I am the one who wanted a baby so desperately," she finished through clenched teeth as another contraction hit.

"Aidan," Colin turned his attention away from his sister. "I need ya on deck. The main sail has broken loose even after being lowered."

Aidan kissed Caitlin quickly. "I love ya. I shall be back."

"I love ya, too," she panted through another contraction.

The hook that secured the main sail had come loose. The wind was batting it around like a tennis ball.

"Fie!" shouted Aidan. "Colin, I have to go up there and secure that hook. Hold the jib still."

"Let me go up."

"Nay. I am used to climbing the rigging. Just keep that jib still."

Aidan climbed the rigging with the agility of a monkey. As he grabbed the hook, a wave swept over the deck, knocking Colin from his feet. Colin struggled to stand and grappled the jib. "Aidan," he coughed out with a mouthful of water. Then, he roared, "Aidan!" He looked up. His friend was nowhere in the rigging.

"God-a-mercy!" he cried. He slipped and slid to the ship's rail, where he saw Aidan, unconscious, being tossed about by the waves.

"Diggory, drop anchor! Aidan is overboard!" he bellowed over the wind.

"I canna drop anchor in this." Diggory came running to the rail just in time to see Colin stripped of his seal skin slicker and shoes about to dive into the water. Diggory grabbed him, "Ya canna go after him, boy. Ya will both be killed."

Another wave pounded the deck, sending both men sprawling. They scrambled to their feet and scoured the water. "There!" pointed Colin. "I must go after him!" He was over the rail before Diggory could stop him or, at least, tie a secure line to him.

Diggory tossed two pieces of balsa wood attached to ropes tied to the rails over the side. A blinding flash showed that Colin had almost reached Aidan's side. Then, another wave sent Diggory flying into the jib. He did not move.

In Elizabeth's cabin, Elizabeth was saying, "Push, Caitlin...I see the baby's head...All roight...Take a deep breath...Push...One more time."

There was instant crying. "Ya have a son, Caitlin. Mary Kate, take care of the baby."

"Lizzie," groaned Caitlin. "I doona think I am done."

"Ya aire roight, honey...Push...Good...Again...Push hard."

"'Tis twins," panted Caitlin.

"At least...Push...One more time...'Tis a boy, too."

Mary Kate took the second baby. "Is that it?" she asked.

"Aye. Mary Kate, I need more towels." Elizabeth looked worried. She came to her daughter's side. "She is hemorrhaging badly. I need towels for packing. Hurry."

Mary Kate hurried as fast as she could. When she got back to the cabin, Caitlin was holding her babies. She looked pale. Elizabeth went to work.

Caitlin smiled at Mary Kate, "Meet yer nephews, Kieran Sean and Rennin Drake O'Rourke."

"They aire handsome boys, Caitlin."

"I want Aidan. Prithee, see if he can come now."

Elizabeth nodded. Mary Kate went on deck.

Mary Kate came on deck to a cold soaking rain. She called loudly, "Aidan!" There was no answer. She called again, "Aidan, Colin!" She heard a faint groaning and followed the sound. She saw Diggory beginning to move. "Papa!" She knelt beside her father and cradled his head in her lap. "Papa, what has happened? Where aire Colin and Aidan?"

Diggory began to regain his senses. "The boys!" he cried frantically. He struggled to his feet and staggered to the rail. He motioned for Mary Kate to come. "Do ya see them, honey? I am so dizzy I can hardly see. Do ya see the boys?"

"Where were they, Papa?"

"Out there." He pointed to the sea.

"In the water?" she said, her voice rising in alarm.

"Aidan was knocked in. Colin went after him. I tried to stop him. He is as stubborn as his sister."

"I doona see them, Papa. We shall get more lanterns and light the area. They aire young and strong and good swimmers. I know they aire alive. I feel it in me heart. Come on. Let us tend to yer head and then come back with the lanterns. I shall help ya look, Papa."

Diggory leaned on Mary Kate until they got to his cabin. He was feeling stronger by the time they arrived.

"Aidan?" said Caitlin weakly as the door opened.

"No. He canna come roight this minute. He and Colin are occupied," Mary Kate told her shakily.

"Momma, Papa is hurt. He hit his head very hard."

Elizabeth looked at Diggory's wound. "Ya will have a headache, but ya will be all roight in a day or two." She bandaged his head. "Doona sleep for a while."

"I canna sleep, woman. I have to find the boys."

"What do ya mean 'find the boys'?"

"They aire overboard. Both of them."

They spoke in hushed tones.

"What aire you keeping from me?" murmured Caitlin.

"Doona worry yer head, honey," said Diggory.

"What has happened to Aidan?" She tried to raise herself, but she was too weak.

"What is the matter with her, Lizzie?" asked Diggory.

"She is dying. I canna stop the bleeding."

"Momma, can ya do something special loike ya did for me?" Mary Kate had walked to her parents.

"I doona know what to do." Elizabeth began to cry. "'Tis me fault. I shan't let her die."

"Aidan," Caitlin said weakly.

Mary Kate went to her friend's side. "'Tis Mary Kate. I am here. I shan't leave ya."

"Mary Kate, take care of me babies. Ya aire their aunt. Love them as if they were yer own."

"No. Oot upon it!" Elizabeth choked the words. "I shan't let her die." She headed for the door.

"Lizzie, where aire ya going," said Diggory, grabbing her arm.

"Do ya not understand? 'Tis me fault." She pounded her fist against her chest. "If I had not pronounced the enchantment that she would conceive in the afternoon, this wouldna have happened."

"What aire ya talking aboot? Enchantment?"

"I doona have time for this now, Diggory."

"Lizzie," he tightened his grip on her arm.

Anger flashed in her eyes and she spat at him coldly, "Diggory, I am a witch. I practice the secret arts. I have since I was little and me mother showed me how to make potions and taught me simple incantations. Me mother was a witch. I am a witch. Now let go of me arm. I have to help Caitlin."

Caitlin began to gasp for air. Mary Kate shrieked, "Momma, do something!"

"Mary Kate, ya aire younger and faster than I am. Run to the hold. Look in the barrel in the farthest back corner. You will find a big black book with the words, *Livre de Morte,* inscribed on it. Bring it to me."

"Elizabeth Gilhooley Danaher! Talk to me!" Diggory was livid by this time.

"I shall talk to ya in a little while. Roight now Caitlin is me priority. I will not allow these children to lose both their parents in the same night."

"Lizzie, ya aire not God."

Arms akimbo, she said through clenched teeth, "No, I am not, but mayhap God put me here for such a time as this."

Diggory let go of her arm.

Mary Kate got back with the book. She collapsed from the exertion.

Elizabeth went to Caitlin. She was white as snow and had stopped breathing.

Elizabeth whispered, "God, forgive me if I am wrong, but I canna let her die." Elizabeth opened the book and read some words in the Gaelic, "Mach fuil augs annsachd beothaich anam. Nach deò." Then she stretched herself over the dead girl and said, "Blood of my blood; breath of my breath; restore sweet Caitlin from the brink of death."

What occurred next made both Diggory and Mary Kate freeze in terror and awe. Elizabeth placed her mouth on Caitlin's and it appeared as if blood passed from one woman to the next. Elizabeth gasped and fell to the floor. Diggory went to her and lifted her in his arms. "Doona die on me, Elizabeth." She was alive, but breathing shallowly.

Diggory laid her in Mary Kate's arms. He went to Caitlin. He heaved a great sigh. "Mary Kate, her color has returned. She breathes."

"Momma is coming around."

"Diggory," Elizabeth called.

He knelt beside her. "It worked. She lives."

"Diggory."

"I canna do this roight now. I have two lost boys to find."

Mary Kate stopped him, "Wait, Papa. I am coming with ya. I shall get extra lanterns and blankets. Ya get the rowboat ready to lower."

Father and daughter met at the rail moments later. They climbed aboard the coracle with blankets and lowered themselves into the water. After hours of searching, the sun began to rise. Finally, they saw a body floating on a piece of wood Diggory had thrown about a hundred yards away.

"Colin!" shouted Mary Kate.

They pulled him aboard the bark. He was alive, but unconscious and suffering from hypothermia. Mary Kate tore his clothes off and stripped herself. She pulled him against her and wrapped them both in blankets. "This will warm him faster, Papa."

"'Twas the roight thing to do."

She held her husband closely as they continued to look for Aidan. Mary Kate broached the subject of Elizabeth carefully. "Papa, aboot Momma."

"Doona speak of it, Mary Kate."

"Papa, at least listen to her. Let her explain. Do it for me."

"Ya ask a lot, wee one."

"Ya love her, aye?"

"Aye."

"Then, ya will hear her out. 'Tis what love does."

"Aye, child. I will let her tell me her story for ya, for her, for me, and for love."

"Much thanks, Papa. I love ya."

They searched until the sun was directly overhead. Finally, they returned to the ship. There was no sign of Aidan.

After they settled Colin for some much needed rest, Diggory sought Elizabeth. He found her in the hold surrounded by all her magical things.

"Talk to me, Elizabeth," he demanded abruptly.

She turned a tear-stained face to him. "All these things belonged to me mother. I remember she always wanted me to call her '*Mami*' because Mother was stuffy and old.' Father always called her Zellie. I thought 'twas her name. Now, I know it was his pet name for her, the way you call me Lizzie.

"I only have a few memories of Mami." She sighed. "One day we went shopping in Wyckeville. She bought me some beautiful silk dresses. Then, we met a man for dinner. He was young and tall and very handsome. He had the most gorgeous green eyes. She called him Alex. When we left she told me not to tell Father we had met a friend and that she would tell me all aboot him someday.

"I remember the day at the brook when the old willow tree died." She lifted a small twig. "I cried because I loved that tree. Mami was going to teach me 'how to make the tree better.' She was teaching me a spell to make the tree look alive again. She said it wouldna be alive, but everybody would think 'twas. Father came upon us. He flew into a rage. Mami was teaching me witchcraft. She had hidden her practices from him.

"The next day me mother was gone. Father told me that she was unstable and she had gone away somewhere so she could get better. She never came back. I was four years old."

Elizabeth closed her eyes and took a deep shuddering breath.

"Years later when Father locked me in the house and forbade me to see ya, I explored every inch of that old house. I found these things locked in a trunk in the attic. I read me mother's journals and studied her books. Her mother had taught her the secret arts. Then, she had been forced to marry a man thirty years her elder as a business alliance. He was a childless widower, harsh and unfeeling. He only came to her bed to create an heir for his fortune. 'Twas when she turned to dark sources for her powers. Then, she met a very young and, yet, unmarried Alex O'Rourke, who shared her secret abilities. She called him her savior. They were only friends until me mother seduced him through magery. She was only thinking of herself. Father was old and harsh. She wanted someone youthful and full of life. She got him through underhanded means.

She also got me. It seems I am Alex's daughter. She never told him, and they were together only that one time. Father never knew aboot Alex."

She rolled her lips together and then bit her bottom lip, bringing blood.

"I never wanted to be loike her, selfish, thinking only of meself. I only wanted to do good, happy things. I swore I never would use black magic. I swore I never would open the *Book of Death*. Now, I have; but how could I let Caitlin die when I had the means to help?"

Diggory listened to her open-mindedly. Then, he said earnestly, "Lizzie, I am glad Caitlin is alive, but it seems ya lost a part of yerself. Sometimes we have to let go of things we love, no matter how hard 'tis." He was feeling a deep loss of his own.

Hugging her mother's journal, Elizabeth mused half to herself, "Mayhap I am finding meself." She looked sharply at Diggory as if it were an attempt to scare him away. Then, she continued, "Oh, Diggory, there is more, and when ya hear it I will lose ya. Of that I am sure.

"Me mother was Spanish. Her surname before she married Father was Morales-Rodriguez. Her name was not Zellie. Look at the initials on the book. They aire Q. M. R.

"Diggory, look at me. Open yer eyes, not yer heart. Me father said I look just loike me mother except me eyes are lighter. Whose face do ya see? Whose raven hair? Think aboot me mother. Ya were a youth when she went away. What did she look loike? Look at me!" She grabbed his face. "Whom do ya see?" Elizabeth ranted.

"Look at me! Think!" Elizabeth railed and then she threw the book across the room and took a step back from Diggory. She screamed, "Doona ya see? Me mother was Quazel Morales-Rodriguez! Now, what do ya think of me? I have betrayed ya! I have betrayed meself! I am just loike her—wicked!"

Diggory saw and understood everything. He grabbed her shoulders and shook her. "Stop it, Lizzie!" She was laughing and crying. Diggory slapped her. She gasped. He pulled her to him.

Diggory was crying as hard as Elizabeth, but he soothed her loosened hair and choked out the words from his heart. "Ya aire not evil. Ya aire me kind, loving, and compassionate Elizabeth. Ya did what ya did with good intentions. Ya never wanted to hurt anyone. I love ya. I have always loved ya. I will love ya until the day I die and thereafter if possible. We will get through this together. Do ya hear me, Lizzie—together?"

19
𝕽𝖊𝖘𝖈𝖚𝖊

Colin awoke from a feverish nightmare screaming, "Aidan! God, no! Aidan!"

"Shh," consoled Mary Kate. "Ya aire safe now."

Wide-awake, Colin struggled to get out of bed. "Where is Aidan?"

Mary Kate's lip trembled. "We couldna find him."

Colin fell back on his pillow, physically and emotionally exhausted. He lay motionless, shedding silent tears. Finally, he summoned enough energy to choke out a feeble explanation. "I had him by the arm. Then, another wave hit us. It pulled us both under. When I came up, I couldna see him. I looked and looked, but he was nowhere to be found. God-a-mercy, h-h-how do I tell Caitlin? Does she know yet?"

"Not yet. She has been asleep all night. Colin, last night was so bizarre. I want to tell ya aboot it, but I doona know if ya aire strong enough to hear it."

Colin reached for her hand. "Tell me," he sighed. "I need to hear something to take me mind off Aidan."

She told him from beginning to end all that had transpired.

When Aidan awoke, he felt warm sand beneath him. The waves lapped at his feet. The sun glared in his eyes. He lifted a leaden hand to shade them. The very movement racked his body, and he gagged and coughed water from his lungs. He rolled over and vomited seawater, and then fell back with a thud and a groan.

At that moment, he heard a low guttural growl beside him. He slowly opened one eye, afraid to move an inch. He was face to face with the biggest black panther he could imagine, even after Diggory's descriptions. Aidan tried to speak, but was only beset with another fit of coughing and vomiting. Thinking he was hallucinating, he reached out a hand and touched the creature beside him. The fur was soft and warm. *Feels like satin.*

The animal growled again and put a mammoth paw on Aidan's chest. Aidan was unable to move beneath the weight.

The young man opened his eyes to see the huge cat scanning the horizon as if he expected to see something.

Yellow eyes reflecting the blazing sun looked down at Aidan. Aidan closed his eyes again. *I might as well be dinner for a panther as supper for sharks.* He lay there expecting to die at any moment.

The panther looked to the sea once more and then back at the golden and bronze angel that lay at his feet. He thought, *something so beautiful to look upon cannot possibly be harmful*; but then, he remembered years of deceptive beauty. *This one must have come from a great distance. There is no ship on the horizon. Could he be the lone survivor of some ill-fated craft? Could he be an innocent who knows nothing of the turmoil of this area?* He felt a strange need to protect this young giant. The look of him brought back a memory long buried for the pain of it. *Has it in truth been twenty years since I last saw hair so golden?* His heart constrained him to care for this one. Why, he did not know.

The next time Aidan awoke he was in a dimly lit cave and covered by warm quilts. Although the quilts were warm, he still shivered. He heard a susurrus to his left and turned his head. He saw glowing eyes and started.

"Welcome back to the world of the living and my home," said a deep raspy voice. "You've been asleep for two days. Now, I must ask you whether you are friend or foe."

Aidan sat up quickly and fell back just as quickly.

The voice moved closer. "Near drowning is a weakening experience, even for one as young and strong as you."

"Is this Draconis?" asked Aidan weakly.

The panther was instantly wary. *This one knows something of the area after all.* "No. We're a week's journey from there. Why do you ask? What do you know of Draconis?"

"Only what a friend told me," answered Aidan cautiously.

"Was this friend a friend of Draconis?"

"That depends. Aire ya referring to the queen's Draconis or the people's Draconis?"

The panther snarled, "There is no queen in Draconis! Answer me now! Are you friend or foe?"

"Friend I hope," said Aidan trying to rise. "I have come on a quest to help free Draconis. Jean Noir is with me."

"Jean…" The voice sounded distant. "Aye, I remember Jean Noir. He disappeared years ago after another man came, a man with good intentions; but his rash actions caused much havoc in Draconis."

"This man. Prithee, tell me of him. Where might I find him?"

"He's one of my kind now and somewhere in hiding even as I am. I shall tell you more when you're stronger. For now, perhaps, 'tis enough that you learn to trust me. I'm called Satin. The Wizard Alexander named me himself, for I was born after the witch showered her evil upon our land.

I'm so called because when Alexander touched me he said I was as smooth as satin. What do they call you?"

"Ai..." *Caution is warranted here.* He coughed to cover his gaff. "Adam. Ya may call me Adam."

"Hmm," grunted the great cat, sensing deception. *Mayhap this boy is being as guarded as I.* "Welcome, Adam, to King Satin's Realm. I am King Satin, and"—He gestured with a paw—"this is my realm," he finished sardonically.

The *Privileged Character* lay anchored for several weeks as the sick and wounded recovered. The weather had cleared, but the ship was shrouded in clouds of mourning. A heavy blanket of fog hovered in front of the vessel.

Caitlin nursed her sons and talked to them incessantly about their father. She told them that soon he would hold them and play with them and tell them all manner of stories. Everyone was deeply concerned for her mental well-being. They thought her denial of reality verged on lunacy. When any of them tried to talk to her she would flare at them. "Aidan is not dead! I feel him. I know he lives, and there is nothing ya can say to change that. I am not crazy. Our bond has not been broken. I would know if he were dead."

Colin was devastated. He blamed himself for Aidan's demise. He hardly ate and moped around the ship doing minor repairs. Three weeks after he was able to be up and around, Diggory found him in the rigging where Aidan had fallen. He was repairing the loose hook and screaming toward the ocean where he had last seen Aidan. "Why were ya so bloody stubborn? Why did ya not let me come up here? Ya left me sister! Ya left yer children! Ya broke Diggory's heart! Ya deserted Draconis! Ya left me to deal with me incompetence!" He began to sob. "Why did ya leave us, ya arse? We need ya. We need yer stability and yer strength. We need yer love and yer friendship. Oh, Aidan. I am so sorry I let go of ya. I need ya. I need me brother and me best friend. Aidan, why did ya leave me?" The big burly man sobbed uncontrollably. He could not be comforted. Diggory left him to his grief.

The old man went to the hold where he was sure he would find Elizabeth. He did.

She had built a huge fire in an empty barrel and was about to throw her mother's journal into the barrel. Diggory caught her hand. "Lizzie, what aire ya doing?"

"I am getting rid of these objects."

"Why?"

"How can ya ask that question?"

He doused the fire. "Lizzie, sit down. I want to talk to ya." He led her to a couple of barrels and they sat down. "Lizzie, love, ya aire who ya aire. Burning these books and things will not change that. Moreover, we might need them. If we have to battle Quazel, ya might have to go against her. I know she is yer mother, but the lady ya knew all those years ago is not the same one on Draconis. The thing there is barely human. She traded all her possibilities for the deceptive lure of the power of evil.

"Think for a moment, Lizzie. Yer father is there, too. Mayhap he will know how to best use these items. If ya destroy them, his resources would be gone.

"Honey, I have been thinking that ya might not know the extent of yer powers. Ya aire descended from two people with magical abilities. Ya might be stronger than the two of them together." He took a deep breath and barely whispered, "Ya aire a necromancer. Caitlin was dead and ya brought her back. When they realize who and what ya aire, they will vie for yer allegiance. That is when ya will have to choose which path to take, good or evil. I will be standing on the side of good. I think that is the path ya will choose. I know yer heart."

"Diggory, aire ya saying we should go to Draconis without Aidan?"

"Aye. Mayhap Aidan was not the one either. Perchance the Promised One is Kieran or Rennin, or both." He shrugged. "I doona know. I do know that we aire not ten days away from Draconis without reason. We have come too far to turn back now. Besides, I have two promises to keep. I must return for Duncan, and I must take Jean home."

"All right. I am beside ya to the end. 'Together' is what ya said. Aye, I believe that together we can do anything. Ya aire me steadier, shield, and strength. Ya aire me bulwark. I love ya, Diggory Danaher. Let us talk to Mary Kate, Colin, and Caitlin. We must away."

Diggory shared his plan with everyone else. They all agreed to finish the journey.

Diggory said, "We came through the fog once already. The storm pushed us back for a reason." He rolled his lips to moisten them. "There is magic at work here. I think we should stop at the little island just before Draconis. I told ya aboot it. Let us stop perchance Aidan washed ashore there." He looked at Caitlin and smiled, holding to the small hope and praying she was right. "Mayhap Caitlin's intuition is roight. Mayhap Aidan did survive."

After three weeks of being moored, *The Privileged Character* grunted and groaned as she resumed her trek.

Meanwhile, Aidan grew stronger under the tender care of a frightening beast and a large winged creature named Draco. It took Aidan two days to comprehend Draco was a dragon, the one Aidan had envisioned. He was as white as snow, and when the sun hit his scales, he reflected all the colors of the rainbow. *They are not all dead.* The thought gave Aidan comfort.

Aidan and Satin liked each other. They felt freedom to talk, yet each guarded his words. One evening as they walked along the beach, Aidan asked Satin to tell him about the man that had once come to Draconis.

"What would you like to know?" queried Satin.

"Was he a tall man loike me? Did he have green eyes and black hair?"

"He did."

"Was his name Duncan O'Rourke?"

"Young man, you know more about my history than you're letting on."

Aidan picked up a seashell and examined it for a moment. "I told ya a friend told me much aboot Draconis and Quazel."

"You dare to speak that name in my presence!" Satin's roar reverberated across the watery expanse.

"I beg pardon." Aidan bowed his head. "I do know what she did to Draconis and to Duncan's crew and to Duncan himself. Prithee, tell me what became of me...of Duncan?"

"You know the man, then?"

"No, but I do know some who knew him."

"I see. I shall tell you what I can. There are some things I don't have liberty to speak."

"Agreed. The same is true for me."

"I told you I was born after Duncan arrived, in truth after Qua—that *bitch*, changed him." The cat shook his head hard. "I apologize for that outburst. I have great difficulty saying that name."

"Why do ya not call her 'Q' if you need to say her name in what ya tell me?"

"Excellent idea. I was born the day he was changed. Duncan was my mentor, along with Alexander. As you've surmised by now, the children Alexander had guarded for years were dragon eggs. Draco is the first born of a new generation. He became my best friend.

"After Q's true form was revealed, civil war broke out on Draconis. Some of the animals sided with Q because they thought she would give them a utopia. Others, who wanted freedom, sided with Duncan. Duncan trained those who followed him in warfare tactics. I fought for freedom with Duncan." Satin stopped and looked aroud as if feeling a presence. He shook his body.

"After several successful battles and much gained territory, I was crowned King of the Panthers. With Duncan's guidance and Alexander's tutelage I tried to rule with fairness and justice. Then, other animals began to come to me for protection; so many that I became known as King Satin, Ruler of all Draconis. Forsooth! That made Q angrier. The war escalated.

"'Twas at this time that Draco was revealed. Draco had just learned to fly when Duncan first came to Draconis. 'Tis how Alexander could travel so fast. Draco had been born a couple of years before Duncan arrived on the island. Alexander cast a spell of protection over the new dragon generation so that Q would be unable to harm them. Q and Alexander are constantly trying to 'out spell' each other: she trying to destroy—he attempting to preserve." The great cat waved a paw in the air.

"After all these years of fighting, allegiances have been defined, obscured, and rebuilt. 'Tis hard to know whom one can trust. The one group we're absolutely sure of is the Wolf Clan. Their allegiance is solely with themselves. At least we know they don't support Q, nor do they believe her lies. We wish to secure them as allies. They would make a formidable addition to our forces.

"To tell you more of Duncan, he's in hiding at this time, even as I am for Q has placed a large bounty to be paid to whoever brings her our heart. There are many who have tried. Some we thought were friends. All have failed.

"I keep abreast of the progress on Draconis because Draco can fly there and back in a matter of hours.

"I can tell you nothing else of Duncan. Only that he's safe and that he still believes in the prophecy. Adam, I've noticed your green eyes. Is Adam your real name?"

Aidan replied cryptically, "Satin, today my name is Adam. On the morrow, I might change it."

Unexpectedly, a shadow hid the sun as Draco flew overhead. He called down, "King Satin, a ship approaches."

Aidan turned. "Caitlin!" was his one word as he ran toward the ocean.

Satin ran beside Aidan. "Adam, do you know this vessel?"

"Aye. 'Tis me ship, *The Privileged Character*, formerly *The Sea Bird*."

"*The Sea Bird*," said Satin with great emotion. He had to turn from Aidan for a moment to regain his composure. Finally, he said to Draco, "Observe that ship!"

Alarmed, Aidan pleaded, "Harm them not. Me family is aboard that vessel."

Satin widened his eyes. "Did I say observe or harm?"

"Observe."

"'Tis exactly what Draco will do; nothing less and nothing more."

A great cloud darkened the sun aboard *The Privileged Character*. Everyone was on deck, including Jean and P.C.

Not looking up from what he was doing, Colin asked, "Is another storm blowing up?"

"No," replied Jean, his voice full of awe at the sight he beheld.

"God save me," said Mary Kate.

Flying above them was a dragon twice the size of the ship.

Oblivious to the dragon above, Caitlin ran to the rail and scanned the shoreline. She was looking for only one thing. Nothing else mattered. She began to scream and point. "There! There! Lower the rowboat, Colin! Lower the rowboat!"

Colin looked up and saw his friend waving to them from the shore. Beside him stood an enormous black cat.

"Colin, hurry!" shouted Caitlin. "Oh, oot up on it!" she hollered. She kicked off her shoes and swam for the shore in her breeches and shirt.

Colin called after his sister, "Caitlin, aire ya batty?"

Satin watched as the young man's face wreathed in smiles. "Caitlin, ya lunatic," Aidan hollered laughingly as he ran into the surf to meet his wife. The two embraced a few yards from shore. For a brief moment, nothing else mattered. They were together again.

They swam ashore and landed at Satin's feet. Aidan kissed Caitlin fiercely, as if it were the first time he had ever touched her lips.

"Oh, Aidan!" squealed Caitlin. "I knew ya were alive. I wouldna believe ya were dead."

He pulled her to him and whispered in her ear, "Call me Adam."

Satin's eyes narrowed. "Aidan O'Rourke," he said accusingly. "You're Duncan's son. Don't look astonished. Aye, I know about Duncan's son. I know about his family. Is your mother aboard the ship, too?" He looked toward the ship, his heart racing.

"I am sorry, King Satin," apologized Aidan. "I thought it best to keep my identity secret. I did not know what danger there might be."

"A wise strategy, but now I know. Do you think you can trust me?"

"Aye. Aye, I do. No, sir, me mother is not aboard. She died almost three years ago. I regret that I canna introduce ya to her, but King Satin, Ruler of Draconis, let me introduce ya to me wife, Caitlin Fitzpatrick O'Rourke."

Caitlin curtsied. "I am honored, Your Highness."

"Don't be silly, girl. 'Tis only a title. Call me Satin." He looked Caitlin over carefully.

"My, but you do have a fiery hue, and from what I have observed, the temperament to match."

"Insooth!" said Aidan. Caitlin flashed her blue eyes at him and then flung her arms around his neck.

Satin cleared his throat. The rest of the crew was coming ashore in the rowboat. He scrutinized each of them as they disembarked. Colin and Diggory got out first and helped the ladies with the babies.

Colin strode up to Aidan. There were no words exchanged, but the two men embraced each other through stifled tears. Colin pulled back, "Methinks there are two little people you want to meet."

Aidan gawked at Caitlin. "Caitlin, two?"

Mary Kate brought the babies forward and handed them to their father. "This is Kieran, and this is Rennin, though I doona know how we manage to tell them apart."

"Satin, look at my sons. 'Twere not born yet when I fell overboard."

Satin sniffed the boys. "You did a good job, Caitlin."

Aidan jested, "She didna do it alone."

"She did the hard part," grunted Satin.

Aidan handed the babies to Caitlin. He finished his introductions. "I would loike ya to meet me dear friend and brother-in-law, Colin Fitzpatrick and his wife, Mary Kate Murphy Fitzpatrick and their children, Declan and Morgan."

"Is he as fiery as his sister?" questioned Satin.

"Aye. I am afraid I am," responded Colin, "but Mary Kate keeps me on an even keel."

Satin looked at Mary Kate. "Pretty." Mary Kate blushed.

Jean jumped from the boat. Satin said, "You must be Jean Noir. You're in truth a legend in Draconis now."

"Imagine that," said Jean with genuine humility.

P.C. encircled Satin's feet. Aidan said, "That is P.C., short for Privileged Character, because all cats think they aire privileged characters." He chuckled. "Some are even made kings."

Satin's whiskers twitched at the young man's jest.

Aidan continued, "She loikes ya. 'Tis the way she behaves when she loikes someone."

Satin gulped. He picked P.C. up in his mouth by the nape of her neck and set her on his back. "There, little one. We don't want you to get lost."

After securing the boat, Diggory walked up to the gathering crowd. Aidan began, "This is me rock, me stalwart friend, and me proxy father, Diggory Danaher."

Satin walked to Diggory. He reared on his hind legs and put his front paws on Diggory's shoulders. "Have you come at last to keep a promise to an old friend?" P. C. dug her claws into the king's fur to keep from sliding off his back.

"I have," Diggory responded

"He has longed for your coming."

The two looked into each other's eyes. Diggory started to speak, but Satin restrained him by placing his paw to his lips. "Not yet," he whispered.

Finally, Elizabeth walked quietly up to the group. Satin whirled at the sight of her. He snarled and sprang at her. "What new magic is this? You are neither temptress nor crone."

"No!" shouted Aidan, as he ran in front of Elizabeth. He pushed her out of the way just as Satin's claws ripped across his chest.

Caitlin screamed.

"No! Not you, boy!" Satin roared. "Draco, take him to the cave!"

"Wait!" said Aidan, holding his chest. "Why did ya attack?"

"'Tis Quazel, boy!"

"No, Satin. 'Tis Elizabeth, Diggory's wife."

"Doona defend me, Aidan," said Elizabeth. "He is almost roight. I shall explain it to both of ya as soon as we take care of ya. That is, King Satin, if ya will allow me to live."

"Your request is granted."

After Aidan was bandaged and Satin had apologized a dozen times, Draco began the conversation. "Peradventure this is vain and selfish, but nobody bothered to introduce me. I'm Draco, friend and confidant to King Satin, and friend to anyone he befriends. Now that *all*"—His vertical pupils constricted to a thin line—"the introductions have been made, mayhap you, Elizabeth, should tell us why you look so much like our arch enemy."

Elizabeth responded, "Good now, I should start at the beginning." She did. She told about her childhood, about her mother's banishment, about finding the books and paraphernalia, about her deep foreboding three years before and how she had whispered a prayer to protect those about to be harmed, about what had transpired with both Mary Kate and Caitlin, and about her deep emotional turmoil. "In conclusion, Your Majesty, I am here to offer me services to the people of Draconis. I would loike to undo what me mother has done."

Satin sat quietly for a while, his tail swishing. "So, you're Quazel and Alexander's daughter as well as Duncan's half-sister. That makes her your aunt, Aidan. This has become quite a little family affair, hasn't it? You're welcome, Elizabeth Danaher, and greatly needed.

"Aidan, methinks your mother is not dead. I know you put a body in the ground, but 'tis not there. She has only been changed. You'll see soon.

"Now, might I suggest we leave your ship moored where 'tis and use Draco's speed to carry us to the mountains and Alexander? There's much to be decided."

"What aboot the bounty on ya?" asked Aidan.

Satin looked keenly at Elizabeth. "Elizabeth will be my bodyguard. Methinks she would sooner tear out her own heart than mine."

It was agreed. Draco made a stop at the ship to obtain the amulet, which Aidan put on; eye coverings, which Elizabeth concocted and which changed the color of Aidan's eyes; the stones; the peacock feathers; the dragon scales, which Diggory had kept since he had left Draconis and which had come from Draco's first molting, though no one had told him where the scales originated; and Elizabeth's magic goods. They shaved Colin's head and placed a blonde wig on Caitlin.

They climbed onto the dragon with Aidan at the very front. A slight voice spoke in Aidan's head. "I hoped you'd come. I was unsure if my words reached you."

Aidan touched Draco's head.

"Yes," the dragon's thought went on. "I'm the one who whispered to you, 'Destiny.' Welcome to my world."

20
Draconis

As they flew over the once lush island, Diggory was astounded. "What happened to the deep forests and the white beaches? They aire decimated."

"Quazel happened," Satin hissed through his teeth. "When her illusion was shattered, she set out to destroy the true beauty of Draconis. Some of the forests have regrown, but they're young and easily damaged. The ravages of war have also taken their toll. Many you cared for have been taken. Orson came between an assassin's spear and me years ago. He was a true friend, even unto the point of death. Hank, too, lost his life in battle. He was struck by an ape's arrow. Michael Flannery sacrificed himself in a raid on the nesting grounds. Much has changed since you were last here, Diggory."

"Including yer speech."

The great cat chuckled. "Twenty years' exposure to a different dialect and the transformation affect many things."

Before they realized that time had passed, Draco landed on a snow-covered peak. He walked a long distance, carrying his cargo gingerly. Finally, they arrived at an opening in the ground where they dismounted and walked behind the graceful creature.

"One would think a being so large would lumber, but Draco is poetry in motion," whispered Mary Kate.

"Many good thanks," Draco acknowledged the compliment. "I hear very well, too."

The passageway descended deep into the earth before it opened into an enormous chamber filled with a multitude of enchanted items. Sitting in a large golden wing-backed chair was a white haired man, absorbed in a hefty purple-bound book.

"Alexander," Draco disturbed the man's concentration. "I've brought visitors."

"Oh, what now?" grumbled the elderly gentleman. "I'm very busy. This book might prove to be Quazel's undoing. Every time I read it, I glean something new."

"You'll want to see these visitors," said Satin with authority.

"Satin!" The aging wizard embraced the shiny black beast.

"'Tis good to see you," whispered the panther. "Speak carefully. These don't yet know all."

"Whom have you brought to brighten an old man's day? Could it be my son has come for a visit?"

Draco stepped to the side and revealed the company he had brought.

Alexander's hands came together in a firm clasp. "Humans! Who might you be?"

Diggory stepped to the front. "Not yer son, Alexander. More. Much more."

"Diggory, is that you?" Alexander was elated and clapped his hands like a child receiving a new toy. He embraced Diggory with enthusiasm. "You've returned at last. Where's my grandson? Which of you is Aidan?"

"I am, Grandfather." Aidan stepped forward.

Alexander hugged Aidan. "How long I've dreamed of holding you in my arms! Let me look at you. You're a strapping fellow. Handsome. Your eyes are blue! They can't be blue. Duncan said they were as green as ours."

"They aire green, Grandfather." Aidan removed the lenses covering his eyes. "Elizabeth crafted these from one of the scales Diggory had. They aire meant to camouflage me true nature. What is good for the goose is good for the gander. If Quazel can hide her appearance, so can I."

"Smart. Sneaky. Just like your father. I like that. One further question. Are you left-handed?"

"Aye, Grandfather."

"Excellent!" He clutched a fist in triumph. "We always thought that the prophecy meant the deliverer would come from the west because west is left on a map. I now believe it means he's left-handed. You've accepted your destiny, then?"

"More than that, Grandfather. I welcome it."

"Good. Good. Well, now, who all have you brought with you?"

"Grandfather, you are just as Diggory said you would be, very insistent! I have brought me whole family. We shall start with me helpmate." Aidan held out his hand for Caitlin. "Take off that preposterous wig. Ya can wear it in public." Aidan pulled the wig off Caitlin and her long copper braids tumbled over her shoulders.

"Grandfather, this is me wife, Caitlin, and our two sons, Kieran and Rennin."

"Exquisite. You're like fine porcelain, Caitlin," praised Alexander.

"Many thanks, Gandfather," said Caitlin. "There is one difference. I am not easily broken. I am as tough as nails."

"Even better," quipped Alexander.

Just then Declan waddled over and tugged on Alexander's robe. Alexander picked up the baby. "Who is this little lad?"

"Good now," said Aidan. "Let us start with Colin, and then mayhap ya had better sit down. It might take a while to sort it all for yer understanding."

"Is it that complicated?"

"Oh, aye, Grandfather."

Alexander carried Declan to his chair and sat down. "I'm ready. I shall see if I can wrap my old brain around the information," said Alexander with a twinkle in his eyes.

Aidan took a deep breath and began. "Declan and Morgan belong to Colin and his wife, Mary Kate. Colin is Caitlin's twin. Believe it or not, his hair is just as red as Caitlin's and he has just as bad a temper. I have a few scars to prove it.

"Belike"—He placed his index finger to his lips—"if I work backward 'twill be easier. Mary Kate is Diggory and Elizabeth's daughter, but she was reared as Logan and Diana Murphy's child. Logan is Ligon's twin. Diggory has only just discovered he has a child. Elizabeth was forced to give the baby up when she was born. On the voyage here Elizabeth deduced Mary Kate to be that child." He took a breath.

"Elizabeth is Diggory's wife. Verily, here is where it gets complicated. Elizabeth grew up thinking that she was Ian and Zellie Gilhooley's daughter."

"Zellie," interrupted Alexander. "I remember her. She was the very young wife of Ian Gilhooley. We were friends. I had dinner once with her and her daughter." He quirked an eyebrow and gazed at Elizabeth. "Zellie dabbled a bit in the mystical arts. She understood me." He waved a hand. "I ramble. Prithee continue."

"Zellie did much more than dabble, Grandfather, and her name was not Zellie. 'Twas what Ian called her. Grandfather, she seduced ya with her magery. Elizabeth is yer daughter. Ian caught Zellie teaching Elizabeth witchcraft and sent her away. He never knew Elizabeth was not his daughter."

The aging wizard shook his head and shivered.

"Grandfather," Adian went on, "Zellie's name was in truth Quazel."

Alexander sat forward. "Aidan, are you telling me I had relations with that woman and made a baby, and I don't remember a thing about it?"

"Aye, Grandfather."

"Boy, I was only sixteen when I knew her, just coming into real manhood. Why me?"

"She knew ya had powers, and she loiked yer physical characteristics. Apparently, Ian Gilhooley was unable to father children, and her time was roight for conception. Here is Quazel's journal." Aidan handed Alexander the black leather book with the golden initials. "Read it and then talk to Elizabeth."

The party, except for Elizabeth, slept that night in the magnificent caves of Draconis. She stayed up all night talking with Alexander. By morning the two were old friends.

Alexander warned Elizabeth, "You must be exceedingly careful. Your mother doesn't know you're here. When she discovers you've arrived, she'll court your affection. Elizabeth, I don't want you to hate your mother, but you must realize Quazel is no longer the person you knew. Granted, she might have been shoved toward the path of evil, but she made her choices, not the least of which was her underhanded way to ensure she conceived a child. I'm not sorry I have you, but both you and I were pawns in her plot. She insooth had genuine affection for you, and mayhap she could've been redeemed all those years ago. I'm sure she has reached the point of no return now. She'll try to manipulate you anyway she can. I'm concerned for your heart, your mind, and your soul." He gave her hand a gentle squeeze. "When temptation is thrown your way, hold to your love for Diggory and Mary Kate. That love will give you strength. Never let Quazel know you have a daughter. If you displease her, she'll go after Mary Kate."

Elizabeth looked like a child at her father's feet. "Alexander, I will heed yer words," she spoke uncertainly.

"I know we have only discovered each other, but I feel a kinship with ya. What should I call ya?"

He smiled. "This old man always dreamed of a little girl to call him 'Da.' Would you mind terribly using that name for me?"

"I would be honored, Da."

"That sounds like music to my ears. I don't know how we can atone for all the lost years. I still haven't made up the loss to Duncan. I'd like to start by telling you how much I wish I'd known you. You seem to be a fine lady. You make me proud."

"Da, we canna recapture the past. We can only start from today and claim our future. Ya must do the same with Duncan. Quazel is using yer guilt aboot the past against ya. Da, I am heeding yer words. Ya must listen to yer own advice."

"You're wise, Elizabeth. Let's claim our future. Do you think we can start with the younger ones? I'd like them to call me 'Seanathair' instead of 'Grandfather.' Seanathair is the old language," He shook his head sadly. "And I do so miss my home."

"That can be arranged." Alexander patted Elizabeth's hand. She laid her head on his knee, and they sat quietly for a while. Elizabeth broke the reverie.

"Da, I have been thinking. What if we manipulate Quazel before she has a chance to manipulate us?"

"What do you have in mind, iníon—daughter?"

21
𝔗𝔥𝔢 𝔅𝔢𝔰𝔱 𝔏𝔞𝔦𝔡 𝔓𝔩𝔞𝔫𝔰

𝕰𝖑𝖎𝖟𝖆𝖇𝖊𝖙𝖍 shared her thoughts. "Quazel will be expecting ya and Duncan to exploit me as much as she would. She will expect ya to try to turn me against her. What if I go to her first, a preemptive strike? What if I make her believe I want to learn from her, to pick up where we left off? I could pass on any information I get to ya, and at the same time, feed her false information."

"No!" snarled Satin as he entered Alexander's sanctuary. "'Tis too risky. When I tried that, I was only in danger of losing my humanity. You, my dear, are in danger of losing your eternal soul! I will not allow it!"

"Careful, Satin," rebuked Alexander.

Satin moderated his approach. "Elizabeth, I thought you'd agreed to be my bodyguard. How can I trust you if there's any possibility of Quazel's discovering your intentions? Know this, Elizabeth: I once tried to fool Quazel into believing I supported her. I lost everything dear to me. Quazel is smart, and she has spies everywhere."

"Gentlemen," argued Elizabeth, "we need to get close to Quazel. We need to earn her trust. I have the best chance of anyone here of gaining her confidence. I doona care who has green eyes or who stands six-feet-four-inches. Quazel is me mother. I am the child she schemed to have. Good sirs, I might be yer only chance."

"As much as I hate to admit it, Elizabeth has a valid point," added Diggory as he entered with a tray of coffee and scones.

"Diggory!" reprimanded Satin. "Do not encourage her in this folly. She is your wife. Talk some sense into her. For God's sake, remember Duncan's fiasco! Do you want Elizabeth to be a beetle?"

"She is me mother for heaven's sake," quarreled Elizabeth.

"Exactly!" roared Satin. "Your judgment will be clouded from the beginning."

"No, it will not!"

"Aye, 'twill. Elizabeth, you want your mother. You've been deprived of her your whole life. Listen to me. Your mother is *dead*! That woman is *not* your mother!" Satin said, adding emphatic tail swishing.

"I understand that."

"No, Elizabeth, you don't. You *think* you understand. Quazel will tear your heart out one memory, one desire at a time. She will twist you into knots. Look over there." With a tilt of his head, Satin indicated Mary Kate and the children as they entered the room. "Quazel will use them any way she can to win. You have a husband, a lover, who was denied to you for years; you have a daughter and two beautiful grandchildren; you have a nephew who has his own family; you have a father you have just met; you have a brother that you have never been able to call brother. All of these Quazel would manipulate, exploit, or harm, especially if she discovered your betrayal. Now, ask yourself if 'tis worth the risk."

"King Satin, with all due respect," Elizabeth strengthened her argument. "When we sailed from Stonebridge, we agreed we would foight for the deliverance of Draconis. We knew the risks when we began. The stakes aire even higher now. Duty brought us here. Blood ties us here. Honor constrains us to foight with all means at our disposal. I will be damned if I will let evil overthrow good. I will give ya me allegiance, me honor, me life to conquer the darkness that has overcome this place if ya will give me the chance to prove meself." Elizabeth stomped her foot, and the cave shook.

All the bystanders were startled, looking around them with wide, wondering eyes. "Well, daughter," said

Alexander after a long moment, "it seems we have one hell of a mage in our midst, if you'll learn to harness and focus your powers."

"Elizabeth"—Satin bowed in deference—"I'm impressed. You're indeed powerful. Peradventure, if you're careful, and I mean extremely careful, you might indeed present us with the opportunity to defeat Quazel. You have my permission to try, but you must listen to everything Alexander tells you. Heed his warnings.

"I shall leave you to work out the details of your masquerade, but guard your heart, my new friend."

Satin leapt to the ledge above and disappeared down a corridor. He could be heard talking to Draco, but the words were indiscernible.

The rest of the group sat down to discuss Elizabeth's plan.

"First," said Alexander, "trust no one from here, save Satin and Draco. Since there are those who would kill Satin in a heartbeat, Draco will be your contact. When you need to communicate with us, go into the cave behind the waterfall. Call Draco loudly. He'll hear you and come to you. You should be safe behind the waterfall. Quazel herself will never follow you there."

At that moment a glistening white horse with a single horn entered with a buttermilk-colored mare. "Ah," Alexander said. "You can trust these ladies." He introduced Eunice, an actual unicorn, and Isabella LaBlanc, Jean's betrothed. Then, he went on with his instructions.

"If, for any reason, you're ever trapped or need to be rescued, call Draco. He'll find you, and we'll send all the forces at our disposal to your aid."

Alexander got up and walked to a massive gilded chest. He opened it, and pulled from it a dagger with an intricately carved ivory handle. "Second, secret this on your person. You never know when you might have to use it. Elizabeth, you're willing to give your life for this cause, but now you must be able and willing to take a life. 'Tis the nature of war.

"Third, Diggory, do you have the stones?"

"Aye." Diggory reached into his pocket and handed Alexander the pouch of stones.

"Elizabeth, since you're going into a place of utter darkness, I'll craft a talisman for you from this onyx. 'Twill be hidden well in the darkness. Never take it off. As long as you wear it, you'll see Quazel for who and what she is. Without it, she'll have the power to cause you to see things that aren't real. She'll find your deepest desire and make you think you have it. She'll manipulate your emotions and your will.

"Fourth, never drink the nectar wine. If you do, you might find yourself losing control of your wits."

Alexander turned once again to Diggory. "A peacock feather please." Diggory handed him a feather from his coat.

"With this I will formulate an elixir to counter the effects of the nectar wine.

"Last, remember how much we all love you."

"Aye," said Satin as he walked back into the underground chamber. "That includes your newfound brother. I've just seen Duncan, but he dares not come into the open yet. He wants you to know he admires your courage and supports you fully. He anxiously awaits the day he can meet you face to face. He also longs to hold each of the rest of you in an embrace, especially you, Aidan."

Satin continued, "Elizabeth 'tis imperative Aidan's identity not be revealed, or he'll be in as grave a danger as Duncan and I are."

Satin turned back to Aidan. "Your father insists you assume a new identity. From this day forward until this war is over, you'll be called Adam Callahan in the public eye. Adam was the name you gave me originally; Callahan was your mother's maidan name. Aidan," Satin finished tenderly, "Duncan wants you to know that his heart is breaking because he can't yet acknowledge you as his son. He longs for the day that he can shout from the mountain tops, 'This man is heart of my heart, blood of my blood, life of my life, and I love him with all of my being.'"

"Satin, prithee tell him I feel the same," gulped Aidan.

"He knows, son." Satin reared onto his hind feet and placed a paw on each of Aidan's shoulders.

Satin looked at Alexander. "After you fashion Elizabeth's talisman, prepare the others." He lowered himself to all-fours and walked to each person as he spoke. "Duncan says to do them in this order: Caitlin is to have the ruby for her hair; give the sapphire to Colin for his azure eyes; the pure white of opal is to go to Mary Kate for her untainted heart; Diggory is to have topaz; and craft the diamond for him once he has regained his human form. You wear it for him until he claims it. Aidan must wear the amulet for strength, wisdom, and protection, as well as the emerald charm. Design breastplates for everyone from the dragon scales born of Draco's first molting. For Draco, weave a vest from flax and the hair of all the women who have descended from Quazel—Elizabeth, Mary Kate, and Morgan."

Satin eyed once again the valiant warriors. "These enchanted pieces won't prevent you from being killed or from being changed, but they will give you an advantage. Even the dragon's hard scales don't cover every inch of him. That's why Draco needs the vest to cover his heart. Although Alexander cast a spell so that Q cannot herself harm Draco, an arrow can potentially pierce his heart.

"Elizabeth, when you go to Quazel, you must go alone. You must make her believe you've come in search of her and you left us against our protests. Believe me, Elizabeth, she knows you've been here. I've brought you a black satin garment, appropriate attire for a dark mage. You must begin your mission at dusk."

22
𝔄 𝕿𝖆𝖓𝖌𝖑𝖊𝖉 𝖂𝖊𝖇

𝕮𝖑𝖆𝖉 in atramentous raiment, Elizabeth embraced her family one by one. She cleaved to Diggory and shuddered. "I didna think I would be so afraid."

"'Tis only natural to be apprehensive aboot such an undertaking, me love." Diggory tried to sound confident.

Elizabeth inhaled sharply. "Doona use that word. It reminds me of death."

"Mayhap endeavor would be better."

"Much." Elizabeth giggled nervously. "I should away."

As Diggory held her once more, he struggled to hold back tears. "I love ya, Lizzie. Ya aire me life," he said huskily.

Elizabeth stroked his brow, his cheek, and his lips with her fingertip. Then she stepped into the twilight.

Elizabeth followed a winding path down the mountain. Shrouded in her charcoal cloak, she was almost invisible against the rapidly darkening sky. She heard the hoot of an owl and clutched the dagger hidden in the folds of her robe. "Doona be silly, Elizabeth. 'Twas only an owl," she chided herself aloud. Her voice echoed ominously through the glen.

A wolf bayed at the rising moon, and Elizabeth caught her breath. She fingered her onyx talisman hidden beneath her blouse. "Doona be so jumpy," she chastised herself again.

As she neared an area that was still heavily wooded, she twisted her small gold wedding band, the only concession to color she displayed. She hoisted her skirt in one hand

and a small valise, which contained a change of clothes, a few toiletries, Quazel's diary, the nectar wine antidote, and several other mystical items, in the other hand as she leapt across a puddle into the forest.

She had walked a short distance into a mosquito-infested glade when a distinctly scratchy feminine voice said, "Be well met, Elizabeth. I've been waiting for you."

Instantly alert, Elizabeth responded, "Mami?"

"Aye. Do you still call me 'Mami'?"

"I doona know what else to call ya."

"I like 'Mami.' It brings back pleasant memories."

"Mami, please show yerself."

The voice maintained its hiding place. "Did Alexander throw you out, or did you leave him behind?

"I came of me own accord to find ya."

"Is it even so?" asked Quazel, not hiding her skepticism.

"Alexander tried to convince me to stay. He told me ya would use me and hurt me, but ya aire me mother."

"So I am, but *he* is your father."

"But I only met him yesterday."

"What about your husband?"

"He has not treated me the same since he discovered that ya aire me mother. I told him I had to find me own way. If he doesna understand, then he has a problem."

"So be it," conceded Quazel as she stepped from the shadows.

Elizabeth jumped as Quazel came into view.

Quazel tested Elizabeth further. "No hug for your long-lost mami?" she hissed.

Elizabeth summoned her courage and walked forward. She embraced Quazel. Despite the icy skin and the hideous appearance, Elizabeth managed to say, "It has been too long, Mami. I can hardly believe I have found ya."

"You've grown into a beautiful woman, but how are your powers?"

"Relatively undeveloped."

"No doubt. How did you manage to escape the old letch?"

"He died ten years ago."

"Did you have anything to do with it?"

"Aye, I put belladonna in his tea."

"Why?"

"He forbade me to see Diggory and then he decided I should take yer place. He should never have come into me bedroom."

"Anger. Vengeance. Good motives for developing strong powers. Tell me, daughter, have you performed any blood magic yet?"

Elizabeth thought of Caitlin. "Aye."

They began to walk. "Did you find my books and study them?"

"I did. I read every word. Your journal is how I knew Alexander was me father, not Ian."

"Have you sensed enchantment in your environment?"

"I have."

Stopping in her tracks, Quazel said, "You give such cryptic answers, Elizabeth. Are you hiding something from me?"

"Only me amateur incompetence. I want ya to respect me abilities."

"What about the small earthquake we had this morning? I didn't have anything to do with it; did you?"

"I did. I was angry and I stomped me foot."

Quazel stood rooted to the spot and gave her daughter an appraising look. "Impressive."

"Alexander said I should harness and focus me energy."

"In that, he's correct." They took up their trek again. "By the way, how is my old nemesis?"

"He appears well."

"You know I once thought I wanted Duncan to reign with me. What a fool I was! Mayhap I should've seduced your father again. With our combined powers we could've been unstoppable, and you would've had a real family. Unfortunately, they're *both* thorns in my flesh now."

After much walking, they arrived at a burned area of forest. The stumps still smoldered. There was a coarse tent in the middle of the fiery stumps.

"What happened here, Mami?"

"I burned them."

"Why"

"I get cold these days."

"Is not there some other way to keep warm?"

"Mayhap, but I was angry today because you were with Alexander. I shall try to restrain my tantrums now that you're here. I wouldn't want to frighten you into going back to Alexander." Quazel sounded almost motherly.

They entered the tent. "Elizabeth, would you like some wine?"

"No, thank you, Mami. I doona imbibe. I prefer to stay in complete control of me faculties. However, some tea would be nice."

"Tea 'tis."

Quazel set about preparing tea and then dinner. "I'm preparing my own meals these days. I'm not much of a cook. Perchance you can help me with that." Quazel served tongue with the tea.

"I am a pretty good cook, or so I have been told." Elizabeth agreed to do the cooking. She gagged as she ate the meal because she was unsure of the kind of tongue she ate. She had no idea whether it was a former human.

Quazel sighed. "I also want to rid you of any trace of the Gaelic. I'd rather hear the Basque. It has been a long time since I spoke to someone in my native tongue."

"Basque, Mami?"

"Oh, yes, but we were forbidden to speak anything but proper Spanish. Our family would've been shunned."

Several weeks passed without any word from Elizabeth. Satin told Draco to fly over the island to see if he could spot her. Draco returned to say Quazel and Elizabeth were walking through the forests and Elizabeth was touching the tops of dead flowers, and they were blooming. He had heard her say, "Just because you hate the inhabitants of this place doesn't mean we must deny ourselves beauty."

Quazel had actually laughed and said, "You in truth are still my little girl."

"I'm worried about Elizabeth," said Draco. "She seemed too cozy with Quazel." His large eyes blinked. "She has already lost the charming accent."

"Don't worry," said Satin, sounding more confident than he was. "Where were they?"

"Near the old walnut grove."

"Methinks I shall walk with P.C." Over the last few weeks, Satin had been showing P.C. the island so she would not get lost. He could not understand why she had not spoken. He felt sure she was human. "Draco, stay close in case I need you."

Satin went in search of P.C. He found her asleep in Alexander's chair. He thought she was the prettiest cat he had ever seen. He nudged her. She stretched and yawned.

"Wake up, little one. Let's walk." He placed her once again on his back. She purred happily and began to knead his fur.

"That tickles," he chuckled. Then, she walked up his back and nibbled his ear. He exclaimed, "Priscilla!" All P.C. did was purr and lick his head. "Alas," sighed King Satin. "That reminded me of days long past." He padded out a secret entrance to the caves.

Draco kept watch from high above.

Quazel and Elizabeth had stopped in a field of dry grass. Elizabeth spread her hands, and the grass became a lush carpet once more.

"Let's sit here for a while, Mami."

"If you'd like. We should review the incantations you learned last night, and then I'd like to ask you some questions."

They went over dozens of spells. Elizabeth only missed one. Quazel seemed pleased. Then, she began to quiz Elizabeth. "What was it you gave old Ian to do him in?"

"Nightshade."

"I thought you said 'twas belladonna."

"Belladonna is a type of nightshade, just as are henbane, trillium, and bittersweet, even tomato." Elizabeth covered her mistake quickly.

"Did you travel from Stonebridge on *The Sea Bird*? Is the old crate still seaworthy?"

"Aye, we came on the same ship. We had to do many repairs to put her in running order, but she held up nicely. I rather enjoyed using Father's money to do something he would have disapproved."

"Whom all did you bring with you?"

"Diggory, of course. He had the ship in dry dock."

"Aye. Aye. Why did you marry such an idiot?"

"Mami, you sound like Father."

The old witch narrowed her eyes to slits. "How dare you compare me to that old reprobate?"

"Then, don't talk about Diggory. No matter how narrow-minded he might be, he's a good man and a great lover." It tore out Elizabeth's heart to disparage Diggory.

"'Tis of no consequence." Quazel waved her hand. "Go on. Tell me. Who else came with you?"

"Colin Fitzpatrick and his wife, Mary Kate. She's Ligon Murphy's niece. Colin and Mary Kate had a set of twins aboard ship. Caitlin Callahan, Colin's sister. Her husband, Adam, came with her. They also had a set of twins on the voyage. Oh, aye, of course, Diggory brought Jean Noir home.

"Priscilla O'Rourke didn't come with you?"

"No, she died three years ago."

"What about Duncan's children?"

"Duncan's child died before he ever came to Draconis."

"Who's the very handsome golden boy? He'd make a pleasing companion."

"'Tis Adam." Elizabeth furrowed her brow. "Mami, is not he a little young for you?"

"What he sees is young and beautiful. What he doesn't know won't hurt him. I could give him pleasure, and I'm certain he would delight me."

"He has a wife."

"That can be easily eliminated."

"Mami, do not you dare hurt Caitlin. She's my friend. She kept my secret for months. I gave her my own blood to save her. I feel that she's a part of me."

"Calm down, Elizabeth. I shan't kill her."

Elizabeth was terrified and repulsed by what Quazel had said. *How can a woman want a man who is the same age as her own grandchild?*

At that moment, a snake slithered up to Quazel and whispered in her ear.

She nodded with a scowl on her face and then said, "Elizabeth, I must meet someone to formulate a battle plan. Can you get back to our tent?"

"Of course. I shall be fine."

As Quazel left with the serpent, Elizabeth saw her chance. She ran to the waterfall.

Behind the cascade, Elizabeth called Draco repeatedly. When he did not come the first time she shouted his name, she panicked. "Draco! Draco, come quickly! Draco, I am scared! Draco, I need you." Elizabeth shivered from the dampness and cold. She paced and started to cry. She called again, "Draco, prithee hurry!"

Five minutes later, Draco splashed through the waterfall. "Elizabeth, are you all right?"

The five minutes had seemed like an eternity to Elizabeth. She ran to the magnificent beast and laid her head on his chest. He enfolded her in his expansive wings. Elizabeth sobbed, "Draco, I am so frightened. Quazel plans to harm Caitlin. She finds Aidan attractive, and she wants him for her companion.

"I doona know how much longer I can keep up this pretense. I had to let Quazel think I am a murderess. She thinks I poisoned my father."

Draco's eyes widened. Elizabeth hastened, "Not Alexander. Ian Gilhooley, the man she married. I often wished him dead, but I did not kill him."

"Elizabeth what do you think she plans to do?" Draco asked.

"I know not, but she did say she would not kill Caitlin. Oh, Draco, she plans to turn her into some wild animal."

"Her forte´," said Draco sarcastically. "We must keep Caitlin in the mountains. None of Quazel's spells can reach her there. Where is Quazel now?"

"She left with a slithering silent serpent. She said she was meeting someone to formulate a battle plan."

Draco touched Elizabeth's shoulder with a talon. "You must return to Quazel's tent now. Prepare supper. Act as if nothing has disturbed you. Elizabeth, you're strong. You can do this. I shall warn Caitlin. Call me, and I'll come. I'll come even if I have to swoop you up right before Quazel's very eyes."

Elizabeth nodded and left the safety of the cave.

Draco flew back to Satin.

While Elizabeth and Draco were in the cave, Satin and P.C. waited at the bottom of the mountain in a small valley filled with lilies. P.C. played hide-and-seek with Satin. She would disappear beneath the white blossoms. Satin laughed in mirth. He had not laughed so hard in twenty years.

Satin had let down his guard. He suddenly sobered as he heard a rustling. He whirled around ready for battle. "What do you want, *witch*?" he snarled as Quazel approached.

"Relax, Duncan."

Satin retreated a step and started to speak.

"I know 'tis you," Quazel preempted his denial. "Those lenses don't fool me even if they might trick most of the imbeciles on this island." Quazel paused and looked around. "Where's your constant guard?"

"Doing a quick flyover. He'll return momentarily; not 'tis any business of yours, *crone*."

"Stop the insults. I've come on a mission of peace," Quazel coaxed.

"I'm listening, *hag*." Duncan stressed another jibe.

"I can't kill you, and you can't kill me. I've come to offer you a proposition, a truce if you please."

Quazel stroked the panther. He recoiled at her touch.

She crooned, "You *are* wonderful to touch. No wonder you call yourself 'Satin.'"

Duncan grew impatient. "Get on with your proposition."

"I once wanted you to reign by my side. We could've been indomitable. I offer you that place once again. Join me, and I'll restore you to the virile, desirable man you once were."

Duncan laughed coldly.

"You wanted me once," inveigled Quazel as she continued to run her hands through Duncan's fur.

"You drugged me! I thought you were Priscilla!"

Quazel cajoled, "I can be whatever you want me to be."

Like lightning, a small ball of white fur flew through the air. Spitting, hissing, screaming, and clawing, P.C. landed on Quazel's face and shrieked in a human voice, "Take your hands off my husband, you harlot, or I'll tear out your eyes!"

Quazel screeched in pain as blood spurted from her face and eyes. She flung the small cat from her. As she flailed she felt a huge paw, full of claws, rip across her middle. Quazel doubled with pain and crawled from the scene in agony.

Duncan called frantically, "Priscilla, where are you?"

"I'm over here," she answered bouncing up to his feet.

"Are you hurt?"

"No. Don't you know that cats always land on their feet?"

"Priscilla!" Duncan licked her from her head to her tail. "Why did you keep silent so long? I knew in my heart 'twas you."

"The time was not right to reveal myself, but I'll burn in Hell before I let some other woman, no matter how hideous, paw you. The problem is that she didn't look hideous to me. You're mine, Duncan O'Rourke, and do *not* ever forget that! You've been mine ever since you rescued me when I was adrift in that small vessel with little memory of my life before, save my name. If that whore touches you again, I'll claw out her eyes," Priscilla finished in a huff.

"I shan't forget, my precious; but as you said, the time wasn't right for you to reveal yourself, so I must remain King Satin for a bit longer. Can you keep my secret?"

"Of course, my love. Should I reveal mine?"

"Quazel knows who you are, so why shouldn't Aidan at least have his mother?"

"Some mother I make. Poor child. Animals for parents."

"What's going on here?" demanded Draco as he swooped in.

"Draco, meet my wife, Priscilla Cecelia Callahan O'Rourke."

23
𝔑𝔢𝔴 𝔍𝔡𝔢𝔫𝔱𝔦𝔱𝔦𝔢𝔰

𝔄𝔦𝔡𝔞𝔫 found it difficult to remember to introduce himself as Adam Callahan. "I am not accustomed to lying. Ya know how straightforward I am. I feel strange changing the color of me eyes. I would rather go oot and find the wench and execute her unceremoniously," he confided one night to Caitlin.

"I know. 'Tis awkward for me, too. First I was Caitlin Fitzpatrick. Then I was Caitlin O'Rourke. Now I am Caitlin Callahan, and my hair changed color." Caitlin grabbed both sides of her head and joked, "I am going mad! I doona know who I am anymore!" She laughed, but when she saw that Aidan did not share her humor she bit her lip. After a moment of contemplation she perked up. "I have an idea."

"Alackaday, this sounds dangerous."

"Where is yer sense of adventure?"

"I married ya, nay?"

"Be a jester if you want. Meet me back here in one hour. Be sure to wear yer blue lenses."

"What aire ya aboot?"

"Away! Talk to Alexander or somebody," Caitlin said pushing Aidan out the wooden door of the suite that Alexander had prepared for them. She bolted the door after him.

Aidan tried the door, "Caitlin."

From behind the door he heard, "Caitlin is not here. Come back in an hour."

He raised his hands in surrender and went to find his grandfather.

Aidan went to Alexander's study area and called, "Seanathair!" Nobody was there. He sank into Alexander's chair and sulked, hating all the waiting and subterfuge. As he languished there, he heard laughter in the corridor above.

Satin jumped down into the sanctuary. P.C. was on his back, and she was laughing.

"What the devil?" exclaimed Aidan, making his presence known.

"Good eve, Aidan. How now, this fine night?" Satin greeted him. Without waiting for an answer, Satin took P.C.'s tiny paw between his two massive ones and said, "Lovely lady, I shall leave you now." Satin pranced toward his secluded hiding place.

Priscilla looked at her bewildered son. "Be well met, Aidan. Do you realize who I am?"

"Mam?" Aidan was speechless.

"Aye, darling."

"Mam, what? How?"

"Methinks it had something to do with Quazel. She forsooth sent a long-distance curse that took all those years to find me. I heard the whammy she pronounced on your father. She said that only tears from someone he loved without bound could set him free. She was trying to keep me from helping Duncan. Cats can't cry tears, Aidan. She thought I was the only person Duncan loved so completely. She didn't, and still doesn't, know about you. I can't free Duncan. When the time comes, you'll have to free him."

"How can I, Mam? I only know yer memories of a man."

"He still loves you with no end. You're his baby."

"I have not even seen him. I shall do what I must do when the time comes, but, Mam, what aboot ya? Why did ya not tell me who ya were?"

Priscilla explained, "I only recently found my voice. As a matter of fact, I first spoke on my walk with Satin today. I tried to show you I loved you. I slept on your bed when you came to Diggory's. I even went to your wedding and sat in my rightful place, albeit in Elizabeth's lap."

"Oh, Mam, I have a million questions. What do ya think of Caitlin?"

"She's remarkable. Stubborn, willful, and headstrong, but wonderful."

"The boys?"

"Precious, and already bigger than I am." Priscilla laughed.

"Mam, ya aire so happy. I have never seen ya so vibrant."

"I've seen Duncan. Satin took me to him when he discovered who I am."

"Mam, I canna wait for Caitlin to know ya." He slapped his head. "Fie me! Caitlin! I am supposed to meet her roight now."

"Away!"

"But, Mam."

"I shall be here on the morrow. Go to your wife. She is *not* a patient person."

When Aidan walked back into his and Caitlin's suite, it had been transformed. There were candles everywhere, strawberries and nectar wine by the bed. Aidan quickly put in his blue lenses.

Caitlin sauntered in from an alcove. She sported a black frock of the sheerest clinging material and her blonde wig. She glided up to Aidan and ran her fingertips up his arm. Affecting a deep, sultry voice, she said, "Good eve, big boy. What beautiful blue eyes ya have. I am Catherine Muldoon. How may I serve ya this eve?"

"Cait..." Caitlin put her finger on Aidan's lips.

"Catherine is the name. What is yers?"

Aidan caught on to her little game. "Adam Callahan."

"Well, Adam Callahan, what is yer pleasure this eve?"

Aidan began to enjoy Caitlin's little intrigue. "Miss Muldoon, I have been under a great deal of anxiety. Would ya mind relaxing the tension in me neck and shoulders?"

"Not at all," soothed Caitlin. She unlaced the leather thongs from the front of Aidan's shirt and slipped it over his head. She led him to the bed. He lay back. Caitlin straddled his legs and massaged his chest and the fronts of his shoulders. Aidan relaxed completely under her touch and responded to her seduction. He turned over and Caitlin continued to rub Aidan's neck, shoulders, and back.

"That feels wonderful, Miss Muldoon," sighed Aidan.

"Call me Catherine," murmured Caitlin. She poured Aidan a glass of wine.

She dipped a strawberry in it and fed it to her husband as he reclined on one elbow watching her move. She took another strawberry and touched it to her lips and slid it down her throat and chest before she gave it to Aidan. Another berry she barely touched to his lips, and then she bit it slowly.

Aidan pulled her close and kissed her hard. He moved his hand along her thigh. Caitlin pulled back from Aidan. He restrained her. He lifted his glass and poured his wine across her breasts.

"Catherine, it seems I have spilled me wine," Aidan whispered.

"Let me get ya some more." She started to slip from the bed.

"No," Aidan crooned. "I wouldna want to waste one drop of this glass." Aidan kissed the top of Caitlin's breasts and pulled her down to him. Through kisses he mumbled, "I doona care what name I use, so long as ya aire by me side."

When Aidan and Caitlin came in for breakfast, there was a commotion, and right in the middle of the hoopla sat a small white cat giving a discourse of what had happened to her.

Caitlin tugged her husband's arm. "Aidan, do ya have any notion what is going on?"

"Well, aye, but I was so preoccupied last night I forgot to tell ya something very important," Aidan answered with a lick to his lips and a pinch to Caitlin's derriere.

Caitlin slapped his hand. "Stop that!" she scolded.

Aidan sighed, "With such an unloving wife, I might be forced to use the services of Miss Muldoon again."

"Ya aire bad, Aidan O'Rourke."

Aidan kissed Caitlin affectionately on the head and said, "I canna wait to show ya just how bad I can be."

Caitlin giggled. Aidan took her hand and said, "Come. There is someone ya must officially meet."

As they approached the raucous bunch, Aidan shouted over the tumult, "Good morrow, everyone."

Aidan bent down and picked up Priscilla. "Forsooth, this feels strange." He turned to Caitlin. "Honey, we have had an imposter in our midst for years. This is none other than Mistress Priscilla Cecelia O'Rourke."

"God's me," Caitlin said in disbelief.

"Is that all you have to say, Caitlin?" asked Priscilla. "I've never known you to be at a loss for words.

"I have no notion what to say, Mistress... Mam...Pris...What do I call ya now?"

"I think Grandma would be nice for the children, but you, my dear, may call me 'Mam' if you like or Priscilla."

"'Mam' 'tis fine with me."

The din of conversations rose again as everyone asked Priscilla questions. As the group prattled, Mary Kate's voice came to a crescendo over everyone else. "Everybody, shut up!"

There was dead silence, for nobody knew that Mary Kate could speak that loudly or that coarsely. Mary Kate resumed her normal speaking voice, only it quivered. "Prithee help. I canna find Declan. He was eating jam and bread before Aidan and Caitlin arrived, and now he has wandered off somewhere."

Colin sprang into action. They split up and searched the caves. When an hour later no one had found the toddler, Mary Kate began to cry. She looked forlornly at the dragon. "Draco?"

"I'm already on my way out, sweet lady," Draco responded before she could voice her request.

Alexander suggested, "We should form teams of two and search around the caves as well. Declan is small enough that he could be hidden beneath foliage, and Draco would miss him. Satin and Priscilla, go north; Diggory and Colin, east; Aidan and Caitlin, to the west, but wear your disguises; I shall go south with Jean; Mary Kate, stay here." Mary Kate started to protest. Alexander stopped her. "In case he comes back, he will want his mother." Mary Kate conceded. The search began.

After her encounter with a riled wife the evening before, Quazel dragged herself back to her tent.

Startled by the sight of her mangled mother, Elizabeth screamed, "Mami, what happened to you?"

"You lied to me, you traitor."

"What aire ya talking aboot?" Elizabeth asked as she helped Quazel to her couch.

"Out upon it! The Irish brogue!" Quazel raised a hand to strike, but reined herself. "Priscilla O'Rourke came with you."

"Mami, Priscilla is dead. I went to her funeral."

"That cat. The little white cat," wailed Quazel.

"Do you mean P.C.?"

"You didn't say there was a cat aboard ship."

"I thought that was in truth what she was—a cat."

"How did you change her into a cat?"

"I did not change anybody into anything."

"You must have," accused Quazel. "The night Priscilla died, what kind of magic did you do?"

"I performed no magic," defended Elizabeth.

"You must have," moaned Quazel.

"I felt a sense of foreboding. I whispered a prayer of protection."

"A prayer! She prayed!" lamented Quazel. Then, she lashed out at Elizabeth. "You fool! That woman was supposed to die. The curse I sent was a curse of death." Quazel cackled, "Duncan has you to thank for having a cat for a wife. That in truth was *not* my fault." She began to laugh uncontrollably. "'Tis just as well. Cats cannot cry. She still can't help him." Quazel laughed so hard she cried. "Oh, Elizabeth, your meddling worked out just fine in the end."

"Mami, are you sure a little cat did this much damage to you?"

"No, stupid! Duncan was with her. Elizabeth, you're an idiot. Give me some wine and get out of my presence."

Elizabeth decided she had had enough. She packed her valise and started for refuge in the arms of her husband.

The night before had been exceptionally dark. Elizabeth had stumbled and fallen many times, and she had totally lost her way. When daylight came she realized that she had only managed to get a few miles from her mother. Bruised and scraped, she began the long trek back to the mountains.

Before she had gone another mile, she heard her mother's voice. "Elizabeth, where are you going?"

"Back to Alexander and Diggory because I am stupid and a fool and an idiot," snapped Elizabeth.

"Sensitive, too," taunted Quazel.

Elizabeth came to the edge of the woods and Quazel followed. "Elizabeth, stop where you are. There's something out there," said Quazel. She looked toward the mountains. "Elizabeth, go back to the tent."

"I do not go where I am unwanted," defied Elizabeth.

"You're wanted. I was angry and hurt last night. I didn't mean those things I called you."

"Is that an apology?"

"Don't push, Elizabeth. 'Tis the best of which I'm capable."

Elizabeth paused. She weighed the risks and the consequences. She was apparently making some headway toward ingratiating herself to Quazel. Elizabeth sighed deeply and turned toward her mother's tent.

"A wise decision." Quazel implied a threat had the decision gone against her. "I shall be back shortly. I want to see what that strange movement is in the lily valley."

Elizabeth looked over her shoulder. *How did she heal so quickly?*

Aidan and Caitlin came into the lily valley fatigued and worried. They had not seen any sign of the missing child. They wondered about the progress of the others, but they felt certain Draco would have told them if Declan had been found.

Aidan squeezed Caitlin's hand. "I shall look this way. Ya go that way, but doona get far from me."

They wandered apart; each looked beneath the immense blooms. Near the end of the valley toward the woods Caitlin heard a small, excited voice, "Nana, Nana!"

She ran toward the sound without hesitation, lest she was imagining what she heard. She saw Declan bouncing and pointing toward a woman that approached. "Nana, Nana!"

"No! Not Nana." Caitlin put the small boy behind her.

The old woman said, "You must be Caitlin. I have heard much about you. Have you lost something?"

Caitlin countered, "You must be the infamous Quazel. I have heard too much aboot ya. My business is no concern of yers."

"Nana!" squealed Declan again.

Caitlin knelt beside the innocent child and whispered, "No, baby, 'tis not Nana." Caitlin pointed to where Aidan would be and whispered again, "Go get Uncle Aidan. Hurry, baby. Aunt Caitlin is in big trouble." Draco had warned her of Quazel's intentions. The little boy ran to find his uncle.

"Where did you send the boy?"

"To get his uncle Adam."

"Oh, goodie," cackled the witch. "I'd love to see the golden boy up close and personal."

"Doona think perverted thoughts aboot me husband. Ya aire old enough to be his grandmother."

"Do I look old to you?"

"Ya look loike a hideous freak of nature."

Quazel was becoming angry, and Caitlin did not know whether to stay and fight or to run.

"Trow you, I usually get what I want," taunted Quazel.

"Not this time!"

"I promised Elizabeth I wouldn't kill you. I shan't lie to my daughter."

Caitlin turned to walk away when she heard Quazel start an incantation:

> *"Blue eyes and hair the color of your fur;*
> *with your temperament you should be a tiger."*

Caitlin instantly felt her body contort. Bones popped and skin stretched. Her nails elongated as she watched, helpless to stop the metamorphosis. She screamed in pain. Aidan heard her at the same instant he felt a small hand tug on his breeches. "Declan, something is wrong with Aunt Caitlin."

Declan nodded and said, "Nana."

"God-a-mercy," cried Aidan, and he snatched the baby up and ran toward Caitlin's scream.

Caitlin whirled around and glared through different eyes at Quazel.

Quazel saw the ruby talisman around Caitlin's neck. "My stone."

"Me necklace. I beg ya to try to take it."

Quazel knew something had gone wrong. "You are orange. You should be a white tiger. I said hair to match your fur."

Caitlin gave a guttural laugh. "Think aboot it, dimwit."

Aidan ran onto the scene. "Oh, God, no. Caitlin!"

Caitlin said calmly, "Adam, aire ya armed at this moment?"

"No."

"Then, stay back. She is *mine*. I might not be able to kill her, but I can make her wish she were dead." With that Caitlin leapt into the air. Her new powerful jaws tore at Quazel's throat.

24
Unraveling

Caitlin tore and mauled Quazel, lunging for her throat. The witch twisted and Caitlin's new powerful jaws found the bitter meat on the old crone's shoulder. Quazel shrieked and reach into the folds of her skirt. Acute pain shot through Caitlin's shoulder. Caitlin roared and slumped to one side. Quazel managed to slip from beneath the weight of the beast she had made and rolled into the underbrush where she lay, wailing in agony. Caitlin dragged herself toward Aidan and Declan. Blood flowed freely from a wound in her shoulder, and Quazel's poniard still protruded from her flesh.

The innocent eyes of the child were round as saucers. Declan clutched Aidan's trousers and cried softly, "Kiki eat Nana. Kiki eat." He was terrified as Caitlin neared him.

Caitlin maintained her wits despite the pain. "Adam," she said in a weak voice. "Put the necklace on Declan."

Aidan slipped the ruby charm from Caitlin's neck and dropped it over Declan's. Even the accepting heart of the child saw Quazel for what she was. He screamed and buried his face in Aidan's neck.

Caitlin collapsed at Aidan's feet. He knelt beside her. Declan reached out a tentative hand and touched the tiger's head. He looked at Aidan and said, "Kiki hurt?"

"No," replied Aidan. "The very good kitty loves Declan." The trusting little boy put both arms around the big cat's neck.

"Oh, Caitlin, 'tis me fault," whispered Aidan. "I was not armed."

Caitlin struggled to speak. "Don't call me Caitlin. Call me Kiki, for I shall not be Caitlin again until that monster is dead." Pleading blue eyes turned to Aidan. "Make it soon, my love."

Aidan pulled the dagger from Caitlin's shoulder and started for the underbrush. Quazel had disappeared.

"Fie! Where could she have gone?" Aidan mumbled.

He whirled around as he heard Declan crying, "Kiki. Kiki." Caitlin was not moving. It dawned on him the dagger blade was poisoned.

He shouted with all his energy, "Draco!" He hardly had time to repeat the call before a huge shadow covered them.

Quazel dragged herself to her tent. Elizabeth gasped, "Oh, Mami, did you meet Duncan again?"

"No," came a surly response. "I met a redhead I didn't know existed."

"What are you ranting about now? You need a surgeon."

"Never mind. I shall tell you later. Give me some wine and the silver vial beside the decanter. I will survive."

Elizabeth poured a glass of wine and brought the vial. Quazel said, "Put two drops, and only two, in the wine."

Elizabeth did as she was told. Quazel drank the wine and fell asleep.

Back in the caves everyone hovered over Caitlin. Mary Kate hugged and scolded Declan interchangeably. Finally, Alexander quieted the group. "Caitlin will live. In a day or two the poison will pass from her system. If the dagger had come from the hand of anyone except Quazel, Caitlin would be dead. Since Quazel is unable to kill any of the animals she made, Caitlin will only be sick a while. However, if Quazel had used that blade before she changed

Caitlin, Caitlin would be dead. I told you all that you must be careful of this woman. She'll kill you or have one of her henchmen kill you in a heartbeat."

Aidan sat by Caitlin's bed for hours. She breathed heavily and never stirred. Mary Kate came into the infirmary. "Aidan, let me sit with her for a while. Ya aire exhausted."

"I canna leave her, Mary Kate. How could I have let this happen to her? 'Tis me fault. If I had taken me pistol or a dagger, this whole nightmare would be over," lamented Aidan.

"Mayhap. Then again, we could have a white stallion lying in that bed and Caitlin sitting beside him whining, "Tis all me fault.' Then, we would have to wait for Declan or Kieran or Rennin to grow up and battle evil." Mary Kate grew terrified in mid-thought. "Oh, Aidan, what if 'tis the plan—our three little boys. They could all grow up to have green eyes. What if we have to wait another twenty years? Is that what ya want? Do ya want Caitlin to be a tigeress for twenty years? Do ya want Kieran and Rennin to risk their lives for Draconis? Stop moping. 'Tis time for a plan of action. I want that fury dead before my son has to contend with her."

Aidan sat there with quiet tears on his cheeks. Mary Kate continued. "Aidan, look at me," she said assertively, but gently. She took Aidan's face in her petite hands. "Caitlin wouldna take this lying down. She wouldna wallow in self-pity and guilt. She would do whatever it might take to restore ya or protect her family. She is lying there because she was protecting Declan and ya. She believes in ya. She thinks ya aire the one who must save this place. If ya doona pull yerself together, ya might look worse than Quazel must have looked when she gets done with ya. Ya know me words aire true." She dropped her hands by her sides.

A smile flickered across Aidan's lips. "Do ya not think a tigress was quite appropriate for me Caitlin?"

"What?"

"If I had ever pictured her as an animal, 'twould have been a tigress—beautiful, strong, courageous, stubborn.

"Aidan, aire ya losing yer mind?"

"No, I am finding it." Aidan kissed Mary Kate on the forehead. "Many thanks, sweet lady. Sometimes methinks ya have more common sense than all of us put together. Little sister, have I ever told ya that I love ya? I do. Ya aire very special. Doona ever forget that. Now," said Aidan rising, "I am going to take yer advice and get some sleep. Wake me when she awakes. Promise."

"I promise."

While Quazel slept, Elizabeth watched her wounds heal. Realizing the properties of the drops Quazel had consumed, Elizabeth quietly transferred some of them to an empty vial in her valise. In only a few hours, Quazel awoke. "Elizabeth!"

"I am right here, Mami. I made you some tea and broth when I saw you begin to stir. I thought you might be hungry after your ordeal."

"'Twas thoughtful. I'm not hungry, but I would like the tea." She drank the tea quickly. Then Quazel commanded, "Elizabeth, pack your bag. There's a very special place I'd like to show you. The trip might require spending several nights."

While Quazel changed her clothes, Elizabeth packed all her belongings because she had an uneasy feeling.

They walked for about two days to a spot in the old desert. Quazel brushed away sand to reveal a trapdoor. She turned a knob and pulled hard. The door creaked. "Come, Elizabeth. It goes straight down."

Elizabeth hesitated.

"Don't be such a coward, daughter. I shall go first." Quazel started down the ladder. Elizabeth followed. Ten feet down, Elizabeth felt a tug on her long braid. Quazel wrapped the braid around her arm and jerked. Elizabeth fell fifteen feet into a dark pit. Quazel lit a lantern at the top of the ladder. Elizabeth could see that the ladder stopped at least ten feet above her head. Quazel sat in the opening above.

Elizabeth slowly took in her surroundings. All around her lay human skeletons and bodies in varying degrees of decay.

Elizabeth shrieked in terror, "Draco!"

"Oh, shut up. By the time he gets here, I shall be gone, and once this door is closed he'll not be able to hear you. Before I go, I want to share my exhilarating experience of a few days ago. It seems one of the little brats wandered out of the caves. He was an adorable little thing with those sandy red curls and brownish-green eyes. Fie me! The adults thought I was going to have him for dinner the way they shielded him from me. He was a tasty little morsel, too."

"Quazel! You did not."

Quazel laughed wickedly. "No, ninny. I didn't eat him, but the funniest thing was that either he thinks he is a banana or he was calling me 'Nana.' I don't think he mistakes himself for a fruit." She laid an index finger to her lower lip. "Just why would he call me 'Nana?' 'Tis such an affectionate term. Could it be a sweet little way of saying grandmother? Why would that child think I was his grandmother? I asked myself those questions all the way home. I have the answer. He thought I was you, Nana." She pointed at Elizabeth. "Why would he call you 'Nana,' Elizabeth? Is there some other deception that should be revealed?"

"I delivered that child. I have been with him his whole life. 'Tis just a sweet way for him to address an older lady who will never have grandchildren."

"No, no, no. You're his grandmother. That makes me his great-grandmother. Now which of his parents is your child, Madre or Padre? Let's think." She tapped her dagger-like index finger against the side of her mouth. "If you were a bad girl and had a baby with Diggory, you could've had redheaded children. You're exceedingly fond of Caitlin, who's obviously a redhead." She waved a dismissive hand as Elizabeth began to speak. "Shut up. I shall tell you that part in a minute. She has a twin brother, who, though hairless at the present time, peradventure has a little red stubble. Of course you could be the mother of that petite mousy brunette. Diggory's short. Your child could be short. Either way, I have a granddaughter and a great-granddaughter. Methinks I'd like to have the great-granddaughter. She hasn't been prejudiced against me yet. How delicious! She could be everything I ever hoped you would be."

"Mami, let me out of here and I shall tell you everything," coaxed Elizabeth.

"Do *not* call me 'Mami' ever again!" snapped Quazel. "Now shut up. I must finish my story before that ridiculous overgrown bat gets here.

"A tall attractive blonde came between the boy and me. She sent him scurrying to find the golden boy. Fie! He is scrumptious to the eye, and now he doesn't have a wife."

"Quazel, what did you do to Caitlin?" screamed Elizabeth.

"I didn't lie to you—unlike you to me. I didn't kill her, although she would've gladly killed me. I simply turned her into a white tiger, but the most unusual thing occurred: she came out orange! 'Twould not have happened if she were blonde. Voila!" She lifted arms as in triumph. "She's a redhead.

"Now I must think one of those two young men must have green eyes. Since the prophecy says one of Alexander's descendents will try to kill me, it must be Colin because he's the father of my great-granddaughter and most likely your offspring, and you're Alexander's bastard. Imagine that: my own grandson possibly being the one who can do me in. How ironic. You did weave a good web, Elizabeth. I shall give you that.

"Alas, you must be punished. This is where I put my political prisoners." She waved a hand as if showing off a prized work of art and puckered her lips. "As you can see, these 'animals' do return to human form. They just don't know it. Don't worry, darling. 'Twill take less than a week. Good-bye." Quazel slammed the trapdoor.

As the door closed, Elizabeth screamed with all her might, "Draco!"

25
𝕰𝖘𝖈𝖆𝖕𝖊

Caitlin awoke briefly. Mary Kate jumped to her feet. "I shall get Aidan."

"No, wait, Mary Kate. I need to talk to you."

"What is it? How can I help?"

"I know you still nurse Morgan twice a day. You're still producing milk. I can't nurse Kieran and Rennin anymore. Mary Kate, will you nurse my babies for me? Will you care for them as if they were your own?"

Mary Kate stroked Caitlin's head. "Ya doona have to ask. Ya know I will."

"Gramercy."

"Now I shall get Aidan."

"No. I'm too tired to talk to him right now. Let him rest, and you have babies to attend. Draco is asleep in the corner if I need anything."

"All right."

Mary Kate went straight to Aidan's door and woke him. She told him what Caitlin had asked.

"Wise request. Ya doona mind? That means another year of nursing."

"Of course, I will care for me nephews. 'Tis time Morgan was weaned anyway. Declan has been weaned for months."

"Gramercy, Mary Kate."

Aidan went to the infirmary where Caitlin slept soundly and Draco snored softly in the corner. The dragon stirred. After a few minutes he arose wide-awake. "Elizabeth summoned me. I must away." He disappeared in a flash of white before Aidan could reply.

Draco flew through the waterfall. "Elizabeth! Where are you?" Draco called.

"She's not here," a timid voice said from behind a boulder.

"Who's there?" Draco inhaled and prepared a blast of fire.

"'Tis Carl Covington." The coyote Duncan had met upon his arrival cowered against the back wall. "Prithee, don't burn me. I shall be dead soon enough when Quazel discovers I've been here, but I had to help Elizabeth. She was always so kind to me. She never kicked me and she always saved me some meat from the meals she cooked."

"How knew you to come here?" asked Draco cautiously.

"I followed Elizabeth the other day. Then, I saw you come in. I knew she was tricking Quazel, but I kept quiet."

"Where is Elizabeth?"

"I'm unsure. She went toward the desert with Quazel. I know she's in trouble because nobody who goes that way with Quazel ever returns. I saw her taking Rory Smythe that direction the day the white cat attacked Quazel. I have not seen him since."

"Where in the desert?"

"I vouchsafe don't know. Now, I'd better get back before I'm missed."

"Wait, Carl. Come with me. I shall take you to Alexander. He'll protect you."

"Why would Alexander want to help me after all these years?" Carl asked with trepidation.

"Peradventure because you've finally come to your senses. Would you rather take your chances with Quazel or Alexander? Which one do you think would be fairer?"

Without hesitation, Carl answered, "Alexander."

"Then, climb aboard."

Carl climbed on Draco's back with a new feeling of freedom and they soared to the caves to report what Carl suspected.

In the pit Elizabeth screamed until she was hoarse. Then, she heard whimpering somewhere behind her. "Is someone else here?" she asked as goosebumps covered her skin.

"'Twill do no good to scream. She'll not come back. She left us here to die. Draco won't hear you either. This dungeon is six inches of lead covered in sand."

"Who are you?"

"Rory Smythe. I'm the snake you saw the other day. Quazel became angry that I didn't realize the little cat was Priscilla O'Rourke."

"Evidently my mother has a bad temper, but I refuse to lie down and wait to die. Mayhap if we work together we can get out of here. Are you willing to try?"

"I suppose. What can I possibly do?"

"I dropped a small travel bag when Quazel threw me in here. I cannot find it in the dark. Can you sense it?"

Rory brightened. "I can do that, aye." After a few minutes Rory called, "Elizabeth, I think I have it. Can you follow the sound of my voice?"

"I shall try. Talk to me."

"What should I talk about?"

"Tell me what you did before Quazel changed you."

"I was a typesetter apprentice. I was planning to be a publisher."

Elizabeth tripped over a body and exclaimed, "Alackaday! 'Tis disgusting! Keep talking, Rory."

"I was a pretty good storyteller, too. I wanted to write books. Ouch!" Elizabeth stepped on Rory's tail.

"I am sorry."

"Good now."

Elizabeth opened her bag and searched for a small piece of manganese and a glass with a small hole in the bottom. Covering the soft, bendable metal with strips of her undergarments, she rubbed pieces of flint from a pocket in her robe, finally causing a spark. Once the glow began, she covered it with the glass, forming a crude lamp. "At least we can see each other now.

"Let us see if we can pile these bones high enough to grab the ladder. Then I can climb to the door. Don't be afraid, Rory. I shan't leave you here."

"Promise?"

"On my oath. I am not my mother."

Elizabeth fell numerous times before they finally had enough bones to get to the ladder. She climbed to the door. "Fie!"

"What's wrong, Elizabeth?"

"There is no knob on this side, and I don't have the strength to push it open."

"'Tis hopeless," whined Rory.

"'Tis not hopeless. We shall think of something else."

Thus, ended the captives' first attempt at escape.

Back in the caves, Diggory was frantic. "We must find Elizabeth!"

"We will find her, Diggory. Draco is flying everywhere looking for any sign of her. If he doesn't find her, we shall search the desert inch by inch." Alexander tried to comfort his son-in-law and old friend.

Draco returned with a downcast countenance. "I didn't see her anywhere. I couldn't hear her."

Diggory fumed. "She must be underground somewhere. That bitch has put her in a dungeon or something. Elizabeth must be terrified. She hates small dark places. Ian used to lock her in the closet to punish her. She will be unable to breathe."

Satin roared above the chaos. "This is what we'll do. We'll need everybody. Mary Kate, prepare some wine skin bottles for the babies. Caitlin or Kiki, whatever you wish to be called, stop moping. I've been a great cat for a long time. You can cope with this. Elizabeth saved your life. Now, she needs *you*. Everybody eat and drink a great deal of water, including you, Diggory. You must be strong for Elizabeth. Everyone be back here in one hour ready to go."

Everyone returned in an hour with knapsacks and water. Mary Kate announced that Eunice had arrived to watch over the little ones. Jean Noir and Isabella LeBlanc, his mate, joined the search party.

Satin had a two-hundred-foot section of rope. He laid out his search plan. "We can't afford to get separated. We will all keep a hold on this rope so that we stay together. We'll be spread approximately twenty feet apart, and we'll search every inch of that desert if necessary. Jean, you and Isabella will be at each end of the rope with it around your necks. Diggory and Colin space yourselves twenty feet apart from Jean. Kiki, go next. I shall go in the middle. Then Aidan and Mary Kate. Alexander, you go next to Isabella. Draco will continue to fly overhead. Away."

The search began.

As the valiant friends searched diligently above, the prisoners tried prying the door loose. They tried digging around the perimeter of the door—all to no avail. Elizabeth pounded the door with her fists and screamed in frustration.

"Elizabeth," said Rory excitedly

"What, Rory?" she said in resignation.

"Don't give up now. I have an idea."

"I shall try anything," Elizabeth said, doubting her slow-witted cellmate would be able to think of a plan.

"If Draco heard you when you first screamed, your friends won't give up the search for you. If he can't see you or hear your scream, mayhap he could hear or at least feel the vibrations from pounding on the metal walls and door."

Shocked at the actual logic of Rory's idea, Elizabeth's jaw dropped. She said, "Start banging."

Rory picked up a femur in the coil of his tail and pounded on the wall.

Elizabeth descended to the bottom wrung and grabbed her own bone mallet. "What is that rhythm, Rory?"

"'Tis a Draconian signal for help."

"Teach it to me." Elizabeth pounded with the same intensity that she had used when she threw her little tantrum and stomped her foot. After a few moments of practice, they were drumming the same, last, desperate call for help.

After hours of flying on the second day of searching, Draco sat down in front of the searchers. "I need some water and five minutes of rest, prithee," he requested.

Everyone sat right where they stopped. Nobody had the energy to speak. They drank water and prepared to continue the search.

Draco stood. "Do any of you feel that?"

"Feel what, Draco?" ask Diggory.

"The ground is trembling."

"I doona feel it."

"Shh. Everyone, be extremely still and quiet," whispered Draco.

Nobody moved a muscle. "Aye, Dun...Diggory, I definitely hear something. This is the sound." Draco tapped the rhythm with his tail.

"'Tis the Draconian signal for help," said Alexander. "It must be Elizabeth."

"Or a trick," cautioned Satin.

The rescuers followed Draco as he tracked the sound. He stopped another mile into the desert. "The sound is coming from here."

"I hear it, too," said Satin.

They all began to dig in the sand. Finally, Diggory shouted, "A door!"

It took Jean's horse strength to pull the door open as they tied the rope around his girth and the knob. There was the haggard face of Elizabeth looking into the frantic eyes of her husband.

"Lizzie! Oh, thank God! Ya aire alive. Give me yer hand."

A small weak voice below said, "Elizabeth."

"Just a minute, Diggory," said Elizabeth as she went back into the pit. She gathered her belongings and draped Rory around her neck. "We did it, my friend," she whispered.

"Aye, we did."

Elizabeth climbed out the door into a sea of loving eyes and arms.

Satin commanded, "Draco, blow sand into this mass grave and let's bury those people properly.

Draco filled in the pit, slammed the door, and covered it so that it looked as if nothing had ever disturbed it.

"Quazel will be in for a surprise the next time she opens *that* door," he gloated as he flew the whole group to safety.

26
𝕶𝖎𝖉𝖓𝖆𝖕𝖕𝖊𝖉

𝕺𝖓 the flight to the cave, Elizabeth and Rory ate and drank. Strengthened, Elizabeth urged, "Draco, fly fast. Quazel has figured out Morgan is my granddaughter. She wants her. Mary Kate is safe for now because Quazel thinks Caitlin and Colin are my children and they got their red hair from Diggory. She assumes Colin is the Promised One because he's Alexander's descendent. Her logic is severely flawed, but her final conclusion is correct. Morgan is her great-granddaughter, and Quazel has every intention of getting my little angel and training her in evil ways. She must be stopped."

Draco flew with new urgency. They arrived at the caves with a sense of relief and refuge. All appeared quiet. The reprieve was short-lived.

When the weary travelers walked into Alexander's sanctuary, they beheld total disarray. It looked as if a tornado had ripped through the cave. Apprehension filled the small band even as Draco informed them, "The babies are crying."

"Where are the babies?" cried Elizabeth in alarm.

"In the nursery with Eunice," answered Satin.

With the realization of the possibilities, the whole group charged to the nursery. Their terrified eyes perceived the mayhem and carnage. Kieran, Rennin, and Declan were wailing. The walls, the cribs, and even the ceiling were spattered with blood. The nursery attendants and several orangutans, scattered over the floor in puddles of blood, had begun to transform back into human form. Eunice lay lifeless beside Morgan's empty bed, an orangutan impaled on her horn.

Unable to endure another moment of despair, Elizabeth sank to the floor, all her energy drained. Mary Kate's eyes examined the room for any sign of her daughter. Then she walked bravely and calmly to her bawling son and held him comfortingly in her arms. Aidan and Diggory cradled the other two infants in strong loving arms.

A faint whimpering came from beneath the changing table. Alexander leaned down and peered into the recess. Carl Covington cowered there. He sobbed, "I tried to help. In truth, I tried to help."

Alexander pulled him from his hiding place. The coyote was mangled and maimed; his left front leg was completely ripped away, and he bled profusely. Colin stripped off his shirt and wrapped the torn appendage to stop the bleeding. Rory inched his way to his old friend. "Hold on, mate. These good people will help you."

"Rory, you're alive." Carl acknowledged his friend weakly.

"Thanks to Elizabeth."

At the sound of her name, Elizabeth revived herself. "Da, the silver vial in my bag. Quazel used its contents when she was mangled worse than Carl. What is it? Can it help anyone here?"

Alexander opened the vial. "'Tis unicorn blood—Eunice's. It has great healing power, but to use it would be a mortal sin."

"Quazel has reached the point of no return," Elizabeth said more to herself than to anyone else. She crawled to Eunice. "I'm too weak to resurrect her."

Mary Kate, to everyone's disbelief, was calm and rational. She spoke, "Colin, take the children and Carl to the infirmary. Surely ya remember some of the procedures yer father performed. Take care of the wounded the best as ya can. Everyone leave Momma and me alone. She needs me strength roight now. Soon we will need to rescue Morgan. I see Draco has already left. Everyone leave us now! Fortify yourselves. We will all need our strength." She looked around the group. "All hell is aboot to break loose."

Everyone obeyed Mary Kate. She sat beside Elizabeth. "Give me yer hand, Momma. We can do this together."

"What are you saying, Mary Kate?"

Mary Kate sighed. "Ya have lost the lilt in yer voice, just loike Seanathair. Does not matter." She grasped Elizabeth's hand. "Draw energy from me. If ya can bring Eunice back the way ya did Caitlin, do it."

"Mary Kate, I can't."

"Then teach me how."

"Mary Kate!"

"Momma, Eunice is the last unicorn on Draconis. One way or another, we will do this."

Holding Mary Kate's hand, Elizabeth repeated the same words and the same procedure she had used on Caitlin. Nothing happened.

"Mary Kate, I can't do it. I don't know why. Mayhap she has been dead too long. Mayhap 'tis because she isn't human and never was."

Mary Kate cried. "Oh, Momma, she was so kind, so gentle, so beautiful. How can we just give up?"

"Honey, sometimes we must let those we love go, no matter how much it hurts."

Mary Kate lay onto the beautiful, mystical creature. Her soft gentle tears fell freely along the unicorn's neck and mane. "Oh, God, I canna believe Ya would allow something so ugly, cruel, and wicked to overcome the goodness and beauty Ya made. I pray Thee, I beseech Thee, bring Eunice back so she can help us defeat the one who mocks the gift Ya gave her, the one who uses her power to destroy rather than to exalt.

"Peradventure I am innocent and naïve, but verily I believe the death of one so rare canna make Ya happy. I am sure Yer heart is breaking, too. An' it please Ya, restore Eunice and help us defeat Quazel. She has plagued this land long enough, and now she wants to continue that tyranny even after her death. She has taken another innocent victim, Morgan.

"Oh, merciful God, give us back *all* our assets and help us put this darkness to flight."

So sweet and honest and trusting was the girl's prayer that Elizabeth felt dwarfed in all power.

"Momma, try again."

"'Tis not up to me," Elizabeth declared. "It never was."

Mary Kate laid her head on Eunice and wept again.

Satin sent forth the proclamation of Eunice's death, and Duncan issued the call to battle immediately. The lull in the fighting was over. The war would resume after Eunice was laid to rest. All the good, honest people of Draconis were heartbroken over the news. Deep lament could be heard throughout the mountainside.

Colin, Aidan, and Satin prepared for a rescue mission. Colin was livid. Aidan had to calm him just so he would think rationally.

Colin took Aidan by the arm. "Take whatever ya think ya need to kill that thing. Do it while we aire there if at all possible. We will get Morgan back, and Draconis can avoid war. Draconis will be free, and we can go home."

"My thoughts exactly," confirmed Aidan.

Satin called his little human group together. "Where are Elizabeth and Mary Kate?"

"Still with Eunice," informed Kiki.

"Get them," Satin commanded. "'Tis time to go forward."

"You don't need to send for us. We are here," came a sweet familiar voice.

All heads turned with awe-stricken faces, for with Elizabeth and Mary Kate stood Eunice, a bit disheveled, but alive.

Satin questioned, "Elizabeth, what did you do?"

"Nothing."

"What happened in there?" Alexander demanded.

"I can't tell you," responded Elizabeth.

"Lizzie, no secrets," reminded Diggory.

"'Tis not it. What happened far surpasses any magic I have ever done or ever will do. It was supernatural, Heavenly. Words cannot express what we experienced."

"Try," chorused all the voices in the room.

"All I can tell you is that Mary Kate prayed," finished Elizabeth.

All eyes turned toward the quiet demure woman.

Flustered, Mary Kate declared, "I prayed. Let us be thankful for our miracle and give glory where 'tis due, to God. Now leave me be. I must find me daughter."

27
𝕭attle 𝕻lans

𝕬t sunrise the next day, Colin, Aidan, Satin, and Draco went on a raiding party to reclaim one small girl. When they arrived at Quazel's encampment, there was no sign of her or Morgan. Her tent was gone. There was no evidence that Quazel had ever been there except for the burned trees.

Colin had held out hope of retrieving his daughter. With this blow, he fell to his knees in despair and wept. Aidan knelt beside his friend and put his hand on his shoulder. "We shall find her, Colin. I swear it."

"Aidan, how can I go back to Mary Kate without Morgan? This might be more than she can bear. 'Tis almost more than I can bear."

"No, Colin, Mary Kate is not as fragile as ya believe. She is strong. She has faith. I wish my faith was as strong as hers." Aidan openly admired his sister-in-law.

"Ya could be roight. She is resilient," agreed Colin.

"He is right," Satin affirmed Aidan's analysis of Mary Kate. "I'm honored to have Mary Kate on my side. I'm certain she's special. As a matter of fact, she could be a prophetess. When she speaks, she speaks words of truth and wisdom. I feel certain this whole campaign would be doomed without her.

"Mary Kate will handle this news in stride. Right now I'm more concerned about you. You need to focus on the whole picture. Defeating Quazel will restore Morgan to you. It will restore many families, including my own." The sleek creature glided closer to the two young men.

"Colin, I lost my son when he was very young. I do know the anguish you feel, but you must stay alert. Your life is in grave danger, young man. Remember Quazel is under the mistaken assumption you are the Promised One.

She would have you assassinated, and then where would Mary Kate, Morgan, and Declan be?

"By tomorrow evening, most of our troops will be assembled. Draconis will be involved in a full-scale war again. Both of you must be exceedingly careful. Draconis can't lose you."

"Colin." Satin placed a paw on the heartsick father's shoulder. "In all our reconnaissance, looking for Morgan will be a priority."

"Many thanks, King Satin," Colin said with more self-confidence. "I came here to help yer world. I shan't let ya down."

The king purred, "Come, lads. Let us away. We have military strategies to plan. I have to meet Duncan tomorrow night."

"May I come to the meeting with me father?" Aidan requested.

"'Tis too risky, Aidan. I shall take Diggory as your representative."

"I came here to foight for Draconis," argued Aidan.

"Your main objective is to get close enough to Quazel to kill her. 'Tis your priority. You must stay alive to do that. Do you understand?" King Satin reprimanded.

"I will not sit and watch while everyone else foights."

Satin roared. Rearing to his full extension on his hind feet, he put his paws on Aidan's shoulders, pinning him to a tree. His golden eyes flashed a momentary green. Satin growled, "You will do exactly as your father commands. You have a purpose, a destiny. If you disobey your orders, I will lock you in a cell until Hell freezes. Now, do you understand?"

Aidan was so shocked that this normally gentle and mild-mannered creature had become so angry that he acquiesced. "Aye, sir. I shall do as I am told. I apologize for my insubordination."

"Humph," Satin grunted. "I, too, apologize for my outburst." He relaxed the pressure he had against Aidan's shoulders. "Aidan, son, there will be times you'll need to fight, but I won't allow you to take any *unnecessary* risks. Either Colin or Caitlin must stay with you at all times. You are too valuable to lose."

Satin mellowed and tried an attempt at humor. "Besides, I'm terrified of your father. I have a title, but he has the power. Duncan himself would rip out my heart if I were to allow any harm to come to you."

Dejected, all four troopers flew back to the mountains.

The next evening, campfires, which Draco had lit, glowed around the entrance to the caves. The citizens of Draconis had responded to the call to battle. The generals met with Duncan to discuss military strategies. There were five major contingencies from Draconis who fought for freedom—the Great Cat Clan, the Bear Clan, the Dog Clan, the Horse Clan, and the Hawk Clan. Diggory attended the meeting as the general for the Human Clan.

As Diggory and Duncan walked down the corridor, Diggory asked, "How aire ya gonna pull off two personalities this eve, old friend, and when aire ya gonna tell Aidan who ya in truth aire?"

"I don't know when I'm going to tell Aidan the truth. I've almost told him a dozen times and almost let it slip more times than that; but something holds me back. I don't know what or why. As for your other question, here is your answer."

Waiting in the shadows was another panther: not quite as large as Duncan, but massive in his own right. Duncan swiped a paw across his eyes to remove his lenses, which stuck to the pads of his feet. "Diggory, keep these safe." Diggory stored them in his doublet pocket.

The two panthers greeted each other warmly, nuzzling cheeks. "Diggory, do you remember young Seamus O'Donnell? He was only twelve when he came on as our cabin boy. Now he is Satin's double when I need to be two entities at once."

"'Tis good to see you faring so well," Diggory greeted his old acquaintance with uneasiness.

"It has been a long time, Mr. Danaher," responded Seamus stiffly.

Satin let out a long puff of air. "Trust, my friends. I trust both of you equally. There is no competition between you."

The two nodded at each other. Diggory paused again as they walked a few more steps. "Duncan, why do the other changelings not recognize yer scent. I mean, the changed humans have all the qualities of the animals they have become."

"Ah," the panther nodded. "Father cast a spell when Seamus and I concocted our ruse to confuse our scents. Even the bloodhounds couldn't track either of us."

"A most excellent solution," mumbled Seamus. "Only Alexander can track us through magic."

Diggory looked at the younger face. The boy Seamus had always had character. The human nodded. Trust formed. The three old comrades entered the great chamber to a chorus of, "Hail, King Satin! Hail, Lord Duncan!"

"Enough," said the new Satin. "We are equals bound to one purpose—the freedom of Draconis. Duncan has some items to discuss with you."

Duncan took the floor. "This new outbreak of fighting is the direct result of Quazel's kidnapping of this man's granddaughter. Quazel wants to train the child to take over her evil reign when she dies.

"The first order of business is to find Quazel and the missing child. She has moved camp, and Draco hasn't spotted her. Samuel Taylor, your hawks and other birds of prey must scout the countryside. Send a platoon to Isla Linda. As afraid as Quazel is of water, I doubt she would have left Draconis; but she's desperate. She'll do anything. Also, get a count and position on Quazel's troops."

"Aye, Commander," answered General Samuel Taylor, a Peregrine falcon who commanded the hawks and other birds of prey.

"Caleb Augustus, have your best hounds track the child. This is her dress."

Duncan took Morgan's dress in his mouth from Diggory's hand and passed it to an English mastiff, who sniffed the garment and replied, "Aye, sir."

"The second order of business this evening is how to win the Wolf Clan as allies. We have tried diplomacy, trickery, bribery, and coercion. Does anyone have an idea?"

"Duncan," said Diggory, "let us humans give it a try."

"Diggory, the wolves are overprotective of their territory," cautioned Duncan.

"I am fully aware of that, but let me ask ya if ya can think of anyone who can make a more convincing argument than Mary Kate Fitzpatrick?"

"No, you're right. She could convince me it was the right thing to do if she wanted me to jump from the cliffs." The panther's whiskers twitched as if to smile.

Diggory amended his suggestion. "She should have an escort. I suggest sending Caitlin and Adam with her."

"Adam, Diggory?"

Diggory smiled. "'Twill give the boy something to make him feel needed."

Duncan nodded with understanding. "You and King Satin meet with them."

28
Allies

𝕯𝖎𝖌𝖌𝖔𝖗𝖞 and Satin called their little team together. Satin presented the mission to the group.

"What aboot the babies?" asked Colin.

"We have numerous female goat-humans who can provide nourishment. Mary Kate will only be gone one day, two at the most," clarified Satin. "Colin, you can care for the children that long."

Turning to Mary Kate, Satin said, "Mary Kate, do you accept this assignment?"

"Yes, Yer Majesty."

"Good. Prepare to leave after breakfast."

Mary Kate lay snuggled in Colin's arms that night. "Colin, should I be apprehensive aboot this mission?"

"Aidan will not let anything happen to ya, and Caitlin will keep him safe."

"Colin, do ya think Quazel took Morgan to that pretty little island, Isla Linda?"

"'Tis a definite possibility. 'Twould explain why Draco has seen no sign of them. She could be using Satin's cave."

"Will ya go there when I return?"

"If Morgan is there, I will take Satin's whole army and get her back."

"Colin, why have ya not asked me what happened with Eunice?"

"Because I trust ya to do what is good and roight." He caressed her arm. "When ya want to tell me, ya will. What is this, honey? Why so many questions?"

"I just want to talk to ya."

"So, talk."

"Colin, I want to grow old with ya. Doona die in this place."

"Love, I doona plan to die here."

"Good. I would never want to be with anyone else."

"Me either," sighed Colin. "I love ya."

They lay quietly holding each other for some time before Mary Kate spoke again. "Colin, do ya realize we have not made love since we got to Draconis?"

"Is that a hint?" teased Colin.

"No. 'Tis a demand."

Early the next morning, King Satin awoke to find that more troops had come. The Elephant Clan, the Elk Clan, the Bison Clan, and a few frightened apes had arrived. Draco showed the new clans to their camping area. The apes cowered at the king's feet as he questioned them. "Why have you decided to come into my camp?"

One timid chimpanzee said, "Sir, we can no longer abide Quazel's tyranny. We've been her slaves long enough. If you can forgive us our stupidity, we'd like to join you."

"You're forgiven, and I rejoice you've had a change of heart. However, know you *will* be watched closely to ensure your conversion is genuine. You must understand my caution."

"Aye, King Satin. God grant you mercy."

"Draco will show you where to camp." The panther flicked his head in a direction.

After breakfast, the three ambassadors left for the caves by the cliffs where the wolves lived. Mary Kate chose to wear a red cloak.

"Why the red cloak?" asked Aidan. "They will see us coming for miles."

Mary Kate smiled. "I am not trying to sneak up on them."

They walked thoughtfully for a while before Mary Kate spoke again. "What do I say when we get there?" she asked her two friends.

"Don't fret about it," said Kiki. "You always come up with the right words."

"Pray," stated Aidan.

As they neared a wooded area on the side of the mountain near the cliffs, a large red wolf leapt into their path. She started to display her fangs, but burst into laughter instead. "What have we here, a little porcelain doll?"

Undaunted, Mary Kate stated, "I am Mary Kate Fitzpatrick. I am on a mission from King Satin and Lord Duncan. I wish to speak with the leader of yer pack."

The red wolf laughed even louder. "Lady, do you know what a tasty morsel you would be?"

Mary Kate squatted to be eye level with the wolf guard. She reached out and touched the wolf's head. "Ya would dare to threaten the emissary of King Satin and Lord Duncan?" She spoke in low tones. "I doona believe ya aire that foolish. On the contrary, methinks ya aire much wiser, wise enough to take us to yer leader, now."

The wolf looked at the dainty woman with wide wondering eyes. *How can one so tiny be so bold?*

"Now," whispered Mary Kate with a gentle pat and a smile.

At the entrance to a large cave, the red wolf stopped and called, "Lightning, Prince among Wolves, I've brought messengers from King Satin and Lord Duncan. They request an audience."

"Who is it this time, the unicorn or the mare?" questioned an insolent voice.

"Neither. 'Tis two humans and a tigress."

"Humans? I shall see them." The wolf prince was intrigued. He had not seen humans other that Alexander and Quazel in eighteen years.

The red wolf escorted the visitors to the wolf prince. The prince eyed them keenly, observing the height, the chiseled features, and the well-defined muscles of the young man and the soft delicate face and gentle smiling eyes of the woman.

He spoke. "Many good thanks, Chanel. You may go." He turned to his company. "I'm Lars Willoughby, former governor of Draconis, but I've used the name Lightning since the beginning of change when Alexander said that I ran as fast as lightning. Lightning is a much better name for a wolf than Lars; don't you agree?"

As Mary Kate sized up this immense black wolf with soulful eyes, she answered, "'Tis a powerful name, a name full of strength and enlightenment. I am Mary Kate Fitzpatrick, and these aire me dear friends, Adam and Caitlin, who now calls herself Kiki, Callahan. We aire here to discuss the future of Draconis with ya."

"Madame," contradicted Lightning, "'tis likely you've come to solicit the wolves' joining the war. I have no wish to endanger the lives of my people unnecessarily."

"'Tis one question for the future I wish to discuss, but there is more. Will ya hear me oot and, peradventure, answer a few questions for me?"

"I'll give you the courtesy of listening."

"God grant you mercy, Yer Excellency."

"Prithee, make yourselves comfortable."

The three ambassadors settled down and made themselves as comfortable as possible.

"Prince Lightning," began Mary Kate, "as ya know King Satin sounded the call to arms because Quazel kidnapped a child in order to train her to carry on her evil ways and the oppression of yer home. That child is me daughter. She is but a baby, not even two years old yet. She is Alexander's granddaughter and Lord Duncan's niece. Her name is Morgan."

Lightning interrupted, "Mrs. Fitzpatrick, I'm deeply sorry for you, but I can't ask my people to go to war for you."

"Prince, ya and yer people live in relative safety on the mountainside, an area almost impervious to Quazel's spells. Alexander has had the whole region under his protection for years. He has never forced ya to do anything. Can ya not find it in yerself to help Alexander rescue his grandchild? Can ya not find it in yer heart to help a man who has given most of his life trying to free Draconis from the clutches of Quazel?"

"Mrs. Fitzpatrick, I do owe Alexander a great deal. If any of my people come upon any information regarding little Morgan, we shall pass it on. Still, I can't ask my people to go to war."

Mary Kate sighed, "'Tis a beginning. What would ya do to repay Lord Duncan, a man who willingly risked and lost his humanity for a land not his own, and a people not his own. He gave up his home and his family, and he has asked only that ya foight by his side for a land that *is* yer own."

"Madame, if I had only myself to consider, I'd be beside Duncan; but I have many families under my care."

"Then, mayhap, Yer Excellency, ya should set the example and go to Duncan's side."

"Who would guide my people?"

"Yer Excellency, the wolves may be under yer care, but peradventure they should make their own decisions. Why not put it to a vote?"

"I've tried that. They're unwilling to fight simply for more territory or to reduce Quazel's possessions."

"Prince Lightning, if ya aire the only one who will stand by Duncan, I will consider this visit a small victory; but what can I say to convince ya to urge yer people to join us?"

"I'm almost persuaded to speak to my people again and to go myself; but short of telling them the Promised One has come, nothing will convince them to fight."

"Then, Prince Lightning, 'tis with great sadness I must leave ya now."

As the emissaries rose, Aidan finally spoke. "Prince Lightning, if ya knew the Promised One was here, could ya keep his identity secret and still convince yer clan to join the battle?"

"I could and I would."

"Then, prithee, call yer troops," Aidan said as he removed his blue lenses. "I am Aidan O'Rourke, son of Duncan and grandson of Alexander."

Lightning sprang to his feet. "We will be in the encampment within twenty-four hours. Chanel will go with you now.

"Chanel!" Prince Lightning gave Chanel her orders. Then, he shook Aidan's hand, laying a large paw in the man's palm.

Aidan replaced his blue lenses and the three messengers left with good news.

On the way back, Caitlin rebuked her husband. "Aidan, how could you reveal yourself?"

"It was necessary and roight," Aidan defended himself. He knitted his brows. "Ya sound different."

Mary Kate stopped the brewing argument. "Aidan did what he had to do, what I knew he *would* do. His secret will be safe with both Lightning and Chanel." She looked toward the red wolf and then placed a hand on Aidan's arm, sending what felt like a lightning bolt through the man without her knowing. "The transformation will change Caitlin in many ways."

29
𝔅attle

𝔄𝔰 Aidan, Mary Kate, Caitlin, and Chanel entered the caves, Samuel and Caleb returned to disclose their findings. Satin was thrilled to have the wolves as allies. "How did you convince them, Mary Kate?"

"'Twas not I, but Aidan."

"Aidan, what did you say?" asked the king.

"Sir, I told them what they needed to know, that the Promised One was among us. They will foight if they believe Quazel can actually be defeated."

Satin stared at Aidan. He loved this young man dearly, but his admiration and respect grew daily for him. *Priscilla did a fantastic job bringing up a boy by herself.*

"Aidan, I can see you did what you thought was right, but I pray you, be careful. The fewer people who know your identity, the safer you are."

"Only Lightning and Chanel know the truth. Lightning is to tell his troops only that the Promised One has arrived. They will be here within the day."

"Well done, son. Well done." Once again Duncan had to fight the urge to tell Aidan his true identity. "Aidan, I'd be honored if you were to stay for the generals' reports."

"'Tis I who am honored." Aidan bowed deferentially.

Satin turned his attentions to the generals who were waiting outside. Samuel Taylor and Caleb Augustus came in with their reports.

General Augustus went first. "We tracked the child to the beach. 'Tis, as Lord Duncan feared. The witch has taken the child and left Draconis."

"Many thanks, Caleb. Samuel, what did your birds find?"

"Someone is living on Isla Linda. We didn't see Quazel, but we briefly saw a small child as a hand snatched her back into a cave."

"I see," said the king. He turned to Aidan. "Adam Callahan, what do you think we should do?"

Aidan sat up very straight and spoke with authority. "We should go to the island, kill Quazel, and take back Morgan. We should surround the island and invade from all sides, leaving no avenue of escape."

"We have no ships, Your Majesty," said General Augustus.

"We have something better and faster," said Aidan. "We have *dragons*. King Satin, prithee, tell me Draco is not the only one. Ya once said he was the *firstborn* of a new generation, not the *only* born."

"Aye, there are others, Adam. They're well hidden for fear of annihilation. Draco, how many other young dragons are ready to fly?"

"Ten, perchance twelve," replied Draco.

The king looked pleased when he said, "Adam, we have our fleet of flyers. Help me plan an invasion."

"What aboot Lord Duncan?" asked Aidan. "I thought he was your military adviser."

"He is. I'll present your plan to him for approval."

Aidan raised one eyebrow. He had the strangest feeling Satin was keeping an important secret about his father. If both Priscilla and Diggory had not seen him, Aidan would have thought he did not exist. "Very well, but at some point, verily, I would loike to speak to Duncan meself," said Aidan.

"You will soon, very soon."

Draco brought twelve young dragons to the mountain peaks to begin training in transportation of troops. None of them were as pearlaceous as Draco. They were either, cream colored, tawny, mahogany, peachy, scarlet, or black as soot. They learned quickly how to help the troops mount and dismount. Within days Aidan's "Dragon Squadron" was ready to take troops to Isla Linda.

Aidan met with the generals and King Satin to present his plan of attack. "The first thing we must do is send an insertion team to set up our bases of operation. I would loike to use Char, the black dragon, and Brindle, the brown dragon, to take the team in under cover of darkness. Draco is going to give them a flyover tonight.

"General Taylor has provided us with the information to make a map of the island." Aidan spread the map onto the table. "Each of ya generals needs to choose a competent captain and three others to set up the bases of operation. We need command points set up in the marked areas. Diggory is making copies of the map for each of ya. They will be ready by morning. Of course, General Taylor and his birds of prey will be in charge of communications. Choose yer soldiers, and we will meet again after supper. At that time we can decide which area best suits your talents. Dismissed."

After the generals left, King Satin approached the young man. "You sound as confident as your father. He's quite pleased with your ideas. You seem to have natural talent."

"No, Yer Highness, I have a natural aversion to that witch, and I want to make this a decisive victory. I dread the thought that this war could drag on with Quazel managing to elude us, but ya know from experience that she is a mistress of deception, trickery, illusion, and escape."

"Where would she go, Aidan?"

"I know not, but she got to Isla Linda somehow. I fear she could hide roight under our noses. Only we humans have the charms to show us her true identity. I must speak to me grandfather aboot extending their range so others can see her as she truly appears."

"Aidan, you can't protect everybody, and only those born *after* Duncan was changed are able to be deceived. Those who were here for Duncan's birthday wish know her for the witch she is."

"I know that, Satin, but I can protect as many as possible, and there are those who *can* be deceived."

"Granted. Talk to Alexander."

Aidan burst into Alexander's sanctuary to find the man playing with three children. It was on the tip of his tongue to admonish his elder for not being serious enough about the upcoming battle when his strong-willed wife brushed against him. "Did ya know they are crawling?" she asked in a brusque tone.

It dawned on Aidan a father did not need to be thousands of miles away to miss the lives of his children. He felt rebuked. For some time he just stood and watched as Kieran and Rennin squealed at the silly antics their great-grandfather performed. He found himself laughing out loud when Declan tried to imitate Alexander and covered himself in green ooze. But when Rennin tried, although ten months younger than Declan and just crawling, a green frog appeared. Aidan's mouth fell open.

Alexander realized his grandson had entered the room. "Come in and join the fun!"

Aidan sat in the middle of the floor and played like a child. He laughed so hard his sides ached. Caitlin got in on the action by giving rides to the boys, but when she jumped on top of Alexander's desk and sent books flying, Alexander put a stop to the rough-housing. Caitlin decided it was naptime. With the three boys holding on tightly to her back, she sidled off to the nursery.

Aidan chuckled, "I needed that release, Seanathair."

"A little comic relief for tension can work miracles," laughed the older man, "but now what is in truth on your mind?"

"Seanathair, will ya and Elizabeth work on a way to increase the range of the gem charms? I would loike more of the troops to be immune to Quazel's deceptions. I was wondering if we had larger stones if ya could place an enchantment on them that has the same effect as these charms." He touched the emerald hanging around his neck. "We could put them at each base of operation, and mayhap make Isla Linda impervious to Quazel's hidden identity."

"'Tis a thought, Aidan. I just don't know where to find large gemstones. There's more on your mind. What is it?"

"My son," he said soberly, pointing toward where Caitlin had gone.

The wise wizard nodded. "Rennin has a great gift, but that's not why you originally came."

"Seanathair, I am worried aboot Elizabeth. What if some of the troops should mistake her for Quazel, the way Declan mistook Quazel for Elizabeth?"

"'Tis a valid concern, but Elizabeth has something Quazel would be too vain to have."

"What is that, Seanathair?"

Alexander laughed because the young man had not noticed the change in Elizabeth. "Aidan, she has many gray streaks in her hair, especially after her ordeal in the pit. Have you truly not noticed?"

"I suppose not. If I have not noticed, and I know her well, someone who barely knows her moight not notice either."

"Good point. Perhaps Elizabeth should wear white. The purity of the color itself would likely burn Quazel's skin."

"Then ya will get Elizabeth to wear white. 'Tis a load off me mind."

"But there is more."

"Aye. One more thing aboot Quazel. Seanathair, is she capable of changing her appearance? I mean, can she make herself look loike one of us or an animal?"

"She never has, but 'tis possible."

"Is there anything ya and Elizabeth can do to preempt that possibility?"

"I shall work on that end. Now, what else is bothering you?"

Alexander sat down in his chair. Aidan plopped on the floor at the old man's feet. He laid his head on his grandfather's knee just like a little boy. "Seanathair, there is something strange going on between me father and King Satin. I feel as if they are conspiring to keep me from seeing me father. Why does me father not want to see me? Am I a disappointment to him?"

"Absolutely not!" Alexander almost shouted. "Duncan adores you. He thinks you're a fine man, a man of honor, integrity, and fortitude. He feels if he were to come to you now, he would greatly endanger your life and your mission. Your father is denying himself your love in order to win the freedom of this place. He watches you, and it breaks his heart not to be able to reveal himself to you."

"Then, he is here?"

"Aye, he's here, but I can't tell you where. Aidan, get close to Satin. The two of them are blood brothers. They would be lost without each other. Satin will tell Duncan anything you have to say. Trust me, Aidan. *Satin* is your key to your father. If you can find it in your heart to do so, love Satin even as you would love Duncan."

"I care a great deal for King Satin. He is a very good friend."

"But do you *love* him? Do you care as much for him as you do Diggory or Colin? Would you come between him and an assassin's weapon?"

Aidan looked at his grandfather. The old man had tears in his eyes. He obviously loved Satin enough to give his own life in his stead. Aidan was convicted to the quick. He was willing to kill Quazel and willing to fight, but was he really willing to die? He answered his grandfather honestly, "I doona know, Seanathair."

The old man leaned forward and kissed the young man's golden curls. "'Tis all right. The time will come."

Satin jumped into the sanctuary without a sound from the ledge above. As he saw the tender moment between the two men, his heart quickened. He had to fight the desire to tell his son who he was. Instead, he cleared his throat and said, "Pardon me."

"Satin, what a surprise," said Alexander. "Aidan and I have been talking about you."

"All good, I hope."

"Could it be anything else?"

"One never knows," said the king. Then he turned to Aidan. "Aidan, we have new allies. The Dolphins have come to our aid. I thought you would want to meet their general."

"Aye, I want to meet him."

"Her," corrected the king.

"Her, then. Seanathair"—Aidan hugged his grandfather—"many good thankings for yer encouragement."

"Any time, my boy."

As Satin and Aidan walked to the beach, Satin explained more about the Dolphin Clan. "Aidan, only a few of the dolphins are former humans. Their general, Danielle Martin, was born a dolphin of former human parents. Her mother was with child when Quazel changed them. She has never known land, only stories from her parents. She is, perhaps, a year or two older than you. You should know, dolphins are intelligent animals, so even the natural dolphins want Quazel gone."

Aidan saw a sleek bottlenose dolphin swimming in the shallow water. As Danielle noticed the two commanders approach, she skimmed across the water in a little dance of greeting. "Be well met, Aidan O'Rourke. 'Tis good to see you have recovered from your near-drowning experience."

Both Satin and Aidan stopped in their tracks. Danielle realized her greeting was out of place. She swam as close as she could get. "I beg your pardon. Hail, Adam Callahan. I'm glad you are alive and well."

"Many thanks," replied Aidan, still puzzled.

Danielle laughed. "Did you think you swam all the way to Isla Linda when you fell overboard? Guess again. A few of my friends and I got you to the beach. You were delirious, of course, so you talked a lot as we swam, but I can tell from the expression on your faces I should pretend I know nothing. Nonetheless, you still need our help. So let me tell you what we dolphins know, and you can decide how to use the information.

"The main thing that will benefit you is the underwater caves on Isla Linda. One of them opens into a grotto, which has a small, narrow opening to the surface. I can tell your hawks or your dragons how to find it. The other one bubbles into a fresh water spring.

"My scouts know how Quazel…"

Satin shivered.

"My apologies, King Satin," Danielle said, "but it's just a name. Anyway. We know how Quazel got to the island. The sharks are circling. Several were seen pushing a boat. And the blasted buzzards helped carry her loyal minions."

"Ah." Satin nodded and flicked his tail. "Go on."

"We dolphins swim fast, too—faster than the damned sharks. Peradventure we can help transport some of you to the island. I shall remain nearby. If you need me, just whistle." Danielle swam away to deeper waters.

"Satin, they may be smart, but they aire definitely free spirits," commented Aidan.

"Indeed," agreed the king. "Especially Danielle. When she becomes human, she will probably be a pixie." Satin sighed, thinking of his own pixie love, his past life. *She reminds me of Priscilla.*

After supper the generals attended another meeting with the teams they had picked. Aidan had his assignments ready.

"Wolves, ya will go in at this point in this wooded section of the island." He showed the area on the map. "Ya will be responsible for most of our covert operations. Mary Kate will be with ya.

"Dogs, ya will go in at this point in this wooded area." He tapped the parchment. "Ya, too, will be privy to me secret plans and in tracking and planning routes. Elizabeth will be with ya. All of ya listen carefully. Elizabeth resembles Quazel; however, take note of Elizabeth's ethereal appearance. She will wear white at all times." He indicated Elizabeth with his hand. "This will serve as protection from her allies, but could also make her vulnerable to attack. Guard her with yer lives. Remember, she is Alexander's daughter and Lord Duncan's sister.

"Cats, I need ya to set up in the grasslands." He ran a hand across the paper. "By nature of yer stealth and speed, ya will serve as me raiding squads. Ya will hit enemy camps quickly and quietly. Do as much damage in as short a time as ya can. Me wife, Caitlin, will be with ya since she is one of ya now. She is the love of me life. Doona let her take any unnecessary risks.

"Bears, set up in this area near the caves." He indicated the place with his index finger. "'Tis most loikely ya will be closest to Quazel. Be prepared for attack and quick defense. Diggory will be with ya.

"Horses, by nature of yer build, ya must take the beach. Ya will be more open than anyone else. Get up yer barricades as quickly as possible. Jean Noir will be with ya.

"Our newest allies, the Dolphins, will take care of the sea, and they have provided a location for me to have as my command post. Colin will remain with me. The rest of ya, doona think ya aire being left oot. Ya will be performing an important role. I need ya to set up a perimeter around Draconis. We doona want Quazel to get back here.

"Aire there any questions?" He was met with silence. "If not, get some rest. We leave before dawn. The rest of our forces will join us in forty-eight hours."

Aidan tried to sleep, but tossed and turned. Caitlin said, "Would you like me to get you some warm milk?"

"Ya know I hate warm milk."

"I used to, but now I like it. I want some. Would you like some cocoa?"

Aidan put his arms around Caitlin, and said wistfully, "What I would loike, I canna have."

"I'm sorry," whispered the great sad tigress.

"I shall settle for cocoa; but, trust me, cocoa does *not* hold a candle to making love to ya."

"I shall be back."

Caitlin returned a few minutes later with a little saddlebag across her back, hot milk in one pouch and cocoa in the other. Aidan drank his cocoa silently. He was asleep within minutes.

Caitlin purred as she licked his curls, "'Tis amazing what a little sleeping powder can do."

The troops congregated on the beach facing Isla Linda and waited for Aidan and King Satin. As the two commanders walked onto the beach a great hush fell on the crowd. The two looked over their brave condottieri. The only reward this group asked was freedom. There was one among the group that did not belong.

Aidan confronted this interloper. "Draco, what aire ya doing here?"

"I'm going with the king. Don't try to stop me."

Satin chuckled. "Adam, Draco takes an oath seriously. He swore he'd never leave my side. I wouldn't suggest trying to dissuade him."

Aidan eyed the enormous beast and said, "I wouldna go without ya, but ya canna go until ya put on yer vest. Hurry. Time is of the essence."

"Well played, Aidan," whispered the king as Draco charged back into the cave.

The three dragons, loaded with troops and supplies, descended upon Isla Linda undetected. They dropped off each squad where they were to set up a base of operation. The squads constructed temporary shelters, and the wolves and the dogs scouted the island. Aidan and Satin found the entrance to the underground grotto and the dolphins awaiting orders.

The troops lay low all day. At evening the captains met with Satin and Aidan in the underground grotto.

Chanel reported Quazel was definitely in the cave King Satin had used when he was on the island, but the entrance was heavily guarded and there were platoons of hyenas, jackals, and dingoes scattered throughout the woods in bands of ten to twenty-five. Quazel's loyal apes had fortifications in the trees, and crocodiles filled the streams and lakes.

Aidan sent Char and Brindle back with the numbers for Duncan and to begin transporting the rest of the troops. After delivering the troops, the dragons were to return to Draconis and fortify the perimeter.

The insertion team settled in for two days of gathering information and determining Quazel's schedule. At noon the second day, Aidan had to restrain Colin when he saw Morgan. Quazel held her hand and walked toward the beach. The child gathered seashells.

"Colin, ya've seen her. Ya know she is unharmed. Bide yer time. We will get Morgan back and eliminate Quazel, too."

The horses' squad held their breath as the witch approached. Their barricades were disguised as sand dunes. It appeared they escaped detection.

The fortifications filled with troops quickly. Aidan, Satin, and Colin were in the grotto planning an offensive strike when Danielle swam into the lagoon. "The apes are attacking the bears and the cats! The dingoes, hyenas, and jackals have struck the wolves and the dogs! The crocodiles are headed for the beach, and the crows are engaging the hawks! Sharks encircle the island. Gentlemen, the war is raging above!"

In one bound, Satin was out the opening to the cave. As he flew to battle, he flung over his shoulder, "Colin, keep Aidan here even if you have to tie him up!"

Despite Satin's orders Aidan tried to follow the king. Colin literally tackled his brother-in-law. "No! Ya will stay here. When we have the chance we will get to Quazel. Yer priority has to be her!"

"Colin, what aboot Satin? He is going into the fray alone."

"He has *Draco*. He is never alone."

Aidan calmed a bit. "And I have you." The timbre of Aidan's voice changed in that second.

The fighting was fierce all afternoon. The crows spotted some of Duncan's forces and sent up the cry. Quazel ordered an immediate attack.

As Satin rushed to the cat fortification, he growled orders. The great cats faced off against armed apes. "Flank and circle," the panther ordered. "Keep your distance from any spears or knives."

The feline warriors never attacked one-on-one, but usually in a triangle to keep the apes off balance, not knowing which way an attack would come.

As the large cats fought the apes, Prince Lightning ordered his wolves to attack in much the same pattern against dingoes, jackals, and coyotes. Yet, often the canines locked in neck-to-neck grapples. Blood flowed freely.

Overhead, screaming eagles engaged crows and vultures. Feathers littered the ground.

As the birds raged in the air, the dolphins and sharks tore into one another beneath the water's surface. Even above the water, the dull thud of dolphins' noses charging into the sides of sharks resounded.

After several hours, Satin returned to the grotto. He was perceptibly tired but otherwise unharmed.

"Satin, what has happened?" Aidan asked anxiously.

Satin gave an account of the day. "Although the fighting was heavy, our casualties have been light today. Quazel's troops have retreated for the night."

"Satin," said Aidan, animated, "mayhap we shouldna stop our pursuit. Peradventure we should attack now, while Quazel wouldn't expect us to attack. Both the wolves and the cats have excellent night vision. 'Tis the perfect opportunity."

"'Tis not a gentlemanly thing to do, Aidan." The great cat listened as his son's speech became Draconian.

"Satin, I have heard it said, 'The rules of fair play do not apply in love and war.' This is *war*!"

"I shall talk to Duncan. I shall return shortly."

"My father is here?"

"Where else would he be?" shouted Satin on his way out.

Satin went to Diggory and discussed Aidan's suggestion with him. "Diggory, should we do it? Should we follow Aidan's plan?"

"Duncan, it could mean capturing Quazel. Ya may feel 'tis ungentlemanly conduct, but Quazel is not a lady. She does not deserve us to behave as gentlemen. We must behave as warriors. Try it Aidan's way."

Eyes flashed a momentary green behind golden lenses. The king noted *the whole group of humans are losing the Irish lilt one by one. Even Diggory's brogue is not as thick, though he still has it.* Duncan knew then he would never leave Draconis. He would never see Ireland again. A lump rose in his throat. He swallowed hard.

"Diggory, get Mary Kate, Elizabeth, and Caitlin and go to Aidan. Send Danielle to get Father. If we capture Quazel, the seven of us will need to be together. I shall lead the attack."

Duncan went straightaway to the cat encampment to find Seamus. Duncan found him asleep under a willow tree. The king nudged the sleeping look-alike, "Wake up, Seamus. We have a raid to run."

Seamus stirred groggily. "Duncan? I'm so tired."

"So am I, Seamus, but we have a mission. I need to be myself later. Rise."

Two platoons each of cats, wolves, and large attack dogs regrouped at the willow tree. Duncan explained the objective. "We are invading Quazel's camp. We want that witch taken to the grotto. The Promised One is there and ready to rid us of this scourge. Also, while we are in the sorceress's camp we are to rescue the child, Morgan. Take the girl to her mother in the grotto. Are there any questions?"

With no answer, he commanded, "Move out!"

Aidan was pacing a trench in the grotto. Colin had thrown enough pebbles into the lagoon to form a dam. The two young men were completely isolated. The waiting took its toll on their already frayed nerves.

Kerplunk! Colin skipped another rock on the water.

"Out upon it, Colin. Would you stop throwing rocks?" snapped Aidan.

"Would ya sit down and stop diggin' an unneeded ditch?" retaliated Colin.

"I seek your pardon. If we don't hear something soon, there could be a small war in here," Aidan joked.

"Ya could be roight. This waiting is killing me." Colin threw another rock.

"Ouch! All that swimming, and I get hit by one of my own. Just my luck." It was Danielle.

"Pardon," said Colin.

"Danielle, do you have any news for us?" Aidan interrogated.

"I have sent a messenger to tell Alexander that he is needed here. I imagine that your friends are on their way. Satin and Duncan are leading a raid on Quazel's fortress."

As Danielle spoke, Diggory and the others arrived. Diggory bore the same news as Danielle. "Alexander will be here soon. Then, all the players will be in one place as soon as Duncan brings Quazel." Diggory put his hand on Aidan's shoulder. "This nightmare could be over tonight."

"I hope so," sighed Aidan. Caitlin rubbed against his leg.

Mary Kate peered through the opening into the darkness. Colin went to her. "Doona worry. All this will soon be over."

Mary Kate turned to her husband with tears on her cheeks. She put her hand in his and whispered, "No, Colin it will not."

The raiding party surprised Quazel's guards, and the fighting was vicious. The cats, wolves, and dogs, armed with only their claws and teeth, struck at vital organs on the apes and the resting dingoes, jackals, and hyenas. The dog-like enemies fought back in kind. The apes armed themselves with lances, spears, daggers, swords, and clubs and returned a ferocious defense.

Duncan, Seamus, Lightning, and Chanel made their way into the inner sanctum. A circle of half-crazed apes, each armed with a poison tipped weapon, enclosed Quazel and Morgan in a circle of protection. The four warriors circled the group. Each waited for an opportunity to strike.

Without warning, there came a blinding light, and the room filled with acrid smoke. The four attackers were on the defensive once again. There was snarling and growling in the confusion. Then came a sharp yelp.

Duncan sounded the retreat. It was impossible to see from which direction the apes attacked and almost impossible to breathe. As he found the entrance to the cave, Duncan heard Seamus bawl in agony. "Seamus!" Duncan screamed, and he tried to re-enter the cave; however, the fumes overcame him. He lay at the maw of the cavern gasping for air. The next thing Duncan knew, he felt teeth clamp into his fur and he was being pulled into the undergrowth by the wolf prince, who also gasped.

After a few minutes of breathing clean air, Duncan said, "Lightning, we must go back. It appears the smoke has cleared."

As the two leaders cautiously re-entered the cave, they could hardly believe their eyes. Chanel lay in the corner, pierced through with a spear. Six apes lay dead from wounds inflicted by the four soldiers. Seven more had succumbed to the smoke. All had begun to morph into human form. There was a trail of blood leading to the wall, but it stopped there. Quazel, Morgan, and Seamus were not to be seen.

Duncan examined the wall. "Quazel must have found some kind of secret entrance or made one. How else could she have disappeared through a wall of solid granite? Worse yet, Lightning, how do I tell my son I let Quazel escape again?"

"Your son, King Satin?" asked Lightning, a bit confused.

Duncan realized he had forgotten to remove his lenses. Several horrible truths dawned on him at once. A moment of confession was necessary. He knew now Lightning was a true ally.

Duncan removed his lenses. "Lightning, Duncan O'Rourke and King Satin are one and the same. Seamus has always played the role of King Satin when both identities had to exist simultaneously. Aidan does not know. I have grown so accustom to these fake eyes I did not realize I had forgotten to remove them. I was supposed to be Duncan right now, not Satin.

"Poor Seamus." Duncan wagged his head. "He is as good as dead, too. Quazel will have him killed. For a brief moment, she thinks she has captured me. She will have him killed either way. She knows the truth. If he were I, she wants me dead, but God only knows what she will do to him when she discovers she has the wrong panther.

"Lightning, I must continue my charade for a bit longer. Prithee promise you will keep quiet about my necessary deception." Duncan replaced his lenses.

"You have my word, friend." Lightning went to his dead captain. "Don't keep your secret too much longer. We aren't guaranteed another day." He rubbed his head on the red wolf, who had become a slim, athletic, strawberry-blonde woman. "I never told her how much I loved her. Don't let your chance slip away with Aidan."

"When we get back to Draconis, I shall tell him, but right now I think this bad news is enough."

Forlornly, the two left for the grotto.

"King Satin, you're hurt," said Aidan as he ran to the big black beast. There was blood seeping from his shoulder. The king had not realized he was wounded.

"'Tis only a flesh wound."

"What happened, Satin?" asked Aidan gently.

"She escaped. I'm so sorry I let you down," groaned Satin as he collapsed from sheer exhaustion.

Mary Kate ripped a piece of her skirt and dressed Satin's wound.

"'Tis not his fault, but he blames himself," said Lightning. Then, he told them of the blinding light, the smoke, and the hidden exit from the cave, which they had been unable to locate. He told them that Duncan and King Satin had decided the majority of the troops should return to Draconis. Only a few from each division should remain on Isla Linda.

"My father?" asked Aidan.

"Safe," was Lightning's only reply.

30
Betrayal

Aidan's troops slowly packed up to return to Draconis. All were deeply saddened by the outcome of the campaign.

Aidan walked to the beach where he had once found refuge. He saw his ship listing idly in the water and longed to sail backward in time to when he and Caitlin were new lovers and discovering each other. Two years would be perfect. *No, perhaps I would sail further back to when I was a baby and my father would take me on little jaunts around Porpoise Point and my mother would never convince him to sail away.*

"A dragon's treasure for your thoughts." King Satin interrupted Aidan's reverie.

"Do you think I can get Char and Brindle to tow *The Privileged Character* into safe harbor on Draconis?" Aidan dared not reveal his melancholy. Satin already blamed himself for the troops' great losses.

"I'm sure that can be arranged."

"Good. I would like to have a little piece of home nearby."

Home. Satin released a hefty sigh. "Aidan, don't blame yourself for this failure. I've dealt with that woman all these years, and I never expected this escape. 'Twas too good to be true. We had her within our reach." He stretched a paw out in front of him. "The only one of us who sensed failure was Mary Kate. I tell you: That girl has the spirit of a prophet. Mayhap we should use her for wise counsel regarding any plans we make in the future."

"That sounds like a good idea. However, I'm sure she would approve of taking the ship into port. Let's go see to the troops."

The two turned from the beach. "Satin, you and Duncan see to getting the troops squared away on Draconis. Colin and I would like to poke around this island a little more."

"That might not be safe for you, Aidan."

"Don't worry. You'll be flying back and forth. You and Draco can come back for us on one last trip. Then we can follow the ship into port. Besides, we're leaving some troops here. If you and Draco don't spot us out and about, we'll be either in your old cave looking for that secret passage or in the grotto. We're both armed and wearing our charms. Mayhap we shall get lucky and find Quazel with her back turned. I would happily put a knife through her cold dark heart."

"Be careful. Her heart of stone might break the blade."

Aidan looked down to see a smirk playing about the panther's mouth, whiskers twitching. "Very funny, Satin."

Far beneath the floor of the king's former abode, Quazel had made a ghastly home. The eerie glow from nests of glowworms provided the only illumination. Thinking all the while that she was on an adventure with Nana, Morgan slept the sleep of innocence in the one room furnished comfortably.

Further down the corridor lay another room behind a heavy stone door, which ape guards swung to the side for Quazel to enter. Inside was a dungeon—a prison a torture chamber. Shackled to the wall were many animals, prisoners of war. Quazel kicked one hyena tethered near the door as she walked by. "You would've dared to try to escape and join Duncan after all these years when 'tis his fault you're as you are? You may have book knowledge, but you in truth are dimwitted, Connor."

"I would've escaped with Duncan years ago had you not enslaved me. I want to watch him rip your heart from your chest someday, you bitch."

"When I discover what the secret ingredient is that you put in those headache powders, I'm going to have one of my loyal subjects chop off your head." Quazel laughed her wicked snort and turned toward the center of the room. "I shan't need you anymore and will have no reason to change you back and forth so you can use your hands." She walked away.

Chained to a stone table in the middle of the room, lay a large black panther. As she walked past, Quazel ran her hand over the creature from his head to his tail, which he cracked like a whip when she touched him. "Still defiant, are you? I would have loved to have run my hands over you like that twenty years ago. You were the most handsome man I'd ever seen, even better looking than Alexander because you were so much more muscular. Look at you now, a whimpering ball of fur. Duncan, do you know what I'm going to do to you first?"

Connor laughed long and loud.

"Shut up you fool, or I shall cut out your tongue." Quazel sighed as she picked up a red-hot poker from the stone furnace.

"Duncan, the first thing I'm going to do is gouge out those gorgeous green eyes. Such a pity." She turned to one of the ape guards and said, "Remove those ridiculous yellow lenses."

The ape went to the panther's face. The panther snarled and tried to bite Quazel's assistant, but his neck was immobilized. The ape touched the eyes of the beast.

"Queen Quazel, there are no lenses. This must be King Satin."

"You idiot! How many times do I have to tell you that King Satin *is* Duncan O'Rourke? This is just some imposter. Well, perchance you can tell me where to find the high and mighty Duncan. Mayhap you can tell me where to find the Promised One. Let's see if we can help each other."

Quazel took on a coaxing voice. "I shall make you a deal. I shall return you to your human form if you cooperate with me. What do you say, big boy?"

"Don't say a word, cat," shouted a small Pekingese chained in the corner.

Quazel picked up a rock and hit the little dog in the head. "That should shut you up for now."

"Go to Hell, Quazel," Seamus snarled, baring his teeth.

"Wrong answer." Quazel calmly walked to the wall where she chose a narrow bamboo cane. She marched back to the table. Quazel screamed and brought the cane down onto the side of the immobile creature.

Seamus winced and writhed, but said nothing.

Quazel resumed a soft soothing voice. "Would you like to try again?"

"I'm King Satin, Ruler of Draconis."

"Wrong answer!" shrieked Quazel, and she picked up the hot poker once more, gouging it into Seamus's left eye.

Seamus roared in agony.

"Would you like to try again?" She smiled, and her canines appeared as fangs. "What is your name? I would like to know what to call you."

"I am"—He labored though the pain—"often called...King Satin."

"When I'm done with you, you will beg to give me information," threatened the evil sorceress.

Duncan took his time sending the troops back to Draconis. He was reluctant to leave Aidan. He gave orders for the dragons to take back one third as many troops on a trip as they had brought on a trip and to fly at half speed.

Diggory, Elizabeth, Alexander, and Caitlin went back on the first trip. Mary Kate refused to go until Colin went.

Meanwhile, Aidan and Colin combed every inch of the beach near Satin's cave and came up empty handed.

"That hidden escape route must be in the cave somewhere," complained Aidan.

"Satin and Lightning searched the cave," reminded Colin.

"Perchance 'tis somewhere they could not reach. Mayhap 'tis in the ceiling."

"Well, time is wasting. Let us check. We shall push every stalagmite and stalactite and kick every rock."

Still, they found nothing.

Through all the days that the Draconian troops were moving out, Seamus endured Quazel's tortures. The witch came into the room carrying a black pot. "Good morrow, *Your Highness*," she bit out. "What are you up for today? What game shall we play?"

Seamus no longer lay secured to the stone table. He hung suspended by his front paws from the ceiling. The massive beast had begun to emaciate. The once regal creature did not answer. He hung perfectly still except for his labored breathing. Each breath he took was a struggle.

His cloudy mind vaguely recalled the last three days. *There was fighting. I was with Duncan. The smoke… Burned my eyes and throat. A lance struck my hip… Must not have been poisoned. I couldn't walk.*

Hard, cold, stone stairs… Dragged down into total darkness. I'm Quazel's prisoner. How could I have been captured? Think. What happened?

Oh, aye. Quazel wants me to tell her something. What? Oh, she wants to know where to find Duncan and the Promised One. Then Duncan isn't here. He wasn't captured. Have I said anything? No. No, I haven't told her anything.

Quazel has tortured me. What has she done? Oh, aye. She put out one of my eyes. Oh, well, mayhap I will look rather dashing with a patch. Oh, that means King Satin will have to wear a patch, too. What else? Her apes hoisted me into the air. After a while of hanging, the sheer weight of my body pulled my shoulders out of place. She took pleasure in watching me suffer.

There's more. She beat me with a cane. I can feel the festered welts. I have fever. The welts must be infected. She burned me with the fire poker. His nose and whiskers twitched. *I can still smell seared flesh. Mayhap, 'tis not the welts, but the blisters that are infected. No. I don't have any blisters. The burns are worse than that. I feel the sores oozing. One of those apes beat me with some sort of hard wooden pole. Quazel must not have had the strength for that one. I know my ribs are broken. That must be why it hurts so much to breathe.*

So cold in here, but I'm so hot, so thirsty. His tongue stuck to the roof of his mouth.

There was something else. What else has the cruel, evil woman done? Oh, aye. The worst thing. How could I forget? She pulled out my claws... Paws still damp with blood.

She's back. Does she never tire? What else can she possibly do? Why doesn't she just kill me and get it over? Oh, that's right. She can't kill me. 'Tis supposed to be a blessing, a form of protection. If I could laugh, I would.

The apes can kill me. Why doesn't she have one of the apes slit my throat or bash my head?

Seamus was drawn back to reality. Quazel was speaking. "What's the matter? No insulting names for me today? Cat got your tongue?" She laughed viciously. "I just love my sense of humor. 'Cat got your tongue.' Was that not funny? No? Alas.

"I've decided to wash your wounds. Verily, one of my assistants is going to take care of you. Paco, take care of the king." She laughed that hideous cackle.

The ape showed his teeth to Seamus. Seamus wondered, *is that supposed to be a smile? He obviously enjoys his work, too.* The ape lowered Seamus to the stone table. He dipped a sponge into the black pot and slowly squeezed the sponge over the panther's racked body. Seamus writhed in pain. The pot contained vinegar and salt.

Seamus shrieked, "Oh, God! Why don't you just kill me?"

Quazel cooed, "But, my dear, I don't want to kill you. I want you to tell me where to find Duncan and his promised savior." Her voice changed to one full of venom, "Now, where the hell are they?"

In his delirium Seamus screamed, "I don't know where they are anymore! They were in the grotto. They're probably gone by now, gone back to Draconis and away from you, bitch!"

"What grotto?"

"The one with the small opening in the middle of the island. Now kill me. I can't bear any more of this," begged the anguished captive.

Quazel shrugged her shoulders. "You heard the man, Paco." She started to leave. "Wait. No." She went back to the suffering panther. "No, I think I shall let you live with your cowardice and your guilt about your betrayal of your friend." She patted Seamus's head in mock sympathy. "Poor baby. You couldn't stand a little pain."

She turned to leave again. "Paco, find that grotto and kill anyone you discover there. Dump this coward on the beach. If he survives, he'll have to live with the fact that he gave me Duncan and his savior."

Paco called three more apes to help him carry Seamus to the beach and raid the grotto. Unknown to anyone, a sneaky hyena had chewed through his tether and slipped out the door of the prison along with the assassin squad.

31
𝕬 𝖁𝖆𝖑𝖎𝖆𝖓𝖙 𝕰𝖋𝖋𝖔𝖗𝖙

𝕬𝖎𝖉𝖆𝖓 and Colin took the rowboat that had been left on the beach of Isla Linda to *The Privileged Character*. Draco hovered over the ship, waiting for the two young men to attach the harnesses with which Char and Brindle would tow the ship to Draconis. It had taken a streak of engineering ability to design harnesses to fit the two enormous dragons. Aidan and Colin were only attaching the half fitted for the ship. The part for the ship was chains. Even now Alexander and Diggory were dressing the two dragons with the leather strapping. The straps were to be connected to the chains. If this little feat worked, Colin proposed engineering as a profession.

Aidan and Colin went back to the grotto. They had explored Satin's cave from top to bottom and wall to wall. They had left no stone unturned: literally, they had moved every rock and pushed every boulder. Satin entered the grotto to round up Mary Kate and the two determined young men.

"Aidan, Colin, 'tis time to go. The last of the troops is loaded."

"Satin, would you and Draco mind coming back once more?" requested Aidan.

"Why?" demanded the king.

"Well, Colin and I have to stay to connect Char and Brindle when they get back. Don't fret, Satin."

"I don't like it at all, Aidan. We still have no idea where Quazel is hiding. Do you *not* know how special you are? Do you *not* know that I love you as if you were my son? I don't care if you have purple eyes and pink hair; you've stolen my heart." He looked at Colin. "I care deeply for you, too. I would die if anything happened to the two of you."

"Satin"—Aidan's big green eyes looked imploringly at the king—"I love you very much, too. Don't worry. Colin and I will be together."

Satin's eyes narrowed. "Aye, that is the problem; two naughty boys together can wreak havoc." He gave a little snort. "You aren't even wearing your lenses."

Aidan quickly put them in.

"I am staying, too," chimed in Mary Kate.

All eyes turned toward her. "I feel the overwhelming need to stay. The only way ya aire going to get me on this transport is to bind and gag me."

"By all means, stay," agreed Satin. "I will never argue with your second sight again." Satin continued, "Don't argue, Colin. I see your mouth about to open. If you two lads stay, she stays. She might just save your arse. Draco and I will be back by nightfall. You *will* go to Draconis then."

"Agreed," they all said together.

Satin stalked out the entrance. He was obviously miffed.

Colin asked, "Why aire we staying here, Aidan?"

He shrugged and shook his head. "I know not. Something inside has said, 'Stay,' over and over. Verily, 'tis odd. I cannot explain the feeling."

Colin worried, "I hope 'tisn't Quazel causing ya to hear voices. What aire we going to do for four hours?"

"Go back to the cave," said Mary Kate.

"Why?" asked Colin.

Mary Kate responded, "I know not, but my instincts tell me to go back to the cave again."

Aidan shrugged his shoulders. "Who are we to argue with a prophetess, Colin?" he jested.

Mary Kate glared at him.

He held up two hands in mock surrender. "I give up. Mary Kate, you've been right too often to ignore your intuition. Let's go back once more, but keep an eye on the sky before we leave. If Satin sees us out, he'll come straight back."

Like naughty children, the three searchers waited to see Draco head for Draconis before they made their way to the cave.

Paco unceremoniously plopped Seamus onto the beach. "Too bad 'tis low tide. You'll have to wait at least twelve hours. Peradventure you'll simply be washed out to sea with all the other rubbish." Paco's lips stretched into that gummy grin. Even in his confusion, Seamus thought how ugly the creature was.

The ape had as many scars on his body as Seamus would have when his wounds healed. The hair had not grown back on the area where his wounds had been inflicted. With his lack of hair, the white ape appeared pink with tufts of white hair. Seamus wondered how many of Paco's scars were battle scars and how many Quazel had inflicted on him.

Paco and his three cohorts started inland to find the grotto. Seamus tried to pull himself toward the cat fortification. Even the flexing of his muscles racked his body with pain. Unable to move, he collapsed.

When Paco and his cronies disappeared into the woods, Connor cautiously made his way to the battered panther. "Don't give up," Connor tried to comfort the anguished animal. "What's your real name? I'm Connor Donohue. I know that I know you."

"Doc? Is that in truth you?" Seamus struggled to speak. "Seamus O'Donnell."

Connor declared, "I'm going to find you some help. In my present state there is little else I can do."

"Bother not. Let me die. I deserve to die. I betrayed Duncan," gulped the great cat.

"Nonsense!" Connor argued. "Quazel has abused your body and broken your spirit. How much torture can one person endure? You were extremely brave, much stronger than I would have been."

"It matters not. I'm useless now and so ashamed."

"Seamus, you know Duncan will forgive you anything. He's a gracious man."

"Not if Aidan dies."

"I'm going to ensure that doesn't happen. Now, be strong. I shall return as soon as I can."

Connor disappeared into the woods at a lope. As he ran, he thought. *Ducan will forgive Seamus, but what about me? Does he know what I have endured? Of Quazel changing me back and forth and forcing me to make more headache powders for her? The beatings? And still I never mentioned Aidan.*

Aidan, Colin, and Mary Kate walked near the edge of the woods following the contour of the beach. As they neared the path to the cave, Mary Kate grabbed Colin's arm.

"What is that?" she asked softly.

Aidan gasped, "Satin!"

"No," said Mary Kate, "it canna be Satin, but whoever 'tis needs our help."

The three young people knelt beside the wounded panther. Mary Kate touched him gently and mused, "What happened to him?" Then, with conviction she added, "Colin, Aidan, we have to take him to the grotto. He is the reason we had to stay."

The three Samaritans lifted the unconscious creature and carried him to the hidden grotto.

Once there, Mary Kate poured a cup of water. By mere instinct, the nearly dead warrior lapped the lifesaving liquid. Then, he fell back, oblivious to where he was or who was with him.

Mary Kate began to tenderly wash his wounds with clean cool water. She whispered, "Poor thing."

Connor found the cat contingency that had stayed behind. He thought if Duncan were on the island, he would be with the cats. Interestingly, he had found a piece of Elizabeth's white garment caught in a bush as he ran.

"Perfect," Connor thought aloud. He carried the piece of white cloth in his teeth as he approached the cats.

A mammoth sandy and tawny lion stepped in front of the hyena. He called over his shoulder, "Behold. One of Quazel's little weasels has come to surrender."

Trembling, Connor found his voice, "I am *not* a weasel. I'm Dr. Connor Donohue. I've been Quazel's slave all these years. I've come to find Duncan O'Rourke. I must speak with him. Under great duress, he has been betrayed. I must warn him. His life and the life of the Promised One are in grave danger."

"So believable," scoffed the lion. He raised his paw to maul Connor.

Connor cowered and thought, *at least I die free.*

A gruff voice boomed, "Lieutenant, what are you doing?" Behind the young lion, stood an older lion with a black mane and a scar across his left eye.

The lieutenant lowered his paw. "Captain O'Leary, I was just about to rid Draconis of some of Quazel's scum."

"Lieutenant, that man carries a white flag. You will not harm him." The captain turned to the cowering hyena. "I'm Captain Patrick O'Leary. Are you in truth surrendering?"

"Escaping," corrected Connor. "Patrick, is that truly you? I'm Connor Donohue."

"Doc?"

"Aye. I must speak with Duncan. Quazel knows where the Promised One has been hiding. She has sent an assassin squad after him."

"Duncan isn't here now. He has flown to Draconis to take back the last troops that are returning. Connor, I don't know where the grotto is. I just took over as captain here. Our first captain knew its location, but he was killed in the last raid Duncan ran. Duncan didn't tell me where the grotto is located yet. Do Quazel's assassins know where 'tis?"

"Not the exact location. Only that 'tis in the center of the island."

"Who makes up the assassin squad?"

"Four apes. Their leader is called Paco. He is white, but he has so much missing hair that he looks pink. There was a black gorilla, a baboon, and an orangutan."

"Good work, Connor." Patrick turned back to his troops.

"Thomas, Sheila, Derrick, Travis," he barked at four cheetahs. They were immediately at attention. "You heard. Go!"

The cheetahs raced into the woods.

Patrick turned back to Connor. "Is there anything else?"

"Aye. A panther. Quazel tortured him mercilessly. She has left him to die on the beach. I can show you where he is."

"Is he the one who ratted?"

"Oh, I beg, don't blame him. He endured days of constant torture. He's badly hurt. When you see him, you'll understand. Pray help him. Patrick, 'tis young Seamus."

Patrick bobbed his head in a nod. "Sandra, George, Tyler, go with Connor. Bring our fallen comrade back to camp."

A few minutes after Seamus's rescuers disappeared into the woods, Sandra, George, and Tyler, along with Connor, ran onto the beach.

"Where is he?" asked George.

"He was right there," Connor defended. "Look. There's blood."

George went to the spot where Seamus had lain. "There was definitely someone here. Big and obviously wounded. Look at this. These are human footprints. Sandra, see if the dogs have any hounds here. Mayhap we can track our victim and take our human friends into safety.

"Dr. Donohue, run back to the cat encampment. Tell Captain O'Leary what we're doing. Lord Duncan should be back very soon. Wait for him. Give him your report."

32
No Greater Love

In the grotto, Mary Kate continued to care for the unknown victim.

"How is he?" asked Aidan. "'Tis it not amazing how much he looks like Satin?"

"I don't think he is quite as big," Mary Kate commented. "Nevertheless, he does make a good twin. Lads, I need medicine from the ship to care for him properly."

Colin came to his wife's side. "'Tis getting late. When Satin and Draco get here, we shall take him to the ship. Ya can dress his wounds on the trip to Draconis. I doona think we shall add much weight to the ship. Two dragons can still tow us."

"'Tis a good, idea," concurred Aidan.

Colin stood. "I hear footsteps. Satin must be back." He started to the entrance.

"No, Colin!" screamed Mary Kate.

In a flash, four apes barged through the hidden opening with swords flailing. The first strike caught Colin across the chest. He fell back, stunned; but he was wearing his dragon-scale breastplate. He lay against the wall, gasping for air. The blow had cracked a rib.

Aidan agilely combatted four apes. "Colin, I could use some help here. 'Tis four against one. I'm good, but not that good." Aidan glanced toward his friend.

Colin struggled to stand. He looked toward Mary Kate, who was crouched near the sleeping panther. His glance drew attention to her position. In horror he saw the big black gorilla go for Mary Kate. Colin coughed, "No!"

Mary Kate screamed and ran toward the water. The gorilla went after her. He lunged toward her. Mary Kate ducked and went under the arm of the gorilla. Blood spurted. Colin was horrified, shocked, and relieved all in one brief moment. The gorilla fell in a heap. Mary Kate's single thrust with her dagger had hit its mark.

The orangutan turned to Colin. Colin pulled his sword. He blocked the orangutan's strike. *Lord, I never knew that broken ribs hurt so much.* He winced.

Seamus groaned and stirred. Mary Kate went to him. Colin fought with the orangutan. The creature was a masterful swordsman. Aidan had to battle Paco and the baboon. Finally, with a spin, Aidan hit his target. Paco's companion fell. Aidan shouted, "I like these odds better."

"Me too," agreed Colin. The orangutan countered Colin's thrust with a high blow. The flat side of the blade caught Colin across the face. Colin hit the wall headfirst. He lost consciousness. Blood seeped from the back of his head. The orangutan poised to strike a fatal blow.

"No, you shall not!" Mary Kate hollered as she jumped onto the orangutan's back. She pulled her dagger and jabbed it into the animal's neck repeatedly. He dropped his sword and threw the small woman into the wall. He fell dead. For Mary Kate, everything went black.

The shadows gathered as Duncan, Draco, Char, and Brindle landed at the cat stronghold. Before Duncan could dismount, Patrick and Connor met him. The magnitude of the moment precluded cordial greetings. The captain tried to tell Connor he was speaking to King Satin, but her poured out his story in breathless fear, knowing the two were one and the same.

"Draco, take me to the grotto now," ordered Duncan.

Draco flew fast and furious. "Duncan, I can't go in there with you. I won't fit."

"Come up through the lagoon," suggested Duncan.

"I shall be there as fast as I can," affirmed Draco.

Inside, Paco managed to knock Aidan's sword to the ground. The ape brought his sword across Aidan's shoulder, yet the young man put a foot in the creature's mid-section. "I will not go down without a fight, you repugnant, grotesque beast."

Paco's next strike cracked Aidan's breastplate and ribs. Paco raised his sword with the intent of decapitation.

As Paco swung his blade, a charcoal streak pushed Aidan with great force, sending him sprawling. The creature's blade cut the entire length of the black blur.

Duncan fell with a thud. Blood flowed freely from his shoulder and side.

Dazed, Mary Kate crawled to the felled king. He lay still, fighting for life. He gasped, "Aidan."

"I'm coming, King Satin." Aidan crawled to the side of the panther.

Paco laughed, "I have done it! My reward will be great!" He came toward Satin to finish the job. *The humans are too weak to help,* he thought. *I shall finish them in a moment.*

Colin regained consciousness. Through blurred vision, he took in the scene. He saw Satin fly through the air and take the blow meant for Aidan. He saw Aidan and Mary Kate kneeling by the downed giant. He inched to join his wife and his friend. "No," groaned Colin.

Mary Kate looked up at Paco. She held up her hand as if to stop the intended blow. Paco put on his hideous smile. "Do you in truth think that tiny paw can stop me?"

"Stay away from him, you repulsive vermin," Mary Kate shouted, all melodic lilt gone from her voice. Even as the words left her lips, a blue flash shot from her hand, striking Paco in the center of his chest, crashing him into the wall behind him. He clutched his chest in disbelief and stared at the small, child-like woman. Then, he knew no more.

Draco's head popped up from the water. He took in the horrendous sight. He howled, "No! No! No!"

Mary Kate cried great teardrops. Satin gasped again, "Aidan."

"I'm here, Satin." Aidan touched the panther's head.

Satin continued, struggling to say each word, "Have...tell...Love you."

The panther closed his eyes and took a sharp, jagged breath. He opened his eyes again and saw Aidan with his head buried on his knees, weeping. "This is my fault, all my fault."

Mary Kate stroked the cat's head. She gasped as she saw one of the yellow eye lenses slip off to reveal vivid emerald eyes.

"Aidan," she said, "look."

Aidan took in the face of the stately beast. His face drained of all color as the truth slapped him.

Duncan struggled to be heard. "Like father; like son."

Aidan bent over the fallen hero. He brushed away the other fake eye. His tears had washed his own blue lenses to the ground. He looked eye-to-eye with his father.

Duncan took another ragged breath. "Aidan, my son." His words could hardly be heard. "Heart of my heart, blood of my blood, life of my life, I love you with all my being."

"No," moaned Aidan. "Daddy, you have to shout it from the mountain top. I pray thee don't die. Don't leave me now. I need you. I love you."

Aidan laid his face on the face of the dying panther. His tears flooded the soft satiny face. The panther's body shook as if in the throes of death. He loosed one long yowl.

Suddenly, before them lay, not an animal, but a wonderfully handsome man with beautiful green eyes, raven black hair with a few streaks of gray at his temples, and perfectly formed muscles.

"Aidan," Duncan whispered. "To hold you with human arms is more than I ever dreamed."

Aidan lifted his father to him. Duncan put his uninjured arm around Aidan's neck. He ran his fingers through his son's golden curls. The hand dropped, lifeless, by his side. His green eyes stared in cold, glassy emptiness.

"No, Daddy. I'm sorry. I'm so sorry," sobbed the grieving son. He pulled Duncan tighter in his arms.

Mary Kate touched Aidan gently. "Aidan, put him down," she commanded softly through her own tears.

Why he obeyed, he did not know; but Aidan laid Duncan down. Mary Kate held Aidan briefly and whispered, "Everything will be all right. You shall see."

Colin put his hand on Aidan's shoulder. Aidan reached up and clasped Colin's fingers.

Seamus had roused enough to witness the last several minutes even as Danielle had popped up beside Draco.

Mary Kate smiled. She lay over the dead man and spoke in a voice full of power. "Oh, God, Your prophet foretold of three men from far away putting an end to the reign of terror from the evil one. Lord, Your words are never wrong. You brought Aidan here at this moment to restore Duncan to manhood, but a dead man cannot fight evil.

"I know You already gave us one miracle with Eunice. In Your infinite wisdom and grace I beg You to grant us another miracle. Give us back father, son, husband, friend, and champion. Give Duncan back to us."

As Mary Kate finished her words, the room filled with a soft blue glow. Everything grew perfectly still. Even the water stopped lapping the shore.

All was silence.

33
To Be Forgiven

Everyone in the grotto held their breath. Duncan's eyes fluttered shut then open. He took a sharp breath.

Aidan stammered, "Oh, God, thanks be unto You."

Duncan still had a gaping gash in his side and shoulder, but he was alive.

"Aidan, give me your shirt. You, too, Colin," Mary Kate demanded. The boys ripped off their shirts. Mary Kate packed Duncan's side and shoulder with the material. She tore her own skirt and wrapped Duncan's torso and shoulder tightly with the strips of cloth.

As she tended Duncan's injuries, three hounds, four cheetahs, a leopard, and two lions charged through the opening to the grotto. They saw three dead humans, all grotesquely disfigured, an unconscious pinkish ape, a severely wounded panther, four humans, a dolphin, and a dragon.

The three young people shielded Duncan's nakedness from curious eyes. Aidan took charge of the situation. "Lord Duncan's faithful troops, I am Aidan O'Rourke, Duncan's son. My father has been seriously wounded. Draco, meet us at the entrance to the grotto." Aidan held his side as he spoke. "My friends and I are injured as well. We need help getting our wounded out of here, so Draco can carry us to *The Privileged Character* and medical supplies. Help us get these two through the entrance."

George ventured, "Are you the Promised One? Where are King Satin and Lord Duncan?"

"Here lies Lord Duncan." He swept his hand toward his father. "His humanity has been restored even as Quazel's own curse foretold."

Aidan had to think quickly. *These people believe they have a king.* It hit him how much the injured panther looked like Satin. Mary Kate had even said he made a good twin. Indicating the panther, Aidan said, "There is King Satin. He battled Quazel herself, but she managed to escape. Now, help me get them out of here."

Aidan had no idea how much truth he told.

Outside the entrance, Aidan hollered, "Char, I need you!"

The glossy black dragon, without explanation, took off. Brindle followed just in case he was needed, too.

Two minutes later Char landed beside his new friend. Aidan ordered, "Char, fly as fast as you can to Draconis. Bring Diggory and Elizabeth to *The Privileged Character*. I need human hands to sail my ship."

Char started to question, "What about..."

"Plans have changed. We need to be *on* the ship."

"What can I do?" asked Brindle.

Realizing the need for diplomacy and sensing a tad of jealousy, Aidan said, "I need you to stay with Captain O'Leary and the troops in case they need to fly quickly. Understood?"

"Aye, sir." He took off back to Captain O'Leary.

Draco landed. He shook like a dog and showered all the bystanders with water. He leaned over his best friend now shrouded in makeshift bandages. He still could hardly believe what he had witnessed. He turned questioning eyes to the miracle worker. "Mary Kate, will he survive?"

"Aye, Draco. God did not give him back just to take him away. He could still get very sick. 'Tis why I need to get him to the ship. We have medicine there to help him and the others, too. Draco, do you know who he is?" Mary Kate asked, pointing.

"Aye, I shall tell you on the way to the ship."

They loaded the wounded carefully onto Draco. He flew them quickly to *The Privileged Character*. He told Seamus's story as he flew. Draco shared with them all about the Duncan and Satin deception. He explained how Seamus had helped all those years to keep Duncan safe. He told them what Connor had said Quazel had done to the creature and how she had finally broken him.

Draco was angry with Seamus. "He should have died before he spoke a word about Duncan."

Aidan spoke kindly. "Draco, do not be harsh on Seamus. Look at him. How much do you think he endured? We all have a breaking point. Some can stand more than others. Draco, from the look of him, I would say he withstood more than most. If you hate Seamus so much, what must you feel about me?"

"What do you mean, Aidan? You're Duncan's son. I love you."

"Draco, if I had left with the last troop transport, none of this would have happened."

Draco said, "That is true, and Duncan would still be a panther."

"As you say, Draco. If Seamus had not broken, my father would still be a panther, and Seamus would probably be dead. Draco, who are we to question *how* God gives our spirits' desires? I, for one, am grateful to have my father. Moreover, I'm content to be God's useful servant. I'm learning that more and more each day I spend with Mary Kate."

"All right, Aidan, I shall give Seamus the benefit of a doubt, but, prithee, do *not* ask me to forgive Quazel."

"No, Draco. We must forgive our fellow man, but evil must be defeated."

By the time they reached the ship, Draco's heart had softened considerably toward Seamus.

Once to the ship, he hovered low and against the vessel. Mary Kate slid down Draco's wing like a giant slide. Colin slid down next. Aidan lowered first Duncan and then Seamus. Finally, Aidan slid down.

"Draco, what will you do?" asked Aidan.

"I shall stay with Duncan."

"How?"

"I shall hover a while, and then I shall float beside you."

Mary Kate set to work patching the wounded. She set up a triage, tending the most seriously injured first. Duncan had to be treated immediately. Mary Kate called Colin and Aidan, "I know you two are in pain, but I cannot do this alone. I wish Momma were here."

A voice said, "Who said that wishes never come true?" It was Elizabeth.

"Momma!"

"Papa and I are here. Char must be the fastest dragon on Earth." She looked at the two disheveled boys and considered the other man. "Is this Duncan?"

"Aye, Momma."

Elizabeth quickly appraised the situation and said, "I've done lots of stitching, Mary Kate. You take care of these two while I tend Duncan."

Elizabeth cleaned and closed Duncan's gaping wound with needle and thread and got him to swallow a few drops of tea made from cinchona bark and meadowsweet oil. He slept soundly.

Meanwhile, Mary Kate stitched Colin's head and wrapped both Colin's and Aidan's ribs. She commanded, "You two, get some sleep."

Aidan argued, "I have to stay with my father."

"Then sleep beside him, but get some rest. You need to be strong for him. You can't do that if you're exhausted." Mary Kate pointed a finger at him. "I mean it."

Knowing Aidan's stubborn streak, Mary Kate made some onion soup and slipped him a sleeping powder.

A few minutes after they had eaten a bowl of soup, Colin watched his friend pass out. Shocked, Colin said, "Mary Kate, how could ya?"

She looked at him and said assertively, "You can both be angry tomorrow. I'm surprised yours is taking so long."

"Ya did *not*!"

Mary Kate kissed Colin softly on his bruised lips. "I did. Now go to bed before I have to drag you to our cabin. I love you, Colin Fitzpatrick. You can scream at me tomorrow."

Colin began to feel the effects of the drug. He staggered to bed, mumbling, "Ya sound different, me love."

"Papa," Mary Kate called.

Diggory came running with fear in his eyes. "Relax, Papa. I only need you to help me get Aidan to bed. I must confess I sneaked a little sleeping powder into his soup. Let's put him with Duncan. I don't want him to be *too* angry tomorrow."

Diggory nodded and smiled. They carried Aidan to be next to his father.

Mary Kate returned to the sick bay she had created. Elizabeth was softly stroking Seamus's head and feeding him some soup.

"Well," Mary Kate said softly, "how is our patient?"

"Much better," Seamus offered hoarsely.

Mary Kate took the creature's face in her hands. "Seamus, you have some badly infected welts and your feet are like raw meat. You're running a high fever. We need to lance and drain the infected areas or gangrene could set in. I can give you some cinchona bark tea for the fever and meadowsweet oil to help the pain, but the lancing will hurt."

"Do you have any whiskey?" Seamus laughed weakly and was overcome by a fit of coughing. When he stopped coughing, he mumbled, "It can't hurt half as badly as the cause. Do what you need to do, sweet lady."

"You're very brave. I need to get a scalpel and sulfur. Momma, give Seamus a couple of shots from Papa's secret bottle."

Elizabeth poured some of Diggory's secret whiskey into a bowl and gave it to Seamus.

"I never drank any of this stuff before," whispered the panther.

"Drink it fast. It tastes disgusting."

Elizabeth followed Mary Kate to where she was boiling the surgical instruments. "I'm worried about that cough. I'm sure he has pneumonia."

"Me too, Momma. After we lance the festers, let's put a camphor poultice on his chest and get some mint and eucalyptus vapors boiling. Three doses of cinchona bark tea a day should help the fever."

"Excellent prescriptions, Mary Kate," praised Elizabeth.

"Ahoy, aboard ship," a woman's voice called.

"Momma, get the supplies ready. I shall see who 'tis."

Mary Kate went to the rail. "Danielle, is that you?"

"Aye. Draco has explained to me about the charade between Seamus and Duncan—the King Satin conspiracy. I *cannot* believe Seamus did *not* even trust *me* with the secret." Her last statement came out shrill and she shook back and forth. "Nonetheless, I just wanted to ask you to tell Seamus that I haven't forgotten him, and I look forward to the day we can see each other with human eyes. Mary Kate, he needs a reason to live. I know him. He's overwrought with guilt about Duncan. Tell him, well…"

"Danielle, do you want me to tell Seamus you love him?"

"Aye. I do."

"'Tis done."

"Many thanks, Mary Kate." Danielle swam away, but stayed near the vessel.

Mary Kate went back to perform minor surgery on Seamus. As she washed her hands, she said, "Seamus, Danielle was outside. She wants me to tell you that she loves you."

"How could she still love someone as vile as I?"

Mary Kate began to lance Seamus's wounds. He winced with each incision. Elizabeth washed the incisions and put in sulfur. As Mary Kate worked, she talked to Seamus. "Danielle still loves you because that is what love does."

"In truth?" said Seamus skeptically.

"Aye, Seamus. Love of all kinds: love between a man and a woman, love in a family, even love between friends."

"Even a friend who has been betrayed?"

"Aye, Seamus. *'Charity suffereth long, and is kind; charity envieth not; charity vaunteth not itself, is not puffed up, doth not behave itself unseemly, seeketh not her own, is not easily provoked, thinketh no evil; rejoiceth not in iniquity, but rejoiceth in the truth; beareth all things, believeth all things, hopeth all things, endureth all things. Charity never faileth.'* Charity is also called love. This is what God's Holy Scripture tells us."

"Do you truly think Duncan can forgive me?"

"Aye, Seamus. You only need ask. Remember this: Aidan doesn't think you sinned against Duncan. Even Draco understands your circumstances. Duncan will forgive you and love you as he always has.

"Now, I'm going to put on a camphor poultice and boil some mint and eucalyptus. Momma and I are afraid you might have contracted pneumonia. Drink this. It contains a sleeping powder and cinchona bark. I want you to rest. Think about Duncan tomorrow."

Mary Kate and Elizabeth left Seamus to sleep. Elizabeth said, "And now you, my dear girl, must rest, too."

Mary Kate looked at Elizabeth, "Oh, Momma!" She fell into Elizabeth's arms and wept tears of relief, weariness, and guilt. "Momma, I almost lost Colin today. I killed two people today. I took two lives."

"No, baby. You defended life. That's not murder. Mary Kate, listen to your own words. What did you say to Seamus about love? Who loves more perfectly than God? Tell Him your heart, and let Him heal your spirit.

"Now, to bed." Elizabeth jutted her chin toward the cabin where Colin slept. "Take one of your own sleeping powders. Those are Momma's orders."

Meanwhile back in the grotto, Paco came to his senses. He saw three graves and knew those were his accomplices. Everyone else was gone. In the cover of the shadows on the beach, Paco uncovered a small canoe. He paddled away to anywhere except where he was. He wanted to escape to one of the small deserted islands for he knew there would be no forgiveness from Quazel for his failure. As great as he had thought his reward would have been, he knew his punishment would be ten times greater. He disappeared into the rising mists.

The next day dawned cold and wet. For the first time since they had come to Draconis, the wayfarers donned heavy cloaks.

Diggory commented, "I have never seen it loike this. Mayhap the weather is reacting to the prevailing temperament of the people. A few smiles aboard ship might bring oot the sun."

Elizabeth looked narrowly at her spouse.

"I shall leave it alone, Lizzie," he backtracked as the two of them breakfasted alone.

Then Diggory went back to the helm, and *Dr. Elizabeth* made rounds. She started with Mary Kate and Colin. With a breakfast tray in hand, she knocked at the cabin door. "Come in," said Mary Kate sweetly.

Elizabeth brought in a sparse breakfast of sea biscuits smothered in honey. "You two look much better."

Mary Kate was dressed and said she was ready to go with Elizabeth. Colin refused to get out of bed.

Elizabeth said, "'Tis the best place for you. You'd be useless with those cracked ribs and head anyway." She smiled at her son-in-law as she and Mary Kate went to check on Seamus. The room smelled of mint, camphor, and eucalyptus. Seamus tried to stand when the ladies came in.

"Be still," scolded Mary Kate. "Chivalry is not necessary at this time. We've brought you some breakfast. I hope pickled herring will meet with your approval. We're having to make do until we get to Draconis."

"Pickled herring sounds great." Seamus coughed. Both Mary Kate and Elizabeth listened to Seamus's chest.

"Will I make it, doctors?" Seamus asked.

"Do you want to?" Mary Kate quizzed.

Seamus opened his eye wide. "Aye, Mary Kate, I do. I want to live very much."

"In that case, I think with a few more days of rest and some food and water you will recuperate nicely. You'll have a few battle scars, but you'll live, my friend."

"About those scars," said Seamus. "Do you think Danielle will find an eye patch appealing?"

Mary Kate teased the quiet man. "If you're wearing it, she'll love it."

Seamus attempted a chuckle. "Oh, don't make me laugh. It hurts."

Mary Kate caressed the panther's head. "We shall leave you to your breakfast now."

The two women clasped hands as they approached Aidan's cabin. Mary Kate worried about how Aidan would react to her having drugged him.

She knocked softly on the door. There was no answer.

"Peradventure they're still asleep," Mary Kate surmised.

"Go in. This tray is cumbersome." Elizabeth was carrying a breakfast tray.

Mary Kate opened the door. Aidan sat in Caitlin's rocking chair, which he had pulled near the bed. His head lay on the pillow near Duncan, and his right hand rested on top of Duncan's hair. His left hand lay on top of his father's hand. He was sound asleep.

Mary Kate sighed. "Well, he obviously woke up at some point last night. Papa and I left him in the bed."

Elizabeth set the tray on Aidan's chest of drawers while Mary Kate gently roused the man.

"Aidan, wake up. Momma and I brought you something to eat."

"I'm not hungry," Aidan replied, still half asleep.

"You must eat. Remember what we talked about last night," argued Mary Kate.

Aidan woke completely. "Aye. I don't recall agreeing to take something to help me sleep. You slipped me a sleeping powder. You're as sneaky as Caitlin."

"Sneakier. I gave one to Colin, too."

Aidan looked at Mary Kate's innocent face. "You were right. I was exhausted. Mary Kate, many thanks for yesterday. Is that what happened with Eunice?"

"Aye."

"'Twas amazing."

"What happened?" Elizabeth demanded to know.

Aidan looked from mother to daughter. "You didn't tell her?"

Mary Kate shook her head. "Duncan died yesterday, Momma. I don't want to talk about it. It takes too much energy. Aidan, prithee, don't spread the news of what happened. God planned yesterday. It was His gift, but if everyone knew, they would expect me to pray over anyone who dies. Two miracles in one lifetime is a lot. Nobody, other than the people on this ship, Draco, and Danielle, knows what happened. It has to stay that way."

"Agreed. I shall issue that order before we leave the ship. Now, to change the subject." He nodded toward Duncan. "When will he wake up?"

In answer to Aidan's question, Duncan moved, groaned, and opened his eyes.

Aidan whispered, "Daddy."

For a moment Duncan was unsure of where he was. His eyes darted nervously around the room. He saw Elizabeth and started.

Aidan caressed Duncan's brow. "'Tis all right, Daddy. You're safe. I'm right here."

Duncan closed his eyes and tried to remember what had happened. He tried to sit up but fell back in excruciating pain.

Elizabeth sprang to his side. "We need to put a clean dressing on his wound. Aidan, get the supplies from the basket on the dressing table."

Aidan obeyed. As Elizabeth touched Duncan's side, he caught her hand. "You're warm," Duncan said in surprise, as if he had expected Elizabeth to be cold.

Elizabeth took Duncan's hand gently. "Duncan, listen to my voice. Focus on my face. Think. Do you know where you are?"

Duncan looked around the room. "Captain's quarters on *The Sea Bird*."

Elizabeth motioned for Aidan to come to her side. "Duncan, who is this man?"

"I don't know." He closed his eyes again.

Aidan's eyes filled with tears, and his voice shook when he said, "Lizzie?"

"'Tis all right, baby boy," she comforted. "Remember the trauma Duncan has suffered."

Mary Kate touched Duncan's hand. He opened his eyes. "I know you. You're my angel. You were glowing. I was floating. I saw you." He looked at Aidan. "You were there, too." Duncan closed his eyes. He was asleep.

Aidan questioned Elizabeth as she put clean dressings on Duncan's wounds, "Lizzie, will he remember?"

"Aye. He just needs to rest. You, young man, eat some breakfast. Stay with your father. If he wakes, let him talk. Don't push. If he asks you something, answer honestly. The memories will come in time."

Aidan toyed with his breakfast. He had very little appetite. He sat in the rocking chair and prayed silently as he watched Duncan sleep. He dozed and started awake when Mary Kate brought him butter and honey on fresh-baked bread, one of his favorite snacks. He set it to the side.

"Aidan," scolded Mary Kate.

"I know. I have to eat to keep up my strength. Mary Kate, what if he does not remember me? Did I find him only to have him so briefly?"

"Aidan, he'll remember. He was disoriented earlier. You must remember that his spirit left his body for a time. Eunice was confused, too, but she has recovered completely. Give it some time."

"You know I lack patience," Aidan confessed.

"Aidan, that's not entirely true. You want things to happen quickly, yet you persevere. That is an admirable quality."

"You're just trying to make me feel better. That's what you do."

"Nay. According to Duncan, I'm a prophetess. I speak words of truth. Now, a word of truth"—She pointed sharply at the tray—"eat something before I tie you up and force feed you."

"You would try." Aidan started to laugh. "Oh, that hurts."

"No, I shan't try. I shall do it, if I must." Mary Kate hugged Aidan carefully so as not to hurt his fractured ribs. Then, she left him to sit with his father.

Aidan forced himself to eat. He surprised himself when he finished the entire meal. He leaned back in the rocking chair and daydreamed of Caitlin. He fell asleep and slept fitfully as Caitlin changed to Mary Kate and back again in his dreams.

Aidan roused from his slumber to a voice calling his name. Duncan was awake. "Aidan," he said tenderly.

Aidan leaned forward and took his father's hand, "Daddy, what do you want?"

"Nothing. I just wanted to make sure I wasn't dreaming."

"No, Daddy, this is real,"

Duncan lifted his hand. "I'm human." He laughed. "Quazel, you're an idiot. Whom could I love without bound more than my son?" He looked at Aidan. "How I look forward to driving a stake through that monster's heart."

"Daddy, I think that might be my job."

Duncan was taken off guard, but true to form, his quick wit kicked in. "I shall hold it while you hammer."

"That is a plan." Aidan kissed his father's hand and held it to his cheek. "Daddy, I'm so sorry I disobeyed you. If I had gone with you on that transport, you would never have been hurt. I beg you, forgive me."

Duncan played with Aidan's curls. "You silly boy. There is nothing to forgive. If you had come on the transport, I would not be human again. This was part of our destiny."

"Why did you not tell me who you were?"

"Foolishness. I thought you would be safer if you didn't know. Father tried to tell me; Diggory tried to tell me; even Lightning tried to tell me. I was wrong. I'm the one who needs to be forgiven. I'm sorry I didn't have enough faith in you. I underestimated you. Can you forgive me?"

"Oh, aye. I know now parents do what they think is best for their children. Sometimes we make mistakes, but love doesn't change."

"Gramercy, Aidan. I cannot believe I'm holding my son. 'Tis still too good to be real."

"'Tis real, Daddy. We're together."

They sat and talked until Duncan fell asleep.

The morning dawned bright, brisk, and blustery. The sails picked up the wind, and the ship flew along toward safe harbor. The weary warriors' spirits were high. Duncan sat up cautiously and ate the cracked barley mush with honey and raisins Elizabeth brought him. By nightfall, Draconis appeared as a shadow on the horizon.

The next day was sunny, but calmer and warmer. Duncan asked to go on deck so that he could feel the warmth of the sun on his skin. Dressed in Aidan's loose pants, Duncan leaned heavily on Diggory and went on deck. He felt the sun on his face, as he had not done in twenty years. He leaned on the rail and absorbed the ocean spray and breathed the salty air. He saw Draconis looming ever closer and remembered the first time he had seen the gorgeous greenness from this same spot. Diggory brought Caitlin's rocking chair on deck, and Duncan relaxed to enjoy a day of glorious beauty. Draco popped over the ship to see for himself that Duncan was recovering. No words needed to be spoken between them.

Seamus was in the cabin Mary Kate had prepared for him. Finally, he was able to walk tentatively on his now clawless and bandaged feet. Mary Kate brought him some boiled venison jerky. He ate with relish.

"You're getting much stronger," said Mary Kate happily.

"I feel stronger. Sweet Mary Kate, do you think I might be able to go on deck today, perchance, to speak to Danielle?"

"I think we can manage that."

Seamus hobbled beside Mary Kate onto the deck of *The Privileged Character*. He put his front paws on the rail of the ship and shook unsteadily. Mary Kate placed a sure arm around his shoulders. "Gramercy," the great cat whispered, embarrassed by his remaining weakness.

Mary Kate smiled softly. Then, she called, "Danielle, come up. I have a surprise for you."

Danielle popped up. She saw Seamus leaning on the rail. Mary Kate backed away to give them a moment alone.

Seamus shyly said, "Danny, I just wanted to tell you that I...I love you. Danny, I know someday we'll be together as humans. Prithee, hold on to that belief. Give your heart to no one else."

"How can I give away something that I no longer own? How can I give my heart to anyone else when you already have it?" Danielle skimmed across the water in her little dance and swam away, but not very far.

Mary Kate helped the tiring giant from the rail. He told her, "I used to come down to the beach and lie in the sun. That's where I met Danielle. She would swim into the shallow waters. Sometimes we would talk for hours. Do you think I could bask in the sun for a while? Just knowing Danielle is swimming nearby gives me renewed energy."

"Of course. Let's go to the other side of the ship where the sun is stronger."

As they came around the stern, Seamus saw Duncan resting in the chair. He took a step backward. "I can't do this," he said.

"Aye, you can. You must," Mary Kate encouraged him.

Duncan heard the voices. He opened one eye. He smiled to himself and spoke, "Seamus! Get over here! You have some explaining to do."

Mary Kate touched the cat's head. "'Tis all right, Seamus. Go on." She left the two friends alone.

Seamus limped to Duncan's chair.

Duncan spoke gruffly, "Well, explain yourself."

Seamus trembled. He wanted to run away. He stammered, "Duncan, I...How can I explain?" Seamus collapsed at Duncan's feet. The strain from his exertion and the mental torment he felt rendered him helpless.

Duncan saw the broken-heartedness of his protégé. To see the sadness in the eye of one so young, of one who was like another son to him, cut him to the quick. Duncan leaned forward laboriously. He put his hand under the chin of the enormous ebony panther and raised his face so that they could look each other in the eye.

"Seamus O'Donnell, you know I love you as I would a son. You have always been my friend and confidant. You are a wonderful person, wise and warm. Do you truly think I could do anything other than to understand what happened to you and to forgive you and to love you as always? Do you have so little faith in our friendship?"

Seamus tried to put his chin down, but Duncan held it firmly in his hand. Seamus's voice quivered. "Duncan, I'm so ashamed of my cowardice, my lack of perseverance. I'm unworthy to be called your friend. I got you killed."

Duncan was indignant. "Cowardice! Is that what Quazel told you? Has she stopped coaxing people into submission by offering the illusion of their greatest desires? Is she now playing on our greatest fears and trying to frighten or beat us into submission? So that is her new strategy."

Duncan's voice softened. "You are no *coward*, Seamus O'Donnell. You are one of the bravest and best men I know. Let go of your guilt. You must be even stronger now, for you will be King Satin, Ruler of Draconis, all by yourself. The people of Draconis need you. I will be your mentor and adviser; and Alexander, Aidan, and I will be your defenders and avengers. Mary Kate, Colin, Diggory, Elizabeth, and Caitlin will be your stalwart companions. Danielle will never leave you. Side by side we will free Draconis. Seamus O'Donnell, hold your head high. 'Tis your time to shine. You must be a king."

Seamus replied humbly, "To be forgiven is all I had hoped."

Part Three

Witch Hunt

34
A New Home

The *Privileged Character* glided into the smooth waters of the natural harbor on Draconis. Alexander, Caitlin, and Priscilla waited anxiously on shore. Aidan stood on deck wearing loose white pants and tight bandages around his ribs. He watched the graceful movement of the vivid orange and black stripes as the majestic tigress, who was his beloved Caitlin, walked along the shore following the ship to a halt. His deepest desire was to bury his face in her hair and let the world melt into nothingness. He closed his eyes and imagined his wife in his arms. Aidan shook his head hard as Caitlin's face became Mary Kate's. "This is preposterous," he muttered to himself. He kept his eyes open and thought of Caitlin.

Alas, reality called as Diggory dropped anchor and the resounding splash brought Aidan from his dream state. He realized his family did not yet know about Duncan's restoration. Duncan was human, his mother was still a lovable white cat, and his wife remained a tigress. With one down, and an entire land to go, the task before him seemed daunting.

Draco positioned himself to be a crosswalk from the ship to the shore. Aidan was tempted to climb onto Draco and fly directly to the mountains. Char could come and get the three on shore. Leaning on Diggory's extra cane, Duncan came to Aidan's side. He put his hand on his son's shoulder. "Are you thinking about running away?"

Aidan gazed at his father. "The thought had crossed my mind. 'Tis hard to look at Caitlin and not be able to do what is natural and right. How are you going to cope with Mam and you?"

"I suppose things in truth have not changed much, have they? We still can't be with the ones we love the way that we want, but 'twill not last forever."

"How have you held onto that belief all these years, Daddy?"

"To do otherwise would mean madness. I would go crazy if I did not hold that hope."

The rest of the ship's passengers assembled on deck. Danielle was beside the ship. Aidan spoke, "Before we go ashore, I want to caution all of you again that what occurred with Mary Kate and Duncan, must remain on this ship for Mary Kate's sake. The only other people, who can know anything about what happened, are those three waiting for us. We are all sworn to secrecy. Now, away home."

As the passengers descended the living crosswalk, Priscilla squealed, "Duncan!" Before anyone could stop her, she raced up Draco's other wing toward the man she had not seen in twenty years. She met Duncan on Draco's back and leapt into his arms. She licked his cheek and his hair before he said, "Priscilla, your tongue is rough."

Pretending to pout, she said, "I'm a cat. What do you expect?"

Alexander looked at Caitlin. "What are we waiting for?"

The two waiting onlookers made their way up Draco's wing as well. Caitlin's first impulse was to engulf Aidan when she realized he was hurt. She began an immediate interrogation. "What happened? Are you all right?"

"Caitlin, I'm fine. 'Tis only a couple of cracked ribs. Colin is worse off than I."

Caitlin looked at her brother. "What happened to you?"

"I have broken ribs and a cracked skull," he said, turning the corners of his mouth down, as if he were truly hurt that she seemed unconcerned about him.

Meanwhile, Alexander had reached Duncan. He stared at himself twenty years earlier, except Duncan was heavier built and had less gray hair than he had had at the same age. Alexander touched his son's cheek. "How? What happened?" He gathered Duncan in his arms.

"I shall tell you all about it later, Father."

Alexander looked around for Elizabeth. He held his hand out to her. "Come here, daughter." He held one child in each arm. "Both my children together. This is more than I ever dreamt could happen. I have my family here." He looked at Caitlin and Priscilla, and then toward Isla Linda where he knew his great-granddaughter to be. "Almost all my family. There is still work to be done. Everybody, sit tight. Draco, take us home."

The next day, nobody could find Aidan. He was nowhere in the cave or near the caves. Draco prepared for a search when Declan piped up, "Unky Ayen ride Char."

Colin knelt down to be on his son's level. "Declan, did ya see Uncle Aidan ride Char this morning?"

The child nodded.

"Declan, tell Da which way he went."

Declan led Colin out the entrance of the cave. He pointed toward the desert.

Colin jumped on Draco, and Duncan pulled himself up behind Colin, grimacing the entire time.

Colin turned around. "Duncan, what do ya think ya aire doing? Ya aire in no condition to go with me."

Duncan listened to the young man's speech. *His speech patterns remain the same. He has not been changed; nor has he killed anyone.* "Don't worry about me," argued Duncan. "I'm not much worse off than you. Your mounting wasn't exactly free from grunts and groans."

"Duncan, I only have a couple of cracked ribs that hurt. Ya could tear open that wound and bleed to death."

"Colin, I shall be fine. I'm going, and there's nothing you can do to stop me."

"Oot upon it!" shouted Colin. "I see where Aidan gets his stubbornness."

"I can settle this," interjected Diggory. "Elizabeth, bring me sword." He climbed in front of Colin and said, "Draco, let us look for Aidan. As far as I am concerned, neither of these two hotheads is able to go looking for anybody. They certainly canna go without somebody who is able to move."

Duncan stared at his friend. *He still has a brogue. His change was incomplete.* The thought brought a smile to his lips. *I hope he doesn't lose it. 'Twould not be Diggory.*

Elizabeth came back with Diggory's sword and the searchers soared off. As they flew, Duncan grumbled, "What do I have to do with that boy to make him understand he cannot run off alone?"

"He's not alone," corrected Draco. "Char is with him. How many times have you and I flown off alone?"

"'Tis different," bickered Duncan.

"Why?" Draco shot back.

"Aidan is special."

"And Char is developing as much love for him as I have for you. Haven't you noticed, Duncan? Since we're on the subject of special friendships between dragons and men, Colin, an' it please you, will you consider asking Brindle to be your bonded dragon? He needs a human. Brindle is a good kid. Admittedly, he's not as bright as Char, and I'm already taken, but he'll be loyal and stand by you 'til the death." Draco looked down. "There they are. They're fine. Char is not six inches away from Aidan. Well, Colin, I'm waiting for an answer."

Colin was surprised by Draco's irritability. "Fine, Draco. I shall talk to him as soon as he gets back from Isla Linda."

"No, I shall take you to him as soon as we settle this nonsense over a grown man riding his bonded dragon. While we're there, we will do another flyover to try and spot Morgan."

Duncan was suddenly worried about the young dragon. "Draco, are you all right? You sound upset."

Draco realized how irritated he sounded. "I beg pardon. It has been a long few weeks, and I need to go to my cave and sleep all day. I might rip Aidan's head off for you, Duncan. I'm too tired for this."

Draco landed next to Char. Aidan realized he had caused some worry when he saw the rescue squad. "What are you all doing here?" he asked.

"That's what I want to ask you," said Duncan angrily.

"Daddy, calm down. Quazel isn't here unless she has learned to tunnel under the ocean. We have the island's perimeter securely guarded. I wanted to see the oasis, or at least where the oasis was located. You've shown me the rest of the island, but you never brought me here. Everybody was still asleep. Char was out and about, so we flew here." He gave a one-shoulder shrug. "I thought we would be back before anyone missed us."

"Aidan, what did I tell you about having Colin or Caitlin with you at all times?"

Aidan waved off the question. "Daddy, walk with me."

Everyone else stayed behind. It was obvious Aidan wanted to talk to Duncan privately. They walked a good distance from the others. Aidan stopped and leaned against a burned tree.

"Daddy, I'm your son, but I am *not* your little boy. I'm no longer a child. I grew up a long time ago. I beg pardon if that sounds cruel, but, Daddy, sometimes I need to be alone with my thoughts. Sometimes they weigh heavily on me. I can't even share them with Caitlin at the time. I usually talk to her sooner or later, but there are times I need to be alone.

Alackaday, you were alone on Isla Linda, miles from anyone."

"I was never alone. *Draco* was with me."

"*Char* is with me."

"Very well," Duncan relented. "We shall leave. I beg pardon, Aidan. By my troth, I'm not certain how to be a father. Stonebridge sent my father away, so I had no example. Quazel took me away from you, so I had no practice. I'm trying very hard."

Aidan embraced Duncan. "Hugs are important. I learned that from watching Colin. He has a terrific father, and I think he learned a lot," Aidan whispered during the embrace.

Duncan held on tightly. "I know why hugs are important. They feel so good." Both men laughed in spite of their injuries.

"Daddy, I don't want you to leave. I needed to think and to breathe. I would've told you my thoughts later today anyway." He ran his hand over the tree stump.

"If Draconis is to be my new home, I need to get to know the land, every inch of it, not merely the parts you think are safe. A war with Quazel won't be waged and won hiding in the caves. If I'm to find this witch, I must learn all I can about her. She is crafty. I must be craftier. One way to learn about her is to see where she lives."

Aidan breathed as deeply as his injuries would allow. "Daddy, I'm going to build a house here. I want to investigate Quazel's former home."

"Aidan, you cannot be serious," Duncan protested.

"I'm quite serious. We can't keep hiding in the mountains. Did the humans live in the mountains before Quazel came?"

"Only a few, here and there."

"The mountains belong to the dragons. Humans inhabited the rest of the island. We must start reclamation of Draconis somewhere. I think I shall start here, right in the heart of Quazel's desire."

"Aidan, this place is uninhabitable."

"Not true. Look, Daddy." Aidan showed Duncan a small palm tree. "Daddy, this place *was* a paradise. Quazel didn't create an illusion; she killed reality."

"Aidan, you're standing just about where Quazel's tent was located."

"I'faith! Then this is where I shall build my house."

Duncan was perplexed, but he trusted his son's instinct. He nodded. "I shall build one across the way. We will start a community."

"Aye!" said Aidan triumphantly.

"Duncan, prithee, may we go now? I'm tired," whined Draco.

"What is the matter with him?" asked Aidan.

"He needs a new home, too."

"What?"

Duncan explained, "I think it must be mating time. He's young, but I think he'll choose a mate early. They will have their own cave in the side of the cliff. He's growing up. It seems we may have new homes all around."

35
The Challenge

The first order of business after Aidan's visit to the decimated oasis was to find a mate for Draco. For the next several days, the dragon's temper flared; he sulked and pouted and moped; he stomped around the caves. Duncan was alarmed at the change of character. "Aidan we have to find Draco a mate. His emotions are all amok. Father told me dragons become very temperamental when 'tis mating time, but this is dangerous."

Aidan approached Char. "Be well met, friend. I need your help."

"What can I do for you?"

"Draco has come to his mating time. We need help finding him a mate. Is there a female who would be interested in Draco?"

Char roared with laughter. "Is there a female? They are all panting after him. That's part of the problem; he doesn't want to hurt anyone's feelings. 'Tis my understanding these things were arranged in the old days by the parents. Of course, we're a new generation and orphans. Alexander is the closest thing we've ever had to a parent."

"'Tis it, Char. You're brilliant. We'll arrange his mate for him, but is there one he would prefer, if he made a choice?"

"Let me see. He *cannot* have Scarlet. She's mine. I'm sorry, but that's that. I don't want to fight, but I will if I have to." The black dragon's agitation began to rival Draco's, and small wisps of smoke wafted from his nostrils.

"Calm yourself." He placed a hand on Char's sleek ebony scales. "I promise we shan't take your girl. Who was the first-born female? That might be the approach to take since Draco was the first-born male."

"A good idea, Aidan. Esmeralda was the first-born female. She's quite beautiful and intelligent. She's vivid green, much like a luna moth when she's in full flight. She would be perfect. Would you like to meet her?"

"Aye. We shall bring Daddy and Seanathair, too."

Alexander, Duncan, Mary Kate, and Aidan flew on Char to the cliff dwellings to meet Esmeralda. She was all in a dither, yet she was gracious and charming. Since Alexander had been the dragons' protector, he brought up the subject.

"Esmeralda, Draco has reached his mating time. We've come to you as the first-born female to see if you'd be willing to become Draco's mate. Remember this is a lifetime commitment. I know 'tis a little early in your life to mate, but the courtship and preparations will take a while. So, what say you?"

Esmarelda asked with hooded eyes. "Does Draco want me?"

"Esmeralda, Draco feels a great responsibility in this matter. He's afraid if he were to choose, he'd hurt a number of young ladies. Since dragon marriages were arranged in the times of old, I have, as the dragons' protector, set out to arrange this marriage. Since you're both first-born of your gender, I feel 'tis only logical you become mates."

Esmeralda was quiet for a while. She pondered her decision carefully.

Finally she spoke. "If Draco is satisfied with the arrangement and if he'll accept my cave as our home, as 'tis the only dowry I have, I'll become his mate."

"Many thanks, Esmeralda," said Alexander, and the marriage brokers left.

Back in the caves, the mate committee sat down for a discussion. "What think you?" Alexander asked the rest of the committee.

"She put a condition on the arrangement," objected Duncan.

Mary Kate spoke softly. "She is pining to become Draco's mate. She doesn't want to seem overly eager and embarrass herself if she's rejected. Her only condition is where they live. Draco has spent his life here." She waved her hand back and forth with her palm up. "If they must have their own place, hers would be logical. Gentlemen, she's perfect."

"Any more discussion?" asked Alexander. Hearing none, he said, "Very well. 'Twould seem the next step is to talk to Draco. Shall we go?"

The marriage brokers found Draco devouring a cow. Mary Kate and Aidan had never watched a dragon eat. It was not a pretty sight. Draco, with a mouthful of food, looked up at his company. He swallowed. "I'm dining. Come back later unless you want to be dessert." He ripped off another leg. The four humans looked at one another. They decided they should wait outside.

Mary Kate threatened, "I sure hope he likes Esmeralda, or I'm going to cover his next meal in sleeping powder."

After a few minutes Draco poked his head out his door. "Oh, I ask pardon. I shan't eat you. Come in."

"Draco," began Alexander, "I'm going to get directly to the point. You've been a terror these past few days. You need a mate as soon as possible. The four of us have taken it upon ourselves to arrange a marriage for you since you have no parents to do it, as in days of old. We have spoken to Esmeralda because you and she are the first-born of this salvaged generation. She has agreed if you'll have her cave as your home. What say you?"

"Esmeralda!" Draco shrieked. "She's the only one who has *not* hinted she wanted to be my mate. She rarely even speaks to me. You vouchsafe she agreed?"

Mary Kate spoke words of assurance. "Draco, she wants to be your mate, but she has a sense of decorum. She doesn't want to make a fool of herself. The question is whether you want her."

"Mary Kate, she's the only one I have ever wanted. I thought she didn't want me the way she has always ignored me. She is absolutely *perfect*. Have you ever noticed the way her scales glisten in the sunlight? Aye. Aye. Aye. I shall live in her cave. I shall find a way to shrink down into the size of a gecko and live in a box with her if that is what she wants. When can we be together?"

"Draco, calm down. I'm happy to see you excited about life again, but you're going to cause a cave-in," Alexander teased the excited young dragon.

The wizard continued, "Draco, she's younger than you. I think you should court her and build your home. You know that because you're both so young, it could be quite a while before you have an egg, and even longer before you have a little dragon of your own."

"Egg, smegg. I'm not worried about that right now. I just want Esmeralda. How did you ever think of her?"

"Char suggested it," said Aidan.

"Tell Char I'm in his debt forever."

Draco set about courting Esmeralda, and the other lady dragons had to deal with their disappointment. Draco's crisis over, Aidan turned his sights to building his home.

Aidan called his crew together, along with Alexander and Duncan. "I've decided to build a house here on

Draconis. I'm building exactly on the site where Quazel had her tent in the oasis. I propose the rest of you build homes for your families. I'd like it if you built near me, but that's your choice. I feel my building a home where Quazel so desired to live will be my first step toward reclaiming Draconis."

Duncan spoke in support of his son. "I, too, am going to build near Aidan. He was right when he said that we cannot continue to hide in the mountains. We are the only humans on Draconis right now. 'Tis our responsibility to start this reclamation process. Father, there are no more eggs for you to protect. Draco, Char, and Brindle, as the three oldest dragons, must form a council to rule their kind. We'll still be allies and friends, but we must begin life anew. Forsooth, I want you to have a home near Aidan and me. The three of us must be close together. I'll begin my house as soon as Aidan's is complete."

Diggory took Elizabeth's hand. She nodded. "We aire with ya, Aidan," said Diggory. "If we all work together, we can build our little town faster. We will build one house at a time."

Colin looked at Mary Kate as if she could read his thoughts. He did not speak at all.

Mary Kate finally spoke after a long sigh. "There will come a time, probably not in our lifetime and mayhap not in our children's lifetime, but there'll come a time when Draconis will be invisible to common men. Now and then, an exceptional man will stumble upon it, but not common men. What we begin here will be the making of a new world, a world that will live only in legend. We must do it right.

"We must be committed to staying here the rest of our lives. Even as I speak, I know that there is no reason for me to ever return to Stonebridge. The two people who had any claim on my life are gone. Only Colin and Caitlin have any draw with the past. The two of you must put your past to rest before we can build the future. Aye, Aidan, I'm willing to stay, and Caitlin has pledged her life to yours, but Colin must make a decision. Then, I must follow *his* lead."

All eyes turned toward Colin. He grew uncomfortable. "Aidan, ya know I am devoted to ya and the cause for which we came, and I will *never* leave this place without me daughter. By the same token, I do not wish to never see me folks again. This decision is too great for me alone. Give me time to think and pray and talk to Mary Kate. In the meantime, start yer house."

The men began to fell logs and plane boards. Colin often disappeared for long periods. He found himself soaring on Brindle, who had agreed to be his bonded dragon. Each time they flew, they went to Isla Linda to speak to the birds of prey who had stayed behind to watch for signs of Morgan. On this trip, Colin spoke to his friend. "Brindle, how can I ever go back? How can I leave this place? Yet, how can I never see me mother and father again? Why does this have to be so hard?"

"I might not be the brightest dragon," said Brindle, "but let me make a proposal. Why not send a hawk squadron with a map and a letter requesting your folks to come here? Draconis is going to need a doctor. If they come here, all your problems are solved."

Colin defended his friend. "Who says ya aire not bright? 'Tis a marvelous idea. Let me talk it over with Mary Kate."

The next day, Colin sent his request in the best talons he could find. He prayed fervently that his parents would accept. Either way, he knew he had to stay.

With a pile of lumber planed and ready for building, Aidan and his construction crew, which was comprised of all the human hands available, plus four dragons for transporting supplies and two horses, Jean Noir and Isabella LeBlanc, for pulling, began to clear the spot where the foundation would be built.

Aidan had drawn the plans himself with Caitlin looking over his shoulder saying. "Add this," or, "I don't like that."

When he finished the architectural drawing, he asked, "Honey, how many rooms do you think we can use?"

Her feelings hurt, Caitlin sniffed, "I plan to have several more children someday, and we need rooms for guests."

Duncan and Diggory had laughed so hard when they saw the size of the house Caitlin wanted, Aidan became angry with them. "Planning this house has made Caitlin happier than I've seen her since she found out she was with child. If she wants a palace, a palace she gets. Now stop making fun of her!"

Duncan apologized, "We beg pardon, Aidan, but 'tis so big. Who's going to be living there? Why not plan something smaller and add on if you have to? If we build this, the rest of us will live in the mountains forever."

Aidan saw the wisdom in Duncan's words, so he talked to Caitlin and they designed something smaller and more practical with space for expansion.

With everything ready, Aidan prepared for groundbreaking. Duncan handed him a pick ax. "Aidan, you get the honors of the first strike. We shall join you once you've started."

Aidan swung the pick ax with all his might. As the point struck the ground, there was an ejulation so loud that the entire group dropped their shovels and pick axes.

"What in God's name was that?" shouted Aidan.

Mary Kate said simply, "It had nothing to do with *God*."

On Isla Linda, the troops were frightened by the wailing they heard; and deep within the underground cavern, Quazel lamented while blood slowly oozed from her chest.

"Nana!" screamed a terrified little girl.

"I shall live, child, but the Promised One has taken back my home. Unless he is killed, I will never be able to live on Draconis again. I must somehow seduce that golden boy into getting rid of him for me."

Once again Quazel took a single drop of Eunice's blood into her mouth. The wound had gone deep, but she knew to use more magic would deplete her store. She hissed as she lay down, "I swear by all that is dark: I will kill you if 'tis the last thing I ever do."

At the groundbreaking Aidan said, "What do you mean, Mary Kate?"

"'Twas Quazel screaming. Somehow that thrust into the ground hurt her," said Mary Kate, her eyes as big as saucers.

"She's right." Elizabeth confirmed, "'Twas Quazel."

"Good," said Aidan, and he struck the ground repeatedly with such rage and force that Caitlin became frightened. She had not seen such anger in his eyes even when she had stowed away on the ship or when Quazel had changed her into a tigress.

The only sounds were Aidan's heavy breathing and grunts of fury. Everyone stood by, looking in all directions, waiting for something more. There were no more eerie screeches. Caitlin realized only the first had done any kind of damage. She screamed, "Aidan, stop!"

Aidan threw the pick to the ground and sat with a plop, his energy expended.

Caitlin put her head on his shoulder. "Hold on to that intensity until you see her face to face. Then, you can dismember her if you so desire."

Aidan laughed bitterly. He encircled the tigress's neck with his arm and buried his face in her warm safe fur. He whispered, "Oh, Caitlin, how I need you."

The big, bold, beautiful tigress licked Aidan's face. "I love you, Aidan O'Rourke. Now, use all that wasted energy and build my house," she purred in his ear.

After weeks of long days, Aidan and Caitlin stood at the door of their new house. Aidan stroked Caitlin's fur. "Sweetheart, there's a small problem."

"What's that?"

"I can't carry you over the threshold."

Caitlin laughed. "I think I shall survive foregoing the tradition."

"I have an idea," Aidan said with a mischievous look on his face.

"Should I trust you and your idea?"

Over his shoulder Aidan called, "I promise 'twill be fun." He scooped two little boys under his arms and carried them like footballs. Kieran and Rennin squealed with delight. Aidan zoomed around their yard-to-be and back to Caitlin. He placed them on her back. "Mam, shall we go into our new home?" Aidan opened the door, and he and his family walked into their new cheerful living room.

Caitlin burst into laughter. "Aidan, there's a small problem."

"What's that?"

"We need furniture."

All during the time the families were building their homes, the troops on Isla Linda kept constant vigil for any sign of Quazel and continued the search for an entrance to Quazel's secret escape. On one occasion, the hawks spotted a little girl gathering flowers near the cave. In a valiant attempt, a large golden eagle swooped down to grab the child. Quazel saw the rescue attempt just in time to pull Morgan back into the cave and disappear. The brave eagle came away with only a talonful of clothing. Nonetheless, General Taylor reported the sighting and the failed attempt to Colin. With renewed assurance that Morgan was safe and still within reach, Colin built his house next to Aidan's. He continued to pray his folks had received his message and would come to Draconis.

After almost a year, there were five new houses built in the once devastated oasis. Thanks to the clearing and the ground being stimulated, rosebushes and honeysuckle vines began to flourish. Mary Kate and Elizabeth planted vegetables. Each time Elizabeth placed a finger in the dirt, a tingle could be felt. The place was alive once more.

A new home was also established in a spacious cave on the cliffside. Draco and Esmeralda set up their home without an ounce of treasure except a golden chain that Duncan had worn when he came to Draconis. It had been a gift from his mother. Duncan gave it to his bonded dragon. "Draco, this is only a small token of my love for you. Hang it above the entrance to your home as an emblem and sign that Draconis will one day be restored to its past glory." It was Esmeralda who engulfed Duncan in her massive wing expanse for Draco could only nod.

Aidan and Colin, in order to keep their bonded dragons from experiencing the same anguish Draco had experienced, made early arrangements for mates to suit

Char and Brindle. Knowing Char already had his sights set on Scarlet, a blood-red beauty, Aidan asked her if she would one day be Char's mate. She readily agreed and their courtship began.

Brindle had a dumbfounded look on his face when Colin asked if there was a female he particularly admired. He slowly shook his head negatively and said, "None of the girls would want me. I'm too stupid."

"Fie me! I have had enough," Colin said, his ire stirred greatly. "Why on Earth do ya think ya aire stupid? Brindle, do ya think I am stupid? Do ya think I would choose a stupid dragon to be bonded to me?"

Brindle's eyes grew wide. "Oh, no, Colin, you aren't stupid, but you only felt sorry for me. 'Tis why you asked me to be your bonded dragon. Everybody knows I'm dimwitted. Alexander dropped my egg before I hatched. I was born with a great big knot on my head. Everybody knows that makes a dragon practically brainless."

"Brindle, that is ridiculous! Granted, I asked ya to be me dragon after Draco suggested it, but I didna know I could have me own special dragon friend. I thought that honor was reserved for Duncan and Aidan. If I had thought ya unworthy to be me bonded dragon, I would have demanded another. I am blessed to have ya. Moreover, ya aire *not* stupid. On the contrary, ya think long and hard before ya act. That prevents rash actions and a multitude of troubles. If anybody says ya aire stupid again, they will have to deal with me. If I must, I will speak to King Satin and have him issue an edict. Do ya understand?"

Brindle nodded his head.

Colin continued, "Now, is there any particular female ya loike?"

"I've never thought much about it. I think Rose is quite pretty, and Periwinkle is soft spoken. Then there is Sandy. Oh, she's so mean. She makes my blood boil. I think I hate her."

"I get the gist," said Colin. "Do ya trust me, Brindle?" He patted the dragon's leg.

"Verily."

"Then, let me take care of this. Ya will have a promised mate by the end of the week."

Colin drafted a letter and sent a copy to every available female dragon. The letter stated:

To all available female dragons:
From Sir Colin Fitzpatrick:

Three golden doubloons to the one who is willing and able to become the betrothed of Brindle, my bonded dragon. Apply for the honor at my house tomorrow morning at sunrise.

The next morning there were eight young female dragons in the oasis, including Rose and Periwinkle. Colin had Mary Kate with him for her female perspective.

They interviewed each lady, and they always ended with the question, "Can you love Brindle for the dragon he is?" After an entire morning of talking to eight eligible ladies, not one of them answered with a definite "aye" to the last question.

Mary Kate said, "I'm not satisfied with any of them. Of the group, Periwinkle has the most admirable qualities. She would be good to Brindle, but something is missing."

A shadow loomed overhead as a glistening beige dragon landed before them. In her talon she held Colin's announcement.

"Colin Fitzpatrick," she spat the words and fire flashed in her eyes as a small stream of steam escaped her nostrils. "I am Sandy. I've read this solicitation a hundred times. 'Tis insulting!" She slammed the letter into Colin's lap. "The very idea that you think you must buy Brindle a wife is *degrading*. How dare you! Brindle does not need your help finding a mate. All he needs to do is open his eyes and grow a little backbone! Some of us have been trying to get his attention since we hatched. If he would *not* believe that absurd story about his being stupid and stop wallowing in self-pity, he might see what is right in front of him."

Colin and Mary Kate looked at each other. Mary Kate spoke, "Sandy, I have one question for you."

Sandy turned her glaring golden eyes toward Mary Kate. "Make it a good one. I'd have thought you would've had better sense than to be a part of this fiasco."

Mary Kate remained calm and asked the same question one last time. "Can you love Brindle for the dragon he is?"

Sandy put her face right in Mary Kate's face so that Mary Kate could feel the radiating heat. "Can I love Brindle for the dragon he is? What do you think I have been ranting about? I *do* love Brindle for the dragon he is. I have loved Brindle for the dragon he is since before my wings sprouted. Now, do you understand?"

Colin spoke, "You have the job, milady." He started to reach into his pocket for the doubloons.

Sandy whipped her head to be nose-to-nose with Colin. He could feel the heat pulsating from her. "If you pull gold from that pocket, you will be a one-handed human. I do not need to be *bought*. Brindle is reward enough." Sandy flew away.

Colin laughed so hard he almost could not breathe. "She is absolutely perfect. I knew she would be. Any time a woman makes a man's blood boil, she has to be perfect for him, but will not Brindle be surprised?"

Surprised was an understatement. Brindle fainted at the news.

One evening after all the families were settled into their new homes and all the mates had been determined, Aidan asked everyone to his and Caitlin's home for supper. They ate outside because there was no way to fit six dragons in the house. Seamus was also invited. He had taken on the role of King Satin admirably. His first act as king was to knight Aidan, Colin, and Diggory.

Aidan had the meal so that he could have a meeting in a relaxed atmosphere. After supper Aidan spoke to the entire group. "The time has come for us to seriously consider a new approach to conquering Quazel and reclaiming Draconis. There could be war again in this land, but we must fight for freedom.

"The one thing that will be certain from this day forward is there will be no more deception or trickery. I fear that the deceitfulness may have contributed to our failures. Lying is too much a part of Quazel's evilness. Let's not stoop to her level.

"I think a straightforward, frontal approach might scare her more than our trying to be sneaky and underhanded. She cannot live in the light or the truth, which is to our advantage. We can adapt to fighting in the dark."

He scanned the faces before him. "Seamus, you are King Satin now. There is no other. Because of what Quazel did to you, you must be a king and no longer a warrior. You must help us plan wisely.

"Daddy and Seanathair, I would like for the two of you to meet me at sunrise on the morrow on the highest mountain peak. There is something I feel compelled to do, but we have to do it together. Bring your swords.

"Mary Kate, I can hear your thoughts. What do you have to say?"

Mary Kate questioned, "Did you verily hear my thoughts?"

"Aye," Aidan replied. "You were thinking, 'I need to give Duncan an explanation and a warning.' So, what is it?"

"Aidan, 'tis exactly what I was thinking. You don't plan to invade my thoughts often, do you?"

Aidan shook his head. "I promise, if you'll do the same," he said with a cloud on his brow that no one seemed to notice.

Mary Kate looked at Duncan. "Duncan, as much as you hate Quazel and want to kill her, you can't do it. You must leave that act to Aidan alone. When you came to Draconis, your motives were impure. You were a mercenary, bought to explore and possibly plunder. Your heart changed, but because your first thoughts were of yourself, you don't have the power to kill the darkness.

"Alexander, you don't have the power either. Your devotion came from rejection, your country's rejection of you and your initial rejection of this land. You never wanted to come here.

"Aidan, you're the only one with the power to kill Quazel. You have the power because you came here of your own free will. You came with the sole purpose of restoration and reclamation. You never sought anything for yourself. Your motives are pure; but know that if you fail, and there will come a strong temptation for you, the burden of defeating the evil in this land will fall on Kieran, Rennin, and Declan. The evil itself will fall on Morgan.

"I can't tell you how long you'll struggle against the darkness before you'll have an opportunity to kill Quazel, but victory will *not* be swift. There will be heartache and tragedy before all is peaceful again, but ultimately, right, truth, and goodness will prevail."

Everyone sat in silence for a time. Mary Kate was totally exhausted after her prophetic declaration. Aidan finally spoke with a touch of humor. "Gee, Mary Kate, I had parlor games planned. You sure know how to take the life from a party."

Mary Kate threw her last bite of bread at Aidan.

Aidan shouted, "Food fight," and began pelting everybody with grapes. Mirth was restored to the gathering.

Just as the gaiety returned, an exhausted hawk landed on Colin's shoulder with a note around his neck. Colin gently set him by his plate and handed him some meat and water. The hawk ate hungrily. Colin removed the note and held his breath. He opened the note to read in his mother's familiar handwriting:

Have followed all directions in regard to the selling of property. Will be with you as soon as possible.

Love,
Mam and Da.

"They aire coming," he breathed.
The party lasted well into the night.

Dawn seemed to come exceptionally early the next day due to the revelry the night before, but three generations of O'Rourke men met on the highest mountain peak of Draconis.

Aidan said, "This might seem silly, but I feel the need to issue a challenge to Quazel. She might not have realized her flawed logic yet, but that doesn't matter. I want her to be afraid, very afraid.

"We three have come from far away. Each of us has taken his own path to get here, but we are at this point in history for a purpose. We must be a united force."

Aidan unsheathed his sword and held it toward Isla Linda. He shouted with all his breath, "Quazel! I am Aidan O'Rourke, son of Duncan and grandson of Alexander. I am here with my father in human form and my grandfather. I have come for you. I will find you. If it takes the rest of my life, I will find you. You are mine!"

Duncan and Alexander were mystically compelled to lay their swords tip to tip with Aidan's. As they did so, a strong force drew the points skyward and a lightning bolt ran from the clouds to the swords. Unharmed, the three men glowed in the aura created by the force.

Deep in her underground chamber Quazel sat up in alarm as she heard her name being called. A chill ran down her spine. She hissed, "Impossible!"

36
New Arrivals

"**Daddy,** Daddy," Kieran and Rennin stormed into the house. The door slammed behind them.

"Boys!" Aidan scolded. "Stop running through the house. Your mother will have your hide." He looked at his two five-year-olds and thought again how much time had passed with no success in fulfilling his destiny.

"Daddy," Kieran began.

"I want to tell him," Rennin interrupted.

"No," said Kieran as he pushed his brother. "I'm gonna tell him."

"Both of you are going to get a spanking if you don't stop fighting," Aidan threatened.

The door slammed again. "I told 'em to walk in, Uncle Aidan," said the vastly superior six-year-old Declan. "There's a ship on the horizon. Now I have to find Da and tell him. It could be Memaw and Papaw Fitzpatrick, but the ship is awfully big for two people. I think 'tis bigger than *The Privileged Character*."

"Declan, you spoiled everything!" the twins shouted together.

"You shouldn't have been fighting," countered Declan as he stuck his tongue out at his cousins.

"Declan Fitzpatrick," Aidan corrected the boy, "do you want me to tell your mam what you just did?"

"No, sir."

"Then straighten up. Put your tongue back in your mouth! Find your da, and meet us on the knoll."

Aidan grabbed his spyglass. "Come on, boys. Let's see who's coming to our island."

Colin, with Declan on his shoulders, jogged up to the knoll. "Aidan," Colin said breathlessly, "is it Mam and Da?"

"No. Not unless they mounted cannons on their ship. I see two. Colin, I don't like this at all."

Aidan lowered the spyglass and raised it again. "Fie! Colin, we have pirates!"

"Aire ya jesting?" said Colin in alarm.

"Look for yourself."

Colin looked through the spyglass. "Alack! Just what we need, human recruits for Quazel."

"Not if I can help it. They're still at least two days out. Kieran, fetch Seanathair and Granddaddy. Declan, find Pap and Nana. Rennin, summon Draco, Char, and Brindle. Colin, round up Mary Kate and the generals. I shall get Caitlin, Seamus, and Danielle. Let's meet in the cave in one hour."

An hour later there was a meeting in the "war room," the big room in Alexander's Cavern. Duncan took charge since there might be military strategy involved.

"I'm open to suggestions on how to keep these cutthroats away from here without giving away our presence."

"Sabotage," said Char. "You'd be surprised what a black dragon can do under cover of darkness. Sails catch fire easily."

"Good," said Duncan. "Anyone else?"

From her special container, a large bamboo box lined with tar and filled with salt water, which Colin had designed, Danielle suggested, "You know that black powder you pour into your pistols. Well, if you could put some of it in several bottles, we dolphins could place them around the ship so that when the ship hits them they'd explode. I bet they'd get a bang from that!"

Danielle's silly comment brought snickers to several lips. Even Duncan smiled in spite of himself. "We could do that, but 'tis not quite that simple to get the powder to ignite. If it gets wet, it won't work."

"Ghosts," said Caitlin. "Pirates are notorious for being superstitious. If they make it to shore, we need ghosts to frighten them away. We ladies can handle ghosts."

"Good idea. Hopefully, they'll be scared away before we need ghosts," Duncan continued. "Anyone else?"

After a time of silence, Duncan was still concerned. "We can implement these ideas, but something is missing. If all else fails, we can fight."

Elizabeth whispered to Alexander, "Daddy, what do you think? Should we take aggressive action?"

"I'm not sure, Elizabeth. I think we must keep the human presence here hidden from the eyes of these interlopers. Aggressive action could have the opposite effect."

Duncan said, "Let's discuss every possibility. You young folks haven't said a word, except Caitlin and Danielle."

Mary Kate, in her usual quiet manner, voiced her opinion. "Uncle Duncan, I think Seanathair and Momma should initially hide the settlement from any prying eyes. 'Tis a time for magic. If for some reason that fails, then implement the other ideas."

Aidan surprisingly supported Mary Kate's idea. "As much as I hate deception, 'tis a time for discretion. We don't need this kind of influx. Let them come ashore, explore, and bury their plunder. They probably won't stay long and will be ready to leave soon. At the worst, they could leave two or three crewmen behind to guard their treasure. We can manage that.

"Seanathair, you and Elizabeth shield any evidence of humans or dragons. 'Twould be good to create some kind of temporary reef near the harbor. At least, make it hard for them to come ashore.

"Animal noises all night will go a long way to frighten men with guilty consciences, and I love the ghost idea." He smiled toward his wife who still inhabitated the body of a tigress. "At least a variation of it would be good, something like intangible voices on the wind.

"Then, if they don't go easily, you wolves, big cats, and bears could get hungry. Not that you'd actually eat them, but they won't know that.

"The last thing we want to do is let these vermin know this place is enchanted or that other humans are here. God forbid Quazel should discover them and form an alliance."

As agreed, Elizabeth and Alexander joined their powers and cast a spell, which made the homes in the oasis appear as an extension of the desert. A coral reef appeared around the harbor, and *The Privileged Character* vanished into thin air. Finally, the entrances to Alexander's Cavern appeared as sheer rock.

The dragons stayed in their caves during the day, and they flew high even in the darkness. The humans who were animals carried on as animals. The ladies stayed in the lsettlement mainly to keep three rambunctious little boys occupied. Alexander went back to the cave and his magic things for the time. Aidan, Duncan, Diggory, and Colin camouflaged themselves and camped in the woods to watch what the pirates would do.

After two days the ship dropped anchor outside the reef. Four camouflaged men watched the proceedings on deck. There appeared to be about twenty-five crewmembers. The captain was a tall, lanky man around Aidan's age. He had black hair and a tan complexion. Across his left cheek was a scar that stretched from his hairline to his chin, just missing his eye.

Near sundown, the captain himself dragged a man who was bound around both his hands and his feet from the hold. The man looked to be about thirty years old. He was stockily built and had light brown hair. The order of the evening was to be an execution.

"We should do something," said Diggory. "They aire going to kill that man." Before anything could be done, a tall blond boy forced the man from the plank into fifty feet of churning waters. Just as the man was being pushed, a petite blonde woman fell to her knees and clutched the arm of the captain. He flung her to the deck where she crumpled into a sobbing heap.

Beneath the waters, Danielle worked fervently to remove the fetters and shackles from the drowning man. However, she was unable to break the chains, and as hard as she tried, by the time she pushed the man into shallow waters, he was dead.

Immediately following the execution, the captain lowered a rowboat. In the boat sat the captain, the blonde woman, a small child, the boy who had pushed the man, and two other pirates.

By the time the small boat rowed ashore it was almost dark. The crewmen built a fire as the four men watched from their perch in the trees. The crewmen were a scraggly lot. One wore a patch and had several missing teeth and a potbelly. Another was tall and skinny with hair that looked as if it fell out in patches, and he scratched his scalp continuously. The third was not much more than a boy, yet he had hard lines in his face and cold, cruel, cobalt eyes. He was the one who pushed the man overboard.

The captain dragged the woman from the boat and threw her to the sand. The child he picked up and set down with much more gentleness.

The woman screamed in stilted British, "You murdering animal! I hope you burn in Hell!"

"Mrs. Montgomery," began the captain. He was surprisingly well spoken although his voice carried a heavy Spanish accent. "Charlotte, I am very sorry for your grief, but I did not murder Malcolm. He was duly tried and executed. I have no intention of killing you or your daughter. I gave Malcolm my word. I might be a thief, but I am not a liar, unlike your dead husband.

"I would *never* have sold out my companions as Malcolm did us. His whole intent when he gave us information about that gold shipment was to ensure our capture. I should have known better than to trust him with our history. None of us will go to prison again. He underestimated my crew. He had to be punished."

"You scum!" shouted the woman called Charlotte. She lunged at the captain.

He grabbed her by the wrists and held her firmly. "Charlotte, I am a ruthless man. Your world made me so. Yet, I have never killed innocent women and children."

Charlotte spat in the man's face. His already hard countenance grew stonier. His coal black eyes flashed venom. "I might make an exception this time," he growled as he held the woman's wrists tighter. Then, he pulled her to him and kissed her forcefully. She struggled against his embrace.

The man leered at Charlotte. "You are a beautiful woman, Charlotte. I have had many beautiful women— some against their will, some willingly. How do you want it to be?"

Charlotte hissed, "I would rather die."

The captain grinned wickedly. "'Tis not as if we have never done this before, but we can do it the hard way if you in truth want to." He forced Charlotte to the ground with one hand and unfastened his pants with the other.

"I can't let this happen," whispered Aidan. Duncan put one hand on Aidan's shoulder. The other hand he put to his lips. Then he pointed in different directions indicating to the men with him which way to go. The four men quietly slipped from the trees.

As they descended, Charlotte felt around with her hand until she found a rock. She bashed the rock into the side of the captain's head. He fell over, more stunned by the fact that she had hit him than by the force of the blow. He touched his hand to his head and bellowed, "You wench!"

In his dazed state, he had not realized Charlotte had pulled his dagger from its sheath. In the next moment, Charlotte plunged the dagger toward the captain's shoulder, missing her target as he rolled over. He grabbed Charlotte's arm again in an attempt to twist the dagger loose. As Charlotte wrenched her body to try to free herself, she rolled forward and landed on the blade point. Charlotte clutched her chest as blood spread over her body. She fell into the outstretched arms of her captor.

"Fie me, Charlotte," said the captain with a catch in his voice. "I would never have hurt you."

Charlotte murmured, "Why, Ricardo? Five years ago I would have followed you to the ends of the earth, but you left me. Why? Miranda. Take. Your..." Charlotte died with her questions lingering in the salty beach air.

The child screamed and ran into the woods. The young boy started after her. "Let her go," said Ricardo as he laid Charlotte gently on the sand. "If she survives here alone, then, I will have kept my word. If she dies, it will not have been by my hand, and I will have kept my word. Bury that box under that big oak, and let us away from here. I do not like this place." He shivered. "I feel a deep, dark, pervasive evil here—far worse than anything I have ever done. We shall come back when 'tis safe to have those things and claim them. It could be a few years. Bury Charlotte beside the box. I shall not leave her like this."

The two crewmen buried the box and the body while the boy helped Ricardo into the boat. When all was settled, they rowed away, leaving the child in the woods.

37
𝔖tirrings and 𝔗raumas

Quazel awoke from a fitful sleep. She had had nightmares all night, dreaming of when she was dragged away to marry a man old enough to be her father. She saw it all as if it had been yesterday; the one person who had loved her, her big brother by one year had been bound by the family servants in order to prevent his helping her to escape. She called his name, "Tomas."

Morgan laid a gentle hand on Quazel's brow. "Nana, wake up."

Quazel sat up. "I'm all right, child. I had a bad dream." She sat perfectly still and quiet, as if trying to hear.

"Nana."

"Shh. Morgan, be quiet. Come quickly." They ran to the entrance of the cave, stopping only long enough to touch the wall, which melted away at a whispered phrase. "Morgan, go to the water's edge. Tell me what you see."

Morgan ran toward the sea and returned a moment later. "Nana, there is a shadow of a ship sailing away."

"Leaving, not coming?"

"Aye, leaving."

"Big or small?"

"Big."

"Tomas? No, it could not have been Tomas. He was killed in a battle with the British just after Elizabeth was born." Quazel was in a state of confusion. "Perhaps it was Pablo, my nephew," she babbled. "I don't know, but I felt a kindred spirit. Somebody on that ship is one of my own."

Quazel and Morgan returned to their beds, but the old witch slept no more that night nor for the rest of the nights of her life. She became a creature of the night, sleeping as the sun shone.

Aboard the ghostly pirate ship all was quiet. Captain Ricardo Morales-Mendez turned from the young blond boy who shadowed him. "I am all right, Trevor."

The boy shook his head hard. He put his fingers to his lips and then looked as if he threw something.

Ricardo sighed. "I know my words were lies. I thought I could frighten her into coming back to me." He placed his hand on the boy's neck. "I was wrong. Now, go to bed. I am tired."

Trevor gusted a breath, tapped Ricardo's chest, and moved away from the door.

Ricardo locked himself in his quarters. He stripped to white drawstring pants and sat on his bed holding a gold locket that hung around his neck. The back of it was inscribed with the words, "For Charlotte. All my love, Ricardo."

As Ricardo laid his head on his pillow, he brought the locket to his lips. Then he let the heavy serpentine chain fall against his skin and lay with his face toward the wall. His body jerked with silent sobs. His badly scarred back heaved as he whispered, "Charlotte."

A voice stabbed his mind. "Tu eres como yo. Vuelve." ("You are like me. Come back.")

He shivered and clutched the locket tighter.

On Draconis an all-out search was underway for a frightened little girl. While Aidan, Duncan, Colin, and Diggory had buried the man's body, they called for the others to search for the child.

"Poor little lamb," Elizabeth said to Mary Kate. "She must be so afraid."

Dawn brought more hope of finding the little girl. Searching by day would be easier. With the ship headed away, the dragons joined the search. By noon, everyone was exhausted and frustrated.

"Did you catch the child's name?" Caitlin asked. "If we call her by name, mayhap she will answer."

Aidan said, "I think the mother said the name Miranda."

"Let us start again. This time, call her name," suggested Caitlin.

"We've been calling that name," Aidan said.

"Perhaps she won't be afraid of a woman," Mary Kate said.

Brindle landed on the beach with three small boys as passengers. Afraid he should not have brought the children, Brindle said, "The little lads insist they can help. They say there are hiding places only a child can get to."

Colin was proud his bonded dragon had once again hit on a workable plan, albeit unwittingly. "'Tis great thinking," he said. Brindle beamed as he always did when he made Colin proud.

Before the parents could decide how to use the boys, the three rascals had themselves disappeared into the woods. Aidan sighed, "Spread out and keep a sharp eye out for the boys."

The boys searched some of their favorite hiding places. Finally, Kieran climbed into a hollow log near where Quazel's camp had been. Curled up inside the log was a small blonde girl who was fast asleep. Kieran started to wake her but thought better and crawled out backward.

Once out of the log, he saw his aunts looking in the shrubbery. He ran up to Mary Kate and grabbed her hand. "Aunt Mary Kate, Aunt Lizzie, over here." He led the ladies to the hollow log. Even Mary Kate was too big to go inside.

She said to her nephew, "Kieran, Aunt Lizzie and I won't fit in there. You'll have to get her out."

"Aye, ma'am," said Kieran as he crawled back into the log.

"Momma, I'm going to the other end. You stay here in case she tries to run," Mary Kate said.

Kieran touched the girl's hair lightly. It looked like spun gold, even lighter than his Daddy's. She looked like a doll lying there. Kieran softly shook the sleeping girl. Her eyes, which reminded Kieran of a doe, fluttered open. She sat up slowly.

"Be well met. I'm Kieran O'Rourke. What's your name?"

She did not say anything. Her big brown eyes brimmed with tears that spilled onto her cheeks. Kieran softly brushed the tears from her face the way his daddy did when he fell and skinned his knees. "'Tis all right," the little gentleman whispered. "I shall take care of you."

Mary Kate looked into the log. Kieran pointed. "Do you see that pretty lady? She's my aunt. She'll take care of you, too. Crawl out to her. She makes the best butter scones you ever tasted."

The little girl looked at Mary Kate who held her hand out for the child, "Come on, sweetie. I shan't hurt you."

At that moment, Rennin peered over Mary Kate's shoulder. The little girl stopped and looked back to see how Kieran got out so fast. He was still there.

Kieran laughed. "Don't worry. That's only Rennin, my twin brother. We look alike, but he's a lot more daring, Mam says. That gets him into more trouble, too. He does crazy things like jumping off the cliff to see if Char is fast enough to catch him. He almost gave Char heart failure. Char was so mad he actually spat fire. That is the only time I have ever seen a dragon actually spit fire. Rennin can be a lot of fun, too. Go on out so you can meet him."

Miranda stared with wide wondering eyes. *Can this boy talk faster than a lightning bolt or what? A dragon? Is there a real dragon here? These people do not seem to be afraid.* She took a deep breath and crawled out to Mary Kate who helped her out and enfolded her in gentle loving arms.

"'Tis all right now, honey. You're safe. Nobody will hurt you now."

Mary Kate carried the frail child to the beach as everyone gathered back there. When Miranda saw the dragons, she held on to Mary Kate so hard the woman winced.

Kieran saw the fear on the girl's face. "'Tis not dangerous, girl. These dragons are our friends." To prove his point he crawled straight up Char's neck and sat on him. "See. There are a lot of things about Draconis that might scare you at first, but you'll soon learn most of them are good. Do you want to come up here with me? I shall hold on to you. I shan't let you fall."

The little girl loosened her grip on Mary Kate's neck and slowly walked to the shiny black beast. She reached out a tentative hand and touched Char's leg.

"'Tis all right, little one," said Char gently in his gravelly voice. "I shan't hurt you."

Miranda gasped and jumped back.

Char said, "I beg pardon. I did not mean to frighten you. I can talk. All of us dragons can talk. Many of the animals here also speak."

"Like me," Caitlin said. "I'm Kieran and Rennin's mother."

Miranda's mouth opened, but now words came out.

Kieran got impatient. "Rennin, help her up."

Rennin protested, "She's a girl, Kieran."

"I know that," snapped Kieran.

Declan walked forward. "Hail, milady. I am Declan Fitzpatrick."

Kieran said in an agitated voice, "Quiet, Declan. I saw her first."

The adults all looked at one another.

Declan continued, "Allow me to help you up." He offered her his hand.

Rennin came to his brother's aid. "Be quiet, Declan. Kieran saw her first." Rennin pushed Declan to the side and turned to the girl.

"Go on. Climb up. Do not be a 'fraidy cat."

Miranda climbed up carefully. When she got to Kieran he said, "You sit up front. I shall make sure you don't fall off." He turned to the boys, "Come on. Time is wasting." Rennin and Declan scampered up.

"Go to my house, Kieran. You may have two scones each, no more," said Mary Kate. "I shall be right behind you".

Char soared off.

Mary Kate turned to the group, "What are we to do about her?"

"She has to stay with someone," Aidan said.

"She can stay with us," Mary Kate said. "I think she trusts me." She turned to Colin. "'Tis all right, is it not, dear?"

"Of course," said Colin. "We have an extra room."

"Good," Mary Kate said as she climbed on Sandy. "I'm going home. The scone tin is probably empty by now."

An hour later, Mary Kate helped Miranda into a hot bath. She talked soothingly to the child as she lathered her hair. "Honey, prithee talk to me? Is your name Miranda?"

The girl nodded her head affirmatively.

Mary Kate talked some more to the still frightened child. "I have a little girl, too. Her name is Morgan. A very bad woman took her, and we are still trying to find her. When she comes home, mayhap the two of you can be like sisters."

Mary Kate helped the little girl from the tub and wrapped her in a soft, fluffy, hand-woven towel. "Does that feel better?"

Miranda looked at Mary Kate and whispered, "The mean man killed my daddy and mommy." Big tears dropped onto the towel.

"I know, baby, but he's gone now. He can't hurt you." Mary Kate hugged the traumatized child tightly. As she embraced the innocent girl, her heart was stirred. She knew someday the pirate would return, not for his treasure, but for *his* child. Mary Kate squeezed her even tighter.

38
A Brief Encounter

For years Colin and Aidan had searched for the secret passage in the cave where Duncan had lived as King Satin. Always, the search came to naught. After eight years of futile searching, Colin sank to the sandy beach in a moment of despair.

"Aidan, I am beginning to think we shall never find Morgan. I canna even picture how she looks anymore. Declan and yer twins doona remember her, and since we found Miranda, Mary Kate pours so much love into that little girl it seems she is trying to replace her emptiness over Morgan with Miranda." He pushed his long red hair back with both hands. "Aidan, doona misunderstand. Miranda is a lovely child, but she canna replace Morgan. Worse is that Morgan probably canna remember us at all. There is no telling how Quazel has poisoned her mind."

Aidan put a brotherly arm around Colin's shoulders. "We can't give up. To find Morgan would mean finding Quazel. That could mean freedom for everyone."

Aidan sighed. "Believe me when I tell you 'tis not easy living with a tigress. I'll love Caitlin until the day I die, but sometimes I have to find a quiet place and weep and scream. Even though Caitlin is with me, sometimes I feel completely alone." Mary Kate's face floated across his mind's eye and he shook his head hard. "I need to feel her in my arms. I need my wife, my lover. At least you can hold Mary Kate and make love to your wife. There must be some comfort in that."

Colin smiled. "I couldna ask for anyone more wonderful than Mary Kate, but, mate, ya have both yer children. There must be some joy in that."

Aidan nodded. "And you will, too, one day soon."

The men heard rustling behind them. Turning, they saw a child dart into the undergrowth.

"Aidan!" said Colin.

"Let's go."

The two fathers followed where the child had gone. They saw her again at the entrance of the cave.

Colin called, "Morgan, wait!"

The young girl turned briefly and saw the two strangers coming toward her. She ran into the cave.

"Morgan, wait! 'Tis Daddy," Colin called frantically, and the two men ran after her.

Morgan placed her hand on the wall of the cave and said, "*Ostium hostusu sequor.*"

Colin and Aidan arrived just as the girl disappeared through the wall. They tried to follow, but the opening became solid rock again.

"'Tis right here, Aidan. 'Tis right in front of us," shouted Colin in frustration.

"Aye, but 'tis opened with magic." Aidan touched the wall and said, "*Sequor.*" He grunted in frustration. "I heard her say that word. We must have missed part of it. We have to talk to Seanathair. Mayhap he can figure out the rest of the phrase."

Colin kicked the wall. "Alackaday, Aidan. We were so close. Oh, Aidan, she didna know me. She was afraid of me, her own father."

Aidan and Colin left to talk to Alexander with hope he could string words together with *sequor* to find the key to the hidden door.

Quazel slept very little at night, so she took the opportunity to rest during the day. This left Morgan mainly unattended and free to do as she pleased. Her favorite thing to do was to dress in breeches and go to the small secluded meadow and just lie in the grass and watch the clouds float by.

One brilliant afternoon, Colin and Aidan flew to Isla Linda to try some of the possible phrases Alexander had put together. They took Declan and Rennin with them. Kieran was somewhere exploring with Miranda as usual.

In the cave, Declan listened to every word with fascination, but Rennin became bored. "Daddy, may I walk on the beach?"

Aidan gave him a stern look. "Aye, but do *not* go into the water. The undertow is strong right now."

"Aye, sir. Declan, do you want to come?"

"No," Declan said with indifference.

Rennin shrugged his shoulders and walked along the beach. Tired of picking up seashells, he meandered through the woods. He never worried about getting lost because his sense of direction was impeccable.

Rennin came upon the little meadow that was Morgan's sanctuary. He saw what he thought was a small dark-haired boy lying in the grass. Surprised to find a playmate, he ran up to the dozing child.

Morgan jumped. Rennin blurted, "Where did you come from? Who are you?"

"I floated here in a ship. I have been here a long time."

"Why have I never seen you before?"

"I've stayed hidden."

"Why?"

"I was afraid."

"Oh, we shan't hurt you," said Rennin with an emphatic head shake, "but my daddy says there's a witch around here that *will* hurt you. I had better get my daddy."

"No! I beg you don't do that. Nana Q would be very angry if she knew I was out here. I would be punished."

"Not if you go with me."

"You don't understand."

"What would your Nana Q do to you?"

"She would beat me and lock me in a dark room with rats. I don't like the dark room. Oh, can you not just play with me for a while? Nobody ever plays with me," begged Morgan. She thought of the few times she had played with Quazel's simian servants.

"My daddy will be mad if I don't tell him about you."

"Will he beat you and put you in a dark room?"

"No, silly. Sometimes I get spanked, but he would never lock me in a dark room. He loves me."

"What do you mean?" Morgan asked with big brown eyes.

"My daddy says when you love somebody, you care more about them than you do yourself."

A sigh gave way to, "That must be nice."

"'Tis. What's your name anyway?"

"Morgan."

"My uncle Colin is looking for somebody named Morgan. Is that you?"

She shrugged. "I don't know anybody named Colin. What's your name?"

"Rennin O'Rourke."

"Well, Rennin O'Rourke, will you be my special secret friend. Mayhap you could love me and care more about me than you do yourself."

"I don't know." The boy knitted his eyebrows in concern.

"I beg you."

"If you *are* the Morgan Uncle Colin is looking for, he would be very sad not to find you."

"Perchance I can meet your uncle another day, but for today can we have fun, only the two of us?"

"Do you promise to meet my uncle another day?"

"I promise. And will you come back and play with me again?"

"Yes."

The two innocent children played, and Rennin returned home with an important secret.

39
𝔉amily 𝔎eunion

𝔅rindle swooped in as Colin helped Mary Kate gather ripe squash, cucumbers, and melons. He was excited. "Colin, a ship is passing Isla Linda."

"Are the pirates back?"

"No. 'Tis a small ship. I saw a gray-haired man and a woman with hair as red as yours."

Colin dropped his basket and looked at Mary Kate.

"Go! Colin, go," she urged him, her face filled with a smile and happy eyes.

"Let me get Caitlin."

Colin burst through Caitlin's door. "Caitlin, they aire here! Mam and Da aire here!"

Caitlin jumped up. "Colin, away!" Then, she stopped in her tracks. "Look at me. How can I go?"

"Caitlin, they know all aboot ya. 'Twas in the letter I sent home."

"I know, but…"

"Sis, away! Get yer arse moving!"

"Aidan isn't here, and the boys are out somewhere."

"Mary Kate will watch them and tell Aidan."

"You're right. Let us away!"

Brother and sister climbed aboard Brindle and took off. On the way Brindle became worried. "Colin, do you think I'll frighten your parents?"

"No, Brindle. I wrote them aboot ya, too. I just want to know what took them so long."

"You can ask them in an hour, Colin," Caitlin said. She was so excited she could hardly sit still.

A shadow overspread the sloop as it glided smoothly along.

"Drake, is there a storm cloud?" asked Martha Fitzpatrick from below deck.

"There was not five minutes ago." Dr. Drake Fitzpatrick looked at the sky. "Martha, ya might want to come up here. Ya will not believe yer eyes."

Martha popped up from the galley carrying two plates. Behind her came Sarah Thames, her housekeeper since before she moved to Stonebridge. "What is it, Drake?" She looked up.

Martha squealed, "Drake, 'tis Colin!"

"Aire ya sure?"

"Forsooth."

Colin waved vigorously. "Brindle, can ya get us close enough for us to board?"

"I'm going to set down in the water and stretch my wing across."

"Many thanks, mate."

Colin and Caitlin boarded the sloop and enveloped their parents. Martha could not believe Caitlin was really in the body of a tigress.

"What took ya so long?" Colin asked.

"We had to sell all the properties, including the Murphy estate when"—Martha shook her head.

Colin took a deep breath. "Yer letter didna say what has become of Mary Kate's parents."

Drake said, "We thought it best to tell ya face-to-face."

"What, Da? How much more pain can my wife stand?"

The doctor released a sad sigh. "Logan shot Diana and then himself. The town was torn apart."

"Mary Kate said her spirit told her they were gone." Colin shook his head.

Caitlin said, "Mary Kate will be fine. After all, she's a prophetess and has unbelievable powers. What else held you up, Da?"

"I had to find a new physician for Stonebridge, and get a ship."

"Selling the houses, especially Elizabeth's, took a long time, but we aire here now," said Martha.

"Ya still have not found Morgan and gotten rid of Quazel?" Drake was flabbergasted. His mouth opened and closed in disbelief.

"Da, ya canna believe how elusive that woman is. We know where she is hiding, but we canna figure oot how to get into her fortress. We know Morgan is safe because we have had glimpses of her over the years. I saw her meself a few months ago. She looks just loike a little version of Mary Kate."

"Colin, why is it so hard to get into Quazel's hiding place?" asked Dr. Fitzpatrick.

"The opening is controlled by a magical phrase. Aidan and I heard the last word one day when we saw Morgan and followed her. It was *sequor*, but we doona know what came before."

"Son, that word means, 'to follow.' She was speaking Latin. Ya and Aidan were following her. What might she have called ya: men, strangers, hunters?"

"Aye, I know the language. Alexander is working on combinations of Latin phrases. Aidan and I went back a few weeks ago and tried two-dozen combinations. Da, mayhap ya can help Alexander since ya have studied Latin."

"I shall be glad to help as much as I can."

"I canna wait for ya to see all yer grandchildren. Mary Kate says Declan reminds her of me. Sometimes he can be overbearing and superior. Was I in truth that insufferable?" Colin laughed.

"Aye," quipped Caitlin.

"There is another little girl who lives with Mary Kate and me. Her name is Miranda Montgomery. Pirates killed her parents, and left her on the island. We have, in a way, adopted her. She is precious. She and Kieran aire practically inseparable."

"Speaking of Kieran, Caitlin, why aire ya so quiet?" asked Martha. "'Tis not normal for ya."

"Well, Mam, Colin has been hogging the conversation."

Martha smiled at Drake. "Some things never change."

Drake furrowed his brow. "Some things do. Caitlin, ya aire speaking differently."

"Aye. The nearest we can figure, the transformation or taking a life here causes many things to change."

Colin shrugged. "Diggory and I still have a brogue. I have yet to kill an enemy, but we doona know why Diggory remains unchanged. Mayhap because his transformation was never complete."

"I understand." Drake said, "Caitlin, honey, tell us aboot yer boys and Aidan. In all truth, I am dying to know what Aidan did when he found ya had stowed away on the ship."

Martha nodded. "Aye. Ya have no idea how distraught we were when we went to Elizabeth's and finally figured oot what ya had done."

"Aye, Sis. Tell Da how ya threw things at yer new husband." Colin teased his sister.

"Shut up, Colin, before I tear out your eyes." She popped out her claws. "I can do it for real now."

"Aye, Caitlin, prithee tell me how many times Aidan has threatened to give ya back to me," laughed Drake.

"Never. We may fight sometimes, but he has never wanted to give me back. He did get livid with me for following him, but my wisdom prevailed. We are together. Do you think I could have stood ten years without him?"

Drake kissed his daughter's head. "Baby, I am glad he makes ya happy."

"Da, I just wish I were human. Aidan is terrific." She blinked her eyes and her whiskers twitched. "He never complains about our situation, and he's a wonderful father.

The boys are identical in appearance, but they act totally different. They're little versions of Aidan. Both of them have golden curls and green eyes. Kieran is practical and thoughtful and obedient. Rennin is my wild child. He's daring and challenges authority at every turn. He's loving and kind, but he wants to do things his own way."

"That reminds me of someone I know and love," teased Drake.

Caitlin said thoughtfully, "I suppose Rennin *is* a lot like me."

Drake and Martha met Brindle who gushed all over them as if they were his own parents. Brindle flew back to Draconis to announce their arrival. Then, the sloop sailed along with Caitlin and Colin aboard until they sailed into harbor and docked beside *The Privileged Character*. Their family, old friends, and new friends gathered to greet them. That night they stayed up late getting to know everyone. Finally, Colin showed them to the house he had built for them.

Happy, but exhausted, everyone slept soundly that night except in a cave across a channel where an old witch stared toward the place she desired, wondering who had arrived on the small ship she saw a few days before.

40
𝔓𝔯𝔦𝔰𝔬𝔫

𝔉𝔞𝔯 away from Draconis, Ricardo Morales and his young blond companion fled from the authorities through the dark streets of Gibraltar. Shots rang out as they darted around corners and into alleys.

The duo collapsed behind a pile of apple barrels in an alley. Ricardo put his hand on his friend's shoulder and felt warm, sticky ooze.

"Trevor, you have been hit!" The boy shook his head and held up his hand in protest, his way of indicating that it was only a minor wound.

The constable turned into the alley. They sank lower behind the containers. Swinging his lantern from side to side, the lawman started back the way he had come when he spotted drops of blood leading behind the crates. He slipped his cudgel from his belt as he kicked over the barrels, which toppled on top of his quarry.

Ricardo struggled with the man until he felt a blow to the back of his head. Everything went black.

Ricardo awoke to a trickle of sunlight through the slit of a window in a dank prison cell. Beside him lay Trevor in a pool of blood. Ricardo knelt beside his young comrade. "Ah, Dios, no. No Trevor." ("Oh, God, no. Not Trevor.")

The young boy touched his friend's hand weakly. Ricardo lifted the boy's head unto his lap. "Do not die, Trevor. You are my only true friend." Trevor smiled and put his fist over his heart to show his love for this man.

The guard walked by and taunted in Ricardo's native Spanish, "Well, Morales, what would you like before they hang you tomorrow?"

"Get Trevor a doctor!"

¿"Por qué? What difference does it make whether he bleeds to death or hangs? Either way he will be dead. Trevor, do you have any last words?" The guard laughed menacingly.

Ricardo charged the bars. "You bastard! You know you cut out his tongue when we were here before, simply to keep him from telling your captain how corrupt you are."

"Shut up, Morales. You had better be glad I put him in here with you so he won't die alone, unlike you. But, of course, you won't be alone either. You will have a cheering crowd."

"I swear, Armando, before I die, you will be dead."

Armando laughed again. "What would you like for your last meal, Morales? Even a condemned man deserves that."

"Tu corazón." ("Your heart.")

"Fine. I shall bring you some bread and water." As Armando walked away, his cruel laugh reverberated throughout the cold stone hallways.

Ricardo knelt beside his friend again. Trevor reached up and touched the gold locket around Ricardo's neck.

"Do you still want me to open this and see if there is anything inside?"

Trevor gave a weak nod.

Ricardo hesitated. "Trevor, I am afraid to look, but I shall do it for you."

Ricardo flicked the little latch. Folded very tiny and stuffed into the locket was a letter. Ricardo turned the folded paper over in his fingers. He looked at Trevor. "I shall read it to you."

The hard lines in the boy's face had softened. He looked angelic. He smiled.

Ricardo read:

My Darling Ricardo,

If you are reading this, I have died and you have returned to Barcelona. I do not understand why you left me. My heart was torn from me when you disappeared. You were my very reason for breathing. I am sure you must have had a good motive to leave, but my heart aches so.

I have given birth to our daughter and named her Miranda, for that is the name you said you would name your little girl one day. I have married Malcolm Montgomery to hide my shame and to give Miranda legitimacy. I only hope you can understand why I married a man I do not love. He was kind to offer your child and me his name. I shall be true to him, but someday when Miranda is old enough to understand, I shall tell her about you.

Wherever you are and whatever happens, I shall always be your devoted and loving

Charlotte.

Ricardo struggled to control his voice. "Oh, God, Trevor, she knew nothing of what her father and Malcolm did. She thought I left her." He clutched his fist to his forehead. "How cruelly I treated her. She must have hated me in the end, yet she tried to tell me. Her last words still ring in my ears. The child." He inhaled sharply. "Trevor, she is *my* child, and I left her on a deserted island filled with wild animals." He placed one hand over his heart. "I am a fool. I must get back there. I must save her and make her understand. I must beg for her forgiveness."

He looked around frantically. "Trevor, we must escape." He felt Trevor's hand slip from his wrist. The boy who had sacrificed himself repeatedly for Ricardo was gone.

"Trevor," gulped a penitent man. "I am so sorry."

Ricardo looked at the locket and chain, which was a thick gold serpentine. He carefully removed the locket and, refolding the letter, replaced it inside. Then he dropped the locket into a pocket on his doublet. The chain, he held in his hand and waited.

A pain shot through his head and a voice whispered. "No se puede cambiar ." ("You cannot change.")

Sometime later, Armando came down the dark, lonely corridor, whistling. "Morales, I brought you your last meal." He slid the wooden bowl filled with rotting, maggot-infested gruel through a slot at the bottom of the door. "Come lap it up, dog."

Ricardo lay still beside his dead friend.

Wondering if both were dead, the guard opened the door. Armando kicked the bowl toward Ricardo who did not move. Armando clutched the club at his side, walked to Ricardo and kicked him. "Get up, Morales," he said viciously.

Ricardo lay perfectly still until the second kick, and then sprang on Armando like a madman. He wrapped the chain from the locket around Armando's throat and pulled. The guard clawed at the gold. Tiny droplets of blood appeared along the edges of the chain. As Armando gagged, Ricardo gloated in his ear, "I told you that you would die before I did. I am glad God has chosen me to mete out justice and retribution for your wickedness, even if I burn in Hell for doing so. Die, you son-of-a-bitch."

Armando's body fell to the ground. Ricardo calmly replaced the locket around his neck and changed clothes with the dead guard. The pants were loose, but he cinched the belt tight. He took the guard's pistol and knelt once more beside Trevor. He placed a gentle kiss on the dead boy's head and whispered, "Adiós, mi amigo. Te quiero. Te extrañaré. Dios vaya contigo igual que mi corazón." ("Good-bye, my friend. I love you. I shall miss you. God go with you as does my heart.")

41
Wayward Son

"Youth!" grumbled Aidan as he plopped onto the davenport. "Caitlin, you talk to Rennin when he comes home. He has disappeared *again*. He gets so angry when I try to talk to him. See if you can talk some sense into him. Why can't he behave more like Kieran?"

"Because he's Rennin, dear."

"I know, but he's going to get into big trouble someday, trouble that I can't protect him from getting into. Doesn't he know it would kill me if something happened to him?"

"Aidan, why don't you say those words to him? They'll get you further than arguing."

"I shall try."

Over the years Rennin had visited Isla Linda with one purpose in mind, spending time with his secret friend. After a while Morgan feared they would be caught in the meadow so they explored the island until they stumbled upon the small entrance into the grotto.

"This place is wonderful," said Morgan. "Bring some lanterns the next time you come."

"I will, but let's go play ball for now."

"I don't want to play ball."

"Morgan, you've been acting peculiar lately. What's wrong with you?"

"Nothing. Let's go play ball."

The two playmates budding on adulthood went to their meadow and tossed Aidan's old ball that was beginning to fall apart. As Morgan tried to elude Rennin, he slide-tackled her, causing her shirt to rip.

Rennin jumped to his feet. "Morgan! You're...You're a girl!"

"I always have been." She pulled her shirt closed. "Does it matter? Aren't you my friend anymore since you know I'm a girl?"

"No, but you should've told me you were a *girl*. It changes many things."

"What does it change?" Morgan asked innocently, sitting up.

"The things we do together; the way I treat you," Rennin responded, flustered.

"You wanted somebody to do boy things with, so I gave you what you wanted."

"I wanted a friend of my own. You should've told me." Rennin plopped down with a huff and frown and pulled grass with his hands.

Morgan moved beside him. "I beg pardon. I'm afraid I don't understand the difference between boy things and girl things. I thought I was caring more for you than myself."

"Morgan, I have to tell Uncle Colin about you."

"No! Nana Q told me she would send someone to kill the men who were looking for me. She would, too, though very few apes still come around. She's very mean."

"Morgan you *must* be the child Uncle Colin and Aunt Mary Kate had stolen from them by an evil sorceress named Quazel, your Nana Q. They have looked for you ever since I can remember."

Morgan clutched Rennin's arm and tears filled her eyes. "Rennin, do you love me? Do you care more for me than yourself?"

Rennin pulled away and stood. "Don't cry. Why do girls always cry? Miranda does that, and it tears Kieran up. 'Tis nothing he won't do for her when water begins to flow." He pointed a sharp finger at her. "'Tis not going to work on me. Do you understand?"

Morgan nodded her head and wiped her eyes. "Aye. Do what you must, but you have no idea how mean Nana Q is."

Morgan tied her torn shirt and walked toward the cave.

"Morgan, wait," Rennin called after her. He caught up with her. "Do you think she would in truth send someone to kill Uncle Colin and my father?"

"Aye, Rennin, she would."

"Then you must tell me how to get to her. My father will take care of her and protect you. You can be with other people who love you."

"Oh, Rennin, then you still love me even if I am a girl?" She threw her arms around his neck.

Rennin awkwardly put his arms around her. He felt his heart quicken at her closeness.

"Aye, Morgan. I love you," he whispered. "Peradventure even more." He held her tighter.

"Can you remember the words if I give them to you?" Morgan asked as she loosened her embrace on Rennin.

"Of course."

"Go into the cave. Touch the wall and say '*Ostium, hostusu, sequor.*' To get out say, '*Ostium, libertas.*' Repeat the phrases."

Rennin said, "To get in, '*Ostium, hostusu, sequor.*' To get out, '*Ostium, libertas.*'"

"Well done."

They walked a short distance hand in hand.

"Don't come at night," said Morgan. "Nana Q sleeps during the day."

"I shall remember. If you need me before I get back, call Smoke. He'll hear you. Go to the meadow and yell, 'Smoke, I need you.' He'll come."

"Gramercy, Rennin." Morgan kissed him softly, the way a woman would kiss a man. "I love you, Rennin." She let go of his hand.

"Morgan," Rennin said her name passionately and pulled her back to him. He kissed her again and then held her closely. "I'm glad you're a girl," he confessed. "I thought I'd fallen in love with a boy, and you can cry any time you want."

Morgan kissed him once more and disappeared into the cave.

Char was at Aidan's house. "Aidan, I have to talk to you. Smoke is my son, and I love him, but lately he disappears. I know I'm young to have had an egg hatch and that thus far Scarlet and I are the only couple to have offspring, but I try to teach Smoke how to behave. I know he has barely learned to fly without wobbling, but I'm afraid to say when Rennin is gone, so is Smoke. The two of them are fast developing a bond, but neither of them weighs the consequences of his actions."

Aidan rubbed his head at the temples. He was quickly getting a headache. "True, Rennin is very headstrong and impulsive. When he gets home this time, I might lock him in his room. I'm sorry he has involved Smoke in his wayward actions."

Char chuckled. "I knew Rennin had a mind of his own the day he jumped off the cliff when he was three. I adore the boy. That's part of his problem; he's really not a boy anymore. All the children are hanging precariously between childhood and adulthood. Living on Draconis, they've grown up too fast. My biggest concern about Rennin is he disappears to Isla Linda."

"So *that* is where he hides." Aidan slapped his leg. "Haven't I explained enough about how sinister Quazel is? Doesn't he understand she'd do anything to anybody to preserve herself?"

Char opened and closed his massive wing span. "Aidan, don't be too harsh on the boy. Methinks Kieran has a few faults you need to address as well."

Aidan's eyes narrowed. "Char, Kieran would never flagrantly disregard my authority."

"No, Kieran rebels silently," said Char quietly, his voice rumbling deep in his throat.

Aidan looked quizzically at his friend. "Char, is there something I should know?"

"Aidan, have you discussed the facts of life with the boys?"

"What?" Aidan's eyes suddenly danced with mirth and he laughed outright. "Of course I have, but here on Draconis it doesn't make much difference."

"On the contrary," argued Char. "From what I witnessed between Kieran and Miranda the other day, mayhap you should make sure he understands, and get Mary Kate to talk to Miranda."

"Kieran is only sixteen," Aidan said in alarm. "They were not?" His pupils dialated as he opened his eyes wide.

"No," Char stopped him short. "But that was only a couple of steps away."

Aidan ran his fingers through his long blond hair. "To think I've been so worried about Rennin when Kieran could be getting into more trouble right here. Rennin would probably thrust a dagger without hesitation into the heart of a woman that might approach him on Isla Linda. He would realize 'twas Quazel, no matter how beautiful she might make herself appear. Char, say a prayer for me. I have more to deal with than I knew."

"Well, here comes one of your challenges with a pretty little blonde girl hanging on his arm. He seems very happy."

"Well," sighed Aidan, "there's no time like the present."

"I leave you. I shall fly toward Isla Linda to look for our duo."

Kieran and Miranda walked hand in hand toward their homes. They saw Aidan and waved. Aidan called, "Kieran, we need to talk about something."

"Coming, Da." Turning toward Miranda, Kieran said, "I shall see you later." He took her face in his hands and kissed her as she slipped her hands up his back and held on to each shoulder.

"Oh, boy," muttered Aidan under his breath. "I hope I'm not too late."

Kieran ran up cheerfully. "What's the problem, Da?"

"Let's go inside and sit down, son. We need to talk about you and Miranda."

Kieran blushed as they sat at the table. "We already had the baby talk, Da."

"Now we're going to have the temptation talk."

"The temptation talk?" Kieran said, a little amused. "What does that mean?"

"Kieran, I know you understand the biological aspects of reproduction, but there's much more involved in making love. Your humours run wild. You don't stop to consider the physical consequences. Kieran, any time you make love, you run the risk or creating a new life. Are you ready to be a father? Are you ready to stop running through the meadow and plant vegetables instead? Are you ready to stop playing ball with your brother, and hold the hand of Miranda while she screams and calls you all manner of names giving birth? Kieran, 'tis obvious you care very much for Miranda, but…"

"Care!" Kieran interrupted. "I love her, Da. I'm going to marry her."

"Kieran, you're barely sixteen."

"Da, this is Draconis, not Stonebridge where convention demands adulthood at twenty-one or even eighteen. Look around." He waved an open palm back and forth. "Show me my other options. Miranda loves me, too. She doesn't want Rennin because he's too wild or Declan because he seems too much like her brother, not to mention that he can be an insufferable prig. She wants me." He poked his own chest with his index finger. "I've wanted her ever since I saw her in that hollow log eleven years ago. She was so beautiful she took my breath away."

The way Kieran was behaving, Aidan thought for a moment that he had gotten the boys mixed up.

"Kieran, I'm not telling you that you can never have Miranda. I just want you to consider the consequences of your actions. Besides, Draconis won't always be like this. One day there will be a multitude of young ladies."

"I'faith! Then why don't you get off your arse and knock down the wall in the cave with a pick ax if you have to? Get rid of the invisible terror so that there can be a normal life on Draconis."

"Kieran!" Aidan was shocked at his son's defiance.

"No, Da. For once I'm going to be like Rennin. I want Miranda now!" Kieran stormed away from the table.

Banging his knee as he stood, Aidan called after the boy, "Kieran!"

His son refused to turn back. "Well, that went well," Aidan growled to himself, thinking, *That's not my son.*

Aidan had barely sat back down when Rennin burst through the door.

"Daddy, I have to talk to you! 'Tis important!"

Already frustrated with Kieran and upset with Rennin, Aidan forgot his words to Caitlin. "I need to talk to you, too. Sit down."

"Daddy, this is no time for sitting. This is important. Where's Uncle Colin?"

"Rennin, I told you sit down."

"No! You have to listen to me!"

Aidan became angry. "Rennin, did you just say 'no' to me?"

"Daddy, I pray pardon. Now listen." Rennin was too excited to notice his father's mood.

"Rennin Drake O'Rourke, I've reached my limit with your insolence. You're rude and disrespectful. You're willful and arrogant. You will sit down and listen to me. You will *not* disappear for days at a time. You will *not* fly off on Smoke to Isla Linda again. Do you understand me?" Aidan slammed his fist on the table.

By this time Rennin was just as angry as his father. "I understand all too well. I'm not your *perfect* Kieran. I'm Rennin Drake O'Rourke. I take chances. I'm not dull and boring. I'm not a child anymore. I'll go where I want, when I want, with whom I want. Apparently, I'm going to have to do the job you came here to do. I have green eyes. Kieran has green eyes, and if I can find Declan, he has green eyes *and* red hair. We're all almost as tall as you." He waved his left hand. "And I'm left handed."

Rennin took a breath and leaned over the table into Aidan's face. He looked more like a man than his father could fathom. "Most importantly," Rennin said through clenched teeth, "I know how to get in."

Aidan was so angry that he did not even hear Rennin's last statement. Before he could stop himself, he slapped his son across the face.

Hot tears stinging his cheeks, Rennin strode from the room and raced toward the clearing where he had left Smoke.

Aidan ran to the door as Rennin disappeared through the trees. "Out upon it, Rennin! Come back! What do you mean you know how to get in?"

Aidan mumbled as he put on his shoes to go after his son, "What the hell is that fool boy up to?"

42
Capture

Before Aidan could get dressed and summon Char, who was half way to Isla Linda when Aidan called him, Rennin had landed Smoke directly on the beach near the entrance to the cave.

"Smoke, go home. I shall call you when I need you."

"Rennin, you should go home."

"I can't, not tonight at least. I'm too hurt and angry."

"Don't do anything rash. Promise me you will *not* confront Quazel by yourself," Smoke entreated his friend.

"I promise. I shall talk to Daddy after we both calm down. Now go home before you get into trouble, too."

Smoke reluctantly flew home.

The sun was low in the sky as Rennin entered the cave. A shiver ran down his spine. He walked to the wall and placed his hand firmly on the cold granite. In a clear, strong voice he said, "*Ostium, hostusu, sequor.*" The wall melted before his eyes.

Rennin entered a dimly lit stairwell. A slight sucking sound caused him to look back and see the wall had resealed in a matter of seconds. He returned his attention to his task.

The hallway's eerie illumination came from a nest of glowworms at the end of the long passageway thirty steps below.

Several doors dotted the corridor. Rennin decided he would peek into each door until he found Morgan. As he took a step forward, the entry at the far end opened. A slightly built woman stepped into the hall. She turned and saw Rennin. Looking around furtively, she ran as fast as she could to him.

Morgan whispered, "Rennin, what are you doing here? You have to go now! Nana Q will wake at any minute. Go to the grotto. I shall come as soon as I can." Pulling Rennin up the stairs, she touched the wall and spoke, "*Ostium, libertas.*" Morgan pushed Rennin through the opening. "Go!" She put her fingers to her lips and blew him a kiss as the wall became solid once more, and the slight vapors of her breath turned to fine icy crystals.

Morgan heard a door behind her. As she descended the stairs, she knew she was trembling. "Nana, you're up." She tried to sound cheerful. "We're having something different tonight. I made omelets with hot chili peppers. I thought you would like that."

Quazel acknowledged her. "That will be fine. Where were you going?"

"I was going to gather some flowers for the table, but they're unnecessary now that you're awake. I'm famished anyway."

Morgan ate hurriedly. Quazel commented, "My, child, you *must* have been hungry. You never eat that quickly."

Morgan said, "I shouldn't have eaten so fast. My stomach feels queasy now. I think I shall go to bed early, Nana."

"Very well. You can work on your spells tomorrow, but clean the dishes before you go to bed. I want to go out tonight anyway. I'm going to get dressed."

In a tiny rivulet that ran along the wall of a chamber used for the kitchen and dining area and out through the cave, Morgan washed the dishes quickly. Then she threw some cheese, fruit, and bread into a bag in the small room where a few animals and stores were kept and where a sliver of a crack appeared fifty feet above the floor of the cave. Stalactites hung like wolves' fangs from the ceiling. The two goats bleated at her as she usually stopped to pet them. At one time, half a dozen apes had slept here, but no more.

She ran to her room and placed pillows under the covers to look as if she were sleeping. She snatched the bag and a blanket and raced down the hall. She put her ear to Quazel's door and heard the witch at her dressing table. Then, she jogged up the stairs.

Morgan touched the wall and whispered, "*Ostium, libertas.*" She grabbed an old lantern and some flintstone from Satin's cave and sprinted nimbly through the gathering darkness. Out of breath, she fell into the entrance of the grotto. "Rennin?"

"I'm here near the water," came the melancholy reply.

Char argued with Aidan all the way to Isla Linda. "Aidan, you should've found Colin. You should *not* have come alone."

"Char, I don't have time to worry about Colin. I have to stop Rennin from doing something dangerous and stupid, just to prove he can do something better than I can."

"Aidan, my dear friend, I love you, but you're as pig-headed, willful, and impulsive as your son. He gets it naturally," Char huffed.

Halfway to the island, they saw Smoke returning. Smoke did not know whether to fly away or go foward. One look from Char told him to keep going.

"Where's Rennin?" Char demanded.

"I left him on the beach near the cave, Father. He told me to go home."

"Then do so and do *not* leave until I return." Small tendrils of smoke curled into the air from Char's nostrils. He growled, "Do one thing. Send Colin to us."

"Aye, Father."

"Well, are you happy, Char? Colin will be here soon," huffed Aidan.

"I hope 'tis not too late to keep you out of trouble," Char stated flatly.

"Me too, Char, but I have to find Rennin." Remorsefully Aidan said, "Char, I slapped him."

"You did what?"

"I slapped him. I have to find him and tell him I'm sorry and I love him."

Char was was so unsettled, his scales rippled. "And dragons have a reputation for having bad tempers," he grunted.

Char and Aidan entered the cave cautiously. Aidan found one of the old lanterns and lit it, and then looked around the cave carefully. There were fresh footprints in the dirt. A man's steps led to the wall.

"Char, look. Mayhap he truly does know how to get in. He was trying to tell me, but I was so angry about the incident with Kieran, I wouldn't let the lad talk."

As he spoke, the wall dissolved before him. There stood the aberration he had wanted to see for so long. With a banshee's scream, Quazel pulled Aidan behind the wall. Char's fire hit solid rock.

Char hollered, "Aidan! Aidan, answer me!" No answer came. Distraught, the black dragon lay down in the cave to wait for Colin.

Behind the granite surface, Quazel hit the off-balance Aidan with a stone, knocking him cold. As she dragged him to her prison she cackled, "I have the golden boy."

When Aidan came to, he found himself chained to the cold, stone wall. His head ached miserably. The room was spectrally lit with the glimmering glowworms.

Aidan jerked his wrists. The shackles were secure. The door creaked, and a tall figure walked in.

"Quazel," gasped Aidan.

"Ah, you know me. I'm afraid I've not had the pleasure of your introduction." Quazel came closer. It was her turn to gasp. "Your eyes! I thought they were blue. You must be Aidan O'Rourke. Coming for me, were you? Well"—The witch clucked her tongue—"it looks as if the shoe is on the other foot."

Quazel blew a yellow powder into Aidan's face. He broke into a fit of coughing.

"What was that, witch? My eyes burn."

"You're tough. I'm going to have fun breaking you. Mayhap I shall get sweet little Morgan to help me."

"Where is Morgan? What have you done to her?"

"She sleeps. Her supper disagreed with her. You should get some rest, too. Tomorrow will be long and grueling. I have a few potions to work on. I probably shan't see you until tomorrow night. I have to get my beauty sleep during the day."

"You need lots of it," snapped Aidan.

"You won't think so for long," countered Quazel.

The aspirant queen left the would-be savior to ponder his situation.

43
Seduction

Morgan dropped her bundle at the entrance to the grotto. She followed Rennin's voice until she found him. The distressed young man grabbed her hand, pulled her close, and held her tightly.

Morgan asked, "Rennin, what's wrong? What happened?" As she soothed his long blond hair from his face, she felt the dampness on his cheeks.

"Daddy was so angry with me for running off that before I could tell him anything, we had a fight. Morgan, he slapped me. He has never been that angry with me before. Morgan, hold me. I need you to hold me."

Rennin laid his head on Morgan's chest. Her heart raced. She cuddled him as she would a child and whispered. "I shan't let you go, Rennin. Everything will be all right."

In the darkness Rennin groped for Morgan's face. He held her face in his hands and kissed her hard.

Morgan pulled away from him. "Rennin," she said breathlessly, "stop."

"Morgan, don't pull away from me. I shan't hurt you. I swear I would never hurt you."

"I'm not pulling away, Rennin. I'm scared. This makes me feel strangely."

Rennin kissed her softly. "I'm sorry. I don't want to frighten you."

"'Tis all right. May we light the lantern I brought? I don't like the dark."

"Of course. I shall get it. You stay here."

Rennin crawled on his hands and knees feeling before him in the pitch-black darkness. He found the bag and the lantern. "Morgan, where is the flint?"

Nervously, she laughed, "In my pocket. I pray pardon. I should have given it to you."

"No concern. Keep talking so I can get back to you."

"Rennin, does anyone know where you are?"

"Only Smoke, but my father will doubtless figure it out."

"Nana Q doesn't know where this place is. You'll be safe here, at least until someone from your island comes to find you."

"I've been thinking about that. When my grandparents came, they had a small sloop. I've been contemplating leaving, just taking the ship and leaving."

Rennin felt Morgan's hand and the stone for sparking. He lit the lantern after several attempts to ignite the wick.

The light illuminated Morgan's face. Her soft sable hair fell over her shoulders. Her big brown eyes brimmed with tears. "Rennin, are you going to leave me? What would I do without you?"

"No! I would never leave you. You'll come with me." Rennin pulled the girl into his arms. Morgan melted in his embrace.

After a few moments of quiet, Morgan said, "Rennin, you know we can't run away like that. Too many people would be hurt."

"I know, but I can dream." He tipped her chin toward him. "You're beautiful, Morgan. How could I not have known there was a woman hiding beneath those baggy pants, ill-fitting shirts, and caps?"

"I think deep down inside you did." Morgan caressed Rennin's cheek. "You said you had fallen in love with me."

Rennin kissed Morgan's lips softly. He kissed her neck. He opened her blouse and kissed her breasts.

"Rennin, stop. What are you doing?"

"Morgan, I want to make love to you. I need to make love to you." Rennin touched Morgan's breasts with trembling hands and kissed her with only a brush of his lips. He glided his fingertips over her thigh beneath her skirt.

Morgan gasped and pulled away. "Rennin, stop. I'm scared."

Rennin breathed, "I'm scared, too, but do you truly want me to stop?" He ran his finger along Morgan's breasts and back to her lips and kissed her again. "I shan't do anything you don't want me to do. But"—He released a breath—"I need to make love to you."

Rennin stood and spread the blanket Morgan had brought. Removing his shirt, he sat on the blanket and opened the bag. He took a ripe mango and bit it. He held the juicy dripping fruit out to the girl.

She walked to the blanket, took the mango and laid it back in the bag. She slipped off her blouse and untied her skirt. It slid to the ground. Kneeling in front of the young, impulsive man, she took his hand and kissed his fingertips. She brushed his hand across her breasts.

Morgan leaned forward and kissed Rennin. He pulled her warm body against his. He kissed her softly, sensuously; then a little harder until he kissed her powerfully and passionately. He laid her gently on the blanket and pulled back to look at her face.

Morgan pulled him back toward her. "I love you, Rennin O'Rourke. I would do anything you ask me, give you anything you want or need. Show me what it means to care more for me than you do yourself. Make love to me."

Colin and Brindle arrived at the cave to find Char lying dejectedly on the floor of the cavern.

Colin asked, "Char what has happened?"

"Rennin said he knew how to get in. He had a fight with Aidan and ran away. Aidan followed. Rennin's footprints led to the door." He flicked his head toward the wall. "The wall melted. Quazel pulled Aidan in. Colin, I fear she has both Rennin and Aidan, and I couldn't stop her."

"How did Rennin figure oot how to get in?"

"I'm not sure. He has been coming here a lot. Peradventure he hid and listened."

"Come on, Char. Lying here feeling guilty will not help. Let us go home and see Duncan and Seanathair. Then, we shall send a spy to hide and listen." Colin looked around. "There aire no more of the witch's supporters. They have all fled."

Quazel must have had some twinge of concern for Morgan because the girl had never been ill. She tiptoed into Morgan's room and sat on the edge of her bed. Reaching out to touch the sleeping girl, she found fluffed pillows beneath the covers.

Infuriated, she screamed, "Where is that little monster?"

Quazel looked in every room. She cautiously opened the secret door. Seeing that the dragon was gone, she searched the cave. She checked the beach because a few times Morgan had sneaked out to play in the surf, but she had never before gone to the trouble of deceiving Quazel.

After searching high and low, Quazel stalked back into the underground cavern. She pulled a chair to the entrance and waited.

Back on Draconis, Kieran and Miranda boarded *The Privileged Character*, where they always went to be alone. They usually sat on the deck and necked. This time Kieran led Miranda into the captain's quarters. "This is where the high and mighty Aidan slept. Are you duly impressed?"

"Kieran, stop it. You and your father will make up soon. Rennin fights with him all the time, and they reconcile. You will, too."

"I'm certain you're correct, but at this moment it feels good to be in his quarters doing something he doesn't want me to do. I see why Rennin does it." Kieran picked Miranda up, his hands around her waist, and kissed her. She kissed him back.

"Miranda, you know I love you."

"I love you, too."

He kissed her again. He touched her. Kieran laid the girl on the bed and started undressing her. The man slipped off his clothes and pulled Miranda to him.

Miranda gasped, "Kieran, stop. I'm not ready for this. Stop." Miranda pushed Kieran.

He grabbed her hands and held her down. "Kieran?" he said in a voice, not his own, and his eyes became black pools.

Miranda started to cry. "Kieran, stop. You're hurting me."

He did not stop. Miranda tried to scream, but he muffled her cry with his mouth.

Kieran lay beside Miranda. She sobbed uncontrollably. He touched her hair. "Miranda."

She screamed, "Do not touch me! I hate you! Don't ever touch me again! You're a liar, Kieran O'Rourke. You said you would never let anyone hurt me, but you hurt me yourself."

Kieran was broken. "Miranda, I beg forgiveness. I thought...I wasn't myself...I thought you wanted me."

"I did want you, but not...not like that. You hurt me, Kieran."

"Oh, Miranda, I am so sorry. I never wanted to hurt you. I only wanted to love you. I don't know what came over me. I cannot bear it if you hate me. Prithee, forgive me. As God is my witness I swear I will never hurt you again. I love you, Miranda." The boy sobbed as hard as the girl.

Miranda turned her back to Kieran and curled into a ball. Kieran touched her arm; she jerked away. He whispered, "I am sorry." Miranda cried herself to sleep.

Near morning they awoke and realized the time. They hurriedly dressed and sneaked home, both feeling shame and guilt and confusion.

Morgan lay cradled in Rennin's arms, her head on his chest. She listened to his even breathing and knew he was asleep. She gently lifted Rennin's arm and slipped from his grasp.

As she dressed, Rennin touched her shoulder. "Don't go. Stay with me."

With her back to him Morgan said, "Rennin, I must go. If Nana Q finds me missing, she'll change the password. Then, no one can get to her."

"Morgan, give me a few more minutes," pleaded Rennin as he slipped his arms around her and buried his face in her hair. "You smell like honeysuckle. I love that smell. Morgan, I love you. How can I let you walk out of here? 'Tis too dangerous."

"Rennin, go back to Draconis. Swallow your pride and apologize to your father. Do whatever you have to do in order to get him over here. Bring Colin with you." She sounded angry.

"Morgan, what's wrong. Why are you angry with me?" He turned her around. She was crying.

"Morgan, whatever I did, I'm sorry."

"Rennin, 'tis not you." She laid a hand on his chest, fingers splayed. "I am *terrified*. I finally understand what that woman has done to me. She wants to turn me into some kind of monster. Rennin, if she finds out about you, she might kill you."

Rennin pulled Morgan into his strong young arms. "I shan't let her hurt you or me, and you couldn't be a monster if you tried. Oh, Morgan, I'm as afraid they won't let us be together back home. You're my cousin. If they try to separate us, I swear I'll leave. Will you go with me?"

"I will follow you to Hell and back, but at this moment, each of us must do whatever it takes to end this nightmare. I love you, but I must go."

"If something goes wrong, what will you do?"

"I'll find a way out, and I'll call Smoke. Then, I'll hide here until you come for me. I shan't go anywhere with anyone else. If you're not with them, how can I trust them?"

Rennin walked out with Morgan. He called Smoke and kissed her once more. She slipped into the night.

Morgan entered the secret passage to find Quazel waiting for her. The old witch grabbed the girl by the hair and snarled, "Where have you been?"

"I went to the meadow to watch the stars. I fell asleep. I'm sorry, Nana."

Quazel raged, "Why did you try to trick me with the pillows?"

"Nana, you get so angry with me. I wasn't thinking straight."

"No, you were not."

Quazel slapped Morgan repeatedly until she caused blood to trickle from her lip. Then, she dragged the girl kicking and screaming down the stairs and the corridor.

Morgan screamed, "No, Nana. Don't put me in there. I pray thee, don't put me in there."

Quazel shoved Morgan into a small room without even the glow from the glowworms. She slammed the door behind the girl and locked it from the outside.

Morgan pounded on the door. "Nana, I pray thee, let me out. I shan't do it again. Prithee, Nana. I'm scared. There are rats in here." Morgan sobbed. She whispered, "Rennin, I need you." She sank to the floor and thought about Rennin until she fell asleep.

Smoke awoke with a jerk as he heard Rennin's voice. He started to wake Char, but realized that would be betraying the sacred trust of his bonded human. He jumped from the cave door and glided downward before he flapped his wings the first time. He flew with all his speed toward his friend.

Smoke picked Rennin up in mid-flight. During the trip home, Smoke eyed his friend curiously. "Was she worth the risk, Rennin?"

"What?"

"The girl. Was she worth the risk?"

"Smoke, she's the best thing that has ever happened to me."

Smoke dropped his passenger in his front yard as the sky began to lighten. Rennin sneaked around back to climb the trellis into his window as he had done on numerous occasions. Three feet above him, his twin brother was having trouble navigating the rickety woodwork.

"Kieran, what are you doing?"

"Trying to get inside before anyone wakes up."

"Here. Let me show you how. Lean into the trellis, not out from it. Come on in my room. I have to know what a novice is doing sneaking in just before daybreak."

The two boys sat on Rennin's bed. "Rennin, I in truth erred."

"You? Not you. I'm the one who errs and causes trouble," Rennin corrected his older brother by ten minutes.

"Not this time."

"What could you possibly have done that was so bad?"

Kieran hung his head and cried. Rennin lifted his chin. "Kieran, what is it?" He was genuinely worried about his twin.

"It was awful...I-I-I felt like something came over me, like I was someone else. I raped Miranda. I couldn't stop."

"What did you say?"

"She said, 'No,' but I didn't stop—I couldn't. Rennin, what kind of man am I?"

"A foolish one, but no more than I. Where is Miranda and how is she?"

"She just sneaked in her window, too. Rennin, she hates me. I don't deserve her love or her forgiveness."

"Do you love her?"

"Aye."

"Then, you'll spend the rest of your days earning her love, but when she forgives you, forgive yourself. Kieran, you won't believe my latest indescretion."

"Prithee, tell me. Mayhap I shall feel better about myself, but you don't seem too distressed."

"I shall start with the good part. I'm in love."

"With whom? There are no girls on Draconis except Miranda."

"All right. Brace yourself." He pushed down on his thighs and puffed out his chest. "I'm in love with Morgan."

"Morgan! How? Start talking, my brother."

Rennin told Kieran all about the years he had played with Morgan and kept her a secret to protect her and about how he had discovered she was actually a girl. He told Kieran about the secret door and his fight with Aidan.

"Is that where you have been tonight, Rennin?"

"Aye."

"Rennin, did you and she make love?"

Rennin did not answer.

"Rennin, your silence is your answer. Are you ashamed?"

"No, 'tis I don't know how Daddy is going to react when he finds out about all this. I'll not tell him the last part. That is a matter of honor, and I will *not* embarrass her in any way. I truly love her, Kieran. I'm going to marry her as soon as possible. I don't care if Daddy thinks me too young. I'll make an honest woman of her. I may be daring, but I'm not a blackguard. I think you should marry Miranda, too."

"I want to, more than anything."

"Methinks we should wake Daddy and get Morgan out of that place. Then, we can court our women and do what's right. Lord, I dread asking Uncle Colin for Morgan's hand."

44
Guardian Angel

The door to Rennin's room burst open. The twins stared at the face of an exceedingly angry tigress, her upper lip pulled back in a snarl and her tail whipping hard enough to make a cracking sound. "Where the hell have you two been?" Caitlin roared. "From Rennin I expect this, but not you, Kieran."

Standing, Rennin greeted his mother happily. "Mam, good you're awake. Where's Daddy? I need to talk to him."

Caitlin snarled and tackled Rennin. "Rennin Drake O'Rourke, right this minute I feel like behaving in every way as my feline persona would behave." She dug her claws into his shoulders deep enough to bring pricks of blood. "I could tear you to ribbons. If you were any other than my own flesh and blood, you would be dead right now."

Kieran came to Rennin's defense. "Mam! Get off. What's wrong with you?"

Caitlin wheeled and snarled at Kieran. Then, she turned back to Rennin. "Your father followed you to Isla Linda. Quazel now has him in her clutches. I swear if any harm comes to him, I will never forgive you. Know this now: Aidan is my life, my reason for waking in the mornings. Perchance someday you will love the way your father and I have loved. Until then, you can have no idea how my heart is breaking."

"Momma, please get off me," Rennin asked in a penitent voice. "I have to find Uncle Colin. I can get into the passage. I know the password."

Colin came through the door. "Caitlin, get off the boy." The tigress stepped to the side and Colin continued to speak. "Rennin, thank God ya aire all roight. We thought

Quazel had both of ya. How can ya possibly know the password?"

Rennin looked at Kieran. Kieran nodded. "You might as well tell him now as later. I shall stay with you Rennin. I shan't leave you. I would never leave you. You're a part of me, no matter what you do."

Rennin gazed at Caitlin who still glared at him. "Momma, I shall get Daddy back. I promise." Rennin sounded so much like the little boy of old that it broke Caitlin's heart to be so angry with him.

"I know you will. Tell your uncle how to get in that place."

Rennin sat on his bed with Kieran beside him. "Uncle Colin, will you please sit down?" Colin sat. "I would also feel better if you were to disarm yourself," the boy went on. "If my own mother wants to kill me, I can only imagine what you'll do. Morgan told me the password."

"Morgan told ya? Ya talked to Morgan?" Colin stood. "Rennin, where is Morgan?"

"With Quazel. Uncle Colin, we have to go there *now*. We have to get Morgan out. She said if Quazel suspected something she would change the password."

Colin went to the window. Tense silence hung in the air. "How long, Rennin?"

"How long what, sir?"

"How long have ya been in contact with Morgan?"

Rennin moved behind Kieran. "Seven years."

Colin whirled around. "Seven years! Ya have kept this a secret for seven years? I moight let yer mother eat ya. How could ya, Rennin?"

"I should've told you in the beginning, but Morgan begged me not to because she was so afraid."

Colin tried to maintain his composure. "Caitlin, Kieran, leave us. I need to talk to Rennin alone."

Kieran said, "No, Uncle Colin. I shan't leave Rennin. He has told me everything tonight. We have no secrets from each other."

Colin's face turned red and he screamed, "Kieran, get out!"

Rennin said, "'Tis all right, Kieran. I shall be fine. I have to make a clean breast someday."

Caitlin, with a reluctant Kieran, left the room.

Colin gripped the chair near the window as his knuckles turned white. "Rennin, ya have seen Morgan, played with Morgan, been with Morgan many times over the last seven years, and ya never said a word. Why?"

"Because I wouldn't do anything to hurt Morgan. She was so afraid of Quazel, of all you looking for her. I was the only one she trusted. I couldn't betray that trust. She's finally able to get free. She asked me to bring you, and she gave me the code, but we must hurry."

"Is that all?" Colin asked. "For some reason I think there is more."

Rennin sat up straight and took a deep breath. "I love her, Uncle Colin. I want to marry her."

"Marry her? Aire ya crazy? She is yer cousin!" Colin clutched his fiery-red hair near his left temple.

"Would we be the first cousins who ever married?"

"Well, no, but, ya aire only sixteen."

"I shall wait for her forever if I must, but, I beg you, don't forbid us to be together."

"How does she feel aboot ya?"

"She loves me, too"

"Of course she does. Who else is there for her to love? Rennin, after *I* talk to Morgan, if she wants ya, ya have me blessing."

"Uncle Colin!" Rennin threw his arms around his uncle.

Colin hugged the boy back and whispered in his ear, "Doona *ever* keep a secret loike this again. 'Twill only tear ya up inside and cause a lot of pain when it comes oot."

Rennin let go of his uncle. "May we go get Morgan and Daddy now?"

"Brindle is waiting for me outside. Peradventure now is the time for the power of seven."

Colin, Caitlin, Mary Kate, Elizabeth, Alexander, Diggory, Duncan, Rennin, and Kieran left for Isla Linda.

Rennin raced to the cave and the wall. He put his hand on the wall and repeated, "*Ostium, hostusu, sequor.*" Nothing happened. He said it again. "No! No! She cannot! Open! Fie me! Open!" Rennin banged on the granite until his hands bled. "Daddy! Daddy!" Frantically, he screamed with all his might, "Morgan! Morgaaaaaan!"

He turned to his uncle in tears. "I swear it opened yesterday. Quazel must have changed the password."

Colin dragged Rennin from the cave. "Rennin, come away. We shall get the new password. I have a plan."

Rennin sat on the beach and sobbed. Colin sat beside him.

"I am so sorry, Uncle Colin. This is my fault. If I had told you about Morgan years ago, if I hadn't been so belligerent with Da, none of this would have happened. Mam won't have to kill me. I shall kill myself."

Colin hugged his nephew. "No, ya will not. Ya have to live for Morgan. We will get both of them. Ya shall see."

Quazel opened the door to the closet and jerked Morgan out. "I have a prisoner I need you to help me care for. He'll need to eat during the day. You'll take care of his needs. Don't bother trying to go out. I've changed the passwords. I shall be dealing with my prisoner in the evenings. At that time you will leave us alone."

"How long have I been in there?" Morgan asked.

"Two days. Would you like to go back?"

"No, Nana. I beg, no."

"Then, do as you're told. I need some sleep now. I've been up since your act of treachery. Take care of the man. I've left the door unlocked." Quazel disappeared into her chambers.

Morgan limped to her room where she bathed and changed her clothes. Her ankle was sprained from being dragged down the hall. She had a black eye and a swollen lip. She put her hand to the tarnished silver that served as a looking glass and cried softly, "Rennin, oh, Rennin, prithee help me."

She suddenly came to her senses. *Quazel has a prisoner.* Morgan ran to the prison door and swung it open, "Rennin? Rennin, are you here?"

"No, I'm not Rennin," intoned a melancholy baritone.

Morgan lit a lantern for more light and saw an older version of Rennin chained to the wall. Quazel had obviously been working on him for his face looked worse than Morgan's.

The man's voice called the girl back to reality. "Morgan, is that you?"

"Aye, I'm Morgan. I shall be back in a moment."

Morgan left and returned with a pan of cool water and a soft cloth. As she washed the man's face she talked. "You know who I am. Who are you? You look just like Rennin. You must be his father."

"Aye. I'm Aidan O'Rourke, Rennin's father and your uncle."

"What did Nana Q do to you, and why are you here at all? Rennin was supposed to bring you and my father back to get me and take care of that witch."

"Quazel didn't seem to like the responses I gave her so she hit me every time I answered her. I'm here because I followed Rennin. I was so afraid Quazel had him, but at least *he* is safe. How do you know Rennin, honey?"

"'Tis a long story."

"I'm not going anywhere unless you have the keys for these cuffs." He jerked his arm.

"I've never seen anyone shackled here." The girl shook her head. "I know not where Nana Q keeps them, but I shall find them sooner or later. We're going to get out of here. I have to get to Rennin. Right now I'm going to get you some food and water. Then, I shall tell you about Rennin."

Morgan came back with soup and bread and cool water. She fed her uncle and talked. She told him how she had met Rennin and how they had played together. "Don't be angry with Rennin for not telling you about me. He only did what I asked. He thought he was protecting me. I thought so, too. We were wrong. Now Quazel has changed the password, and I can't get out. Don't blame Rennin. I know you can get very angry. He told me."

"'Tis why I followed him. I wanted to tell him how sorry I was. Morgan, I love Rennin very much. I was wrong for getting so angry and for slapping him."

"You were in truth going to apologize for punishing him?" The girl's eyes widened in wonder.

"Morgan, that was no proper way to punish him, and I would *never* have forbidden him to come here if I'd known he was seeing you. I would've come myself and rescued you from this place."

They talked all day and before they knew what was happening, Quazel walked in. "Morgan, you've not made supper! Leave us now."

Morgan quivered. Aidan whispered, "'Tis all right. Go on. I shall be fine."

For hours, Morgan sat by the door hoping to hear what was happening to her uncle, but through the thickness of the door, she could only hear muffled groans. Finally, from sheer exhaustion she went to bed, only to dream of a monster's hand pulling her down into quicksand and Rennin's hand trying to reach her. Their fingertips touched, but the monster with its green, scaly skin and blood soaked claws pulled her again. She awoke drenched in perspiration although the cavern was cold.

The next morning, Morgan took Aidan some tea and toast. When she saw the blood on his clothes and bamboo shoots under each fingernail, she dropped the tray in horror. Morgan tediously removed each shoot and soaked Aidan's hands before she tenderly bandaged them. "Uncle Aidan, why is she doing this to you?"

"She's like a cat with a mouse. She's toying with me before she kills me," Aidan said with a sardonic smirk on his face.

Tears dripped down Morgan's cheeks.

Aidan whispered, "How have you stayed so sweet living with that woman? How has she not corrupted you?"

Morgan honestly answered, "Rennin thinks she wants to turn me into some kind of monster like she is, but she has never tried to make me do any of the cruel things she does. She has taught me a few spells, but I'm not very good at doing them. Mayhap she was in truth lonely and took me to keep her company, although she's mean and I don't want to stay with her. I want to be with Rennin."

Aidan spoke kindly. "I see your face, Morgan. I see the kinds of things she does to you. You are little more than her slave. This is the price I pay for being Duncan's son and for being the one who was *supposed* to kill her. Morgan, around my neck there's a gold chain with an emerald attached. I don't need it. I know what she really is. You may feel her evilness, but you've never truly seen her. Take the necklace and wear it hidden under your clothes. If I don't get out of here, somehow get it to Rennin. He'll need it. Tell him I love him, and I'm proud to be his father."

"Uncle Aidan, prithee, don't talk like that. We'll escape together." Morgan put the emerald charm around her neck and dropped it in her blouse. "Are you sure you don't need this?"

Aidan nodded. "You need it more, sweetheart."

Quazel walked in. Aidan could not help himself as his naturally stubborn streak rose to the surface and he said, "And there was morning and evening and it was the...how many days has it been?"

Morgan stood, gawking at the hideous creature that stood before her. Quazel commanded, "Morgan! Leave us!"

Morgan ran as fast as she could. Outside the door she prayed, "God, help me. I beg You, help me."

Outside the secret entrance, a barn owl took up residence. Every day he waited and watched. Days stretched into weeks. He asked himself if the witch or the girl ever came out. Surely one of them would have to come out sooner or later to gather vegetables from the garden near the cave or to claim the trapped animals for meat.

Every week General Taylor took a report back to Colin, always the same: no comings or goings; no secret code.

Morgan began sleeping by her door, hoping Quazel would go out, and she could hear the new pass code. Otherwise, they would soon be eating only mushrooms, maybe the rats from the dark room.

During the day Morgan took care of Aidan. Lately, he appeared to be drunk every morning. Quazel had stopped inflicting pain on him. Morgan was confused.

As the days became weeks, six weeks to be exact, Morgan became pale; and several times she fled the room in a wave of nausea after bringing Aidan breakfast.

Quazel had changed Aidan's shackles so he could sit. Morgan would keep her head on his lap, and he would stroke her hair after he sobered from whatever drugged state Quazel had put him in the night before. He often thought how much Morgan looked and acted like her mother.

After the third morning of her running from the room, Aidan said to the miserable girl, "I've seen this before. Is there something you want to tell me about you and Rennin?"

"What do you mean, Uncle Aidan?"

"Morgan, have you and Rennin had relations?"

She looked at him with questioning eyes. Aidan realized this girl honestly did not understand.

Aidan said softly, "Morgan, don't be afraid to tell me the truth. Have you and Rennin made love?"

Morgan's face brightened. "Oh, yes."

"Honey, do you truly not know babies are made when a woman and a man make love?"

She shook her head. "Do you mean I made a baby with Rennin? Where is it?"

Aidan was dumbfounded. Quazel had told Morgan nothing. He found himself explaining the facts of life to a sweet innocent girl, a child who had made love without knowing the consequences, but Rennin knew. *Why would he do such a thing? They're obviously in love with each other, but still... Rennin has no idea she doesn't know. He thinks she's just innocent, not ignorant.*

Morgan put her hand on her stomach. She started to cry. "Uncle Aidan, did we do a very bad thing? I love Rennin so much. I only wanted to do what he asked. Am I being punished? Will Rennin be punished, too?"

Aidan continued his explanation. "What you did should be reserved for your marriage bed, but you're not being punished. 'Tis the way God gives humans babies. The sickness will pass, but you'll get large and in a few months you'll have a lot of pain before you have a little baby."

"Oh, I'll marry Rennin if we ever get out of here."

Aidan smiled. "Aye, you will."

As Aidan looked up from the sweet face, a new realization and horror struck him. *Quazel has not tutored this girl in witchcraft. The stone table, the bloodletting dishes, the ceremonial dagger, the virgin: Oh, God! Morgan is not Quazel's protégé. She was to be her sacrifice. Quazel must have some kind of deep, dark magic to prolong her life and her youth.* Aidan started laughing. He startled Morgan.

"Uncle Aidan, what's wrong?"

"You aren't a virgin anymore. Rennin might just have unwittingly saved your life and thwarted Quazel's plans. Oh, my wayward son, you are a hero unawares."

Days came and days went with little change in the routine until Quazel entered the prison chamber in a good mood in the middle of the day. "Morgan, would you be so kind as to make me one of those very special milk baths? I'd like to soak for a while. I feel tonight is going to be quite good indeed. After you prepare the bath you may come back and visit with your uncle until I come."

Morgan obediently left, but she turned back to see Quazel run a long bony finger down Aidan's cheek and say, "I am so looking forward to being with you tonight."

Morgan went to her great-grandmother's rooms and mumbled as she went, "Over my dead body." She prepared the bath and returned. Quazel practically scampered from the room.

Aidan was disoriented. "Uncle Aidan, what's wrong? Look at me." Morgan took Aidan's face in her hands. "Listen to my voice."

Aidan tried to focus on Morgan. "I'm all right, just groggy. Yellow powder always makes me groggy. Wears off."

Morgan washed Aidan's face with cold water, which seemed to help restore him to his senses. Then, she asked, "What does Quazel do to you during the night?"

"I don't remember. She always blows that yellow powder into my face. I don't remember anything from that time until you come in. I don't think I want to know what she does."

"Aye, you do so you can fight it."

"Morgan, there's a part of me that doesn't want to fight. My recollections seem to be pleasant."

"Uncle Aidan, fight for me."

"I shall try, my little guardian angel."

"Uncle Aidan, I truly don't feel well today. Can you tell me why?"

"Are you eating well?"

"I have no appetite."

"You must eat for the baby. That is my grandchild."

"I shall try, but we're almost out of food since I haven't been able to go outside."

Toward evening, Quazel returned. "Morgan, you need to go now."

Aidan squeezed her hand and nodded. With a deep sigh Morgan left.

Morgan decided to bathe. She lay back in the water with closed eyes. Silently she prayed, "God, help me. I don't know what to do. Uncle Aidan is in serious trouble."

As she stood and reached for her towel, a sharp stabbing pain shot through her abdomen, and she fell to the floor. She let out a little cry. *Uncle Aidan said it would be several months.* Another pain hit her. She dressed slowly. With no regard for Quazel's reaction, she held the wall and groped for the door to the prison. She stumbled into an appalling scene.

Her uncle and Quazel lay naked, entwined in each other's arms. He kissed her the way Rennin had kissed Morgan.

Morgan gasped, "Uncle Aidan, no!" Another pain hit her abdomen and she felt warm, sticky blood trickle down her leg. "Uncle Aidan, help me. Something's wrong."

Quazel let go of her embrace on Aidan and hissed, "What are you doing here?" She jerked Morgan's arm to push her from the room.

Morgan whimpered, "My baby. Something's wrong with my baby."

Quazel screamed. She ran her hand over the girl's abdomen. "You have defiled yourself." She looked back at Aidan. "And with one of his spawn." She touched Morgan's abdomen. "Fie! 'Tis a boy, too! Away with you! You are useless to me now!"

Aidan in his doped state held out his hand. "Caitlin, come back to me. I want you now."

Quazel screamed again and put her hands to her head. "You have ruined everything, Morgan. I finally had him where I wanted him. He was to be mine tonight. Now, my head is splitting."

Morgan laughed softly. "With any good fortune, your head will burst and you'll die."

Quazel slapped Morgan with all her might, knocking her to the floor.

"I have to lie down. Make me a headache powder and then get out. I never want to see you again."

Morgan stumbled to the medicine. At first she obediently scooped the level measure of ground butterrut into a glass of warm milk. Then she dumped the whole container into the glass and gave it to the old witch. Quazel drank every drop. The girl smiled to herself. She said, "I can't go if I don't know how to get out."

Quazel moaned, "*Patefacio, licentia.*"

Holding her side, Morgan went back to the prison. Quazel had had the presence of mind to chain Aidan back to the wall; however, she left him naked. He was sound asleep.

Morgan whispered, "Damn you to Hell, Quazel." Suddenly, she remembered a glint of silver she had just seen around the witch's neck.

The girl eased into Quazel's bedroom. The socceress was out cold. The terrified young woman lifted the silver chain and jerked as hard as she could. Quazel only moaned. Morgan held a small key.

As she groped her way back to the prison another severe pain shot through her, but she fought through the pain and kept going. In the prison, the key fit the cuffs. Morgan unlocked Aidan. She took the washbasin that she had furnished him and threw the water in his face.

Aidan awoke with a start. Morgan threw his clothes at him. "Uncle Aidan, get dressed. We are getting out now."

In his sluggish state he asked, "Why am I naked?"

"You thought Quazel was Aunt Caitlin."

The very words sobered him. He looked at his niece and saw that something was wrong, but he was still so drunk he could hardly stand.

Morgan took the necklace from her neck. She gently dropped it over Aidan's head. "I think you need this more than I do right now. I have my sheer hatred to protect me, no matter how she looks."

"Morgan, my eyes burn so badly."

Morgan wet the end of her blouse in Aidan's cup and squeezed the water into his eyes. "Does that help?"

"Aye." Aidan was finally coming around. "Morgan, what's wrong?"

She shook her head. "I don't know. I hurt, Uncle Aidan, and I'm bleeding." She crumpled to the floor as another pain hit her.

Aidan lifted the wisp of a woman in his arms. "Let us away," he said as he kissed her forehead.

Aidan carried Morgan to the entrance where she leaned forward and touched the wall. Weakly she said, "*Patefacio, licentia.*"

Before he stepped through, he asked, "Do you know how to get in?"

"No, Uncle Aidan, but I never want to come here again."

"I know, baby." He went through the opening and it closed solidly behind them.

"Take me to the meadow," Morgan begged.

Aidan ran with the girl to the small, secluded meadow where the child had known her only happiness. Morgan whispered, "This is Rennin's and my meadow." From deep within her soul, she summoned all the energy she could muster and yelled, "Smoke, I need you!"

Her head fell onto Aidan's chest. He realized he was covered in her blood. He whispered, "Don't die, sweet angel."

He felt her stir. "I shan't leave Rennin, Uncle Aidan. Wait for him in the grotto. He *will* come."

45
𝕽𝖊𝖙𝖚𝖗𝖓

𝕸𝖔𝖗𝖌𝖆𝖓 could hear voices. One was familiar. Someone was holding her hand. The bed was soft and cozy. The room smelled like roses. She felt warm lips on her fingertips. She tried to open her eyes. The room was bright, filled with sunlight. She listened to the voices. She found her power of speech. "Uncle Aidan?"

"Morgan!" She felt a kiss on her lips. Her eyes fluttered open. Rennin held her hand. She reached up and touched his face, thinking she was dreaming. Rennin had a black eye. She wondered why.

"Rennin, are you real?"

"Aye, I'm real. You're safe now."

"Uncle Aidan?"

"Right here, angel." Aidan came to her other side. "We got out together, just like you said."

There was a man standing beside Aidan. He knelt beside her bed and started to take her hand, but stopped. He had tears in his eyes.

"Daddy?"

Colin could no longer control himself. He gathered the girl in his arms and wept openly. "My Morgan. My precious Morgan." After a moment Colin laid her gently back on the pillow. A woman had come to stand beside Rennin. Morgan saw herself looking down at her.

"Mommy!" Morgan had vague recollections of this woman holding her and singing to her. Mary Kate bent down and kissed her daughter's head.

"Hello, my joy. Welcome home."

Morgan lost sight of Rennin. "Rennin, don't leave me."

He came back to her bedside. "I'm not going anywhere unless Uncle Colin throws me out." He touched his eye gingerly and sat back down, taking Morgan's hand and kissing it.

Finally, realizing that she was truly safe, she relaxed, but held Rennin's hand tightly. She closed her eyes. Then, she opened them and looked at Rennin with a light in her eyes. "Rennin, we made a baby."

The room became quiet. Everyone slipped from the room except Rennin and Colin. Colin put a hand on Rennin's shoulder and left, too.

Alone, Rennin kissed Morgan again. "Morgan, there's not a baby anymore. You had a miscarriage. The baby died."

Silent tears flowed down Morgan's cheeks. "I'm sorry, Rennin. I didn't mean to."

"Morgan, 'twas not your fault. These things happen sometimes. I'm the one who should be sorry. Daddy told me you didn't understand what we were doing. I should never have taken advantage of you like that."

"Are you sorry we made love?"

"No, Morgan. I love you more than anything. That was the best night of my life, but I wish we had waited until we were married. Then, again, I'm glad we didn't wait. Daddy told me not being a virgin saved your life. I couldn't have stood losing you."

Morgan closed her eyes and smiled. "Then, I haven't ruined everything. You still love me."

"You made everything right. You got out, and you got Daddy out. You even remembered to call Smoke."

"I'm glad," Morgan sighed.

"Morgan, do you feel like talking a little more, or are you tired?"

"Talk to me, Rennin. I want to hear your voice."

"This is important."

She opened her eyes. "I shan't go to sleep. I feel as if I have slept forever."

"Morgan Celeste Fitzpatrick, 'tis your whole name. I love you. I love you more than my own life. I would die for you or kill for you. When I'm with you, I'm happier than I ever knew I could be. Will you marry me? Uncle Colin says that if you want me, we have his blessing, especially now that I put the cart before the horse." Rennin felt his eye again.

"Oh, Rennin, do you in truth want me? I'm not much. I'm small and weak. I can't cast a spell. I hate the dark. I can cook. That's one thing I can do. Do you verily want me?"

Rennin laughed. "You're the perfect size for me, and you're the strongest person I know. I don't want you to cast any spells. We can always have a lantern, but I *am* glad you can cook. Aye, I want you. I would never have made love to somebody I didn't want."

Morgan teased Rennin, "Will we make love?"

"Whenever we like as often as we like."

Morgan laughed. "Often. Aye, Rennin. I shall marry you. I love you so much. I don't want to live without you." Morgan flung her arms around Rennin and he held her, inhaling the soft honeysuckle scented hair and knowing that life could be good, even in a world that has true evil.

There was a soft knock at the door. "May I come in?"

Not letting go of Morgan, Rennin replied, "Aye, Uncle Colin, you may come in."

Colin folded his arms across his chest when he opened the door. "Do ya two think ya can wait until ya aire wed?"

Morgan lay back on her pillow. Rennin replied, "Aye, Uncle Colin, I promise we'll wait until we marry." He touched his eye again. "This one still hurts. I wouldn't want another."

Morgan's big brown eyes got even bigger. "Daddy, you did that to Rennin? Why?"

"Fathers do impulsive things when someone hurts their little girls."

"Rennin didn't hurt me. Hit Quazel if you want to hurt someone."

"I deserved it, Morgan," said Rennin.

Colin sat down on the bed. "Morgan, I have something far more permanent in mind for Quazel than a black eye. Honey, do ya have any idea how Uncle Aidan and I can get into that cavern?"

"No, Daddy. Quazel changed the password when she found me coming back into the chamber after I had been with Rennin. She only gave me the exit code to get rid of me because she said I had defiled myself and I was useless to her. She said my baby was a boy and I had ruined everything. I think at least I stopped her from defiling Uncle Aidan."

"What does that mean?" Aidan walked into the room.

"Uncle Aidan, do you not remember anything about that night?"

"Very little, angel. Tell me what you know. I have to know what happened."

Morgan looked around the room full of men and blushed. "'Tis rather embarrassing, Uncle Aidan."

"Will you tell me if we're alone? We've talked about some very personal things before."

She clutched Rennin's hand. "I shall tell you with Rennin and Daddy here, if you'll not get embarrassed."

"I've survived worse." Aidan delivered his winsome smile.

"*We* have survived worse," said Morgan with more confidence. "When I came into the prison room, you and Quazel were lying naked together. You kissed her the way

Rennin kisses me. When she came to me you called her back, but you called her Caitlin. I don't think you actually had relations with her because she was angry with me for ruining things. She said you were to *have been* hers that night, not you *had been*. I think you must have resisted her charms even without the emerald. Mayhap 'tis because you love Aunt Caitlin so much, but it appeared even you were about to give in to Quazel."

Aidan covered his face in an attempt to control his emotions. Rennin let go of Morgan's hand and embraced his father.

Aidan sobbed."Rennin, your mother is my heart, my life. How could I betray her?"

Rennin comforted his father. "'Tis not your fault, Daddy. You were under the influence of a powerful spell. Mam will understand."

"No! I shan't tell her."

"You must. Uncle Colin, tell him what secrets like that can do."

"Listen to the lad, Aidan. He has learned the hard way."

"I know you're both right, but 'twill be the hardest thing I've ever had to do."

Aidan knelt beside the bed and stroked Morgan's hair. He kissed her forehead. "I owe you everything, my little guardian angel. I owe you my life, my freedom, my virtue, my honor. I love you, sweet girl. I'll be proud to call you not only my niece, but my daughter also." Aidan left to find Caitlin. He had to bare his soul.

On Isla Linda a small skiff slid onto the sand just as the sun began to set. An exhausted man fell onto the beach. He looked toward Draconis and spoke aloud in his native Spanish. "Seguiré mañana, para debo descansar un rato." ("I shall go on tomorrow, but I must rest for a while.")

Examining his surroundings, Ricardo Morales-Mendez looked for shelter for the night. He came upon the cave once inhabited by King Satin. To his trained eye he saw it had once been used for shelter. He found a lantern and lit it with a piece of flint lying beside it. He saw an old straw cot and fell upon it. He slept the dead sleep of a weary man.

Ricardo awoke when he felt frigid breath on his face. Standing over him was a gorgeous Mediterranean-looking woman. He could have been looking at someone from his hometown. The woman was breathtaking. When she spoke, her voice was cold and piercing, but the words were in his native tongue. "Who are you and what are you doing here?"

Ever the charmer with the ladies, Ricardo rose to his full height and bowed low. Taking the woman's icy hand in his, he kissed it. A bitter taste remained on his lips, yet he flattered her, the words flowing like honey as he spoke his mother language. "Most beautiful lady, allow me to introduce myself. I am Ricardo Morales-Mendez, your most humble servant."

At the name, Quazel was intrigued. "And your father?

Not sure why this woman could possibly care about his ancestry, Ricardo graciously answered, "Pablo Morales-Martinez."

"Your grandfather was Tomas Morales-Rodriguez, killed in battle with the British."

"Sí, my lady. How do you know?"

"Let's just say that I am a distant relative. I'm called Quazel."

"It is a pleasure to meet a fellow Barcelonan so far from home."

"You were here years ago. I felt your presence."

"Sí, I was here doing a very foolish thing."

"An' it please you, come into my humble abode and tell me all about yourself. I shall prepare supper, and you can have a proper rest."

"Much thanks for your kindness."

Quazel asked, "Will you bring the basket of vegetables I gathered?"

"Of course."

Quazel placed her hand delicately on the wall and said, "*Ianitor, invado.*"

The unsuspecting fly entered the spider's lair, and a small barn owl began a long trek to Draconis.

Quazel showed Ricardo to Morgan's old room where he bathed and shaved, the first in a long time. Quazel also provided Ricardo with a change of clothes for the next day and one of her infamous white suits to wear for supper.

Ricardo came to supper looking like a new man. Quazel commented, "Ricardo, you're quite dashing when you're cleaned and dressed properly."

"Gracias." Ricardo stared at the figure before him. Quazel wore black clinging silk, cut low to reveal perfectly formed breasts. Her glistening raven hair fell in volumes over her shoulders and bare back. Ricardo whispered, "Breathtaking."

"Ricardo, was that comment meant for me?"

"Sí."

"Gracias."

The air was heavy with a strange, sweet, sensuous scent. It was intoxicating. Quazel seemed to float as she served the food. "Ricardo, pour the wine. I think you'll find it exquisite. It's nectar wine, found only in this region."

The former pirate sipped the wine. It was the sweetest flavor he had ever tasted. "Delightful."

Ricardo could have been eating tree bark, and he would not have noticed so potent was the magic spell Quazel wove. She questioned him, "Now, Ricardo, what foolish thing could you possibly have done on Draconis all those years ago?"

Drunk from the magic perfume and the nectar wine, Ricardo's lips were loose. "Years ago I lived as a pirate, a looter of the seas. I came to these waters to seek vengeance on an old foe, a man who had me unjustly imprisoned and sold into galley slavery, and married the woman I loved." He held the goblet aloft and circled his hand. "I executed him in these very waters, only closer to the large island. I, then, rowed ashore with his wife and daughter with the intent of having my way with the woman, my old lover who I thought had betrayed me. She was, however, innocent and had no knowledge of the plot hatched by the man she married and her father. She fought my advances and was killed accidentally. Being a man of my word, I left the child on the island for I had promised not to kill her. Sometime after that, I discovered that the child was my own. I have returned in the hope that she survived on a deserted island, alone."

"You have a daughter? How old would she be?"

"Sixteen."

"Ricardo, I am certain she is well, for the island is inhabited by a few humans. They have peradventure cared for her; but if they were to discover she is a relative of mine, she could be in danger." Her lips twitched in a quasi-smile. "They banished me from their midst because I practice the black arts. You should go and rescue the girl on the morrow. Bring her back here to meet me before you decide to leave."

The evil witch spun her web tighter. She walked behind the man and began her seductive massage. "Ricardo, how long has it been since you have had the warmth and comfort of a woman?"

"Too long."

"I should like to remedy that." Quazel took Ricardo's hand and led him to her boudoir. The intoxicating fragrance was even stronger there, and a strange yellow powder floated in the air. She removed his doublet and kissed him sensuously. Completely lost to her spell, Ricardo swept her into his arms and took her to bed.

Ricardo awoke at dawn. Quazel slept soundly beside him. He quietly slipped from her bed and returned to the room she had given to him. He bathed and changed clothes. He wandered around the cavern and into each room. Finally, he opened the door to the prison chamber.

Not unfamiliar with the black arts, he recognized many of the magical objects, including the bloodletting instruments and the ceremonial dagger. He picked up an open book and read short passages dealing with human sacrifice of a virgin and prolonged youth by the consumption of a virgin's blood.

Ricardo carefully replaced the book and left the room. He looked into Quazel's chambers where she slept still. He closed the door without sound. Shivering in the gloomy light of glowworms, he touched the wall and said the words Quazel had spoken the day before. Nothing happened.

He made a swishing sound with his lips. *Obviously to leave I will have to wake the woman.* As pleasurable as the night had been, the morning's exploration brought disconcerted feelings to his heart. He had a strong desire to protect Miranda from the influence of this woman. A voice wafted on the air. "Vas a fracasar. Tú eres igual que yo." ("You will fail. You are just like me.") He had experienced enough evil and sin in his life to know something was amiss. It was time to leave.

He entered Quazel's room and gently shook her. "Quazel, wake up."

"What do you want? It's day. I sleep during the day. I'm a creature of the night."

"I wish to go to the big island to find my daughter. The words you spoke yesterday will not let me out. How do I get out? You may go back to sleep as soon as I leave."

"Very well. I wish you would stay longer. Last night was more than pleasant. It was exhilarating. Please bring your daughter to me. I should love to meet her. Touch the wall and say, '*Patefacio, licentia.*' Will you at least kiss me good-bye?"

Ricardo kissed her and whispered, "Gracias for a most memorable evening."

He left as quickly as he could. The lips that had been so sweet by night were as bitter as gall by day. Once outside the cave, he became sick and had to vomit. He spoke aloud, "If I find Miranda and she forgives me, I shall not bring her here. Oh, God, I promised You I would change. What did I do last night? Why did I succumb so easily to that woman's wiles? I pray help me to be stronger in the face of temptation. Help me to be worthy to be loved by someone better than that woman. And, right now, God, my head is splitting. I beg You give me some relief." Ricardo vomited again and heard a taunting laugh.

The air was still and the sea was glassy smooth, making the sail useless on the small craft, so Ricardo rowed toward Draconis. The going was slow. When the sun rose high in the sky, Ricardo stopped for a short rest and a bite to eat. The glare only made him feel sicker.

As Ricardo ate his meager repast, a barn owl landed with a thump in front of him. Ricardo was surprised to see this nocturnal animal in the noonday sun. When the owl sputtered, "Too hot. Too far to fly. Can't find Danielle," Ricardo almost jumped overboard.

Just as the man began to regain his composure and blame his headache, the heat, and his isolation at sea for thinking he heard an owl speak, Danielle popped up. "Hey, mister, tell Simon I'm here."

Ricardo grasped the oar tightly with the intent of using it to hit the creature, but first he closed his eyes, took a deep breath, and said aloud to himself, "Esto no puede ser. Esa mujer debe haberme embrujada mucho más de lo que creía, o me estoy perdiendo mi mente lejos he estado solo y en el mar demasiado tiempo. Por favor, Dios, haz que estas apariciones desaparecen. Restaurar mi cordura." He opened his eyes. The beautiful silvery-gray dolphin was still there.

"Take it easy, mister. Now, will you be so kind as to repeat what you said in a language I can understand?"

Unable to think what else to do, Ricardo repeated what he had said in English because the strange speaking animals spoke English to him. "This cannot be. That woman must have bewitched me far more than I realized, or I am losing my mind for I have been alone and at sea far too long. Prithee, God, make these apparitions disappear. Restore my sanity."

The dolphin called Danielle interpreted what Ricardo had said. "By 'that woman' you must mean Quazel. I don't know what she might have done to you, but I know what she did to us. You think you're losing your mind, but you're not. We're talking to you because we were once human. Quazel is a powerful, but wicked, sorceress who changed all of us. Don't worry. We're harmless, but you are *not*," Danielle finished as she recognized Ricardo. "You're that pirate who killed that man and woman. Your treasure is right where you left it. Take it and go." Danielle started to swim away.

"Wait! Prithee," Ricardo beseeched Danielle. "I am not the same man who came here ten years ago. The body is the same, but the heart is different. I have not come for the treasure. It can stay buried for all I care, although it was rightfully mine in the beginning." Ricardo touched the locket that hung around his neck. "This is the only gold I need or desire anymore."

"Then, why are you here?" demanded Danielle.

"The child I left." Ricardo dropped his head in shame. "I had to come back to make sure she survived and to give her this." He still fondled the locket. "'Twas her mother's."

Danielle eyed the man curiously. She was unsure whether to trust him, but he seemed genuine. He was almost too broken and contrite. *Mayhap, he has truly repented of his evil ways.* Danielle's naturally perky spirit wanted to console him; however, she refrained and instead she warned, "I'll personally keep an eye on you. Now, wake Simon and tell him Danielle is here."

Ricardo nudged the owl with his toe. He did not move. Ricardo nudged him a little harder. Still he did not move.

"Señorita Danielle Dolphin, I think he is dead."

"He can't be dead," said Danielle impatiently. "If he were dead, he would be human again."

Danielle saw Ricardo back away from where Simon lay. In frustration she jumped onto the side of the boat and held on with her flippers. She saw the body of a middle-aged man lying there. "Simon!" Danielle screamed. "No! He can't be dead. The only reason he would've started a flight to Draconis would've been if he had discovered the password to the secret entrance. Now, we'll have to start over again."

Still shocked, Ricardo said, "By 'password' do you mean the Latin phrase Quazel uses to enter her home?"

"Aye. We've tried to get it for years."

Ricardo's acute mind saw an entrance into this strange and mystical land and, perhaps, a way to atone for some of the pain and suffering he had caused. "I know the words she spoke last night. Mayhap I can be of some help."

46
𝔉irst 𝔏obe

𝔉or several days the little settlement on Draconis had been in a bustle. There was to be a wedding. The bride must have a distinct dress. Special foods had to be prepared. Morgan and Rennin simply sat back and watched everyone else plan their day.

Morgan whispered to Rennin, "You would think *they* were getting married."

Rennin replied, "'Tis too bad we can't elope and leave them to their fun."

"Rennin, isn't there something we can do to plan our own wedding? I haven't even had a say about my dress. I'll be using my mother's wedding dress."

"Aye, Morgan there is." He smiled at his bride-to-be. "I don't think the wedding planners have thought once about who will perform the ceremony. That owl I talked to once, I believe he called himself Devereaux, said he had been a priest but was excommunicated. As far as I know, there's only one person on Draconis who can legally marry us, and I've not seen him involved in the ado. Let's visit Granddaddy. We can at least plan our own vows."

Rennin took Morgan's hand, and they happily skipped to Duncan's house where they found him watching the frenzy from his window.

Rennin knocked and opened the door, calling, "Granddaddy?"

Duncan turned. "Ah, come in. I'm surprised you two haven't taken the sloop and sailed away. I would have."

Rennin sighed, "Oh, good. A kindred spirit," and hugged his grandfather.

Morgan stood by the door. Every time she saw Duncan she stood in awe of him. To her the man who had defied

Quazel all those years was godlike. He was the most handsome man she had ever seen, even more so than Rennin. He towered over even her Uncle Aidan, and at sixty-one he still had very little gray in his ebony hair. His eyes sparkled like emeralds, only finely etched with lines. He had a quiet peaceful dignity that touched everything in its path.

Duncan, too, had a heartfelt respect and reverence for the angel that had finally graced their lives. He marveled at the goodness that had survived in the face of pure evil and saw Morgan as a miracle and a promise that the future would still be bright.

As the two surveyed each other Duncan spoke. "Morgan, come in and sit down. I want to talk to you." She promptly obeyed.

Duncan sat on the table in front of the trembling girl and took her hand. "Morgan, take me off that pedestal where you've put me. I'm just a man, and I have no desire to be a god. That job is already taken and performed quite well. Tomorrow you're to become my granddaughter; that is, if you actually marry this rogue behind me. Before that, I want us to be friends. I'm not some all-powerful being. I've sinned many times and failed those I love many times. So, right now I want you to give me a hug just the way Rennin did and see that I'm no more or less human than you."

Morgan giggled shyly and put her arms under Duncan's and around his waist as he smoothed her hair. He whispered to her, "Little girl, you're with people who love you and who will protect you with their very lives, especially Rennin. He's devoted to you. Give him your honor and respect. Turn the rakish fun-loving boy into a loving, compassionate man."

Morgan spoke softly, "I'll love him with all my being until the day I die, Granddaddy, and I'll vow it before God tomorrow." She sat back down.

Duncan held his hand out to his grandson. "Rennin, come here." Rennin sat beside Morgan and Duncan put their hands together as he held them between his own. "You two will conquer a world yet unknown to us, but that will be another day. Today, you came here for a reason. What was it?"

Rennin said, "Granddaddy, you're the only person I know who can legally marry us, if I recall my studies correctly. Unless we recognize that owl, Devereaux, as a minister, he can't. Will you perform the ceremony?"

Duncan laughed joyfully. "I would be honored, but you'll have to wed aboard *The Privileged Character* because I only have the authority to marry people if we're at sea. Your marriage wouldn't be legal if I performed the ceremony on land, but that is something we will need to remedy soon."

"'Tis fine with us. As a matter of fact, I like the idea," said Rennin.

"Me too." Morgan agreed. "At least 'tis a plan we've made for ourselves."

"Granddaddy, besides the traditional vows, Morgan and I would like to say something special to each other. Is that all right?"

"If you want me to say 'will you' and you answer 'I will' and nothing else, we can do that."

Morgan laughed comfortably for the first time in Duncan's presence. "Even for me, that's a little too simple."

"Very well, you two let your mothers know the plan so they can put their flowers all over the ship. Tell me what kind of vows you want, and we'll astonish everyone tomorrow."

So, Duncan conspired with the two young people to have something of their very own on their special day.

The Privileged Character was decked in flowers and vines early in the morning for the ladies of the island had planned an all-day affair. The wedding was to take place at ten o'clock with a celebration afterward. The magical platform Alexander had conjured so that the ship could be dry-docked vanished and the vessel listed in the sea, a mile from shore.

Morgan wore the same dress Mary Kate had worn when she and Colin had had a double wedding with Aidan and Caitlin. In her hair she wore only a wreath of miniature white rosebuds and honeysuckle. She carried a nosegay of miniature white rose buds and honeysuckle entwined with English ivy.

Duncan found and wore his military uniform, which surprisingly still fit him. He beamed at his fellow conspirators for none of the guests had any idea there would be anything other than traditional vows

Duncan addressed first the guests: "You have come today to witness the richest and deepest magic in the world, the magic wrought in the hearts of a man and a woman as they pledge their lives to each other. Next to the bond between God and man, there is none stronger than the love God gave to be shared between a man and a woman. As you witness this man and this woman pledge themselves to each other for all eternity, remember the vows you took if you are married, or ponder the sanctity of the vows you will one day take when you pledge yourself to another."

Duncan turned to Colin "Who gives this woman to be married?"

Colin almost could not choke the words out. "I do." He had only found his baby, just to give her away again. Colin laid Morgan's hand in Rennin's and gave him a cold hard glare before tears welled in his eyes. Unexpectedly, Colin pulled Rennin into an embrace and whispered, "If ya doona take care of her, I shall kill ya. Seriously, Rennin, I love ya. I always have. I pray pardon for the black eye."

Rennin whispered back, "I swear I shall take care of her, and I love you, too, Uncle Colin."

Colin sat down as decorum demanded.

Duncan addressed Rennin: "Rennin, as a father Colin has entrusted you with his most precious gift, his daughter. Will you have this woman to be you wife?"

Rennin answered confidently, "I will."

"Then, repeat after me: 'I, Rennin Drake O'Rourke, take thee, Morgan Celeste Fitzpatrick, to be my wife, to have and to hold from this day forward, for better for worse, for richer for poorer, in sickness and in health, to love and to cherish, until we are separated by death.'"

Rennin repeated the words strongly for all to hear and see.

"Rennin, you have requested to say your own vows to Morgan as well. Will you share your heart with her now?"

Rennin's voice shook as he spoke the words from his heart. "Morgan, you blew into my life like a summer breeze and have filled my heart from that day forward. As God is my witness, I will be your protector, your provider, your lover, and your friend all the days of my life. I have heard my father speak these words to my mother every day of my life and since I could have had no better example, I now make them my pledge to you, 'Heart of my heart, life of my life, you are my reason for breathing, and I will love you until the day I die."

Duncan, then, turned to Morgan: "Morgan, as Rennin desires to share his life with you, will you have this man to be your husband?"

In her sweet clear voice Morgan answered, "I will."

"Then, repeat after me: 'I, Morgan Celeste Fitzpatrick, take thee, Rennin Drake O'Rourke, to be my husband, to have and to hold from this day forward, for better for worse, for richer for poorer, in sickness and in health, to love and to cherish, until we are separated by death.'"

Morgan repeated the words phrase by phrase with more confidence than anyone had ever heard in her voice.

"Morgan, you also have something special you would like to say to Rennin. Do so now."

Morgan touched Rennin's cheek as she spoke. "Rennin, for years you were my only joy, my only happiness, my only hope. You were my savior. I owe you all that I am and ever hope to be. Today, I pledge myself to you. I will be your joy, your happiness, your hope every day of my life."

Duncan spoke slowly for the children's words had touched him deeply. "Rennin, your father has made something for you just for this day." Duncan held out two small golden bands, which Rennin recognized to be made from the chain on Aidan's watch.

Rennin looked at Aidan. "Gramercy, Daddy."

Rennin took one small band and repeated after Duncan as he placed the ring on Morgan's finger, "With this ring I thee wed, and with all my worldly goods I thee endow."

Morgan took the other band, which was not a usual custom for the day, and placed it on Rennin's finger and repeated after Duncan, "With this ring I thee wed, and with all my worldly goods I thee endow."

Duncan leaned forward and kissed both young people on the forehead and said, "Rennin and Morgan, as much as you have pledged your lives to each other by the exchanging of vows and the giving and receiving of rings, I pronounce that you are husband and wife. Rennin, you may kiss your bride."

Rennin softly and tenderly kissed his new bride.

As Rennin pulled back from Morgan, Danielle shouted, "I have waited quite some time because I hate to interrupt such an important day, but this man knows the password to Quazel's chambers."

A small sailboat pulled beside *The Privileged Character*. Miranda let out a stifled scream and slid behind

Kieran. She whispered in his ear, "'Tis the man that killed my parents. I pray thee, don't let him hurt me, Kieran."

Kieran pulled Miranda into his arms and whispered back, "I shall kill him if I must." It was the first time Miranda had let Kieran touch her since the night on *The Privileged Character.*

47
Confrontation

Ricardo addressed Duncan because he was the only one who wore a uniform, "Permission to come aboard?"

"She's not my ship anymore. You need to ask my son."

Aidan leaned over the rail and instantly recognized Ricardo. "Permission denied. We can talk on shore." Aidan and Ricardo locked eyes. A silent understanding passed between them.

"I shall meet you on shore, Captain?"

"O'Rourke."

With a deferential nod, Ricardo said, "I shall meet you on shore, Captain O'Rourke." Ricardo steered closer to shore.

Aidan said, "Danielle, do you have any idea who that is?"

"Aye, I recognized him, too, but Simon is dead, and he knows the password. We must at least listen to him."

"What happened to Simon?"

"No, Aidan. I know what you're thinking. Ricardo, 'tis his name, didn't harm Simon. He landed in the boat and died. 'Tis that simple. His body is there now, and we will need to bury him."

"All right, Danielle. We shall meet in the war room and listen to what he has to say."

Aidan went to Rennin. "Son, I'm sorry this day hasn't gone as planned, but 'tis still your wedding day. Draco has a surprise for you. Go with him."

"Daddy, if you go, I should go with you."

"We shan't go anywhere for a couple of days. I will *never* jump into a plan blindly again. After all these years, two more days won't matter. You and Morgan deserve this day. Besides, you don't want to offend the dragons."

Rennin panned the sea of dragon friends surrounding the ship. "As you wish, Daddy, but, prithee, let me know what that man tells you."

"I will."

Rennin took Morgan's hand. "Let's go, Morgan. Daddy wants us to go with Draco."

"Rennin, what's happening?"

"I am unsure, but Daddy will come for us if he goes to Isla Linda. Draco has a surprise for us. We should accept his gift graciously."

Rennin and Morgan left with Draco.

Duncan took Aidan to the side. "Aidan, at first I think you and I should talk to this criminal alone. He might balk under the scrutiny of many eyes."

Kieran interrupted the tête-à-tête. "Da, I want to go with you."

"Not yet," said Aidan.

"Da, Miranda recognized him. I must protect her."

Duncan spoke sharply to his grandson. "Kieran, Aidan and I are going to talk to this Ricardo alone at first. When I get back later, I want you at *my* house. We'll have a talk about how to protect Miranda. Go there and wait for me."

Duncan had never spoken angrily to Kieran in all the years the grandson could remember. He immediately obeyed.

"Daddy, what was that about?" Aidan asked.

"Kieran will tell you when he's able. Let it go for now. We have a pirate to meet."

Aidan and Duncan asked Char to carry them to shore. When they searched for Ricardo, they found him beside Charlotte's grave. Aidan started for him, but Duncan detained him. The older man put his finger to his lips and then his ear to indicate that he wanted to hear what the man said.

Ricardo was confessing his sins to the ghost he had left behind as he knelt in contrition.

"Charlotte, I am so sorry. If I could trade places with you, I would. You did not deserve to die. I have cheated death so many times. I do not deserve to live. I only pray that our daughter can find it in her heart to forgive such a cruel and wicked man." The penitent man ran the locket between his thumb and index finger.

"Charlotte, I am a changed man. I want a new life. I want to be loved and to love. The only hope I have is Miranda. If she cannot forgive me, then I would just as soon join you.

"I wish you could tell me what to do. I met a strange woman." He took a shaky breath. "She held a power over me so strongly I felt smothered. I am verily afraid. I keep hearing her voice—taunting, condemning.

"There are people here who want to destroy this woman. I think they are likely correct, and I can help them. Charlotte, I do not want to be the cause of any more suffering or death, but I fear she wishes to harm Miranda. Can you not, I beg you, find a way to tell me what to do?"

Aidan could stand the eavesdropping no longer. He came forward. "I'm sure she'd tell you to help us."

"How long have you been listening to me?"

"Long enough."

Duncan stood beside Aidan. "Ricardo, I'm Duncan O'Rourke. Prithee, excuse my son. He's not a patient man. I, too, have been held under Quazel's spell. I know the fear and confusion. Ricardo, the woman is pure evil. We were here long enough to hear you claim Miranda as your child. Let me tell you what Quazel wants with your daughter. She wants to sacrifice her and to use her blood to prolong her own miserable life. Does that help you make a decision?"

"Sí."

"Good," said Aidan. "Then, let us away. There are a few people you should meet. Tell us everything you know." Aidan softened slightly. "Peradventure you can find a new life here on Draconis."

Aidan called Char. Ricardo asked, "Do you truly expect me to mount that thing?"

Still feeling some need for Ricardo's punishment, Aidan replied, "He only eats bad humans."

Ricardo climbed on Char's back carefully. The dragon chuckled all the way to Alexander's Cavern.

Draco took Rennin and Morgan to a fabulously furnished chamber on the cliffs. He said, "'Tis my understanding humans take a wedding trip called a honeymoon. Since you can't go anywhere, we dragons brought the honeymoon to you. Each dragon contributed to make this chamber as your mothers said an inn should be. I hope it meets with your approval."

Morgan pulled the dragon's head down and kissed him. "'Tis wonderful, Draco."

Rennin hugged the beast. "Many thanks, Draco. We couldn't ask for anything more perfect."

The white dragon was pleased as he said, "Then, I shall leave you alone. I think I'm supposed to say congratulations and best wishes." Draco flew immediately to the caves.

Morgan sat on the bed and ran her hand over the sheets, "Rennin, the sheets are satin."

Rennin sat beside his bride. "This is much nicer than an old blanket on the ground."

"'Tis beautiful," said the bride. "So, why am I still so afraid?"

Rennin looked into his wife's gorgeous brown eyes. "Would you like me to put your fears to rest, Mrs. O'Rourke?"

"I like the sound of that, Mr. O'Rourke, but I'm very afraid. It could take a while to allay my fears."

"Then I should get started with this." Rennin kissed Morgan softly as he unpinned the flowers from her hair. He slowly ran one fingertip across her lips and traced a path across her chin, her throat, her shoulder, and her breasts.

Morgan closed her eyes and sighed with contentment as she whispered, "Again."

The groom's hands trembled as he unbuttoned the looped buttons on Morgan's wedding dress and slipped it from her shoulders to perform the ritual again, this time touching soft skin.

Morgan lifted Rennin's shirt over his head and dropped it to the floor. She kissed his chest and nibbled his neck until her mouth found his.

Rennin whispered, "Mrs. O'Rourke, you seem to be overcoming your fears."

Morgan breathed, "Give me time to practice and we shall see who is scared."

Rennin laughed, "Is that a promise?"

Morgan pushed Rennin down onto the bed. "Rennin, you talk too much," she laughed as she kissed him passionately.

Aidan and Duncan escorted Ricardo into the one place on Draconis that retained any of the island's past glory, Alexander's Cavern. Ricardo took in the room, the furnishings, and the magical trinkets. In awe he breathed, "Spectacular! And all of Draconis was once this majestic?"

Aidan spoke curtly, "So I'm told. I've never seen it so."

A white haired man with clear sparkling green eyes came to the visitor. "An' it please you, sit down." He offered Ricardo a plate of food and a goblet. Ricardo reluctantly accepted the food and cautiously tasted a bite.

Alexander said, "'Tis not poisoned or drugged. 'Tis exactly as it appears, nourishment and cool clear water."

Ricardo, feeling a bit ashamed of his distrust, said, "Much thanks for your hospitality."

"You're welcome. I'm Alexander O'Rourke. I wish to tell you some things before we ask any response from you. I know you still doubt your senses. Who wouldn't after a night with Quazel? She appears to be very desirable, but you'll see when I'm done she is anything but desirable.

"I came here years ago when Draconis was glorious. Not long afterward, a dark beauty wrecked on our shores. I saw her change an entire land and annihilate a race with the exception of a few gestating eggs."

The aging wizard sat beside the confused newcomer. "However, there was a prophecy in Draconian history that foretold of a tall man with green eyes, a relative of mine who would come with the power to destroy the evil one. When my son appeared here we thought he must be the one. We were wrong. He, too, was changed, but with a different curse that could be broken without Quazel's death, but a curse she thought could never be broken even with her death because she didn't know Aidan existed. As you can see the curse on him alone has been broken."

Ricardo nodded with some hesitation.

The magic user continued. "Miraculously, God sent my grandson. As you can see, he must be the one who was prophesied. He's our hope for a bright future, but he can't fulfill his calling if he's unable to get to the evil. That's where you come into the scenario."

Ricardo scanned the faces of those around him. The group was not large, but he felt intimidated. There was an urgency here that made his heart quake.

Duncan spoke to this man for whom he felt a strange bond. "Ricardo, don't fear us. Let me introduce you to everyone."

"You have already met Danielle and Aidan, so we will start with the fearless leader of Draconis, Seamus O'Donnell. To those living as animals, he is known as King Satin."

"Hardly fearless," said Seamus. "Sir, I, too, have experienced Quazel in a very personal way." He put a paw to the patch over his eye.

Duncan continued, "This is my lovely daughter-in-law, Aidan's wife, Caitlin. She's actually a breathtaking redhead."

Caitlin acknowledged the introduction. "I am as you see me because the witch wanted my husband."

"Meet our dragon council: Draco, the first born of a new generation and eldest dragon council member; Char, who did not eat you; and Brindle.

"These are Colin and Mary Kate Fitzpatrick, and last, but not least, my oldest friend, Diggory Danaher and his wife and my sister and Quazel's daughter, Elizabeth."

Ricardo spoke slowly, not knowing what to say. "I am awed in your presence. I am Ricardo Morales-Mendez."

Elizabeth interrupted, "Did you say Morales?"

"Sí, my lady."

"Who was your father?"

"Quazel asked the same question."

"'Tis important."

"Pablo Morales-Martinez, and my grandfather was Tomas Morales-Rodriguez."

"Quazel's brother!"

"Señora, are you saying this woman who seduced me is more than eighty years old and related to me? This is the aunt of whom no one will speak?"

"Aye. 'Tis why she seduced you. Ricardo, why did you come back?"

"To ask my daughter's forgiveness."

"Miranda. She's in grave danger," said Elizabeth. "Quazel wants to attempt a blood offering. 'Tis why she took Morgan. She must have the blood of a young virgin and one who shares the same family line as she. Morgan is her great-granddaughter. That plan has been thwarted, but Miranda is her great-grandniece."

"No!" shouted Ricardo.

Duncan spoke calmly, "Miranda is in no danger. Kieran will take care of her."

"But..." began Elizabeth.

Duncan took on his old authority. "Elizabeth, trust me."

Ricardo saw how no one argued with Duncan. It was obvious who led this group.

Mary Kate spoke, "Mr. Morales, what do you want from us?"

Ricardo was taken aback. He thought they wanted something from him. "I wish to have one hour with my daughter to beg her forgiveness and to give her this." He touched the locket. "It belonged to her mother."

Mary Kate stood and pounded her tiny fist on the table. "No! You almost destroyed that child! I have loved her as my own for the last ten years. The only father she has in this room is Colin! I will *not* let you hurt her. Do you understand?"

"I ask only one hour. You may be present if you wish, Mrs. Fitzpatrick."

Mary Kate sat down. She whispered, "One hour. Not a minute more."

Duncan said, "Ricardo, there is one more thing I wish to show you. I think 'twill seal your decision to help us." Duncan removed a gold chain from around his neck. On the end hung a perfect, multi-faceted diamond. "Wear this and remember your night with Quazel. Then, tell me how beautiful and desirable she is. You have heard our words, but you must see it yourself." Duncan dropped the necklace over Ricardo's head.

The night he spent with Quazel flashed before him. He saw even in his memories the monster she truly was. He saw the hideousness that evil had wrought in her life. Ricardo screamed, "Take it off!"

Duncan removed the charm and led Ricardo to a corner and a pan because the pirate was nauseous again. Duncan whispered, "I vomited when I saw her, too, almost forty years ago."

Ricardo fell on Duncan's neck and whispered, "*Ianitor, invado.*"

"What?"

"Those are the words to get in, '*Ianitor, invado.*' To get out say, '*Patefacio, licentia.*' Go and do what must be done. Do it quickly for I fear if I do not bring Miranda soon, she will suspect something is amiss."

Only a voice Ricardo heard said, "Usted tendrá que pagar un precio alto por esta traición . Voy a tomar todo de ti—tu amor, tu cordura, tu futuro, su vida misma. No puedes ganar." ("You will pay dearly for this betrayal. I will take everything from you—your love, your sanity, your future, your very life. You cannot win.") He shivered.

"I have one thing to do for Miranda before we can leave," said Duncan.

Turning to the group, he said, "Draco, take me home. The rest of you prepare to go to Quazel's lair at first light."

Aidan said, "Rennin."

"Leave Rennin alone," Duncan commanded. "He and Morgan aren't a part of the power of seven. We are all here."

Draco dropped Duncan at his house and went home to rest before morning. They would be leaving at first light.

Duncan walked into his living room where the lantern had almost gone out. Priscilla was curled up in Duncan's chair, and Kieran slept on the couch.

Duncan carried Priscilla to bed. She stirred and said, "Kieran is downstairs. He says you're angry with him. What has the boy done?"

"I shall tell you another time, my sweet, but I shall tell you something to dream on now. Tomorrow at this time, I think I shall be looking into your beautiful face once more. Good night."

Duncan sat in his chair and looked at his grandson. He rubbed his hands across his face and spoke aloud to the sleeping boy. "Oh, Kieran, if you had half the backbone your brother has, you would have been married weeks ago. I hope you are truly penitent. You have always outwardly been the good son while inwardly you screamed to be yourself. Rennin was himself. He has never tried to be anything else. Oh, my beautiful, sweet little boy. 'Tis time to grow up and be your own man," Duncan finished as he caressed Kieran's hair.

"Kieran, wake up," Duncan spoke sharply.

"Granddaddy, what time is it?"

"'Tis late, but that doesn't matter. We must talk. Tomorrow we leave for Quazel's lair."

"What time do we leave?"

"You aren't going. Listen! If something goes wrong, you, Rennin, and Declan, as Alexander's descendants, will be the hope for the future."

Kieran nodded his acquiescence.

"I want to talk to you about Miranda. Kieran, I don't have time to bandy words. You have shamed that girl."

"What do you mean, Granddaddy?"

"Kieran, don't play innocent with me!" Duncan slapped his thigh. "You have lain with that girl, and for some reason, I think it was against her will. 'Tis in her eyes. She never looks anyone in the eye anymore. 'Tis in her voice when she speaks nowadays. She hardly ever speaks anymore when she used to talk gaily all the time. 'Tis in the way she carries herself and covers herself with clothes that hide her beauty. I've seen her when she thought she was alone, shedding silent tears. I've watched her shy away from you. Kieran Sean O'Rourke, I am appalled. You should go to Miranda this very evening and fall on your face. Beg her forgiveness and marry her!"

"Oh, Granddaddy! I am so ashamed." Kieran buried his face in his hands and wept. "I have asked her to forgive me and she says she does. That is what hurts so much. I am not worthy of her. How can I ask her to share her life with someone as despicable as I?" The boy's green eyes glistened with remorse.

"You should have thought about that before you forced yourself on her!"

Duncan walked to the fireplace and stoked the embers. "Kieran, who else knows about this?"

"Only Rennin."

"Rennin knows?" He glanced over his shoulder. "Of course he does. You and he are two sides of the same coin. What did he say to you?"

"He told me I was a fool and that I should spend the rest of my life earning Miranda's love. He told me to forgive myself and marry her as soon as possible. Then, he told me about him and Morgan."

"Wise words from one so young. Kieran, listen to your brother. You should also know the pirate, Ricardo, is actually Miranda's father. She doesn't know. How much sorrow can she bear? Kieran, go to her tonight."

Duncan opened a wooden box on the mantle. "Kieran, this is the wedding ring Alexander gave my mother. She asked me to give it to my firstborn son when he was ready to marry. I wasn't there for Aidan when that happened, but I think she would be happy if I gave it to my firstborn grandson. Ask the girl to marry you. I don't know which father's permission you'll need to seek, Colin or Ricardo. You may need to ask both."

"'Tis it not a little late to wake Uncle Colin and Aunt Mary Kate?"

"They are staying in the mountains. The only other person at home is Declan."

Kieran hugged Duncan. "Granddaddy, can you ever think highly of me again?"

"I love you, Kieran. That will never change. Live up to your responsibilities and you will earn my respect. You can start right now."

"Gramercy, Granddaddy." He started out the door but turned back. "Granddaddy, 'twas like a force drove me that night. I had no control over my actions."

Duncan knitted his brow. "I believe you, but *you* must still make it right."

With a nod, Kieran fairly danced down the lane. His heart was lighter than it had been in months.

Kieran started to knock on the door but decided he did not want to wake Declan. Instead, he picked six each of his mother's red, white, and yellow roses. He tied them together and climbed the trellis beneath Miranda's window. He tapped lightly.

Miranda, who was not yet asleep, cracked the window. "Kieran, what are you doing here? Are you crazy? You're going to fall and break your neck."

"Let me in."

Miranda looked over her shoulder. "Kieran, 'tis my bedroom."

"Miranda, I beg you. I swear I shan't hurt you." He handed her the roses. "Prithee?"

Miranda opened the window wide enough for Kieran to come in. She hastily put on her dressing gown.

"Oh, Miranda, do you feel such revulsion for me you hide yourself from me?" Kieran reached out to brush a stray wisp of hair from her face.

Miranda put up her hand. "If you touch me, Kieran, I will call Declan."

"Miranda, your words say you forgive me, but your actions say something else."

"Kieran, 'tis not a matter of forgiving, but trusting."

"What can I do to regain your trust? I shall do anything you ask."

Miranda looked at her suitor. The pain still showed in her eyes. "Can you give me back my innocence and honor? Kieran, how can I ever give myself to another man after what you took from me? I'm just glad God has seen fit to let you keep your sordid little secret. At least I'm not with child."

"Miranda, what other man?"

She narrowed her eyes to slits. "Declan would marry me tomorrow if I gave him half a thought I might want him, but God help me, I still love you even after what you did to me." Fresh tears flowed down her cheeks.

The sorrowful young man knelt at the girl's feet. "Miranda, I will confess my sin to the world. I will fall prostrate before you. I will grovel and beg and plead. I will do anything to win you back. I was a fool and a coward. I will not make excuses. I accept full responsibility. Miranda, I love you with my whole being, my heart, my soul, my mind, and, *yes*, my body. No, my love, I cannot restore your innocence, but your honor was never lost. Mine was— it was stolen from me that night. *You* were stolen from me.

"Miranda, without you I'm only half a man. I know I have nothing to offer you save myself, which is, indeed, small; but I want to be with you all the days of my life. I will spend each day earning your love and trust if you will only have me."

Kieran reached a trembling hand into his pocket. "This is the ring my great-grandfather gave to his wife on their wedding day. I want to place it on your finger in front of everyone and then shout openly and honestly, 'This woman is mine, and I am hers. I will love her all the days of my life and thereafter if it be possible.'

"Miranda, prithee, marry me. Marry me as soon as Granddaddy gets back from Isla Linda and can perform the ceremony."

"Kieran," whispered Miranda as she stroked the golden curls on her beau's bowed head. He was sobbing. "Kieran." Miranda took a step closer to the broken lover.

Kieran wrapped his arms around Miranda's hips, laid his flushed face against her abdomen, and rested on the soft cotton dressing gown, his energy spent.

"Kieran, stand." Miranda pulled him to his feet. She caressed his cheek and he kissed the palm of her hand. There was softness in her eyes the young man had not seen in months.

"Aye, Kieran, I'll marry you." She took his hand and led him to her bed. She nestled into his arms, and they fell asleep.

For some the dawn came quickly; for others it came slowly; nonetheless, dawn came. The small troupe that had waited for this one act for fifteen years donned their instruments of battle. Each carried a dagger and sword and wore a dragon-scale breastplate and gemstone charm, except Alexander who needed no charm. Caitlin carried no weapon, save her claws. Aidan once again placed the golden amulet around his neck.

Ricardo watched the preparations in silence before he asked, "Do you wish me to come with you?"

Duncan shook his head. "No, Ricardo. We eight have known this day would one day come for us. We have longed for it, but 'tis something that only we can do."

Aidan handed Ricardo an envelope. "If I don't return, give this to my son, Kieran. He'll see you have your hour with Miranda."

The valiant few climbed aboard the three dragons, who were their most loyal friends, and zoomed into a date with history.

Smoke, who had eavesdropped from the ledge above the cave, paced to and fro, debating with himself. *Aidan promised to get Rennin if he went to Isla Linda. He lied. Even if Rennin doesn't go into Quazel's chamber, he can wait on the beach nearby. Rennin will be upset. Oh, but he's on his honeymoon, and that's very special. He can go back to his honeymoon.* Smoke made a decision and flew to the honeymoon chamber.

The groom's most special friend arrived at the entrance to the sound of laughter. He crept into the chamber and saw Rennin chasing Morgan around the room. Rennin wore only a towel while Morgan wore Rennin's shirt. Rennin caught her, and she did not seem to really be trying to get away, he wove his fingers into her hair and kissed her. When Morgan let Rennin's towel fall to the ground, Smoke figured he should let his presence be known.

"Excuse me. I'm sorry to interrupt your honeymoon, but Aidan and the others went after Quazel. I thought you should know." Smoke turned to leave.

"Smoke, wait," Rennin called after the young dragon as he dressed quickly. "What do you mean?"

"The chosen ones left at dawn to finally kill Quazel."

"Out upon it, Daddy! I suppose he thinks he's protecting me. Morgan, get dressed."

"I'm ready." She had thrown her dress over her head when Smoke spoke. "Let's go, and don't attempt to leave me behind."

Rennin touched her face. "Never. Now, let's get Kieran and Declan, and I suppose Miranda, too."

Rennin ran into Kieran's room. He wasn't there. "Grandma's," said Rennin. He barged into his grandparents' house. Kieran wasn't there.

"Rennin, before you disturb Memaw and Papaw, see if he spent the night with Declan. We have to wake him anyway." Morgan gave her new husband a lopsided grin.

Rennin banged on the Fitzpatricks' door. Bleary-eyed, Declan opened. "Rennin, what the devil?"

"Declan, they went to Quazel's without us. Get dressed. Is Kieran here?"

"No."

"I shall get Miranda," offered Morgan.

Morgan tapped on the door and went in. When she saw Miranda in Kieran's arms, she locked the door and shook the sleeping lovers. "Both of you wake up. Kieran, do you want Declan to find you here?"

"Morgan, nothing happened," Kieran defended. "We just slept."

"Convince Declan and Daddy of that, not me. You saw what Daddy did to Rennin."

"He speaks the truth," said Miranda.

"I know," said Morgan, pointing. "He's dressed except for his shoes, but do you think the men of the house would believe it?"

Rennin knocked on the door. Morgan responded. "Miranda is dressing," which she did hurriedly. "She has an idea where to find Kieran. Go to the kitchen and grab some boiled eggs, bread, and milk so we can eat on the way."

"What's happening?" whispered Kieran.

"We're on our way to Isla Linda. Our folks went there this morning. They have the password and are going after

Quazel," Morgan explained as she pushed Kieran out the window and threw his shoes to the ground.

"I know. Granddaddy told me not to come."

Morgan saw the roses still tied together in a glass of water. She snatched them and looked out the window. "Kieran, catch. Bring them to the front door. Tell them you went to gather Miranda some early morning flowers. We're going anyway."

The girls opened the door. Rennin leaned against the jamb with his arms folded and his ankles crossed.

"Did you push him out the window? Don't worry. Declan is in the kitchen. Did he break anything going down the trellis?"

"You know not of what you speak," said Morgan and she took Miranda's hand and led her down the stairs just as Kieran knocked.

Rennin said, "Let me get it. Gee, I wonder if that could be my brother." He opened the door and jerked Kieran in as he whispered, "Get the leaves from your hair. You truly aren't very good at this sneaking business."

In fifteen minutes they were at the cave where they found Ricardo reading one of Alexander's books.

Rennin grabbed the man by the shirt. "We don't have time for niceties. My father is confronting Quazel. She has almost killed him twice before. What's the code?"

"*Ianitor, invado.*" Ricardo did not hesitate to tell the impatient young man. "Prithee, allow me to come with you."

Miranda clutched Kieran's arm. Rennin replied, "Fine, but if you make any attempt to assist that perversion of nature, I'll personally cut out your heart."

Another minute and they were winging their way to Isla Linda. As they flew, they saw Seamus on the beach with Danielle in the shallow waters.

"They are waiting to see each other as humans," said Ricardo.

The chosen few stepped into the cave with drawn swords while the dragons guarded the entrance. Duncan put his hand on the wall and prayed Quazel had not changed the code. He spoke the words Ricardo had given them. "*Ianitor, invado.*"

The passage opened. The group entered quickly and quietly. They were surprised there were no guards, but they had been told Quazel's troops had scattered after Duncan had been restored.

Even stranger was that they heard humming in the prison chamber. Quazel had not yet gone to bed. The door stood open. Quazel was preparing the sacrificial elements.

Caitlin, Colin, Mary Kate, Diggory, and Elizabeth quietly encircled Quazel while the three O'Rourke men filled the doorway and touched the tips of their swords. Electricity crackled upon the blades and ran the length of Aidan's edge. His sword glowed ethereal blue. Duncan moved to the side, Alexander stayed in the doorway, and Aidan stepped forward.

At the crackling noise Quazel raised her head. Aidan spoke, "Quazel, I have come for you."

The sorceress wheeled around and saw she was surrounded. The circle tightened. No matter which way she stepped, someone blocked her path. The witch saw that each member of the group wore a gemstone charm. "I've been betrayed *again* by my own blood. The girl is *not* a virgin or that fool father would have had her here by this evening."

Outside, Rennin was pleading with Draco to let them pass. "Draco, if something should go wrong, Daddy might need me. I'm here and ready, willing, and able to complete the task."

Draco stood his ground. "Duncan forbids you to come in."

"Fie, Draco! I've never defied your authority, or Granddaddy's as far as that goes, but that's my father who's putting his life on the line in there." He stabbed the air with a sharp index finger. "I've let him down too many times. I'll not do it today."

Rennin turned as if to go back to the little band of people. Suddenly and unexpectedly, he whirled around and darted behind Draco's hind leg. He was to the wall and saying, "*Ianitor, invado.*" Almost before Draco turned around, he was inside.

Draco narrowed his eyes at the rest of the group. With a deep throaty growl, he blew a ring of fire around those who waited and said, "Would anyone else like to pull a dido like Rennin?"

Rennin ran up behind Alexander who quickly quieted him. The boy stood there, a spectator.

Quazel lifted her hands in surrender. "I am defeated," she uttered as she fell to her knees. "I have one final request, Aidan O'Rourke. Even a condemned woman is afforded that."

Aidan nodded.

She said, "Make it quick with one swift swing of your blade."

The crone bent her head as Aidan raised his sword. In a lightning's flash Quazel lifted her hand and thrust the ceremonial dagger under Aidan's breastplate. Aidan dropped to his knees and spat blood from his mouth.

Rennin yelled, "Daddy!" He tried to pass Alexander.

Aidan leaned on his sword and spoke with authority, "Stay back, Rennin. This is *my* destiny. If she gets to that door, she's yours, but I don't think she'll make it that far."

Quazel laughed bitterly. "The morning I heard the echo of your voice saying you'd come for me, I swore I'd kill you if 'twas the last thing I did. So be it."

Aidan coughed and spat more blood and struggled to stand.

Quazel made as if to pass him. Alexander raised his hand, an ice bolt prepared to be thown. Tiny ice crystrals floated from the zig-zag shape in his hands, nullifying any spell the sorceress might cast.

As a droplet of water condensed on her skin, Quazel let out a shriek that could be heard beyond the granite wall. She gave Alexander a snarl in which her canines elongated. The witch tried the other direction.

Caitlin roared and raised a paw, claws spread wide. The circle tightened, cutting off any avenue of escape. Duncan held tightly to his son's right arm and helped him stand. Blood drizzled from Aidan's mouth.

Quazel cackled. "Do you really think this is the end?"

Aidan raised his sword and with one swing Quazel's head flew across the room.

He fell to the floor gasping for air.

Diggory bellowed in agony and there was a cracking sound.

The room began to spin for Aidan.

Caitlin screamed and loud popping sounds filled the air for several seconds, and then Aidan saw her face. Duncan had covered her with his cloak. Aidan reached his hand up and touched her cheek. "Heart of my heart, life of my life, you are my reason for breathing, and I will love you until the day I die." Rennin knelt beside Caitlin.

Aidan struggled to speak, "Rennin...don't let...mother do...foolish."

Aidan closed his eyes. "Caitlin...cold. Take me...sunlight."

Diggory hurried forward and invoked the exit words.

Duncan carried Aidan to the beach. Draco let his prisoners go.

Kieran knelt by his brother; tears streamed down his face. Duncan still held his son.

Aidan looked for Caitlin. "Caitlin, I love you." Aidan's body went limp in Duncan's arms.

Duncan laid his son in the sand. Caitlin refused to let go of his hand. Mary Kate touched Caitlin. "Let me try. Remember Eunice and Duncan."

An hour later, Aidan lay still and rigid. Mary Kate sobbed, "Why will it not work for Aidan? Oh, God, he sacrificed himself freely. Why?"

Elizabeth touched Mary Kate. Mary Kate sobbed, "Momma, you do something."

Elizabeth looked at the crowd. Without another thought, she stretched herself over Aidan uttering the incantation in the ancient language and then, "Blood of my blood, breath of my breath, restore sweet Aidan from the brink of death."

Nothing happened.

Duncan commanded, "'Tis over. Let him go."

Part Four

New Lives for Old

48

Restoration

Draconis was in uproar! Celebration reigned!

After several long moments of screams and pops, sounding like pistols firing in rapid succession, naked humans ran across sand, through grassland, among woodland, all across Draconis.

On the beach Seamus enveloped Danielle. "'Tis over, Danny. 'Tis truly over!" They danced around, momentarily oblivious to the fact that they were naked.

Danielle stroked Seamus's slightly graying chestnut hair that hung halfway down his back. "Your eyes are blue. I knew they would be blue."

"Do not you mean eye, Danny?" Seamus said with a wry grin. "Look at you! You are absolutely gorgeous! I should have known you would be a redhead. Your strong-willed independence should have told me that. You look like a sunset."

Seamus was six feet tall with a broad chest. Standing beside the petite auburn-haired, brown-eyed Danielle, he looked like a giant. Seamus lifted her and she wrapped herself around him.

"Danny, marry me. Marry me the minute Duncan gets back."

"Aye, but I shan't wait another minute to be with you."

Feigning surprise, Seamus said "Here? Now?"

"Right here. Right now."

"As you wish, milady." Seamus kissed Danielle the way he had dreamed for so many years as they sank into the warm inviting sand, and the waves lapped in rhythm to the beating of their hearts.

Duncan gathered Aidan in his arms and spoke compassionately to his daughter-in-law. "Caitlin, honey, you have to let go now. Let's take him home."

Caitlin walked with Duncan as if in a trance. She shed no tears, showed no emotion at all. Draco placed the dejected father and wife on his back.

Rennin and Morgan were already on Smoke. Rennin addressed his brother, "Kieran, are you coming?" Miranda took Kieran's hand and they slowly climbed on Smoke.

Alexander said, "Go on. I shall come with Char in a little while. We have some business to attend. Ricardo, will you stay and help me? I need the help of someone younger and stronger."

Realizing how much of an outsider he was, he replied, "Sí, sir. I shall gladly assist you."

Everyone else mounted Brindle, and the victorious, yet grieved, family flew home.

As the dragons approached Draconis, the conquering heroes were greeted with cheers and adulation. They, however, hardly noticed the welcome, but flew to Alexander's Cavern. No one spoke much. Victory and freedom had come at a high price.

Seamus, cuddling on the beach with Danielle, said, "Something's wrong. Char isn't with them." Seamus and Danielle went aboard *The Privileged Character* and borrowed some clothes. Esmeralda circled the island as she waited for Draco's return. Seamus called, "Esmeralda, will you give us a lift to the caves?"

"Who are you? I'm sure I know you, but I don't recognize anyone."

"Seamus and Danielle."

Esmeralda appraised them. "Not bad for humans. Climb aboard." They followed closely behind the returning heroes.

On Isla Linda, Alexander and Ricardo, with Char's help, built a fire where they burned Quazel's body. The old man asked as they worked, "Ricardo, do you practice the secret arts?"

Surprised by the question, he answered honestly. "I have dabbled in my younger days, but I have no desire to replace my ill-fated aunt."

A wind tickled Ricardo's ear. "Usted es demasiado débil para reemplazarme." ("You are too weak to replace me.") Ricardo inhaled sharply.

Alexander tilted his head to the side and scowled. He shook his head. "I'm glad to hear that, but my daughter will need an assistant when I'm gone. None of my male offspring seem to be interested in the practice, though one has remarkable ability. I sense a great hidden talent in you."

"Where are you going, sir?"

"Nowhere any time soon, I hope, but I shan't live forever. You said you want a new life. Will you consider apprenticing with Elizabeth and me?"

"I would not know where to begin."

"Books, my boy, books."

Ricardo was thoughtful for a long time before he replied. "After I meet my daughter, I shall consider your proposal."

With a nod, Alexander said, "I understand. Many thanks for your help today, Ricardo. Now we must return to Draconis. I need to mourn my grandson, as does Char."

They buried the few bones that had not turned to ash and left for Draconis with a feeling of desolation.

Char's brow ridge drew down hard in confusion. Large dragon tears fell to the sea below.

Seamus and Danielle arrived at Alexander's Cavern to see Kieran and Rennin spread a clean white satin sheet over Alexander's table. Duncan held Aidan in his arms and spoke. "Caitlin, get the clothes he wore to Rennin's wedding. They will do nicely for a burial shroud." Caitlin obeyed, still in her trance-like state.

Seamus came to Duncan's side. "Duncan, let me help."

Duncan stared blankly at Seamus for a few moments before recognizing the boy who had sailed from Draconis with him. "Seamus?" He turned to the attractive auburn-haired lady, "Danielle?"

Seamus repeated, "Let me help."

Duncan acquiesced. "Aye, of course. Seamus, I need to get Priscilla. Will you help Caitlin and the boys change Aidan's clothes? We can't bury him covered in blood."

Duncan climbed onto Draco's back. "Draco, how do I tell his mother? I can't do this."

"Aye, you can, Duncan. You must," said Draco. A large tear wove its way down his scaled face, landing on the ground with a slight sizzle. "I'll be with you. Draw from my strength."

The revelry and celebration came to an abrupt halt as word spread that Aidan had given his life to free Draconis from Quazel's curse. The island was once again shrouded in sorrow. Aidan lay in state in Alexander's Cavern. His grandfather insisted on two full days to give all the inhabitants the opportunity to pay their final respects. He whispered a spell of coolness to preserve the body from rapid decay.

Those who came found Caitlin holding her husband's hand. She refused to let go. Finally, on the night before Aidan's funeral, Rennin and Kieran pried Caitlin's hand loose. Kieran carried his mother like a baby, and the boys took her home.

The household tried to sleep, but Rennin tossed so much Morgan insisted he get some warm milk. When he went downstairs, he found Caitlin in the kitchen holding Aidan's dagger to her chest.

"Mam!" Rennin wrestled the blade from his mother. "What are you doing?"

A single tear traced a path down each of Caitlin's cheeks. "I want to be with Aidan."

Rennin pulled his mother into his arms and wept into her hair. "I know, Momma, but you can't leave Kieran and me, too. We need you. You have to live for us and for the grandchildren we'll one day give you. Do you think Daddy would want this?" He held up the dagger.

Finally, Caitlin lost control and crumpled into her son's embrace. She sobbed, "How can I live without him, Rennin? He's my life."

Rennin sat with Caitlin for a long time and let her cry. At long last, she cried herself to sleep, and Rennin carried her to bed.

Exhausted and in much need of his own comfort, Rennin went to his wife. Morgan was gone.

In the quiet deserted cave as morning streaked the sky, Morgan dismounted Smoke. "Prithee, wait outside. I want a few minutes alone with Uncle Aidan before they put him in the ground."

"Morgan, are you going to be all right? Rennin will be angry with me if I let anything happen to you."

"Aye, Smoke. I shall be fine. I need to say good-bye alone."

"If you insist, but call me if you need me. I cannot lose Rennin too. My own father is curled in our cave and will not leave. He says he can still feel Aidan." Smoke walked out the entrance to wait. He heaved a great sigh. His heart was heavy.

Morgan approached her uncle quietly. She touched his hair and held the hand that Caitlin refused to release. It was surprisingly warm. "Uncle Aidan, I should have been with you. I'm your guardian angel, remember? Why do you have to leave us? Rennin still needs you, and Kieran needs you more than ever." She looked toward where Smoke waited. "Char is devastated."

Morgan kissed her uncle's hand and spoke again. "God, Quazel never told me about You, so I only have a little faith. I suppose it comes from my mother's teaching when I was very young, but she believes You perform miracles. She told me how You restored Eunice and Granddaddy Duncan. She told me how much You hate evil. God, I have known such evil in my short life. Mayhap I'm not worthy to even speak to You, but Momma says You forgive and heal. God, if You hate evil so much, why does it have to be that although Quazel has been defeated and a deep dark evil has been lifted, she seems to have had one more victory in killing Uncle Aidan? God, I suppose 'tis too late to ask You to give Uncle Aidan back, but I want to have the kind of faith my mother has. So, if You would only show me that You're real, I would tell everyone I meet about Your power. Amen."

Morgan kissed Aidan softly on the lips. "Alas, this is good-bye. Many thanks to you for having someone as wonderful as Rennin. I love you, Uncle Aidan."

As Morgan laid Aidan's hand down, suddenly the fingers tightened on her hand. She screamed, "Smoke! Smoke!"

The dragon charged into the cave ready to blow his first breath of fire. Morgan commanded, "Get Rennin! Get Rennin now!"

Rennin banged on Colin's door. His uncle answered the door sleepily, "Rennin, what's wrong?"

"Is Morgan here?"

"No. Why?"

"I sat with Mam for a while, and when I went back to bed, she was gone."

"Gone where?"

"I don't know, Uncle Colin. 'Tis why I'm here."

Smoke swooped down. "Rennin, Morgan needs you in the cave now!" Smoke picked up Rennin in his talons and swung him onto his back.

"What's wrong, Smoke?" Rennin demanded to know.

"I don't know. She wanted to say good-bye to Aidan alone. Then, she screamed for me to get you." The leaves swirled as the young dragon took wing, leaving Colin to shield his eyes from flying debris.

Rennin jumped from Smoke before he stopped moving. "Morgan!"

"Rennin, come quickly!" shouted Morgan. "He's alive!"

"Impossible," said Rennin, noticing Char standing against the wall, tapping his talons together as if clapping.

Morgan whispered, "God can do anything."

Rennin touched Aidan. He was warm. Rennin gently shook his father. "Daddy. Daddy, 'tis Rennin. Open your eyes."

Aidan's eyes fluttered open and he spoke hoarsely and haltingly, "Did...you...keep..." He licked his dry lips. "Your...mother...from...doing...anything...foolish?"

"Daddy, you're alive!" Rennin bear-hugged his father. Aidan winced.

"Easy, son. That wound hurts."

"How?" asked Rennin in wonder and amazement.

Char danced up and back. He rumbled, "I knew I could hear your thoughts."

Aidan gave his bonded dragon a smile. His muscles working better, Aidan said, "Quazel's dagger must have been tipped with the juice from the *Chondrodendron* vine. Remember that her minions often had poison-tipped daggers, spears, and arrows. She had the dagger, planning to use it on Miranda. She must have intended to paralyze her before the bloodletting. I was never dead; but she figured if the wound didn't kill me, then you would bury me, and I would die. Either way, she thought I would be dead. I'm glad Seanathair delayed my funeral to give everybody a chance to pay their final respects. And the unintended benefit from her poison is that my blood loss all but stopped."

He tried to lift his hand, but could barely raise his fingers. "I couldn't move, but I could hear everything you all said—the prayers, the spells, the promises, the confessions. I'm going to have a long talk with Kieran."

"Daddy, plan a wedding and leave it alone. They have both suffered enough," Rennin defended his brother. "Now, I think we should take you to Mam."

"I agree. I can't wait to hold her in my arms. It has been too long."

After a few more minutes, Aidan tried to stand. "Rennin, I need your help. The effects of the poison haven't completely worn off."

Rennin said, "Forget going home right now. Stay here and recover. Morgan, will you bring Mam to Daddy?"

"Of course I will." Morgan hugged Aidan. "I'm so glad you're alive."

Aidan closed his eyes and channeled a thought directly to Char. *She's not gone.*

She has to be. I burned her bones.

Holding a cup of coffee flavored with cocoa, Caitlin sat at her dining table with Kieran. He had made her favorite in an attempt to lift her spirits.

"Mam, you need to eat something. You haven't eaten a bite in two days."

"I'm not hungry."

"At least drink your coffee. I made your favorite."

"Your father made this same coffee for me the morning we set sail for Draconis. He thought it would cheer me, too. You were both wrong."

"Mam, I miss him, too, but Da would want us to live. He loved us more than anything."

"Correction," said Morgan's lilting voice. "*Loves* us. Aunt Caitlin, Kieran, he's alive."

Caitlin looked at her daughter-in-law in disbelief. "What did you say?"

"Don't take my word for it. Come on. He wants you now."

Caitlin and Kieran followed Morgan. Morgan stopped. "You two go on. I need to get Granddaddy Duncan and Grandma Priscilla."

Caitlin and Kieran flew off.

Draco lay on the ground outside Duncan's home. He gave Morgan a wide-eyed stare. His talon's clicked the hard packed dirt. *Is it true?* His thoughts reached into her young mind.

She gasped, but nodded. The white dragon jutted his chin toward Duncan's home. *You tell him.*

Morgan knocked on Duncan's door. The man who opened it was a different man than the one who had performed Morgan's wedding ceremony only a few days before. He appeared stooped and had dark circles under his eyes.

"Hello, child. Is there something I can do for you?" Duncan greeted half-heartedly.

"No, Granddaddy. There's something I can do for you. Look at me."

Duncan turned to the gentle young woman, his face wet with tears. "Priscilla won't get out of bed. She says she refuses to put another baby in the ground."

"Good." Morgan smiled. "Go and drag her out and tell her there's no need to put Aidan in the ground. He's alive."

Duncan grabbed Morgan's shoulders. "What did you say?"

"He's alive!"

"How?"

"He said something about a poison on Quazel's dagger, but he was *always* alive."

Duncan swung the dainty girl through the air before he ran upstairs and literally dragged Priscilla from bed.

Caitlin laughed and cried and kissed Aidan for many minutes before she could speak. "How? What happened?"

Before he had finished his explanation, Duncan and Priscilla blew into the cave with Draco behind them, and he had to start all over. Within hours the funeral gathering had turned into a joyous celebration of life and freedom that lasted well into the night.

49
𝔗𝔯𝔞𝔤𝔢𝔡𝔶

𝔉𝔦𝔫𝔞𝔩𝔩𝔶, able to move his extremities and walk with ease a few days later, Aidan went home. The gaiety continued anew all around the settlement. Alexander broke out his hidden store of nectar wine. In the lane where the immigrants from Stonebridge had made their home there was as big a celebration as there was all around them. Of course, those who lived there, Aidan and Caitlin; Duncan and Priscilla; Colin and Mary Kate; Diggory, sans his hump, and Elizabeth; Rennin and Morgan, Kieran and Miranda; Alexander; Declan; Drake and Martha Fitzpatrick; and Sarah Thames, attended. Jean Noir and Isabella LeBlanc, no longer horses, were there, as were Seamus and Danielle and Lars Willoughby, former governor of the island and former wolf. Many of Duncan's crew, such as Ligon Murphy, Patrick O'Leary, and Connor Donohue, were there. Eunice in all her unicorn glory graced the gathering. All the generals who had fought with Duncan attended, and Alexander had kindly invited Ricardo to join the celebration saying, "Without your help we wouldn't be celebrating at all. You're welcome to spend the night in my home."

Many dragons celebrated with their bonded humans.

After a time of becoming reacquainted with old friends in new bodies, Alexander proposed a toast, "Ladies and gentlemen, to courage, honor, perseverance, and a job well-done and to Aidan. Long live the vanquishing hero!"

The crowd cheered and raised their glasses in salute with calls of, "Speech! Speech!"

Aidan had to take the spotlight. "I'm not a man of many words. I leave that job to Caitlin." The crowd laughed at Aidan's jibe. "This isn't my night. 'Tis a night for gratitude to God and praise to everyone who ever fought the evil that held Draconis." Aidan raised his glass. "I salute all of you, my friends and loved ones. Without you this day never would have come." He drank the glass to the bottom. "Now, celebrate for tomorrow we rebuild a great land."

Aidan gathered Caitlin in his arms. "I hate making speeches."

Caitlin pinched his ribs. "Ouch! What did I do?" he said.

She teased, "So, I talk too much, do I?"

"Can you not take a jest?"

"From you? Aye." She kissed him hungrily.

Aidan said, "Caitlin, I hardly think this is the place for that kind of behavior."

"Do you think we can slip away unnoticed?"

"My, my, beautiful lady, what do you have in mind?"

She kissed her husband again. "Peradventure a visit from Catherine is in order. She has been dormant far too long."

Aidan kissed Caitlin in return. "I would rather have a visit from this gorgeous redhead I know. I've missed her and she's more to my liking."

"That can be arranged for I know how much she has missed you." Caitlin took Aidan's hand, and they disappeared into the house.

Alexander stood beside Ricardo, who drank very little. "You don't enjoy the wine?" the wizard asked.

"I do not wish to lose control of my faculties."

Alexander chuckled. "I suppose someone should keep a clear head, but it shan't be I tonight. I've looked forward to this celebration for almost sixty years."

"And you should enjoy it." Ricardo tapped glasses with Alexander and took a sip of his wine.

Alexander became serious for a moment. "You've watched Miranda dance all night. Talk to her."

"The young man, Aidan's other son, is her lover, is he not?"

Alexander looked at Ricardo with a little concern. "He's her betrothed. Lover? I don't know."

He lies to protect the boy. Ricardo sighed. "I remember when Charlotte and I looked at each other as they look at each other, before her father and my competitor sold me into galley slavery. I would give anything for a woman to look at me like that again. There's nothing more wonderful, except, perhaps, the love of a child. Alexander, if she cannot forgive me, what do I do then?"

"Live. Make a new life for yourself. It could take some time for her to accept the truth, but you can never give up. Even if she can't forgive you right away, mayhap, in time, after she sees you're truly a changed man, she'll be able to forgive you."

"So, you think I should speak with her tonight, without Mrs. Fitzpatrick?"

"Definitely without Mary Kate. She means well, but she's too emotionally involved this time. She does love Miranda as if she were her own daughter. Go on; talk to her. I shall take care of Kieran."

The two men approached the couple as they danced. Kieran glared at the Spaniard as Ricardo spoke, "Señorita Montgomery, I would like a moment to speak with you."

Kieran declared, "You have nothing to say to her."

Ricardo leveled a gaze at Kieran. "On the contrary, I have a great deal to say. I would also like very much to speak to *you* later. I believe there is something you have neglected to ask me."

Kieran was ready to punch Ricardo when Alexander grabbed his arm. "Kieran, you don't want to do that."

"Aye, I do, Seanathair."

Ricardo spoke. "Sí, he does, Alexander, and he has my permission to do so if I may return the action later when we talk."

"That sounds good to me," said a rash Kieran.

Alexander released the boy's arm, and Kieran hit Ricardo with a punch that put the older man on the ground and brought blood to his lip. Ricardo stood, licking the blood. "Would you like another turn, young Señor O'Rourke?"

"Aye!"

Miranda screamed, "Stop it! I shall talk to you briefly. Let's go to the gazebo behind Momma's house. Kieran stay here. I think I shall be fine. If not, I can scream loudly." She gave Ricardo a sneer. "And dragons could hear if I whispered."

Miranda and Ricardo went to the gazebo. Her voice quivered as she said, "Talk. I'm listening, and prithee stop staring at me."

"I am sorry. You look so much like you mother."

"My dead mother that you killed. Don't look so shocked. Did you in truth think I wouldn't remember you?"

"No. I knew you recognized me, Miranda."

"Excuse me, but Miss Montgomery will do."

Ricardo closed his eyes and tears escaped through his long lashes. He breathed deeply.

With the unexpected response to her harsh tone, Miranda relented. "Very well. You may call me Miranda."

Ricardo opened his eyes. "Miranda, I never intended to kill Charlotte. I never wanted to hurt her."

"You tried to rape my mother. Mr. Morales, rape is hurtful even if you love the person who did it. I know."

"How would you know?" He took a deep breath, the answer already imbedded in his mind.

"Never mind. Say what you need to say."

He nodded slowly. "The words you speak are true. I was a cruel and wicked man, but I have changed. I came back here to find you and to beg you to forgive me."

"Forgive you for murdering my parents and for leaving me to die on what you thought was a deserted island? You ask a lot."

"There is more. Miranda, I once loved you mother even as Kieran loves you." He rolled his lips together, thinking just how similar that love was. "Her father and Malcolm Montgomery conspired to sell me into galley slavery. That is where I rowed for pirates and had the whip put to me and learned to hate. I thought your mother knew about my betrayal. I was wrong. She thought I had abandoned her. She died before either of us knew the truth about the other."

Ricardo took off the locket. "I gave this to your mother before I was sold. There is something in it your mother wrote. I read it for the first time long after I left you here. I would like you to read it for I fear you would not believe my words. If, after you read it, you can find it in your heart to forgive a fool, I shall be staying with Alexander. On the other hand, if you cannot forgive me, I shall go to live in Alexander's Cavern, and you never need see me again." Ricardo handed Miranda the locket and left her alone.

The former pirate returned to the party and found Alexander and Kieran. "Pardon me, gentlemen. Kieran, I believe you and I have some unfinished business. Let us take it somewhere private."

Kieran looked at Alexander. The aged wizard replied to Kieran's silent question. "You brought this on yourself." *In more ways than one.*

Behind Alexander's house, Ricardo pinned Kieran to the wall. "You want to beat the hell out of me because of what I did to Miranda. You are right to feel such anger toward one who would hurt the woman you love. Now let me ask you what kind of anger a father should feel for a man who would rape his daughter?" He ground his teeth. "I want to *kill* you, but I will not because my daughter loves you. I understand you are to be married. I suppose you have my permission, but I think you should ask your uncle for formal permission. His wrath might be even greater than mine, and know this: If you ever hurt her again, I will kill you. You will not be the first man whose life I have taken." Ricardo punched Kieran as hard as he could. "Now, we are even and our agreement is complete. Miranda probably needs you right about now. Go to her."

Two peas in a pod, went through both men's minds, one in Draconian English; the other, Spanish.

Kieran, with a broken nose, found Miranda crying in the gazebo. "Miranda, what did he do to you?" he asked.

Miranda handed Kieran the letter from the locket. "Kieran, he's my *father*. He never knew. He wants my forgiveness. What do I do?"

"Miranda, do you truly forgive me for what I did to you?"

"Aye."

"Have I sinned any less against you than he has?"

"Kieran, I don't understand."

"Ricardo sinned against you when he thought you were a total stranger, even the daughter of a man who had cheated him of his life and his love. I sinned against you when I loved you. If you can find it in your heart to forgive me, I think you have the capacity to forgive him."

"Kieran what did he do to you?"

"He was honest with me. He wants to kill me because he knows what I did to you, but he loves you. He has given us his permission to marry, but he wants me to ask Uncle Colin for formal permission." He touched his nose gingerly. "Then, he returned my punch, but I think he hits harder."

Miranda gently touched Kieran's nose. "'Tis broken."

"I know. Mayhap now I shan't look *exactly* like Rennin."

Kieran and Miranda embraced. "Forgive him, Miranda. Give him a chance for a new life. I'm not telling you to love him or to have a close relationship with him, but forgive him. I think it will give you peace."

"I shall try, but it could take a long time."

When Kieran and Miranda returned to the party, Ricardo was talking with Alexander. "I think I shall go to bed. I see Colin's parents are leaving, too. Many thanks, Alexander, for making me feel welcome."

Miranda approached the two men. "Are you leaving the party without a dance with your daughter?"

Ricardo looked at the girl with a broad grin. "Do you truly want to dance with me?"

"'Tis one step. I can't promise I'll ever love you the way you might want, but I'm willing to try to forgive you, and I'd like to know the man who gave me my start. Don't expect me to call you 'Daddy.' You must realize I love Colin like a father. He'll always be special to me."

"As he should be. He has done a fine job as your father. Call me Ricardo. Many thanks."

"Don't thank me. Thank the man with the broken nose. Now, dance with me before you go to bed."

"Gladly."

The voice came to him again, speaking his native tongue. "Tan galante. ¡Ha! Es solamente un acto. Ella te odia." ("So gallant. Ha! It is only an act. She hates you.")

The two danced beautifully together while Alexander and Kieran watched. Alexander asked, "Is the fighting over?"

"Aye, Seanathair."

Alexander looked across the way. "I have my doubts. Here comes Colin, and he has been drinking heavily. Ricardo was sober."

"Kieran, lad," said Colin loudly as he put his arm around his nephew's shoulders. "We need to talk."

"Aye, Uncle Colin, we do, but 'tis not the right time."

"Not the roight time? 'Tis no time loike the present."

"Uncle Colin, you're drunk."

"Aye, I am. That gives ya an advantage. Perchance I shan't break *every* bone in yer body, only some of them."

"Why would you want to break my bones?"

"Let us walk and I shall tell ya."

Kieran appealed to Alexander. "Seanathair?"

Alexander shrugged. Miranda saw Kieran and Colin leaving. "Ricardo, Colin will kill him if he knows anything. I know what he did to Rennin, and Rennin did not force himself on Morgan. Do something. I pray you. I love him."

"I shall follow them to make sure Kieran stays alive, but he will have to fight his own battle."

Ricardo followed Kieran and Colin to the gazebo and watched from a distance. Colin said, "Kieran, why would Quazel say Miranda is not a virgin? When did she give herself to ya?"

"Uncle Colin, you're talking about the words of a witch. Miranda has never given herself to me."

"If she didna give herself to ya, then why is she not a virgin?"

"Uncle Colin, you're drunk. Sleep it off. On the morrow I shall come to your house and ask formal permission to marry Miranda." Kieran started to leave.

Colin grabbed his arm. "I may be drunk, but I am not stupid. Ya have been with Miranda. 'Tis why Duncan knew she was in no danger from Quazel's little spell on Ricardo." He wiggled his fingers on his left hand in the air. "How on Earth have ya and yer brother developed such low morals? Yer father would never have behaved in such a way."

"Uncle Colin, I love Miranda. I want to marry her. Ricardo has already given us his permission, but I want your blessing, too. Now forget what some evil woman told you, and let's have a drink together."

"Kieran, ya will marry Miranda, and I will have a drink with ya after I teach ya a lesson. If ya loike ya can hit back, although I doona think ya have the nerve for that."

"I would never hit you, Uncle Colin."

"That makes me job easier. It looks loike somebody else had the same idea," Colin said circling Kieran's nose with his index finger. "Was it an angry father?"

"Aye. So take your best shot and get it over."

"Ya aire just as arrogant a little prig as Rennin, aire ya not?" Colin hit Kieran harder than Ricardo had. Kieran lost his balance and fell. "Get up!" Colin shouted at the boy. "Ya aire worse than yer brother. If she had given herself to ya, I would stop; but since ya obviously forced the issue, ya deserve more. Get up!"

Kieran stood. "Go ahead, Uncle Colin. I deserve it."

"Aye, ya do." Colin hit Kieran again. He kept his feet. "Boy what I would loike to do to ya is illegal. At least I think castration is illegal. Mayhap 'tis not illegal on Draconis." Colin hit Kieran again. The boy's mouth bled, and his eye swelled. Colin's next punch went to the midsection. Kieran doubled over and dropped to his knees.

Grabbing Kieran by the hair and yanking his head upward Colin snarled, "Get up!"

Ricardo stepped forward. "Kieran, stay down. Colin, 'tis enough. If Miranda forgives the young fool, then, we should let bygones be bygones. Let Kieran marry Miranda and do what is right. Come on. As Miranda's two angry fathers, let us have a drink together. Then, I am going to bed, and you should sleep off the wine you have imbibed."

Ricardo turned to Kieran. "Find Miranda and let her clean you up. Then go home and go to bed. You did deserve it." *But no more than I.* He helped Kieran stand.

Caitlin lay in Aidan's arms when she heard her brother. "Aidan, what is Colin hollering about? He sounds angry."

Aidan groaned, "Do I have to let go of you even for a second. I truly don't care what has Colin so riled."

"I shall keep your place warm."

Aidan reluctantly pulled the sheet around him and went to the window to see what was going on. He came back to bed. "Colin is beating the hell out of Kieran. Now, come here." Aidan pulled Caitlin to him.

She pushed away. "Aidan, why is Colin hurting my child?"

"Because he deserves it. Now come here."

"Aidan, what has he done?"

"Caitlin, you in truth don't want to know."

"Aye, I do."

"No, you don't."

"Aye, I do!"

"Caitlin!"

"Aidan!"

"Alackaday!" He slapped the pillow. "He raped Miranda. Are you happy?"

"I knew about that a long time ago. I heard him tell Rennin what happened. He is getting what he deserves. I am surprised it took Colin so long."

"Caitlin! You didn't tell me."

"I wanted Kieran to tell you himself."

"He did——when he thought I was dead."

"He was in all likelihood afraid he would get worse than Colin is giving him."

"He would have."

"And now?"

"Now? Now, I shall plan a wedding and leave it alone. They have both suffered enough, but first!" Aidan laughed wickedly. "I shall have my way with my wife." Aidan pulled Caitlin on top of him. She squealed.

After a while, the revelers became quiet, and all was peaceful. Many of the happy people built bonfires and camped where they had celebrated.

In the wee hours of the morning, the winds blew hard, but most of the sleeping people felt the effects of much wine and slept contentedly.

In his room in Alexander's house, Ricardo awoke to the smell of smoke. As he opened his eyes he saw a bright orange glow. Somewhere in his half-awake state, it dawned on Ricardo what he saw was not a bonfire.

Without changing from his night clothes, Ricardo bounded from the house, yelling into Alexander's room as he went by, "Alexander, the doctor's house is on fire!"

So full of wine were the campers that they did not hear Ricardo's shouts immediately. At last, several people awoke. Alexander pounded on Colin's door.

Ricardo lost no time running into the burning house. In a few minutes he carried an unconscious man from billowing smoke. Seamus saw Ricardo stagger out the door. He took Dr. Fitzpatrick and laid him at a safe distance. Ricardo coughed from the smoke as Seamus asked, "Mrs. Fitzpatrick? Miss Thames?"

Breathing hard, Ricardo replied, "I did not see the ladies. I shall go back; let me catch my breath."

"I shall go," said Seamus.

Many men and women bustled with buckets of water as the houses emptied. Elizabeth and Alexander began to throw ice crystals toward the blaze. Colin ran after Seamus. Within minutes, Colin stumbled from the house, his hands badly burned. He coughed, "Seamus ran upstairs. I started to follow, but the stairs fell in. I canna get up."

The crowd heard glass shatter. Looking up, they saw Seamus at the window with Martha Fitzpatrick in his arms. Sarah Thames stood behind him.

Even as several men surged ahead to catch the trapped victims and Seamus leaned forward to drop Martha into their waiting arms, the roof crackled loudly and caved in around the three people.

Danielle screamed, "Seamus! No!" She ran toward the engulfed house.

Ricardo raced after her. "Danielle Dolphin, come back! 'Tis too late!" He pulled her from the very flames of the door and held her so securely there were bruises on her the next day.

Danielle dissolved into hysterical sobs. Ricardo held her tightly and whispered words of comfort, "'Twill be all right, Danielle Dolphin. On my oath, everything will be all right."

That familiar voice snorted. "No eres un héroe." ("You are no hero.")

50
𝕬 𝕸𝖆𝖗𝖗𝖎𝖆𝖌𝖊 𝖔𝖋 𝕮𝖔𝖓𝖛𝖊𝖓𝖎𝖊𝖓𝖈𝖊

The morning broke with gloomy, heavy-laden clouds. As Diggory had often surmised, the weather reflected the mood of the people. The clouds unleashed their tears about midday.

The inhabitants of Draconis had lost many friends over the years; but this time they had lost the man who had so admirably assumed the role of a king, a man who had ruled wisely and justly, always thinking of his people before himself for nearly fifteen years.

Most grieved was Danielle. She stayed in one of Caitlin's guest rooms. So heartbroken was the former dolphin that she would not get out of bed for the funeral services.

Through his grief, Drake Fitzpatrick heralded the courage and selflessness of the men who had risked their lives to save him and his household, one who survived, one who sacrificed all, as well as his own son who sat in their midst, hands bandaged.

The week after the funerals, Dr. Fitzpatrick came into his daughter-in-law's kitchen. Miranda and Morgan were there talking in hushed tones. With a kiss and a smile for both girls Drake asked, "What is the big conspiracy?"

"Nothing, Papaw," answered the girls together.

"Could it be wedding plans?" Drake's eyes misted.

Miranda said apologetically, "Mayhap we should wait on the wedding. 'Tis too soon after such a tragedy."

Drake scoffed, though his voice caught, "Nonsense! Martha would have encouraged ya to go on with yer plans. She was so excited she had already started scouting the young ladies to find Declan a wife. I shall tell ya what: Go on with yer wedding, sweetheart, and name one of yer daughters after Martha. That would be the highest tribute ya could give her."

"Are you sure, Papaw?"

"I insist."

Miranda hugged Drake. "Gramercy, Papaw." She skipped out the door calling, "Kieran!"

Several weeks later Ricardo made his weekly pilgrimage to put flowers on Charlotte's grave. The strongbox he had buried remained in the ground beside her. As he neared the grave, he saw Danielle in the waves up to her chest.

¿"Ah, Dios, qué hace esa mujer"? ("Oh, God, what is that woman doing?") he said aloud to himself. Then, he yelled at her, "Danielle, do not be foolish! Come back!"

Danielle looked back but started further into the sea, ignoring Ricardo. The man kicked off his shoes and reached Danielle as a wave knocked her from her feet. He wrestled her to shore.

Huffing and coughing he shouted, "Danielle Dolphin, are you crazy? How many times must I keep you from harming yourself?"

The petite auburn-haired woman calmly replied, "Ricardo, the sea has been my home since the day I was born. I only want to go home. Being human is *not* all 'tis thought to be."

Ricardo was angry with this woman without understanding his reason. "Why? Because your heart is aching? Because you lost someone you loved? Danielle, pain is as much a part of life as joy. If you give it a chance, you will have joy, too."

"You sound so sure."

"I am sure. Look at me. I was joyous when I was with Charlotte. Then, I was miserable for years. Now, I have found happiness, or at least contentment."

Danielle sat up just as angry as Ricardo. "All right, Mr. Contentment, why have you not dug up your chest?" She jabbed a finger toward where the box was buried.

"It reminds me of what I was."

"So? Do we not need to confront our past to forge our future? I shall make a deal with you. I shan't attempt suicide again if you will dig up that box and show me what's inside."

Ricardo looked at the place where the box was buried. "Alack. I do not have tools for digging, but we shall come back tomorrow and dig it up together."

True to his word, Ricardo and Danielle hitched a ride on Brindle the next afternoon. Ricardo brought a shovel and dug. He hoisted the trunk to the beach and said, "Are you ready for this powerful treasure, Danielle Dolphin?"

Ricardo opened the box. A bunch of papers lay on top.

Brindle asked disappointedly, "Is there no gold? I thought you were a pirate."

"Ah, Brindle," laughed Ricardo, "spoken like a true dragon."

Ricardo lifted the papers and below was a tray of sparkling jewels. Danielle gasped at their brilliance.

"I did not steal them, Danielle. I took them back. They were mine before I was sold into slavery. The papers prove my ownership of a number of business ventures that Malcolm Montgomery and Victor Jordan, Charlotte's father, claimed as their own."

The former pirate picked out a large multifaceted diamond and chuckled. "Brindle, catch!" He tossed it.

Quick as a flash Brindle caught the jewel. Ricardo said, "'Tis yours to start your new treasure stash."

Ricardo started to place the coffer back in the ground.

"What are you doing?" asked Danielle. "These things are valuable and important."

"Not to me." His long black hair, tied back with a ribbon, fell over his shoulder as he shook his head. "I am home, Danielle. I do not want to go back to that life."

Danielle argued, "At least put them in Alexander's Cavern. They might come in handy someday."

"Very well," Ricardo relented. "I will if you will promise to live, truly live."

"I shall try." Danielle smiled sadly.

Kieran and Miranda's wedding day dawned clear and perfect. Miranda had solved the problem of which father would give her away. She walked with one on each side as she wore a lovely linen dress with puffed peasant sleeves and carried one white rose, one yellow rose, and one red rose, reminiscent of the flowers Kieran had brought her when he proposed.

The wedding was simple and to the point with no distractions. The only deviation from tradition came when Kieran placed his great-grandmother's ring on Miranda's finger; and Kieran surprised Miranda as he said, "With this ring I declare openly and honestly before all those present that this woman is mine and I am hers. I will love her all the days of my life and thereafter if it be possible."

"Kieran!" Miranda had tears in her eyes.

"I told you I would shout it to the world."

Duncan finally said, "I pronounce you husband and wife. Kieran, kiss your bride before she floods the ship."

The big event for Kieran and Miranda was the uninterrupted wedding reception. There was island music and dancing and food and wine.

As Kieran danced his first dance with his wife, he looked deeply into her eyes and said, "I love you, Miranda.

I've loved you since I saw you sleeping in that hollow log." They stopped dancing and kissed each other long and passionately.

Rennin harassed his brother. "Kieran, save it for tonight. I promise 'twill be worth the wait."

The guests roared with laughter. Miranda kissed a blushing Kieran on the cheek and whispered, "I promise it *will* be worth the wait."

Colin rescued the embarrassed couple. "Miranda, I think 'tis time for me dance. Kieran, dance with your mother."

Miranda kissed Colin. "I love you, Daddy. I always will. Thank you for adopting me and loving me." Miranda looked at Ricardo who stood with Alexander and Danielle. She sighed. "I think I should dance with Ricardo now. Do you understand?"

"Verily, I do, honey." Colin danced close to Ricardo and handed Miranda off. Ricardo beamed and danced with his daughter.

He whispered, "I am proud of the woman you have become. I owe Colin and Mary Kate a debt of gratitude."

Miranda smiled softly. "Mayhap I owe you a debt of gratitude. If Malcolm Montgomery was the kind of man you say he was, I was better off living with people like Colin and Mary Kate."

The party continued. Ricardo went back to his safe little enclave, Alexander and Danielle. Ricardo asked her, "Will you dance with me?"

"I don't think so."

"You promised me you would live."

"Alack. One dance."

Ricardo whirled Danielle around until she laughed aloud. He asked, "Did that hurt?"

"No, but I'm feeling faint. Will you take me home?"

"Aye, of course. Kieran and Miranda are leaving anyway."

Draco flew Kieran and Miranda to the honeymoon chamber. Draco chuckled, "I suppose Declan will be next. Did you notice all the girls swarming around him?"

"Uh-huh," mumbled the happy couple as they kissed each other.

Draco wagged his head. "And I thought Rennin and Morgan were bad." Draco dropped Kieran and Miranda and made a hasty exit. "Good luck," he shouted on his way out.

Miranda laughed, "I hope we didn't offend him."

"I think he in truth understands," assured Kieran. "What would you like to do now, Mrs. O'Rourke? I like the sound of that. I think I shall stop calling you Miranda."

"Don't you dare!"

"All right, my Miranda, what would you like to do?"

"I shall show you." Miranda slipped Kieran's shirt over his head and dropped it on the floor. Then, she pushed him backward toward the bed as she fumbled with his breeches.

"Miranda!"

"Now I want you, Kieran. This is the way 'tis supposed to be."

Kieran kissed Miranda as she pushed him onto the bed.

The next morning Caitlin came down the stairs to the kitchen late. At the table she found Morgan with a cold cloth on her face and Danielle with her face buried on her arms.

"What is this, too much wine?" Caitlin asked brightly.

"No," moaned Morgan. "This is the third day I have felt like this. Aunt Caitlin, I'm with child. I'm just too sick to tell Rennin."

"Vomit on him. He'll get the message." Caitlin laughed. "This is so exciting! Morgan, Danielle, can you keep a secret? I'm with child, too."

"How nice," sobbed Danielle. "Both of you are married."

Caitlin and Morgan suddenly realized that their joyous news was heartbreaking news for Danielle.

Caitlin asked candidly, "Danielle, are you expecting?"

Danielle nodded and started crying, "And Seamus is dead. What am I to do?"

Caitlin put her arms around Danielle. "You're going to have a little Seamus and tell him what a brave and wonderful father he had."

"Caitlin, Seamus and I weren't married. People are going to think I'm an immoral person. My baby will be branded a bastard."

"Danielle, you'll always be a part of this family, and I'll not let people treat you like that. Did you have a mate as a dolphin?"

"No. Seamus and I waited all those years for each other. He asked me to marry him. Then we thought Aidan was dead and found out he was alive and celebrated. We just had not gone to Duncan yet."

"Go talk to Duncan. Mayhap he will say he married you quietly."

Danielle wailed, "Nobody will believe *King Satin* wed without the whole island knowing. Oh, I'm going for a walk. I shall think of something."

Danielle walked and cried and thought and cried some more. She could think of only one course of action to keep her honor intact, and her decision broke her heart even more. Finally, she went to Alexander's house. No one was home.

Declan, who was pruning his mother's blackberry vines with three young ladies chattering at him, told Danielle that Alexander, Elizabeth, and Ricardo had gone to the cave early. There were things there Alexander wanted to teach Ricardo.

Danielle looked toward the mountains and some words Mary Kate had read once came to her memory. *I will lift mine eyes unto the hills from whence cometh my help.*

Danielle asked, "Declan, which dragon is in the clearing today?"

"I think Smoke came today. The parents had too much celebration yesterday."

Danielle walked briskly to the clearing where a dragon waited each day for the dear people in the settlement should they need to fly quickly. Thinking her decision had been confirmed with the memory of the words Mary Kate had read, Danielle asked Smoke to take her to Alexander.

With his usual genuine concern for the humans in the settlement, Smoke asked, "Is everything all right, Danielle? You seem anxious."

"I think everything will be all right later today, Smoke. Many thanks for caring."

Danielle found Alexander alone for Elizabeth and Ricardo were gathering herbs, but Ricardo returned as Danielle spoke with Alexander. He stayed in the shadows to hear what the woman wanted. He had an uneasy feeling it was not good.

Danielle sought the wizard's aid. "Alexander, I need your help."

"What is it, dear child?" Alexander sensed a deep sadness in the woman who had always been so blithe, even in times of war.

"Alexander, I'm with child. I can't have this child without Seamus. I need you to help me. I pray thee, make me a rue tea, and my dilemma will be over by morning."

Alexander's face went ashen. "No, Danielle. I will *not* do it. I'll not give you an abortifacient. I'll not help you kill an unborn child. I don't think 'tis what you want anyway. You sit here and have a cup of chamomile and ponder what you're asking. I'm going to find Elizabeth. I want *her* to talk to you."

Danielle sank into Alexander's chair as he left her alone. Her tears flowed freely once again.

Ricardo entered the room and spoke softly to the distraught woman. "Danielle Dolphin, I will help you."

A chuckle only he heard was followed by, "¡Sí! Mátalo. Y su." ("Yes! Kill it. And *her*!")

He shook it off.

She flashed angry eyes at him and went on a tirade. "Why am I not surprised? I should've come to you first. I should've known you wouldn't hesitate to give me a poison to rid me of this baby. Verily, you're a thief and a rapist and a murderer. What's one more innocent life to you?"

Ricardo set his basket of herbs on the table with trembling hands. His face was dark with his eyes half closed and his mouth in a thin line, but he spoke calmly. "I have no intention of giving you a poison of any kind. I will not help you kill this baby any more than Alexander. You do not want to kill it anyway. Your heart is breaking at the thought. No, Danielle, I have another solution to offer you."

Danielle saw she had cut the man, who had saved her life twice, to the quick. "I'm sorry, Ricardo. My words were cruel, and I didn't mean them. I'm hurting, and you were an easy target. Forgive me."

"'Tis forgiven and forgotten. Will you hear my proposal?"

"Aye."

Ricardo came to Danielle and knelt beside the chair. He took her hand. "Danielle, you are a beautiful woman. Your charms and attributes have not gone unnoticed by me. I am a very lonely man. You befriended me before anyone else.

Marry me, Danielle Dolphin. I will gladly give you and your baby my name and protect your honor. I am not asking you to love me or even to share my bed; only let me take care of you. Be my friend and companion. If someday something more grows between us, I would be overjoyed; but I am not asking for anything."

Danielle sat there, stunned and unable to respond. Finally, she asked, "You would be content to be a father to another man's child and husband in name only to a woman whose heart belongs to a dead man? Ricardo, 'twould be unfair to you. You deserve to be loved."

Ricardo shrugged. "Peradventure, one day you will have some affection for me. I would be honored to be a father to your child."

"But this is Seamus's baby. I'd want the child to know about his father."

"As he should. I will be his adoptive father. His father died a hero before he was born."

"What about his name?"

"Name him Seamus O'Donnell Morales if 'tis a boy. If 'tis a girl, would you consider naming her Charlotte, after my first love?"

Danielle giggled. "We're talking as if I've agreed to this preposterous plan."

He leaned his head to the side. "Have you not?"

"I suppose I have."

"Let us talk to Duncan. I will leave Alexander a note that I have left and to meet us on *The Privileged Character*. Since he knows your situation, he can be one of our witnesses. Whom else would you like to be a witness?"

"Caitlin. She knows."

Ricardo scribbled a hasty note to Alexander and he and Danielle left.

Duncan graciously performed a quiet ceremony for Ricardo and Danielle, and Danielle moved in with Ricardo and Alexander. That night Ricardo made a bed on his floor. Danielle asked, "What are you doing?"

"Going to sleep."

"Don't be ridiculous. This bed is big enough for two people to sleep."

"I have not asked you to share my bed. That was part of our agreement. I am a man of my word."

"Ricardo, I said 'sleep.' That's what I meant."

The man acquiesced. Ricardo lay beside his new wife and fought a great temptation to touch her.

The ever-present voice said, "Llévatela. Usted sabe que quiere." ("Take her. You know you want it.")

This marriage of convenience is going to be hard. He sighed.

51
Second Chances

Aidan, Duncan, Colin, and Rennin felled logs to build the newlyweds their own houses. Kieran would join them when he and Miranda returned. The morning after the impromptu wedding, Ricardo joined the men, saying that he thought Danielle should have her own house, too.

At noon Morgan showed up with two baskets, one for the workers and one for her and Rennin. She sweetly informed the older men, "I'm stealing him for a few hours." Of course, the men teased him mercilessly, but he left laughing with his wife.

Morgan spread Rennin's baby blanket, which Caitlin had knitted, on the ground by the brook. She had baby's breath in a jar for a centerpiece. She wore a baby-blue frock. Last, she served baby beef on bread cut into the shape of baby booties and milk.

Rennin plopped down and began to devour the food. "I'm starved," he informed Morgan.

"Obviously," said the young wife with disappointment in her voice.

"What's wrong?"

"Rennin, didn't you notice the theme of this meal?"

"We're having a picnic. 'Twas very sweet of you to do this."

"No. Rennin, look at the bread before you gulp it down."

"Cute, but little. I shall have to eat a dozen to stop my hunger."

"What are the flowers?"

"I don't know." He shrugged. "'Tis some fragile looking little white stuff."

"What is beneath us?"

"A very small blanket. Forsooth, it's not big enough for us to make love on it. Is that what you had in mind?" Rennin snuggled close to Morgan.

"Mayhap, but not if you don't catch on pretty soon."

"Give me another hint."

"Oh, marry! What color am I wearing?"

"Blue."

"What shade of blue?"

"Light-blue."

"Rennin you're dense!" Morgan started to cry. "Baby-blue, baby blanket, baby's breath. Hint, hint, hint."

The confused husband kissed his bride. "Oh, honey, just tell me you want to make a baby. I will gladly oblige."

"Not want to. Have. I was trying to tell you."

"Have? Are you? Are we?"

"Aye, dimwit." She spread her hand across the repast. "'Tis what all this is about."

Rennin kissed Morgan again. "I beg pardon I'm so dense. When?"

"About seven and a half months according to Papaw and Elizabeth."

"May I tell everybody else?"

"Aye, but I'd like to see the look on Uncle Aidan's and Daddy's faces when they find out they're going to be grandfathers."

"Let's go tell them and see who says, 'I'm too young to be a grandfather.'"

"We can tell them after our picnic, and I *did* have something else in mind. Do you want to forego that activity?"

"Not on your life."

Morgan and Rennin returned to the log site after a while, both smiling broadly.

Colin teased them. "What took so long?"

"We had to discuss something," Rennin quipped.

"Loike what?" Colin refused to let Rennin get the last word.

"Like the fact that you and Daddy are getting old."

"Who's old?" asked Aidan.

"You and Uncle Colin," said Rennin matter-of-factly.

"Colin might be, but I'm not," argued Aidan.

"Grandfathers have to be old," said Rennin as Morgan started to laugh.

Duncan said, "Pardon me?"

"Not you, Granddaddy."

"I'm the only grandfather here."

"Only for about seven more months."

"Oh, good grief," said Aidan as he picked Morgan up and hugged her. "I'm too young to be a grandfather, but Colin isn't." He turned and gave Rennin a hug. "Does your mother know? I want to start calling her Seanmháthair."

"I would hold off on that if I were you," said Morgan.

Colin hugged his daughter. "I am happy for ya, but I think I shall be called Pop or something young sounding."

Duncan laughed as the men went back to work. "Ricardo, you could be the next one to have that hammer fall."

"I hope they wait a while. I am just getting accustomed to the idea of becoming someone's father from the beginning." Ricardo said with a grimace, "Grandfather?" and shook his head.

Aidan came home worn to a frazzle. No one seemed to be around. He called, "Caitlin?"

"I'm upstairs."

Aidan found renewed energy at the sound of Caitlin's voice and trotted up the stairs. "Where is everybody?" he questioned as he neared the top.

"Staying at Colin and Mary Kate's tonight. We're alone."

Aidan entered their bedroom. Caitlin had been at work. Supper waited on a table with two long white tapers. Cinnamon incense burned by the bed. Aidan leaned against the wall and laughed to himself. "I must be getting old."

Temptingly Caitlin said, "Aidan, come on in." Aidan walked in, kicking off his shoes and pulling off his shirt at the same time. Caitlin was up to her neck in bubbles in a large oval tub. She motioned for him to come to her.

Aidan leaned down and kissed his vivacious redhead. "Care to join me?" she asked naughtily.

Aidan laughed. "I don't know if this grandfather-to-be has enough energy."

"Well, this grandmother-to-be has enough energy for both of us, and she has already been cheated out of too many years. Now get in here," Caitlin said, lacing wet sudsy hands around Aidan's neck.

Aidan slid into the steamy water and leaned back against Caitlin. She wrapped her arms around him and pulled his head onto her chest. Caitlin massaged Aidan's neck and shoulders.

He sighed, "You always did have magic hands. I'm feeling stronger by the minute."

Caitlin slid her hands down Aidan's chest and whispered, "We're magic together. I love you, Aidan. I've loved you since the first time I saw you take Colin down with a perfect slide tackle and steal the ball for a goal in practice. I knew that if you were strong enough to put Colin in his place, you could handle a fiery demon like me. You can handle anything that's thrown at you, even becoming a grandfather. Are you terribly upset?"

"No, I just feel too young. Of course Rennin and Morgan are a lot younger than we were when we had a baby."

"Only four years."

"Four years would make me forty. Grandfather at forty sounds a lot better than grandfather at thirty-six. Caitlin, we should not be grandparents. We should still be having our own babies."

"I'm glad you feel that way."

"Why?"

She hugged her husband tighter. "Because we *are* having our own baby."

Aidan sat upright. "What?"

Caitlin repeated, "We're having our own baby."

Aidan turned to face Caitlin and put his hand on her abdomen. "Caitlin, are you sure?"

"Aye, I went to see both Elizabeth and Da today. We have a little less than eight months to wait."

Aidan had a faraway look in his eyes. Caitlin said, "Aidan, are you paying attention to me?"

With his other hand, Aidan touched Caitlin's cheek. "I was just hoping this is a little girl who looks just like her mother. You can dress her fancy, and I can spoil her rotten. I promise I shan't be thrown overboard and miss the birth this time; and I shan't leave, no matter how hard Lizzie tries to get rid of me."

Aidan moved his hand down, and Caitlin jumped. Aidan leaned back in the tub and pulled Caitlin on top of him and kissed her. He breathed, "Make love to me, Caitlin. Make me feel twenty years old again."

A little shyly Caitlin said, "In the bathtub?"

Aidan ran his fingers through her hair. "Why not? We've never done that before, and I don't want to leave the comfort of these steamy suds yet."

New homes sprang up all over Draconis—near the beaches, in the grasslands and forests, in the foothills of the mountains, and in the oasis. The desert area became a small strip less than a day's journey wide. Duncan was a busy man performing wedding ceremonies, and *The Privileged Character* became the temporary chapel. His first changeling wedding was Jean Noir and Isabella LeBlanc, though they had been mates for years and had three children.

The inhabitants of the little settlement in the oasis jokingly began to call their village King Satin's Realm, but the name stuck, prompting the other settlements to want names. The beach settlement became known as Waterford; the grasslands were called Prairieville; the woodland town was known as Wildwood; and the foothill settlers called their area Sierra Bluff.

As in any loose settlement, the need for a government arose, especially since Draconis no longer had a king. Members from each town came to Duncan to ask him to be governor of Draconis. Among them was Lars Willoughby. Duncan modestly asked, "Lars, why don't you re-assume the position you once held?"

"No, Duncan, I'm content at this stage of my life to be the mayor of Sierra Bluff. We've all come together and decided we'd like for each town to have its own mayor and two council members for every fifty people with a minimum of two council members and then one fair and impartial governor for the island. We want you to be that governor for we all know you were King Satin before you handed the role to Seamus O'Donnell after you became human again. You ruled us well then. You can do it again. The position of governor will be a lifetime position to be voted on by the people for a successor, but you're to be the first. The mayor and council for each township will be elected every five years."

Duncan said, "It sounds as if you have a very fine plan to implement. 'Tis why I think you should be governor."

"Duncan, the people want you," argued Lars.

Priscilla squeezed Duncan's hand. Duncan replied to Lars and the other representatives, "I'll agree on these conditions: First, that the position be elected every seven years and not be a lifetime position, for if the people become disgruntled, I wouldn't like to end up at the end of an assassin's lance; second, that the dragon council be included as town representatives; third, that the town governments meet monthly while the state government meets quarterly; and last, that women have as many rights and privileges as men on Draconis."

The representatives talked among themselves. Lars said, "Duncan, about that last condition."

Duncan stopped him. "Lars, the women of Draconis fought just as hard as the men to win freedom. They died side-by-side with their male counterparts. Have you so easily forgotten Chanel? 'Tis only fair now they're human again they should be afforded the same rights and privileges as men, even to be elected to positions of power."

The representatives talked again. "Agreed," Lars said.

Draconian government was re-established, and King Satin's Realm had to elect its officers. They decided Aidan would be mayor and that Colin and Diggory would be council members.

Life in King Satin's Realm took on an easy routine. Everyone did the work needed to be done each day. In the evenings, three constantly growing pregnant women came together to knit and sew and crochet. They were often joined by the other ladies, while the men gambled for toothpicks. Ricardo usually won the games of chance.

Alexander jibed, "I think it must be the pirate in him cheating."

At first, the comment stung, but Ricardo eventually realized Alexander was just making good-natured fun. So, on the occasions when Alexander won, Ricardo returned the taunt. "It must be the wizard enchanting the cards."

Life went on this way while the new houses were being built. While Morgan and Miranda had hands-on work with their houses, Ricardo insisted Danielle's be a complete surprise when she walked in for the first time.

Naturally, Ricardo chose a day when the governments met to take Danielle to her house. He wanted as much privacy as possible. Danielle in her excitement turned the knob of the front door and started in.

"One moment, Señora Morales." Ricardo detained her.

He took out his silk handkerchief, blindfolded Danielle and lifted her in his arms. "I believe this is one tradition I should like to keep." He crossed the threshold and shut the door with his foot.

Danielle said, "You can put me down now. I can walk."

"I think not. Which room would you like to see first?"

"All of them," she laughed.

"How about the nursery?"

"That will be fine."

Ricardo started up the stairs. Danielle fussed at him. "Ricardo let me walk. I'm quite heavy these days. You'll hurt yourself."

"Nonsense! Let me have my fun. Quiet, woman!"

Danielle laughed. Ricardo opened the door tediously, but stepped through and set Danielle down. He untied the blindfold, and she started crying. "Ricardo, 'tis beautiful." She caressed the hand carved mahogany cradle and matching chest of drawers, dresser, and bentwood rocker. "You did all this by yourself?" Danielle threw her arms around Ricardo's neck. "Gramercy."

He said cheerily, "I thought the sunshine yellow and white trim would make for a sunny disposition. Do you like the colors? I can change them if you do not."

"'Tis wonderful. I wouldn't change a thing."

"Would you like to see your room?"

"My room? Don't you mean our room?"

"No, Danielle. You have your own room."

"Ricardo, why do we have separate rooms?"

He was surprised by the question. "Danielle Dolphin, I may not be a scoundrel any more, but I *am* a man. I have found it very difficult not to ask anything of you."

"I see. 'Tis just that I've grown accustomed to having you beside me. I feel safe with you there."

"I shall be right across the hall if you need me."

Danielle took a deep breath to control her tears. "Show me my room and yours, too, if you don't mind." Timidly, Danielle put her hand in Ricardo's. "Lead on," she said sweetly.

Danielle's room was white with pink rosebuds stenciled on one wall, a white canopy bed, dresser, and chest of drawers, and white linen curtains. "'Tis very soft and feminine, just what any lady would like," she said somewhat sadly.

"What is wrong?" Ricardo asked. "Is there something you want me to change?"

Danielle answered honestly, "Aye, but 'tis something I should like to change myself after the baby comes. You'll have to wait to see it just like I had to wait." She turned and winked playfully. "Now show me your room."

The room across the hall was pleasant with mahogany furnishings and beige paint. In addition to the regular bedroom furnishings there was a bookshelf with Ricardo's books that Alexander had given him. Danielle picked up one of the books and turned to Ricardo with a new light in her eyes. "Ricardo, will you teach me to read?"

"I would love to. That will pass the evening hours admirably."

Danielle loved her new house with one exception she kept to herself, and Ricardo left the evening card and dice games for a while to teach his wife to read.

Danielle learned quickly. One evening as they read together, Ricardo dropped his book and grabbed his head. He screamed, "Stop it! Leave me alone!"

Danielle was terrified. She knelt by her husband and stroked his hair, "Ricardo, what's wrong?"

"My head hurts so badly. Prithee, get Dr. Fitzpatrick." As Danielle stood to leave, Ricardo caught her hand. "Get Alexander too. I am afraid, Danielle. I can hear Quazel's voice."

Danielle ran as quickly as her body would allow and interrupted the men's card game. "Dr. Fitzpatrick, come quickly. Something's wrong with Ricardo. He asked for you and Alexander."

The doctor went to his house to get his bag, but Alexander went with Danielle.

Alexander asked, "Is he hearing Quazel's voice again?"

Wide-eyed Danielle asked, "This has happened before?"

"Twice that he's told me. And I'm sure his head is splitting just the way Quazel's used to."

They entered the house to see Ricardo holding his head and rocking back and forth. He was saying, "Vayase y dejanme solo. Yo no soy como tu." ("Go away and leave me alone. I am not like you.")

Danielle made Ricardo go to his room and lie down. She sat beside him and held his head on her lap. The doctor gave Ricardo a butterbur-mixed-with-poppy-seed syrup. Dr. Fitzpatrick took Danielle and Alexander into the hall.

"He suffers from migraine headaches. 'Tis a condition that is often inherited. The headaches aire excruciating and aire often accompanied by nausea. Light and sound will aggravate them. He has probably had the headaches his whole life from time to time. I will leave ya some mixture for when the headaches occur. What concerns me more aire the voices he hears."

"Not voices, Doctor, Quazel's voice," Danielle said angrily. "I will *not* let that witch torment him from the grave."

Alexander asked, "Danielle, did he tell you what the voice said?"

"Aye, she tells him he's just like her; that they're of the same blood. She says he'll never be happy and isn't worthy of being loved because he's evil. I won't let her get away with that. That bitch is *dead*, and I'll find a way to get her out of Ricardo's head. I'm going to be with my husband now. Good night, gentlemen." She stomped inside.

On the front porch Drake said to Alexander, "I thought this was a marriage of convenience. That sounded like a woman with an agenda."

"Aye, I know," said Alexander with a smile.

52
𝕭𝖆𝖇𝖞 𝕭𝖔𝖔𝖒

𝕬𝖗𝖔𝖚𝖓𝖉 midnight Ricardo awoke to find Danielle beside him with her arm around him. He turned over and looked at the sleeping redhead. He gently moved the hair from her face and whispered, "Un hombre puede sonar." ("A man can dream.")

At the sound of Ricardo's voice Danielle opened her eyes. He asked, "What are you doing here?"

"Making sure you're all right. I have an obligation to take care of you."

"I am much better. The doctor's headache mixture is very strong. It makes the pain subside unlike anything I have ever tried. The headaches are not new, only the voice. Even that I have heard from time to time. You do not need to look after me any more, but 'tis nice to know I am in good hands." Ricardo squeezed Danielle's hand.

Feeling rejected, the woman, heavy with child, stood but sat back down quickly. "Ricardo, I'm not moving." She clutched his hand. "'Tis your turn to get the doctor. My Water just broke."

Ricardo ran from the house half dressed and barefoot. He met Rennin in the lane. He said, "Morgan, too?"

Rennin nodded with a look of terror on his face. Ricardo put a steady hand on the boy's shoulder. "Does Morgan want your grandfather or her grandmother?"

"Papaw. He was there after he left you earlier. Morgan has been having contractions all night. Papaw said to get him when the pains were close."

"We just started. Get your grandfather, and I shall get Elizabeth."

The two men returned with their respective doctor and midwife. Elizabeth had spent several month's teaching

Drake the proper way to deliver babies. The midwife and mage was glad to have help and enlightened men to work with.

Elizabeth stopped in with Danielle and examined her. "You have hours to go. I would like to check on Morgan. She should be having a baby within the hour. I shall be back."

Danielle held onto Ricardo's hand. "Don't leave me."

"I will not move a foot."

Down the lane, Elizabeth came in as Morgan groaned and tried to breathe. She took control even if Drake was there. "Rennin, you should wait outside."

Morgan looked at Elizabeth. "Like hell. He was there for the fun part. He stays for the hard part."

Rennin shrugged. "Get used to it, Aunt Elizabeth. 'Tis the new order of things on Draconis. Fathers stay. I know Daddy is planning to stay, and I think you'll be hard pressed to throw Ricardo out."

Morgan groaned again. "Rennin, hold my hand!"

Drake said, "Morgan, push with the next contraction. It should hit any second."

It did. "Morgan, push. Good. Again."

As Morgan screamed one soft scream, a baby cried. Drake exclaimed, "Ya have a son!"

Rennin asked, "Just one, Papaw?"

Drake said, "Just one. No twins this time."

Elizabeth cleaned the baby and wrapped him in a blanket while Drake finished with the mother. She handed the new little O'Rourke to Rennin who took him to his mother. Morgan held him delicately and like most new mothers marveled at the little fingers and toes, making sure he had ten of each. She barely mumbled, "Good. Not six on each foot and hand." She smiled her unassuming smile. "Nana, Papaw, meet Donovan Alexander O'Rourke."

The great-grandparents oohed and cooed for a while. Then, Elizabeth said, "We need to check on Danielle."

Morgan asked sweetly, "Is she in labor tonight, too?"

Elizabeth nodded. Morgan said, "Give her a hug from me and tell her I survived."

The two grandparents walked down the lane. As they walked, Drake said, "I'm glad Declan has decided to study medicine with Connor and me. I am getting too old for this."

Elizabeth laughed. "How many women have you attended?"

"Not many back in Ireland, but this is a new world."

"At least Caitlin is waiting."

They entered the Morales home unannounced. They could hear Danielle upstairs, obviously in the middle of a contraction. Ricardo gently talked her through it. They heard him say, "Good. Relax and wait for the next one."

Elizabeth and Drake entered the bedroom. "How aire we doing?" asked Drake.

"I am a bundle of nerves," said Ricardo. "Danielle is great."

Drake examined Danielle and asked, "How close aire the contractions?"

Ricardo said, "They are never exactly the same."

Drake patted Danielle's leg, "We have a long day ahead of us, dear. Ricardo, let Elizabeth know now if ya aire staying through this. She will try to throw ya oot."

Danielle grabbed her husband's hand, "Ricardo?"

"I will not move a foot, on my oath."

Elizabeth sighed, "Forsooth, 'tis the new order of things."

Drake told Elizabeth to make some coffee and a bite of breakfast. "Danielle, will ya let Ricardo leave long enough to eat?"

She nodded, and then shook her head as another contraction hit. Ricardo said, "I will be fine. I will not leave Danielle."

After the contraction subsided, Drake insisted Ricardo eat to preclude the onset of another headache so near the last one. He explained he did not want food brought into the room for fear the smell could make Danielle nauseous. Ricardo relented, but ate hurriedly to return to his wife's side.

The day came and went and night fell. Still Danielle had not given birth although the pains were close and hard.

Drake took Elizabeth into the hall. "Elizabeth, I am worried aboot her. She has not dilated at all. Do ya have any suggestions?"

"Two. First I have a tea I've used to help women progress. The other one you will likely find barbaric because it goes beyond simply cutting the mother open to take out the baby. We'll talk about that if the tea fails."

"Make the tea."

Ricardo started into the hall. Danielle held his hand tighter, "Don't leave me. Please, don't leave me. I'm scared, Ricardo."

He sat back down and rubbed Danielle's brow with a cool cloth. Then, he kissed her forehead and whispered, "I am not going to leave you, love."

Elizabeth gave Danielle the tincture of blue cohosh every hour. After midnight, Drake said to Elizabeth, "I think 'tis time to try yer other solution. She has no strength left to push."

Elizabeth told Drake what she had done to Mary Kate. He said, "'Tis not barbaric, Elizabeth. Many physicians perform Caesarian sections, but we often lose the mother in the process. This is much better. Sometimes extreme measures *aire* necessary. Teach me to do it yer way."

Elizabeth ran home to get the things necessary for the procedure. When she got back she heard Danielle screaming. As she came into the room Drake said, "Elizabeth, I shall have to learn yer full procedure another day. All of a sudden everything just started working right.

Come on, Danielle, one more push." Another little boy graced Draconis.

Danielle said weakly, "Let me hold him."

Drake laid the baby on Danielle's chest for a minute and then said, "Let Elizabeth clean him. We aire not quite through."

A few minutes later Danielle held her son again. She also held Ricardo's hand. The new mother spoke softly. "Seamus Manuel Morales, meet your Daddy."

Ricardo started. "I thought you said..."

"I changed my mind."

"But Manuel is my middle name."

"I know."

A week later the day dawned cool and crisp. Aidan had plans to fly to Isla Linda where another group had decided to settle. They wanted to begin building right away, but wanted Aidan to survey the land to determine where the best place for a village would be. Caitlin said at breakfast, "I want to go with you."

Aidan said a little concerned, "Are you sure you should right now? You should've had this baby last week."

"I feel wonderful, and we'll only be a couple of hours away. From past experience I think it takes longer than a couple of hours."

"All right."

Caitlin packed a picnic basket and planned to make a day of the trip. "We can have dinner in that little meadow where Rennin used to meet Morgan. Don't let anybody build there. Get your father to declare 'tis a park."

"Aye, ma'am."

Aidan surveyed the area and determined the best place to build would be the area where the cats had had their military encampment.

Caitlin had spread dinner when he came back to the meadow, but she was sitting there crying.

"Honey, what's wrong?"

She looked at him with her big blue eyes and melted his heart. "You'll be angry."

"Nay, I shan't. What's wrong?"

"My Water broke."

Aidan started laughing. "Let's go home. We have several hours."

"I don't think so." Caitlin lay back and screamed.

She said, "My contractions are already near time. You're going to have to deliver this baby."

Aidan panicked and Char went into frenzy, shooting a stream of fire skyward.

Caitlin screamed again. "Aidan Duncan O'Rourke, you had better get ready to catch this baby."

Aidan tried to stay calm as he said, "Caitlin, it can't be that close."

"Oh, no? Take a look."

Looking, Aidan hollered, "Caitlin, do something. I can see the baby's head."

"I *am* doing something. I'm pushing."

Five minutes later Aidan held his new baby daughter. She already had a tuft of red hair. He laughed, "Mam, meet our impatient little angel."

Caitlin held her baby. "She's perfect. Aidan, we have to name her. How do you feel about Genevieve Marie?"

"That was my grandmother's name."

"I know. We can call her Ginny."

"Ginny O'Rourke. I like it."

53
Husband in Every Way

The children grew as the parents watched, helpless to slow time. No one watched more closely than Danielle. She watched as Ricardo played with Seamus and acted as if he were his own. She watched as Ricardo turned ashen the day Miranda told him he was going to be a grandfather. She watched as Ricardo had terrible headaches and fought the voice in his head. She watched her husband go alone into his room each night, but she did not see the man on the other side of the door whisper her name and wait in hope that her footsteps would come to his door.

Finally, she could watch no longer. So she sought the council of her best friend, Caitlin. Mary Kate joined them for tea and Danielle laid her dilemma in their hands.

She said, "I don't know what to do. First, I want to get that voice to leave Ricardo alone. He's trying so hard to be an upright man. He's good and kind and understanding. What can I do?"

Mary Kate asked, "What does the voice say?"

Danielle explained, "It sounds like Quazel to him. She tells him he's evil and just like her and that they're of the same blood. Then, she laughs and taunts him and tells him he's unworthy of being loved."

Mary Kate asked honestly, "Danielle, do you love the man'?"

Danielle blushed and looked at Caitlin for support. "Well?" said Caitlin.

"Let me explain our situation," Danielle said. "You know Ricardo married me for the sake of my baby. It was a kind and generous thing to do. He promised he would never ask me to share his bed. He hasn't. We sleep in separate rooms."

Mary Kate said, "'Twas not the question. Do you *love* him?"

"I care for him."

"'Tis not the same. Miranda still can't say that she loves him either," said Mary Kate.

Caitlin changed the subject. "Danielle, do you want to share his bed?"

Danielle's face turned the same color as her hair. "Aye, but he won't ask me. Not ever. He's a man of his word."

Caitlin said, "In that case, you must take over."

"How?"

"This is definitely your area, Caitlin," laughed Mary Kate. "I deal with the heart, love, not lust."

"Seduce him, Danielle," said Caitlin

"I wouldn't know how to start. I've only been with Seamus, and only once. I waited my whole life for him."

Mary Kate said, "Danielle, if you ever want to love Ricardo, you must let Seamus go. I believe he would want you to have love, and I think your loving Ricardo would exorcise his demons. Your voice would be a lot louder than the voice which makes him doubt himself."

Caitlin said, "I have a plan. First, when are you going to wean Seamus?"

"He has all but weaned himself. He only nurses to go to sleep."

"'Tis time to give him a cup. Wean him completely. As soon as you have done that, Mary Kate has the perfect white nightgown for you to borrow. Anything I have would be too long for you. You're about the same height as Mary Kate. Put on the gown and use whatever pretext you have to use in order to get into his room. You could probably slip the thing off and stand there. He would get the idea. Perhaps you could wait in his bed with candles all around. I promise you if you let him know you want him, he won't say no."

"How can you be so certain, Caitlin?"

Caitlin and Mary Kate looked at each other and chorused, "He's a *man*."

Time passed and exactly two years went by from the day Ricardo had given Danielle his name. A few weeks after she sought help from her friends on how to seduce a man, he came in to a romantic supper. Danielle made roast pheasant, potatoes whipped to fluffiness, salad, and fresh-baked bread. She had opened a bottle of nectar wine, and she wore a soft pink dress.

"What is this?" asked Ricardo.

"I thought we should do something special for our second anniversary. Did you not realize we've been married two years?"

"Verily." Ricardo looked guilty.

"'Tis all right. This marriage is at the least unusual, but we've managed not to kill each other for two years, so that deserves celebration."

"Do I have time to bathe and change my clothes?"

Danielle laughed. "I shan't start without you."

Danielle lit the candles and waited. Ricardo returned carrying Seamus. He grinned. "Look who was awake."

"I see someone who has already had his supper and is supposed to be asleep." She put her hands on her hips.

Seamus squealed and wrapped his arms around Ricardo and said, "Da."

"So you think Daddy will let you stay up and play." Danielle folded her arms. "Gents, you have five minutes before my supper is ruined."

Ricardo hugged the adorable brown-haired, blue-eyed boy and whispered conspiratorially in Spanish, "Oye, amigo, nosotros no queremos que Mamá se enoje. Es tiempo para duermas. Papá se muere de hambre. Vamos, te me remeteré." ("Hey, buddy, we do not want to make

Momma mad. It is time for you to go to sleep. Daddy is starving. Come on. I will tuck you in.")

Ricardo returned alone. "He did not argue at all. He just wanted to see Da. Does he really call me that?"

"All the time," replied Danielle. She put on pouting lips. "He never says Momma."

"Da is easier," laughed Ricardo. "Danielle, this looks wonderful. Would you like me to pour the wine?"

"Aye. I wanted to make something special. I hope you like it."

Ricardo took a bite. "Fabulous."

"I got the recipe from Elizabeth."

"You did a great job, but I have never tasted anything better than your fresh-baked bread."

They ate supper and made small talk, but Danielle was nervous throughout the entire meal. After supper, they finished their wine; Ricardo put his head back on the divan. Danielle took the opportunity to untie the ribbon that held Ricardo's long raven hair back and to rub his temples. Relaxing to her touch momentarily, Ricardo jumped up.

"I think I should go to bed now. It has been a long day. Good night, Danielle."

As Ricardo reached the top of the stairs, Danielle threw her glass against the wall.

Ricardo called, "Danielle, what was that?"

"Nothing. I dropped my glass," she said curtly.

As she cleaned up the shattered glass, she muttered to herself, "I shan't give up that easily. *Señor* Morales, you're in for a big surprise."

Danielle went to her room and put on only the robe that went with the gown Mary Kate had given her. She brushed her hair and splashed herself with the toilet water Caitlin had given her. Danielle took a deep breath and said, "I shall give you a second chance, Señor Morales. I'm not easily daunted."

From under the door Danielle saw a light, so she knew Ricardo was not asleep. She knocked softly and called, "Ricardo, may I come in for a moment." She looked at the small cut she had received while cleaning up the broken glass. "Any pretext," she mumbled. Then, more loudly, "I cut myself cleaning up the glass. I need your help."

Ricardo opened the door quickly, wearing only drawstring pants. "Danielle, are you hurt?"

She breezed past him into his room and stood with her back to him. She whispered, "Aye, badly."

Ricardo turned her to face him, "Where?"

Danielle untied the belt to her robe and let the garment slide to the floor. She took Ricardo's hand and placed it on her breast. "Here."

"Danielle, what are you doing?"

"Something that should've been done a long time ago." She slipped her fingers into Ricardo's loosened hair and kissed him. "Ricardo, I want you; I need you. Make love to me. Make me your wife in every way."

Ricardo held Danielle's hands tightly as he pushed her from him and looked desperately into her eyes. "*Every* way, Danielle? Do you *love* me? You said you 'want me, need me,' but, Danielle Dolphin, do you love me? I cannot—I *will not* be with you unless you love me."

Danielle's heart raced. She looked into Ricardo's eyes and saw the longing he had tried so hard to hide. Her heart melted. She answered. "Aye, Ricardo, I love you. You're the one thing that has been missing from my room. I don't want my room anymore. I want you."

"Say it again, Danielle, for I love you more than I ever thought possible. My heart cannot bear it if you are only speaking words."

Danielle took her hands from Ricardo's and ran them up his chest. "I love you, Ricardo Manuel Morales-Mendez. I never thought it possible to love again as deeply as I once had, but I think I love you even more." She kissed him again.

Ricardo pulled her to him and kissed her deeply and passionately. He lifted her in his arms and took her as his wife.

54
𝔉ighting 𝔉ire with 𝔉ire

𝔇anielle Morales reached for her husband in her sleep, but she felt nothing but cool sheets. She awoke and called for him, "Ricardo, where are you?"

She heard a sound like weeping and followed it until she found Ricardo huddled in the corner, holding his head. Danielle pulled her lover into her arms. She kissed his head. "Ricardo, let me get you a headache mixture."

"Danielle, the voice—Help me. Make the voice stop."

Danielle spoke angrily. "Ricardo, don't listen to *that* voice. Listen to me. Listen to *my* voice." She took her husband's face in her hands. "Ricardo, look at me. I can't make the headaches stop, but the doctor gave you medicine. I can make the voice stop, but you have to help me. Ricardo, don't listen. That voice is lying. You're a good man. Just because you're related to Quazel doesn't make you bad. Elizabeth, Mary Kate, and Morgan are her direct descendents. Are they evil? No! Neither are you!"

The woman cradled her husband. "Ricardo, you're worthy to be loved. Seamus adores you. Ricardo, *I* love you."

Danielle shouted, "Do you hear me, Quazel? I love Ricardo! Leave him alone, you bitch! You're dead. I won't allow you to torment him. Leave him alone. I love him. Do you hear? I love Ricardo, and there's not a damned thing you can do to change that. You have *lost*. Ricardo is mine!"

"Danielle, I heard the voice a few times before I met her."

"'Tis still a lie. I love you. That is truth. Claim it."

She gave him a headache solution and held him until he fell asleep. She spoke to some invisible force again, "I shan't let you torture him, Quazel or whatever you are, no matter what it takes."

When Ricardo awoke the next morning, he found himself cradled in Danielle's arms, his face against her bare breasts. He realized that beneath the covers neither of them was dressed. Memories from the previous night slowly flooded his mind. He whispered softly, "No fue un sueño." He raised his head onto his elbow and watched Danielle sleep.

His slight movement made her stir. She opened her eyes and smiled brightly, "Good morrow, Señor Morales."

Ricardo traced her cheek with his finger. "I thought I must have been dreaming, but you are truly here beside me. Tell me again, Danielle. I need to hear those words again."

Danielle kissed Ricardo's chest. "I." She kissed his neck. "Love." She kissed his cheek. "You." She kissed his mouth, and he responded. She whispered, "Would you like me to show you how much?"

He answered as he ran his hand up her thigh, "Sí, very much."

As he kissed her again, from the nursery they heard, "Da, Da, Da."

Both laughed. Danielle said, "If we ignore him for a few minutes, mayhap he will go back to sleep."

The call for Da continued. Ricardo shrugged. "He wins. I surrender. Madre, I think Seamus wants breakfast. I am a little hungry myself." Ricardo stood, but sat back down quickly. "Danielle, my head still hurts. 'Tis not as bad, but when I stand, it becomes worse."

She got up and put on her robe. She handed Ricardo his loose pants and said, "You're staying in bed today. Alexander will understand." Danielle fluffed an extra pillow and Ricardo leaned back. She put a glass of water and a vial of headache solution on the nightstand. "Just in case," she said. "Now I shall make some breakfast." She started out the door but came back and kissed him again. She traced the scar on his cheek. "I truly do love you. Those are not just words."

The mother and wife left but returned in a few minutes with a little boy. "He wants to wait with Daddy for breakfast. Do you feel up to having company?"

Ricardo smiled. "Always. Come here, amigo, and snuggle with Da. Tell Momma, 'Tenemos hambre. Apurate'. (We are hungry. Hurry.)"

Waving a little fist in the air, Seamus said, "Apuro."

"Very funny," said Danielle, and she threw a small pillow at Ricardo.

After breakfast, Danielle once again took matters into her own hands. First, she found Alexander and asked him to go to her house because Ricardo was suffering with a headache and she did not want to leave him alone. Then, she paid a visit to Aidan.

"Aidan, verily, I need to talk to you," she declared.

"Do you want to talk alone, or may Caitlin stay?"

"Caitlin is welcome. She might be able to help more than you know."

Caitlin served three cups of coffee and said, "Before you start, I'd like to ask how your little plot is progressing?" Caitlin winked.

Danielle blushed and replied, "Let's just say that the egg hatched."

Aidan looked at the two women. "What was that all about? Am I safe here with the two of you?"

Caitlin reprimanded him. "It has nothing to do with *you*. 'Tis girl talk. Besides, Danielle is here about something else today. What is it?"

"I shall get directly to the point," said Danielle. "Aidan, do you ever hear Quazel's voice?"

"Do you mean like Ricardo?"

"At all. In any form."

Aidan looked into his coffee cup. "Sometimes I have nightmares, but I've written them off as bad memories."

Danielle beseeched, "Prithee tell me about them. It might help Ricardo. I'm afraid if I don't stop the voice in his head it will drive him mad."

Aidan shuddered. "Sometimes I dream I'm still in Quazel's prison, but I want to be there. She tells me I can never defeat her and we're perfect together. It gets worse after that because I do things with her I would never do with anyone but Caitlin. I wake up in a cold sweat. Sometimes I dream her head keeps talking even after I sever it. It taunts me and tells me I can't kill her. The worst dream that instills the most fear, is when I dream I didn't wake up in the cave and I was buried alive. Quazel is in the grave with me and taunts me that she told me she would kill me. I dig and scratch the dirt, but I can't find sunlight, only darkness and Quazel's voice. I wake up having trouble breathing." He swallowed a gulp of coffee. "Danielle, do you think I'm suffering from the same hallucinations as Ricardo, only mine don't manifest while I'm awake?"

"Aidan before you killed Quazel, what were your greatest fears?"

"I was afraid I wouldn't be able to kill her, and I was deeply ashamed she came so close to seducing me."

Danielle explained, "Ricardo is terribly afraid he can't get away from what he once was, that he can't really change. He's afraid because he's related to Quazel there's some inherent evil in him. He's terrified no one can ever truly love him. It sounds as if your dreams and his voices are playing on your worst fears. Aidan, what if some of the poisons or potions she gave you have that effect? If we can determine just what she gave you, we might find something to counter the effects."

Aidan was thoughtful. "Mayhap Seanathair can examine the herbs and potions to see if there's something that would cause these things. Then he could concoct something to counteract the effects. 'Tis worth a try. I'd love to rid myself of the dreams, and I know Ricardo wants to free himself of the voice."

Danielle asked Aidan two more favors. "Aidan, when can we go to Isla Linda to see what we can find?"

"We can go now."

"Ricardo isn't able to go today. He has one of his headaches."

"And the voice?"

Danielle nodded.

"Then let's plan to go on the morrow."

"Aidan, there's one more thing I would like to ask. Would you tell Ricardo about your dreams? Mayhap if he knows he's not alone, he can fight the voice in his head."

Aidan took Danielle's hand. "Danielle, have you fallen in love with Ricardo?"

"Does it show? I hope it shows."

"'Tis all over your face and in your voice. I'm happy for both of you. Danielle, he has loved you for a very long time. Did you know that?"

"All I care is that he loves me now."

"Good girl. I shall talk to him. It might be healing for both of us."

"God yield you. I have another person I'd like to talk to today about love and forgiveness."

"Are you going to see Miranda?" asked Caitlin.

"Aye. 'Tis time for her to open her heart. Ricardo has punished himself far more than any authority could have. 'Tis time for her forgiveness to take on a more active role."

While Aidan went to visit Ricardo, Danielle walked half a mile the other direction to visit a very pregnant Miranda. Danielle knew they would be alone because Kieran and Rennin had taken the sloop out to catch fish for the settlement, but she was more afraid to talk to this girl than she had even thought about with Aidan. Aidan was her friend and had not been wronged by Ricardo. Danielle was afraid Miranda would reject any possibility of love for her father.

She knocked with more confidence than she felt. Miranda opened the door. "Danielle, what a surprise. I don't think you've ever come to visit me before. Come in."

"Gramercy. Miranda, I've come with a purpose."

"I'm sure it has something to do with Ricardo. What is it, Danielle? Sit down and tell me what he wants."

"He doesn't want anything." Danielle's breath came in quick angry huffs. "Verily, he doesn't know I'm here. Miranda, why can't you have some small affection for the man? Hasn't he proven to you over the last two years he has become a new person? What does he have to do—die for you?"

Miranda was taken by surprise at her stepmother's outburst. "Danielle, I don't want him to die. I don't hate him anymore."

"No, you tolerate him and do perfunctory things like let him walk you down the aisle with Colin or dance one and only one dance at your wedding reception or make a required trip to let him know you're having a baby, *after* you told Colin. Miranda, I know you love Colin, and you should, but Ricardo's your father. He's trying very hard not to complicate your life and let you come to him in your own time, but he needs you desperately right now."

Miranda's eyes flashed. "You're one to talk. You let him marry you for your own sake. You let him fawn all over that little bastard of yours and make a fool of himself when everyone knows he's not the child's father. You've kept him at arms' length for two years when you should perform certain obligations as his wife. Let's not have the pot call the kettle black."

It took every ounce of control Danielle could muster not to slap Miranda. Rather, she held the back of the ladder-back chair at the dining table so tightly her knuckles turned white. "You're right, Miranda," she said in a measured tone. "Ricardo graciously offered Seamus and me his name and preserved my honor; but he loves my son, and Seamus adores him. You're wrong about the other part. I haven't kept him at arms' length; he has kept *me* there. I shall tell you this moment that I respect Ricardo for the man he has become. He has overcome a sordid history, tarnished reputation, and abusive background. You've never seen the scars on his back, let alone the scars on his heart. I'll also tell you this: I *love* Ricardo very much, and I'll not let a voice in his head or an upstart little daughter full of bitterness hurt him anymore. You can think what you like of me; but if you *ever* say anything so cruel about Ricardo or my son again, I will slap your face. Let me remind you that you're exactly the same as my son—a bastard who was provided legitimacy by someone other than her own father."

"You love him?" Miranda was shocked by Danielle's invective. "What voice in his head? Do you truly think I'm bitter?"

Miranda sat down. "Pray, sit down, Danielle. I beg pardon for my harsh words. What's wrong with Ricardo?"

"Kieran hasn't told you about your father's headaches or that he hears Quazel's voice when they come upon him?"

Miranda shook her head. "Forsooth he doesn't want to distress me right now."

Danielle asked, "Would it truly trouble you if there was something the matter with Ricardo?"

"Danielle, I don't hate him. I don't want any harm to come to him."

The wife pled her case for her husband. "I pray thee, don't think Ricardo is crazy. Aidan has been having similar problems, only his voice comes in his sleep. Ricardo suffers from migraine headaches. Dr. Fitzpatrick says the headaches are inherited. Alexander says Quazel had them, too. When Ricardo gets a headache, he hears Quazel's voice telling him how evil he is and no one will ever love him. Miranda, I *do* love him, and for your information, we no longer have separate rooms. I don't know if my love alone is enough to help him fight the voice he hears. If you could find it in your heart to love him just a little"—She held up her index finger and thumb to show about an inch—"it might heal some of the wounds in his heart. Miranda, he loves you very much, and he loved your mother."

"Danielle, 'tis hard for me. I still have the memories of a five-year-old who saw her mother and the man she thought was her father die."

"Miranda, think back." She clasped her hands together as if in deep prayer. "Tell me exactly what you saw that night on the beach. I saw what happened to Malcolm Montgomery. I tried to rescue him."

"Ricardo brought Mommy and me ashore. He was rough with my mother, and he tried to defend what he had done to Malcolm by saying it was an execution, not murder. Mommy was angry. She hit Ricardo and spat on him. That made him irate. He tried to rape her. He truly did, Danielle." The girl ran her fingers through her long blonde hair.

"I know. He has told me. Prithee, go on."

"Mommy hit Ricardo with a rock and knocked him off her. Then, he stabbed her."

"Are you sure? Think very hard, Miranda. I know you were a very frightened little girl, but you must remember everything."

Miranda put her head in her hands. "Mommy had his dagger. She pulled it from its sheath while he had her pinned. Danielle, Mommy tried to stab Ricardo. They fought over the dagger and she fell. Oh, *Danielle*! He didn't stab her on purpose; she fell on the point. He held her in his arms and *cried*. He told her he would never have hurt her, and he refused to leave her unburied. Danielle, he didn't murder Mommy. 'Twas an accident."

"Think about that for a while, Miranda. I'm going home. I beg pardon for getting angry with you."

Alexander, Ricardo, Danielle, and Aidan flew to Isla Linda the next morning. Ricardo's headache lingered, but he insisted he was able to go with them. As they approached, they could still see the black smudge on the beach where Alexander and Ricardo had burned Quazel's body and the small mound where her few remains had been buried.

Inside the chamber where Quazel had lived the last years of her life, both Aidan and Ricardo trembled. Alexander reassured them, "She is *dead*, lads."

Alexander examined the herbs and potions and asked each man if Quazel had ever used the concoctions on them. He did not find one that had been used on both men until he opened a vial of yellow powder.

Aidan said, "She blew that substance in my face every time she came into this room. It made my eyes burn terribly."

"Sí," said Ricardo. "There was a yellow powder floating in Quazel's bedroom."

"This has to be it," said Alexander. "Let me examine it for content and properties."

In the cave on Draconis, Alexander examined and tested the powder for all kinds of things. He discovered ground mushrooms and rye. Further examination showed the rye had a fungus on it.

Alexander told the men, "I've determined you've ingested and breathed some form of poisoned mushrooms and ergot. The effect of the mushrooms should've subsided long before now; however, I do know ergot can have effect long after consumption. At this time I don't have anything to counter the result. Lads, you might have to live with the outcome."

Aidan said, "It in truth is like Quazel is haunting us, but at least we know the cause."

Ricardo sighed, "I hope the ergot *is* the cause. There is some small comfort in knowing I am not losing my mind. Knowing the voice in my head is drug-induced and not real, helps. Still, I hope we can discover some antidote." He scowled, knowing he had heard the voice vaguely before that night with Quazel. *But not before I came here the first time.*

Danielle took Ricardo's hand. He looked down at her. She said, "I have your antidote right here." With that she kissed Ricardo in front of Aidan and Alexander. "I love you. If you hear that voice, tell it Danielle loves you."

Aidan teased the couple, "Should we leave for a little while? Do you need some time alone?"

The woman got a gleam in her eyes.

Aidan said, "Oh, no. I recognize that look. Caitlin gets it frequently. Ricardo, you're in for trouble now."

"Amusing, Aidan," said Danielle. "Seriously, would you and Caitlin watch Seamus for a few days? Ricardo and I never had a honeymoon. Why can't we take a little trip right now?"

"Are you serious?" asked Ricardo.

"In all truth," said Danielle.

Alexander piped, "I think 'tis an excellent idea. You should have some time alone. By all means, go. Go now. You don't need anything from home."

Aidan whispered to Ricardo, "I told you that you were in trouble."

Ricardo whispered back, "I think I like this trouble."

"I know what you mean," laughed Aidan.

"What's the secret?" asked Danielle.

Aidan folded his arms. "Nothing. Just man talk. Does that answer sound familiar?"

55
𝔇𝔢𝔪𝔬𝔫𝔰

𝔇𝔯𝔞𝔠𝔬 popped in right after Alexander called him and Alexander said, "Draco, take Danielle and Ricardo to the honeymoon suite. They never have taken their wedding trip."

"Humph," said Draco. "I thought Declan would be next, but come on. Just don't be completely rude and ignore the transport service."

Danielle kissed Draco's nose. "We could never ignore you."

Draco dropped the couple off for a few days alone, and left whistling because they had talked to him all the way there.

Danielle contentedly watched Ricardo sleep peacefully. He hardly ever slept so soundly. With all the tension in his face relaxed, he looked ten years younger; and he was really a handsome man, despite the disfiguring scar across his cheek. Danielle found herself wondering how he had received it as well as the scars on his back. She softly traced the scars with her fingertip, wishing she could erase them and all the pain associated with them.

Ricardo stirred and reached for his wife. "Danielle, are you there?"

"Vouchsafe, I'm here. Where else would I be?"

The former pirate scooted close to the woman he loved and put his head in her lap. "Were you trying to exorcise my demons?"

"I was wishing I could erase whatever caused you all that pain. Ricardo, tell me what happened."

He sighed, "I was not an obedient slave. The scars on my back are from floggings."

Danielle inhaled sharply. "They beat you? They were as evil as Quazel. What could you have done to deserve that?"

"I tried to escape several times. The only reason they did not kill me is because I was strong and they had paid a tidy sum for me."

Danielle slowly traced each scar. Ricardo wrapped an arm around her. "When you touch me like that, I am almost glad I have the scars."

She touched his cheek. "How did you get this one?"

"You will not like that story."

"Tell me anyway. I want to know everything about you."

"Oh, Danielle, you truly do not." Remorse weighed heavily in his tone.

"Aye, I do. How can I help you heal the hidden scars if I don't know what caused them?"

"Danielle, I am afraid if you know about me and how awful I was, you will stop loving me."

"Ricardo, sit up and look at me." He put his pillow behind his back and looked at her. She caressed the scarred cheek and kissed him softly. "I will never stop loving you. I'm not Charlotte. I am your Danielle Dolphin."

"I got the scar on my face when I decided not to be a slave anymore. I fought back and started a mutiny." The former pirate breathed deeply. "I broke the neck of the man who dragged me from the hold to flog me. I took his sword and keys. I unlocked the other prisoners, and we battled for our freedom. During the melee I fought with the captain. He thought I was some vagabond who was sold to pay his debts. He had no idea I was from a wealthy family and I had been well-educated and well-trained in fencing. Knowing he was ignorant of my prowess, I ran him through, but not before his blade slashed my face." He covered the scar with his hand. "Now, my love, are those the kinds of things you truly want to know about me?"

With tenderness and understanding, she said, "Ricardo, I don't think that was murder any more than I murdered the sharks during our battle for freedom. Now, how did you become captain?"

"The men reckoned if I was brave enough or *crazy* enough to start a rebellion, I deserved to be captain. After that, only twice did anyone usurp my authority because, Danielle, I slit both men's throats. Others dared not challenge me.

"I swore I would never be dominated by another man. During all those years, I slept with a dagger under my pillow. I had underlings taste my food to see if it might be poisoned, or prepared it myself. All that time I trusted only one person, Trevor, the young boy you saw push Malcolm Montgomery into the ocean." The penitent man shivered. "The authorities were going to execute Trevor because he could not pay the debt his father left when he died. He was thirteen, Danielle, thirteen, a child. I convinced the jailor to sell him with me just to keep him alive. From that day forward, the boy never left my side except for brief periods of sleep. At one time when we were imprisoned in Barcelona, the guard cut out his tongue to keep him from revealing his crookedness. Trevor died because he came between a bullet and me, and the same guard who cut out his tongue would not get him a doctor.

"Even the night after I decided to change my life, I killed the guard who had sold me for Malcolm and Charlotte's father and who had cut out Trevor's tongue and let him bleed to death. I truly hated that man. I was a terrible person, Danielle."

Ricardo became agitated, but Danielle continued to ask him questions. "Ricardo, would you have raped Charlotte if she hadn't hit you?"

"Sí, I would have." The Spaniard's eyes grew dark. "I stupidly thought that if I could be with her again, she would love me again. Danielle, I never raped a woman. I boarded both transport ships and merchant ships and took whatever I wanted whether it be gold, jewels, supplies, or women, but I never forced myself on them." He gave her a faint smile. "I charmed them. Yes, I was a lover to many. But that day with Charlotte—something darker than anything I had ever done came over me.

"Now, have I told you enough to make you hate me? I certainly do not deserve to be loved by someone as wonderful as you."

"Ricardo Morales!" Danielle huffed. "I told you I would *not* stop loving you. I don't lie. Your past life has helped to make you the man you are today. I don't *approve* of what you did. I'm even *appalled* by parts of it, but 'tis over. My love, the only person who hates you is *you*. You've changed. You've prayed to be forgiven. If you want to exorcise your demons, you must forgive yourself."

Ricardo caressed Danielle's cheek. "You are so beautiful when you are angry. I think you could even be dangerous. You are like an erupting volcano, dangerous and beautiful at the same time. My beautiful, dangerous, Danielle Dolphin, do you truly believe in me that strongly?"

Danielle slipped into Ricardo's arms. "Aye, I believe in you, and I love you. I'll say it until you believe it, too."

"I believe you. I believe your love can help me through anything. I pray thee, do not ever stop loving me. Help me put my demons to rest."

She barely brushed her husband's lips with her own. "Ricardo, sometimes I'm afraid, too. I am afraid of losing you. I'm afraid that voice will take you from me. Don't leave me. Don't *ever* leave me."

"Wild horses could not drag me from you." He tipped her face to his. "I vow I will fight my demons, and with your help we will vanquish them." He kissed her fiercely.

Danielle pushed away, a little frightened by the intensity of Ricardo's passion. Heretofore, he had loved her softly, gently, tenderly, never with such forceful fervor. He entangled his fingers in his wife's hair and pulled her head back. He panted, "Do not be afraid, Danielle. I promise I will not hurt you." He kissed her again, hard. It did hurt, but at the same time it exhilarated every fiber of her being. Ricardo pulled back and searched Danielle's face for the fear he had seen a moment before. There was none. It had been replaced with a look of anticipation. She returned his fire with her own, and she willingly succumbed to her lover's ardor.

Aidan sprang from his bed and ran from the room screaming, "No, Ginny!"

Caitlin followed him closely asking, "Aidan, what's wrong?"

Aidan flew into his daughter's room where she slept soundly beside Seamus. Aidan closed the door and leaned against the outside. Caitlin demanded, "Aidan, what's the matter with you?"

Still trembling, he replied, "I had another nightmare, but this time she had Ginny. I realize it was only a dream, but when I first awoke, I was so scared."

Caitlin wrapped her arms around Aidan. "'Tis all right. Go back to bed. I shall get you some cocoa."

Bringing two cups of cocoa, Caitlin sat beside her husband and sipped the warm soothing liquid. "Aidan, I've been thinking. Do you think there's any chance there's something mystical at work here? Could it be demonic? Perhaps what we need is an actual exorcism."

"Caitlin!" Aidan was terrified at the thought. "Do you think I'm possessed? Seanathair found a strong hallucinogen that has long-term effects in that yellow powder. Nobody else besides Ricardo has been affected. We're the only two who breathed any of that stuff."

"Perhaps the powder only opens your mind to the evil presence." Caitlin was up for an argument.

"Quazel is dead! I'm having nightmares. 'Tis as simple as that." Aidan was disconcerted. His body tensed all over.

Caitlin became a bit angry herself. "Aidan, do you have trouble believing in ghosts after all we've seen here?"

"'Twould mean Quazel is not *dead*, Caitlin, and I know I killed her. Seanathair burned her body and buried the few bones that survived the fire."

Caitlin took Aidan's hand. "Honey, listen. What if her spirit hasn't gone to Hell? There must be more to the power of seven than merely surrounding Quazel and Duncan helping you stand. Seanathair's ice spell doesn't count—he was never one of the seven. You took care of her physical form. What if the power of seven has to do with destroying her spirit and sending it where it should be?"

"The very thought scares the hell out of me. I don't know how to fight what I can't see. For Pete's sake, we need a priest or at least a church."

"So build a church, and we have Mary Kate. And we should seek out Devereaux—remember the old owl? We haven't seen him since the restoration. Honey, think. Right now only you and Ricardo are affected, probably because you had the most direct hands in Quazel's demise. You actually killed her, but you couldn't have done so if Ricardo hadn't given us the secret words. What if you're only the beginning? Morgan helped you escape before that. What if she's next? What about Lizzie, who tried to deceive her own mother, and God only knows how much Quazel hated Duncan?"

"Have it your way, Caitlin. When Ricardo gets back, I shall talk to him. If he thinks 'tis worth a try, we shall do it. I would like to sleep one night without waking terrified."

Caitlin snuggled into Aidan's arms and they sat quietly for some time before Aidan broke the silence. "Caitlin, if I'm being exorcised, I can't be a part of the power of seven. Who would take my place?"

"'Tis obvious. Danielle. There must be someone who would die for Ricardo."

"You're right, but for this moment would you hold me and keep me from trembling? I need you right now Caitlin, more than I ever have."

Caitlin held Aidan tightly, and he fell asleep. However, Caitlin stayed awake a while longer and spoke to an evil presence. "Quazel, you've made a mistake this time. You have angered two women who love their husbands. I promise we *will* send you to the pit of Hell where you belong once and for all."

When Danielle awoke, she saw Ricardo at the cavern entrance. His mind seemed to be far away. The chamber was chilly in the early morning, so Danielle wrapped the covers around her and tiptoed to her husband. She wrapped her arms around him from behind and laid her cheek against his back. "Honey, aren't you cold over here?" she asked.

"No," answered Ricardo huskily.

Concern poured over the woman. "Ricardo, what's wrong?"

He took Danielle's hand and led her back to the bed. He had obviously been crying. "Danielle, have you looked at yourself this morning?"

With a quizzical expression on her face, she shook her head. Ricardo gently pulled her arms from beneath the sheets. Her arms, her chest, and her inner thighs were bruised, definite imprints of fingers visible. Ricardo said remorsefully. "I am sorry. I hurt you. I was too rough. I swear I shall never hurt you again."

Danielle ignored the bruises. "I'm fine. I don't remember complaining, but why were you so angry? At least, you seemed angry."

"I think all the memories stirred some part of me that I have tried to bury. I am so sorry."

"Ricardo, don't bury your passion. You didn't hurt me. Rather, you excited me." Danielle looked at her bruises. "Don't worry about these. I've always bruised easily, and they'll heal."

Ricardo held Danielle in his normal gentle manner. She said, "May I ask you something?"

"Anything, except I do not want to talk about my past. Will you respect that request?"

"I shan't ever ask you again, but if you ever want to talk about it, I shall listen."

"'Tis a deal. Now, what do you want to ask me?"

"First, I want to confess something to you."

Ricardo scowled lightly. "What could you possibly need to confess?"

"I lied to you."

"When and about what?"

"On our anniversary. I tried to seduce you with supper and the massage."

Ricardo laughed. "Is that all? Well, lady, you were succeeding until I ran out on you."

"'Tis when I lied. You made me very angry. I threw my glass against the wall in a fit of rage. I honestly felt like slapping your face because I felt rejected. Will you forgive me?"

"There is nothing to forgive. I am glad you are stubborn and pigheaded and did not give up. I think you lied about being cut, too," Ricardo teased.

"No, I cut myself, but it was a tiny little nick." Danielle laughed.

"I never figured you for deception; temper, but not deception."

"'Twas Caitlin's influence."

Ricardo chortled. "*That* I see, but you have not asked me anything yet."

"I'm a little afraid of this question, but here 'tis. Do you think the voice you hear is from the drug Quazel gave you, or is it possible her evil spirit really is at work here?"

"Honestly, Danielle, I think she talks to me. I have not heard the voice once since we have been in the mountains. Do I not remember Alexander saying Quazel's spells could not abide the cold? The ergot is in my system, so I think it would affect me wherever I was, but not Quazel herself. Danielle, if the voice comes back when we go home, would you consider giving up your house and bringing Seamus and living in Alexander's Cavern?"

"Ricardo, I'll live wherever you live, but before we give up our home, let's explore all our alternatives. Mayhap 'tis the ergot, and Alexander will have found an antidote by the time we get home."

The couple had pulled apart to talk. Danielle opened her arms and said, "Come here. We have one more day up here alone. Let's enjoy every minute."

Ricardo snuggled back under the covers with his wife. "Well, Señora Morales. I do like the sound of that—Señora Morales. I have not said it aloud enough. Señora Morales, how would you like to pass the time we have left?"

Danielle's face took on a naughty grin. She whispered in Ricardo's ear as if she were afraid someone would hear her. "Peradventure I shall make you angry, and we can repeat last night."

In total shock Ricardo exclaimed, "Danielle!"

The woman giggled as she put her leg over Ricardo. "Don't act so surprised. Mayhap I'm a firebrand after all."

Ricardo and Danielle walked leisurely up the lane toward Aidan and Caitlin's house. Caitlin sat on the porch with the babies. When Seamus spotted the couple he danced up and down and squealed, "Da! Da! Da!" Unable to contain his own excitement, Ricardo kissed Danielle hastily and jogged to the porch. Scooping Seamus into his strong arms, he whirled the toddler around and planted a big kiss on his cheek. Then he hugged the little boy close and whispered, "Papá le perdió, también." ("Daddy missed you, too.")

Visiting with Mary Kate across the lane, Miranda watched the scene from the window. Mary Kate stood beside the girl she had claimed as her own. "Are you wondering if he would have loved you that much if he had been given the opportunity?"

"I suppose I am, Momma."

"Why not give him the chance, now?"

Miranda said, "But how would that make Daddy feel?"

Mary Kate reassured, "Honey, Colin is resigned to the fact you should have a relationship with Ricardo. 'Tis understandable even to me, and I resented his return more than anyone, he's a new man."

Miranda sighed. "I was about to go home and make supper. I think I shall stop and greet him. Perchance, we can at least become friends. I shall see you later, Momma." She kissed Mary Kate and left.

As she would have done before Danielle's visit, Miranda did not walk straight home. Rather, she crossed the lane and greeted both Ricardo and Danielle with a kiss on the cheek. Before she left, she surprised herself when she suggested Ricardo, Danielle, and Seamus meet her and Kieran for a picnic on Saturday.

When Miranda left, Ricardo said in disbelief, "Did my daughter in truth invite us to have a picnic with her and her husband?"

Caitlin said, "Aye, she did. Now, I'm inviting you to stay for supper tonight. Verily, Aidan and I need to talk to you."

After a delicious supper of pot roast with potatoes and carrots, biscuits, and blackberry cobbler, the two couples sat down to talk while their little ones played on the rug near the hearth. Aidan began to pace.

Caitlin said, "Aidan, sit down and relax."

He snapped, "Caitlin, I'm too nervous to sit down. I'm not certain I can even bring up the subject."

Sensing a great deal of angst in Aidan, Ricardo asked, "Is this about our mutual affliction?"

Aidan nodded. "Caitlin thinks we're being haunted or perhaps we're possessed. Whichever, she thinks we should have an exorcism."

Taking Danielle's hand, Ricardo spoke softly. "Aidan, I think she is correct."

Stunned by Ricardo's reply, Aidan sat down with a thud. "Why?"

Ricardo explained, "I did not hear the voice once while Danielle and I were in the mountains. I have already heard faint laughter and taunting since Miranda asked us to join her and Kieran for a picnic. The voice was telling me she would poison the food so she could be rid of me. I have had headaches all my life. Aidan, I hear the voice without the headaches, but 'tis louder with the headaches. I am weaker then. I am willing to try anything to rid my head of that woman's voice."

Aidan confessed quietly. "My dreams have changed, too. While you were away, I dreamed she took Ginny."

Long black hair moved from shoulder to shoulder as the former pirate shook his head. "'Tis to instill fear in you, Aidan. Because of the bloodline, Ginny would be useless to her, but Miranda's child if 'tis a girl would be very useful. So would any daughter Morgan or Declan might have. If this *is* Quazel's spirit and she could control the thoughts of an innocent little girl, the evil could start anew."

"I hadn't thought that far into the future." Aidan breathed deeply. "Aye, for the sake of those I love, I'll do anything, but how are we to do this without a church or a priest?"

Ricardo suggested, "Let us build a church on the morrow. A priest?" He shrugged. "I do not know. Perchance, one will shipwreck very soon."

56
Confirmation

Saturday arrived in grand style. The sun shone brilliantly and a light breeze blew. Danielle baked a cake for the picnic, but when she went into the kitchen to get it, she found a little boy covered in chocolate icing. She scolded loudly, "Seamus Manuel Morales!"

At the sound of Danielle's angered voice, Ricardo popped into the kitchen. When he saw Seamus covered in chocolate and Danielle red in the face, he laughed so hard he cried.

Danielle grew angrier. "Ricardo, 'tis not funny! I worked hard to make that cake. Now, I shall have to make something else. You take this little scalawag and clean him up before I spank both of you! Go on to the picnic. I shall be a little late now that I have to bake the apple tarts we were to have tomorrow."

As Ricardo bathed and changed Seamus, he asked still laughing, "¿El bizcocho estaba bueno no amigo?" ("Was the cake good, buddy?")

The boy grinned and said, "Goo."

On the way out, Ricardo and Seamus peeked into the kitchen. Laughter still hovered around Ricardo's mouth. Danielle threw her potholder at them and said, "Go!"

When Ricardo and Seamus got to the brook, Miranda was there without Kieran. She explained, "Kieran will be a little late. He and Aidan had a few more logs to plane for the church, but he'll be here. Where's Danielle?"

"She will be late, also." Ricardo started laughing again. "Someone very small ate the cake she had baked, and she insisted on making apple tarts to replace it."

Miranda put her hands on her hips and said lightly to the little boy, "Did you eat your Momma's cake?"

Seamus nodded, and Ricardo described the scene in the kitchen. By the end of the story, Miranda was laughing, too.

She said, "We shall have some lemonade and if we get hungry before they come, we will eat without them. Seamus, how would you like to go with me and wiggle your toes in the water?"

Seamus nodded. Miranda took off his shoes and her own and they started to the brook. Seamus turned and said, "Da."

Unsure if Miranda wanted him to come, Ricardo excused himself by saying, "I think I shall have a glass of lemonade first. I shall join you in a little while."

Miranda and Seamus splashed in the water. She took the boy's hand and walked around a bend in the creek. When they had not returned in a few minutes, Ricardo felt uneasy. He slipped off his shoes and followed in the direction they had gone. When he rounded the bend, he still did not see them. He walked on a little further and called, "Miranda, Seamus, where are you?"

He heard a reply. "In here. Come see what we found."

Ricardo followed the sound to a small opening in the creek bank. If the creek was high, the hole would be hidden, but the water was low. He stuck his head in the hole and said, "Miranda?"

She answered. "Come in and see what we found. Be careful. You'll need to crawl at first."

Ricardo crawled on his hands and knees for a little way before the passage opened into a small cave. The light filtered in, but it was rather dim. In a little space at the top of the cave was a nest of glowworms.

A chill ran over Ricardo. "Miranda, let us leave here. This place reminds me too much of the cave where Quazel lived."

"I've never been inside. Was it like this?"

"Somewhat. It was illuminated only by glowworms."

Miranda sensed a real fear in the man. "All right, let's go. Come on, baby." She took Seamus's hand.

Without warning, there was a strange crackling sound. Miranda asked, "What was that?"

With a great leap and a shout of, "Bajense!" ("Get down!") Ricardo knocked Miranda and Seamus to the ground. The entrance to the little cave fell all around them.

After a little while Ricardo sat up and asked, "Are you all right?"

Seamus cried and Ricardo pulled him close and comforted him. "Esta bien, niño. Papá está aquí. Yo te cuidaré." ("'Tis all right, buddy. Daddy is here. I will take care of you.")

Ricardo turned to Miranda. "Miranda, are you injured?"

"No, but I don't think I am all right."

"What is the matter?"

"My Water broke, and I just had a contraction."

Ricardo could hardly make out Miranda's silhouette in the eerie light of the glowworms as he felt for her hand. She sniffled, "I'm scared. I want Kieran."

Her father tried to comfort her. "Miranda, listen to me. I want you to hold Seamus's hand. Seamus I want you to stroke your sister's hair."

Miranda thought briefly, *this is my little brother.*

Ricardo continued, "Miranda, when you have a contraction, breathe through it. That's what they told Danielle. I am going to try to move those rocks so we can get out."

"I shall try," she whimpered.

Danielle and Kieran arrived at the picnic site about the same time. "Where's everybody?" asked Kieran as he swiped a drumstick and handed Danielle one. "I'm starved."

Pointing to the three pairs of shoes, Danielle said. "It looks as if they went wading. Mayhap they waded around the bend. Let's give them a few minutes before we start a search." Half an hour later, they started a search. An hour later, the whole village and a strange old man, who came up with Alexander, joined the search.

In the little cave, Ricardo sat down and kicked a rock in frustration. He realized the entire tunnel was blocked. A voice taunted him, "Usted es un fracaso. Sus niños y su nieto morirán, y usted no los puede ayudar." ("You are a failure. Both your children and your grandchild are going to die, and you cannot help them.") Ricardo grabbed his head as pain crept up his neck and shot through his temples. "No!" he growled.

"Da." A little voice and a small hand on his cheek pulled Ricardo to his senses. Ricardo took the little one in his arms. "Saldremos. Yo lo juro. Te quiero, mi pequeñito." ("We will get out. I swear it. I love you, my little darling.")

Miranda let out a weak cry. Ricardo went to his daughter. His eyes had adjusted to the dimness. "How close are the pains? Elizabeth says when they are close, it is time."

"I don't know for sure, but I don't think 'twill take me as long as Danielle did." She clutched Ricardo's hand. "It hurts, Da." She tried to hold in her cry.

"Miranda," Ricardo sounded like a commander. "Do not stifle your screams. Scream loudly. Kieran and Danielle might hear you." Miranda obeyed. Then, she relaxed.

Ricardo smoothed her hair. "Miranda, did you call me 'Da'?"

She looked at her father, but before she could answer, another labor pain overwhelmed her.

Ricardo said, "God, they cannot be that close yet." He placed a hand over his mouth. "Honey, I have to take a look."

Miranda nodded.

Ricardo examined his daughter, feeling squeamish and embarassed. "Miranda, you are correct. 'Twill not take you much longer. I can see the baby's head."

Miranda screamed loudly again. "Da, when can I push?"

"Not yet. A little longer." He tried to remember exactly what Dr. Fitzpatrick and Elizabeth had done during Danielle's delivery.

"Hold my hand I beg you, Da. I'm scared, not of having a baby, but of being trapped in here."

"I will get us out, but right now I have to worry about this baby." Ricardo grabbed his head. "No, I shall not listen to you. Leave me alone."

Miranda screamed again. "Don't listen, Da. Tell that voice to shut up. I need you." Miranda shrieked. "You tell her she's a lying bitch and your daughter loves you."

Ricardo hardly had time to hear what Miranda said before he told her to push. A few minutes later Ricardo announced, "Miranda, you have a girl."

Miranda breathed, "Martha Nadine." Ricardo laid baby Martha in her mother's arms.

He set Seamus down to watch the baby and went back to pulling rocks. He prayed silently, "Ah, Dios, es una chica. Por favor, ayudanos a salir. Tengo que alejar a la bebé del espíritu de Quazel, pero gracias que Miranda me quiere." ("Oh, God, 'tis a girl. Prithee, help me get us out. I have to get the baby away from Quazel's spirit, but thank you that Miranda loves me.")

As long as he prayed, the voice was silent.

Outside Kieran and Danielle teamed up to look for the three missing loved ones. Kieran stopped and leaned against the bank. He jumped. "Danielle, did you hear that?"

"Aye, Kieran. It sounded like a faint scream."

"Where?"

Danielle's keen sense of hearing as a dolphin remained sharp. "Kieran, it sounded as if it came from behind these rocks."

Kieran commanded, "Danielle, get help. I shall start moving rocks."

Danielle ran back to the picnic site where she found that Rennin and Morgan with Donovan as well as Duncan and Priscilla had returned. She told Priscilla to stay with Donovan. The rest went to help Kieran. Priscilla nodded, her graying blonde hair twisted into braids around her head and her amber eyes misty with concern. Small enough to be a child herself, she knew the best place for her was watching over the young ones.

A little way into the tunnel the screaming stopped, and Kieran heard grating sounds. Kieran hollered, "Hail. Is anyone in there? Can you hear me?"

Ricardo rejoiced, and Kieran heard a muffled reply. "Kieran, is that you?'

"Aye."

"There is a cave in here. The tunnel collapsed while we were exploring," Ricardo yelled.

"Relax," said Kieran. "We're on our way."

"Is Danielle with you?"

"Aye."

"Tell her we are unharmed."

Kieran asked fearfully, "What about Miranda?"

Ricardo said, "She and Martha are just fine."

"Martha?" Kieran asked confused.

"Kieran, you are a father."

The young man's heart skipped a beat. "Many thanks, Ricardo. You sit back. Let us work from this side. We shall have you out soon."

Ricardo leaned against the wall of the cave. His hands bled from the jagged pieces of rock, but he and his children were getting out. Seamus curled up in Ricardo's arms. He and the child slept, as did Miranda and Martha.

It took another hour before Kieran broke through into the cave. When the rocks fell, Ricardo started awake. "Kieran?"

"Where's Miranda?"

"Asleep." Ricardo grabbed his son-in-law's arm. "Kieran, when you get them out, take them directly to Alexander's Cavern."

"Why?"

"Kieran, what Aidan and I have been experiencing is *not* from a drug or a potion. I am convinced Quazel's evil spirit has returned. I am afraid for your daughter. I pray you, do as I ask."

"You're serious." Kieran saw Ricardo's fear. "Aye, aye. I shall take them."

In the sunlight again, Ricardo gathered Danielle and Seamus in one embrace. Danielle gasped, "The blood on Seamus's shirt is from your hands."

"I will be fine. Where is Aidan?"

Aidan answered, "Here I am. Kieran says you've insisted he take Miranda and the baby to the mountains immediately."

With urgency Ricardo told Aidan, "We have to do this exorcism as soon as possible. I am certain now the voice is Quazel's spirit. She talked to me in there. I prayed. As long as I prayed she was quiet. Her evil presence could not tolerate the presence of God."

"'Tis why I've come," said an aged, crackling, and unfamiliar voice. Standing with Alexander was a wizened old man, small in stature and bent almost double. His white hair lay only in a ring around the back of his head from ear to ear, but his gray eyes sparkled, alert and alive.

"You were right to send the child to safety. Allow me to re-introduce myself to some and introduce myself to others. I am François Devereaux."

"The owl I spoke to years ago?" Rennin interrupted.

"Yes." The hoary head nodded. "I came to these shores only days after Alexander. I was driven into exile because I followed my conscience and voiced my disagreement with many practices of the Church. I have lived most of my years on Draconis as an owl, but in France many years ago, I was a priest. Although the Church excommunicated me, I believe I was called of God, not the Church.

"A week ago it came to me in a dream to seek Aidan O'Rourke and his friend who where tormented by one they thought to be dead and gone. I've come to rid you of the evil completely and finally, but you must realize 'tis not Quazel herself you're fighting, but the evil that once inhabited her form. Even she didn't always have the evil in her." He looked from man to man. "And some are spirits that never plagued her."

Aidan nodded. "My wife said we should seek you out. I'm glad you found us."

"'Tis my understanding you will have the first church on Draconis built soon. We'll consecrate it, and then we'll vanquish your demons, for there are many. There is a spirit of *fear*, a spirit of *lust*, a spirit of *greed*, a spirit of *hate*, a spirit of *murder*, a spirit of *oppression*, and a spirit of *confusion*. Most of these manifested themselves in Quazel and are seeking a new body to inhabit. Thus far, fear, confusion and oppression have found temporary homes because Quazel's drug has weakened your defenses. The others have toyed with your thoughts even if you were not conscious of their presence, and others of the group aren't immune from their influence.

"Gentlemen, Monday morning, let us work tirelessly to build our church. As soon as 'tis finished, we shall consecrate it. Then, we'll send these spirits where they belong."

Caitlin said, "Father Devereaux."

The old man interrupted, "Reverend, prithee. I prefer that term."

Caitlin corrected herself. "Reverend Devereaux, come home with us. There's plenty of room, and I insist you stay with us."

"I would be delighted, Mrs. O'Rourke, but first, let us send this new baby to safety.

Aidan said, "They've left with Draco and Dr. Fitzpatrick."

"Good," said the old priest. "Mrs. O'Rourke."

Caitlin interrupted him. "Call me Caitlin. With all the Mrs. O'Rourkes around we must use first names to avoid confusion."

The old man patted her hand. "Caitlin, I should like to meet with each man and with each of the seven of you who need to be present to pray and support the participants in this exorcism."

"You know of the seven?" she asked with an arched brow.

"Oh, yes."

"Do you need to meet with us separately or together?" Aidan inquired.

"Together will be fine, but I have a message for each individual."

Caitlin suggested, "On the morrow, gather at our house for a late dinner. I shall provide the main course. Everyone else, bring something, and we will have a feast."

57
Confessions

Everyone went home. Danielle took her two men home and fed them. She bathed Seamus and put him to bed. He was asleep before his head hit his pillow.

Danielle went to her and Ricardo's room. The brooding man stood at the window looking toward the mountains. She put a gentle hand on her husband's shoulder. "They're safe. Now, 'tis your turn."

Ricardo chuckled. "Are you going to bathe me and put me to bed?"

"Aye," she replied. "I have a hot tub of water waiting for you."

With a wink Ricardo asked, "Will you join me?"

"I thought you'd never ask," laughed Danielle. They walked down the hall arm in arm.

"I want to tell you something wonderful," Ricardo said as he slipped into the hot water with Danielle in front of him.

"What?" she asked as she gently washed Ricardo's raw hands.

"Miranda said she loves me. She called me 'Da.'"

She kissed her husband. "I'm glad. I want you to be close to Miranda. I must confess to you I had a talk with her. It became a heated argument, and we said some unpleasant things to each other. Then we talked, and we both apologized."

Ricardo smiled. "Gramercy." He lay back in the water and soaked. After a moment he sat up. "Guess what else," he laughed. "I am a grandfather. Tell me, my love, do I look that old?"

Danielle ran soapy hands up Ricardo's chest and around his neck. "You look marvelous to me." She rinsed the suds and stepped from the tub. "Come on," she said as she wrapped Ricardo in a towel. "You're falling asleep in the tub, Grandpa. What is the Spanish word for grandfather?"

"Abuelo."

"Let us get some rest, Abuelo."

Every family in the little village, all of whom was kin, descended on Caitlin's backyard Sunday afternoon except for Kieran and Miranda. Caitlin prepared a huge ham as the main course, and it would have appeared the other ladies of the village communicated about what each should bring because the assortment of food was vast. The three little ones played happily under a tree while the adults socialized and got to know the newest adult of the community.

The reverend was an amicable man with a dry wit. He was also learned and knowledgeable. Ricardo bonded with him immediately. The two men discussed all manner of subjects. Ricardo shared with him many advances in the areas of science and world exploration Devereaux had never heard. The old man was delighted to hear something new and exciting. Rennin found himself listening to their conversation. He absorbed every word.

Finally, the reverend began to take each person to the side one-by-one to speak with them privately. He began with Elizabeth. "My dear, before you can stand strong and firm for your friends, there is a deep bitterness you must abandon."

Elizabeth looked confused. "I have no bitterness toward anyone here, Reverend. I love every person here."

"Aye, you do, but you still harbor a deep grudge against your dead father. You must put that behind you. Elizabeth, I know he denied you the love of your life and your child for years, but you now have them and much happiness with them."

Elizabeth's hands trembled and tears filled her eyes. "Reverend, you don't know all he did to me. Even Diggory doesn't know because I can't talk about the abomination." She laughed bitterly. "'Tis funny. Only Quazel knew what he did to me, and she thought I killed him for it. I suppose I did kill him in my thoughts, but the old letch died in his sleep without suffering for what he did. Even now, I become nauseous when I remember his coming to my bed. Unless he somehow learned he didn't sire me, he thought he was my father—a double autrocity. How can I ever let that go?"

The old man of God took Elizabeth's hand. "Although it might seem to us evil goes unpunished, the unrepentant soul is punished forever. Elizabeth, let us pray together for your pain to be removed, then tell your husband. His love can help mend your broken heart."

The two prayed together and returned to the crowd. Diggory approached his wife and the old man with a look of consternation for he saw Elizabeth's wet cheeks.

Before he could respond, Reverend Devereaux found himself pinned to a tree, Diggory holding him by the front of his shirt. "What did ya do to me wife?"

A number of people started toward them, but Devereaux shook his head and said, "Diggory, let's talk, then take your wife home and mend her broken spirit." Even as Diggory's mouth fell open, the reverend indicated the small, secluded apple orchard he and Elizabeth had recently exited. Diggory followed hesitantly, not wanting to leave Elizabeth alone.

François Devereaux said, "I shall come straight to the crux of the matter. Although you live a good and selfless life, you've coveted something not yours for many years while not fully appreciating what God gave you."

Diggory was speechless for a moment. "What have I coveted? I am content with me life."

"Aidan. You've coveted your best friend's son. You've wished many times he were your son while you haven't fully appreciated the wonderful daughter you have. Aye, you love Mary Kate, but you've felt cheated for not having a child to carry on your name. Even if Mary Kate can't carry on the family name, she can carry on your legacy of selfless love. Let go of your desire for what you can never have. Love what you have."

Diggory's eyes filled with tears. "I *never* would have hurt Duncan intentionally. The heart can be deceptive. I canna stop loving Aidan. He gave an old decrepit man a reason to live."

The reverend placed a hand on Diggory's shoulder. "You don't need to stop loving him, only love him as your nephew, not your son. Love your daughter as your legacy."

Diggory nodded. "Will ya pray with me to have the strength to do so and to recognize me error?"

"Of course." The two prayed together and Diggory took Elizabeth home.

Caitlin was curious why Elizabeth and Diggory left. The reverend said, "They need time alone, as do we, Caitlin." He indicated with his hand for her to follow. "Come and talk with me for a while."

Airily Caitlin prattled as they entered the orchard. The reverend patiently waited for her to be quiet and then indicated a soft patch of grass to sit upon. The two got comfortable and Devereaux spoke. "Caitlin, your lively personality is delightful, but I need you to be serious for a time. You're willful, pigheaded, and stubborn. Those traits can be useful at times. I'd like to talk to you about your need to dominate your husband."

Springing to her feet, red in the face, Caitlin said, "What?"

He inclined his head to the side and she sat back down like a petulant child. "My dear, you have the need to *always* get your way, no matter if what you want goes totally against your husband's wishes. When he doesn't agree with you, you will stoop to coercion, manipulation, even deceit to gain the upper hand. Aidan has loved you despite this flaw, but imagine how he must feel when others point it out to him. You must allow him to be his own man and make decisions concerning his family. Sometimes, you must lose the battle, even if you must force yourself to let Aidan be wrong."

Caitlin's blue eyes welled with tears. "I never realized I could be such a..."

"Don't call yourself names. Now that you see your error, can you let your husband lead you?"

"I shall try. Will you pray for me to have the discernment to be a proper wife?"

"We'll pray together." They did.

Colin held Mary Kate's hand as he saw Caitlin come from the orchard. "The reverend is speaking to everyone privately. I suppose I shall go to him and get me chastisement done. I am sure I have some hidden faults to confess."

Colin interrupted the reverend during a moment of silence. "Pardon me. I can come back later, but I thought since ya were talking to everyone I moight as well talk to ya now."

The old man's kind eyes smiled softly without his lips moving. "Aye, Colin, I shall talk to you. You're a fine man with many admirable qualities. I'm sure Aidan is proud to call you his friend. However, I'd like to address your jealousy."

Colin questioned, "Jealousy?" The expression on his face looked so much like his twin's the old man almost chuckled.

"'Tis true you've suffered in silence, but you're jealous of your dear friend, Aidan. You've been jealous since your youth. In your heart you've longed for the respect, admiration, and recognition Aidan has received. You've wished silently just once someone would sing your praises as loudly as Aidan's. Your own daughter praises her uncle for rescuing her, a feat you were unable to do. Even now, you're jealous Aidan has been able to have another child, when you know you and your wife can't."

Colin sat down in total dismay. "How do ya know I have felt as if I were always in Aidan's shadow? I do love him. He is me brother-in-law, for goodness sake."

"I know you love him, but you must put aside your feelings of jealousy if you're to help him now. Believe me when I tell you, you do *not* want to be in his shoes at this time."

"I would give me life for Aidan, but I suppose all I have wanted is for someone to recognize I, too, have sacrificed all I have or am for this place, for someone to say, 'Colin, a job well done.'"

"Colin, all these years, Aidan would have been lost without you. You've been a great friend, but don't envy the man you call brother. Rather, he deserves your pity and love. I'll pray for you now if you'd like."

"Aye, an' it please ya." The two men bowed their heads and prayed.

"Now, send me your wife." Devereaux smiled. Colin started out of the grove. The old man called him back. He put a hand on the younger man's shoulder. "Colin, a job well done."

Colin nodded with tears in his eyes and went out to Mary Kate. "He wants ya. Get ready to find oot how imperfect ya aire," Colin said wryly.

Mary Kate walked into the little orchard nervously. "Come to me, dear. I don't bite," said Reverend Devereaux. "Ah, my sweet lady with the gifts of healing and prophecy, you're terrified of what I might reveal to you."

"Aye. I know how imperfect I am."

"Aye, but sometimes you see yourself as much better than those around you. You would never have made love to

Colin before your wedding night. Danielle, Rennin, Kieran, Ricardo, even Elizabeth and Diggory have a moral fault. You're easier on Morgan because she did not know what she was doing, and Miranda was forced. You'd never have deserted an innocent child. Ricardo must be wicked and cruel. Mary Kate, self-righteousness is petty. You must rise above your judgments. The others I've spoken to have only to repent of their actions, but I want you to talk to Ricardo. Though you've said it to others, let *him* know you've come to a place where you can forgive him and accept him. I know 'twill be hard for you, but you must do it."

"I will."

"Give me your hand. We'll pray for your strength to look beyond human fault once it has been confronted and forgiven and for your strength to admit your wrong to Ricardo."

They prayed, and then the reverend put Mary Kate's arm on his. "I would like a glass of lemonade before I talk to anyone else. Will you walk with me?"

Reverend Devereaux mingled with the crowd and made his way to Danielle's chocolate cake. This one had survived little fingers because Danielle had made Seamus his own cake. Danielle handed the reverend a glass of lemonade. "You can't eat chocolate cake without either milk or lemonade. All we have today is lemonade, so I thought I'd get you a glass," she said cordially.

"Many thanks, Danielle. Dear, are you aware you'll be taking Aidan's place with his group of rescuers?"

Danielle blinked with astonishment. "No. I thought Aidan would pass his charm to one of his sons, but I'd be at the exorcism no matter. I'll be with Ricardo."

"Do you truly love your husband so much?" asked the reverend.

Danielle flared. "Aye, I love Ricardo. Why does everyone have such a hard time believing that?"

Frankly the reverend said, "Because a part of your heart still belongs to a dead man. The one thing I want you to do is to visit Seamus's grave and let him go before you stand beside Ricardo in this endeavor. He needs your whole heart without reserve."

"But…"

"Danielle, first admit to yourself that you've reserved some part of your heart for your first love."

"Reverend, how can I ever forget Seamus?" Tears dripped down the woman's cheeks. "He's the father of my child who is his spitting image. I loved him my whole life."

"Don't *forget* him. Put his memory into perspective. Never compare the two men."

"I suppose I have compared them, but I truly do love Ricardo."

"Then tell Seamus good-bye." Devereaux took Danielle's hand and prayed for her to wholly love her husband.

As evening fell and the families started home, Reverend Devereaux walked with Duncan to his home. So much was the respect Duncan commanded, the reverend would not speak to him in public, lest they be overheard. Once inside, even Priscilla excused herself.

The ancient minister graciously sat down to have coffee with Duncan. He began, "Duncan, you know I've spoken with the other six who will assist me with the ritual I've come to perform. You're the seventh. I must speak with you about an unconfessed sin in your life." He sipped the beverage he had been given.

"Duncan, although you're a just man, you sin against yourself constantly. You've allowed guilt for the woes of this world and the ones you love to take a foothold in your heart. You feel guilty you were unable to free Draconis; you feel guilty you left your son fatherless to be reared by his mother alone; you feel guilty your crew will never return home; you feel guilty so many died in the civil wars.

The list goes on. Duncan, these things were not your fault. You must stop blaming yourself. Until you're free from your self-imposed guilt, you can't help Aidan now. Of *that* you will be guilty."

"Whom do I blame?" asked Duncan sadly.

"Blame the evil we fight."

Humbly Duncan said, "I saw you praying with Danielle. Will you pray with me?"

"'Twas my plan." The old man placed a hand on the dark hair as Duncan bowed his head and prayed for Duncan's freedom from guilt and peace of mind. When the old man left, Duncan's spirit was light.

58
Conviction

Ricardo's hands were too bruised and cut to work on the building of the church during the first few days, so he stayed home and worked on formulating an eggshell-colored whitewash for the outside, with the thought that the color would look clean and pure without showing the weathering as quickly as stark white. As he worked, Reverend Devereaux interrupted Ricardo's concentration.

"Ricardo, we must discuss the demons that have been hounding you. I thought you'd prefer to speak alone."

Ricardo responded, "I appreciate your thoughtfulness, but I have no secrets from Danielle."

"None? What about the spirits of hate and murder that have been plaguing you?"

Ricardo looked perplexed. "I do not understand. I have not thought of murdering anyone for a very long time. I do not hate anyone here."

"You do not hate anyone here, and you have not thought of killing anyone in a very long time except *yourself*. Self-hate is one of the worst forms of hatred. I think Danielle has even confronted you on that subject. I dare say this is a struggle you've had long before you ever encountered Quazel."

The man in question puffed out his cheeks at the memories—mostly his remorse over Charlotte.

"Ricardo, how many times have you toyed with your pistol when Danielle wasn't around and the voice taunted you?" Devereaux continued. "How many times has the voice encouraged you to end it all because you were worthless?"

"Too many, but my love for Danielle and Seamus has kept me from doing anything that would cause them pain.

Danielle is my rudder and stabilizer. She has helped me get beyond my self-loathing, for the most part."

"I know. One of your other demons has used your love for Danielle to manifest itself."

"How?"

"This house, for example. Although wanting a nice home for your wife isn't wrong, did you do it for Danielle or to prove to everyone else you and Danielle were just as good as they? Wanting to be as good, or better, than those around you is a subtle form of greed."

Ricardo became a little upset and spoke through clenched teeth. "Surely, you do not want us to give up our home."

"Of course not. I only want you to beware of the trickery and deceit these spirits will use. Ricardo, mainly I want you to know how many demons you're fighting. You're well aware of oppression and confusion. Those two have been blatant in their attack."

Ricardo walked around for a moment. "So, five of the little devils are mine. Was I such an easy target? Why?"

"Your desperate need to be loved."

Wistfully Ricardo sighed, "Does that mean the love of my children and my wife will give me strength?"

"Ricardo, you must learn to love the man God wants to make you, whether or not anyone else loves you." The bent old soul hugged the suffering man and whispered a prayer to keep the demons at bay before he left.

As Devereaux left Ricardo in order to find Aidan, Mary Kate approached the Morales home with a basket. She greeted the minister and walked on to Ricardo. The former pirate stared blankly at the woman who ordinarily would not have given him the time of day, let alone visit. "Mrs. Fitzpatrick, is there something I can do for you?"

Mary Kate lowered her eyes. "No. 'Tis I that can do something." She looked Ricardo in the eye and summoned her courage. "I've come to apologize to you. I've held on to my resentment of you long after you proved yourself to be a new man. I felt threatened by you, and I let those feelings fester. I'm sorry, and I wish to change the nature of our relationship. I want us to become friends. Shall we start with your calling me Mary Kate?"

"Your apology is accepted. I would like very much to be friends." Ricardo replied graciously.

Mary Kate breathed a sigh of relief. "That was easier than I thought 'twould be." The prophetess laughed nervously. "Danielle's still working at the church. I brought you some dinner because I know if youre anything like Colin, with Danielle and Seamus gone for the day, you'll either go hungry or pilfer the biscuit jar rather than actually make dinner."

Ricardo smiled with charm. "Mary Kate, I would be honored to have dinner, if you will join me."

"I would be delighted."

Animosity behind them, the two former antagonists shared a meal and began to know the real people behind the masks they had worn.

After dinner Mary Kate went home, and Ricardo was compelled to talk to Danielle. Not finding her at the church site, he searched for her. Finding Danielle at Seamus's grave, he could not bear to approach her; neither could he tear himself away. He sat behind a tree and his wounded heart listened.

Danielle first cried unshed tears as the thought of her love for the dead man overwhelmed her.

"Seamus O'Donnell, I loved you for so long. My heart was completely broken when you left me. I was angry with you. I know 'twas not your fault, but I was so alone. However, you did leave me a part of you. We have a son. He's remarkable. I named him Seamus. Someday when he is old enough to understand, I shall tell him what a brave and wonderful father he had, but that is not why I've finally had to come to you." The former dolphin ran her hand over the grave.

"Seamus, I must tell you good-bye. Miraculously, I've fallen in love again. You won't believe with whom. Seamus, 'tis Ricardo. I know how much we all distrusted him, but if you could only know the man I know, you'd understand. He's my knight in shining armor. He's my hero. I have to let you go completely so my life with Ricardo can be all it should be.

"Seamus, Ricardo and I are married. He loves me, and he adores your son. I know you're Seamus's father, but Ricardo is his da. Those two were meant for each other.

"I don't know the words I need to say to you. I know you would want me to live and be happy. Ricardo makes me truly happy. I'm going to leave you now, my King Satin, my Seamus, my past. My present and my future await me. Good-bye." Danielle kissed her hand and touched Seamus's headstone.

During Danielle's discourse, Ricardo had quietly slipped from his hiding place and stood behind his wife. She stood and turned around directly into the tall, dark, brooding man that had stolen her heart. The sheer fact that she had thought she was alone made her scream.

"I beg pardon, Danielle. I intruded upon your time with Seamus, but do you truly mean the things you said? I would not want to live without you, Danielle Dolphin. I do truly love you above all else. To be your hero, your knight, to make you happy is my greatest desire."

She threw her arms around Ricardo and kissed him as though she were afraid she would never be able to kiss him again. "Ricardo, you're my joy. You give me reason to live. I love you to the depths of my very soul."

Ricardo ran his fingers into Danielle's hair and turned her face to his. "You have told me you love me many times, but to hear you tell the one person, who has meant as much or more to you than I, truly convinces me you do love me. Danielle, I all but worship you. You are my reason for breathing." Ricardo kissed her and lost his sadness, his anger, his insecurity.

As he buried his face in her neck and hair, she whispered, "Let's go home."

With trembling voice Ricardo said, "I cannot wait that long. I want you now, Danielle."

"Yes, you can. Let's go home."

François Devereaux found Aidan and asked, "Aidan, walk with me to the desert's edge."

"Why so far?" asked Aidan.

"I want to be sure we're away from everyone. You will *not* want anyone to overhear our conversation."

They walked and talked about nothing in particular until they reached the desert's edge. They sat and leaned against the ruins of the gate Jean Noir had once guarded.

The reverend spoke softly, but clearly. "Aidan Duncan O'Rourke, you're not a man who appreciates deception or hem-hawing. Contrarily, you like candor, so I shall be candid. You're aware of the spirit of fear that has come upon you. That one you have fought with all your power and energy. I'm concerned about the other demon you will have a hard time admitting has plagued you for a long time—many years before your capture by Quazel."

"What other demon?" Aidan asked defensively.

"Did you really think Ricardo had *all* the other ones I named that day by the brook? Ho! No, no. My dear man, you've been consumed with lust."

Aidan shouted, "Lust! I've never been unfaithful to Caitlin. Mayhap you should re-evaluate your demons." Aidan stood to leave.

Devereaux, in a voice with authority reminiscent of Duncan, said forcefully, "Sit down."

Like a naughty child who had been caught with his hand in the biscuit jar, Aidan obeyed.

"In actions, you haven't been unfaithful, but in your thoughts and in your heart you've been most unfaithful. You've lusted after your best friend's wife on numerous occasions. Not only have you dreamed about her, but also in your waking thoughts you've fantasized about her."

Aidan stammered, "How can you possibly know my thoughts?"

"I can't answer that question, Aidan. I don't know how I've had these revelations at this time. I never had this ability before, so it must be solely for the purpose of vanquishing these demons. Suffice to say I *do* know."

Aidan rubbed his hands across his face and through his hair. "Oh, God, help me. When Caitlin was a tigress and I so desperately needed to feel her arms around me, I made excuses my fleeting thoughts were because I was lonely. Mary Kate never encouraged my thoughts. God-a-mercy, she would be mortified if she even suspected. She was her innocent, caring self. When she would talk to me or in passing take my hand in compassion and sympathy, I can't even voice the thoughts I had or the things I did in secret. I'm ashamed, but I thought it had passed." He blew out a breath. "When Caitlin was restored, the thoughts stopped, until recently. They're stronger and even more perverted. I've fought them. I've of late avoided a dear friend and even been rude to her to keep the thoughts from coming, but it doesn't work.

"Reverend, lately I've had thoughts far worse than what Kieran did. Are his and Rennin's immoral behavior a result of my lust?"

"Aidan, they're responsible for their own actions. We're talking about you."

"Reverend, are you telling me these thoughts aren't my own, but are being placed in my head by some evil spirit?"

"That's exactly what I'm saying."

A look of utter terror spread over Aidan's face, all color draining from his cheeks. "Could this spirit cause me somehow to act upon these ideas? Is there a possibility I could put deeds to the thoughts?"

The reverend lowered his head. "That's my greatest fear for you." The old man took a deep breath. "You need to know—the day Kieran acted so rashly, the spirit left you and went after him."

"Oh, God! What can I do?" He clutched a fist over his heart. "I would never willingly be unfaithful to Caitlin; or, God forbid, hurt Mary Kate. And I'd never wish the evil on anyone else—most of all, my son. Reverend, right now that spirit of fear is really strong."

"No, Aidan"—Devereaux shook his head—"that's reasonable fear. That's *real* fear. Short of alerting the parties involved of the danger, I don't know what to tell you to do."

Aidan laughed sardonically. "Reverend, I might be straightforward most of the time, but I'm not a complete and total fool. There's no way on God's green Earth I'll *ever* tell Colin I had impure thoughts about his wife. I'd like to live to a ripe old age. Prithee, think of some other solution."

"Is there someone you can tell about your dilemma who will become your constant companion?"

"Char? No, he would be willing, but he cannot keep company with me *constantly*. I really don't want *anyone* to know exactly what this spirit is doing to me."

I know, Aidan. Char's voice sounded in the man's mind.

Then, help me.

I will do all I can.

The reverend smiled. "I'm going to tell you something. Ricardo needs someone to keep him from harming himself. One of his demons taunts him to kill himself. Perhaps the two of you can keep each other from doing anything stupid."

"Isn't that the blind leading the blind?"

"Look at it as a purpose to keep you busy until the church is finished."

"Reverend, why do we have to have a church building? Isn't God capable of defeating evil without a building to house the event?"

"The building is for your and Ricardo's privacy."

"So, we could do this anywhere? The church itself isn't necessary?"

"Oui."

"I say let's go to *The Privileged Character* tonight. I'm sure Ricardo would agree. We can build the church with clean spirits."

"Not tonight," objected the reverend. "I want all the participants to take twenty-four hours to fast and pray before the ceremony. If Ricardo is agreeable, let's start a fast at sundown tonight. Tomorrow night we rid you of this torture."

As with all the others, François Devereaux prayed with Aidan for strength to fight his demons and someone with whom to share his strife that would understand and not judge.

59
Exorcism

𝕬𝖎𝖉𝖆𝖓 himself went to Ricardo who was more than agreeable; he was insistent. While Aidan was there, he gave his charm to Danielle.

"My dear friend, I think you must wear this for now."

"Gramercy, Aidan." Danielle hugged him.

He laughed sadly. "You might not want to hug me if you knew what one of my demons is."

As Aidan left, Ricardo joined him on the porch. In a manly embrace, Ricardo whispered in Aidan's ear, "Lust. 'Twas the only one I did not have other than fear. Besides, I have seen the way you have looked at Mary Kate. It concerned me because I recognized the look from my previous life, and it was so unlike you. If you want to talk, we can fast somewhere together."

"Gramercy," said Aidan. "Tonight, I'm going to my sure haven, Caitlin. On the morrow I may seek you, my friend."

Ricardo Morales tossed and turned all night, so Danielle suggested they pray together. During a lull in their prayers, Ricardo walked onto the porch for a breath of the cool night air. In a moment panic struck; he saw a furtive shadow lurking around the Fitzpatricks' window. He shouted over his shoulder, "Danielle, I love you. I shall see you tomorrow evening. I know now why I could not sleep a wink."

Not taking the time to put on his shoes, Ricardo ran as fast as he could to the hedge where he had seen the shadow. He found Aidan trying to pry open the window. Grabbing broad shoulders he growled softly, "What are you doing,

Aidan?" Whirling his friend around, he became aware Aidan had no idea he was even outside. The eyes staring at him were blank and empty and dark.

Ricardo shook Aidan to try to wake him. A guttural voice, totally unrecognizable, hissed at the Spaniard, "I will have that woman. She'll rue the day she was born. How dare she resurrect Duncan? I'll make her forget her morality. She'll beg me for more and scoff in the face of that milksop she married."

Although Aidan was three inches taller than Ricardo and outweighed him by twenty pounds, something inside the former pirate bubbled out, and with one blow, he punched Aidan, knocking him cold. With an almost inaudible whisper Ricardo said, "You will thank me in the light of day." Ricardo lifted Aidan across his back and carried him to the clearing where he called, "Char, come quickly. Aidan needs you."

The sleepy dragon was on the spot within minutes. Ricardo started his explanation immediately as Char eyed his unconscious friend, and smoke swirled from his nostrils. "Before you eat me, let me explain. Take us to the suite the newlyweds use. I will explain on the way."

Char intoned, "I think I know. I lost connection to Aidan for a while."

Knowing Char would never betray his dearest friend, Ricardo told him everything.

Char left the men in the suite. "Call me if you need me."

Ricardo said, "If I do not call before sunset, come then and take us to *The Privileged Character*."

"Verily, I shall be here."

Ricardo washed Aidan's face with cool water and he started wide-awake. "Where am I? What am I doing here? Ricardo? What's going on?"

Ricardo told Aidan of the incident outside Mary Kate's window. "I do not know if that demon had the intention of raping Mary Kate, of getting you killed, or both. I do know part of the anger toward her had something to do with Duncan's resurrection."

Aidan sat in stunned silence. "How can I ever repay you?"

Ricardo laughed lightly. "Have Caitlin make her pot roast again."

Aidan grinned. "You have a deal. 'Tis a standing invitation. Every Friday night for the rest of our lives, our families dine together." The two men shook hands. Then, Ricardo laughed loudly.

"What's so funny?"

Ricardo affected as feminine a voice as he could. "Dear, we *are* in the honeymoon suite." Then, he said seriously. "At least here we can pray and fast in relative safety."

Danielle watched Ricardo belt Aidan and carry him away. Unsure exactly what was afoot, she bundled Seamus and went to Caitlin. The door was ajar, so with great apprehension Danielle entered her friend's house. She laid Seamus, who still slept, on the rug by the hearth and went in search of Caitlin.

In the doorway of the master bedroom, Danielle found the woman of the house, half-conscious, naked, and beaten. She dropped to her knees and lifted her friend's head with an exclamation. "Caitlin!"

Caitlin responded groggily, "Danielle?" Suddenly, fully cognitive, she screamed, "Where is Aidan? I have to stop him!"

Danielle chided her. "Don't worry about Aidan. Ricardo's taking care of him."

"Then, he didn't hurt Mary Kate?"

Danielle shook her head. "No. I saw Ricardo hit him and then carry him way. I don't know where they went, but I trust my husband to see to Aidan."

As Danielle helped Caitlin slip into her robe, Caitlin began to weep. "Danielle, it was so horrible. Aidan had gone to sleep. I couldn't sleep, so I sat in the rocker and prayed silently. I must have dozed because when I woke, Aidan was standing over me, but 'twas *not* Aidan. 'Twas Aidan's body, but 'twas not Aidan. This malicious voice started telling me how I was only half a woman and couldn't satisfy my husband, but he would gladly fulfill my desires. I was so scared." The terrified wife wiped tears from her cheeks. "I tried to run from the room, but he grabbed my hair and jerked me backward. Then, he hit me over and over. I tried to scream, but he choked me. I thought he was going to kill me." Caitlin let loose another stream of tears as her friend hugged her. The tall redhead choked out her next words. "He forced himself on me, Danielle."

Caitlin sobbed in Danielle's arms for a while before she continued her story. The smaller woman did not know how to comfort her friend, except to remind her it was not Aidan. She whispered tenderly as a mother would to a child who had a nightmare. "Shh. 'Tis all right now. You're safe. Caitlin, remember 'twas not Aidan. 'Twas one of his demons."

Caitlin, through strangled sobs, continued her account of the night. "When he got off me, he started laughing and said, 'Guess what I'm going to do now? I'm going to show that Fitzpatrick bitch what a real man is like. I'm sure she has never had one unless your precious Aidan gave her what she wanted and needed.' I ran after him and he pushed me into the wall with his hands around my throat. I must have passed out because the next thing I remember is you. Danielle, I have to see Mary Kate. I have to know she's unharmed."

Danielle said, "All right, Caitlin. Bathe and dress. I shall bring Mary Kate to you."

Danielle left Caitlin and went to wake Mary Kate. However, Colin answered the door. "Danielle, what's the matter?"

Nervously she answered, "Something has happened to Caitlin. She wants Mary Kate."

Mary Kate appeared behind Colin. "What happened?"

Discreetly Danielle said, "I think you should hear it from Caitlin."

Both Colin and Mary Kate were dressed except for their shoes. They had obviously fallen asleep in their clothes. Colin went with his wife. Knowing she could not stop him, Danielle caught his arm. "Colin, whatever you see and hear, remember Aidan's not himself right now. Don't react rashly." A look of consternation spread across Colin's face.

Danielle saw light in the kitchen so she took Colin and Mary Kate to the back door and they went in. When Colin saw his sister's face, he bellowed, "Where's Aidan?"

Danielle said calmly, "Ricardo took him away. I know not where."

Caitlin pointed her finger at her brother. "Stop right now. I asked for Mary Kate, not you. This isn't Aidan's fault. Remember why we're praying and fasting before you lose your head." Her tears began to trickle.

Colin said tenderly, "Katie," and took her in his arms. It was the first time he had called her his pet name since they were ten years old and she had fallen from the top of the tree she was not supposed to have climbed and broke her arm. "Why did ya want Mary Kate?"

Caitlin looked cautiously at her brother. "That fiend inside Aidan's head was going to do the same thing to Mary Kate, but Ricardo stopped him."

Colin said, "The same thing? Exactly what did he do?"

Caitlin looked soberly at her twin and mumbled, "Think about it, Colin. I'm sure your mind is sharp enough to read between the lines."

Colin sat down in one of the dining chairs. "I had no idea Aidan was dealing with something of this magnitude. No wonder Reverend Devereaux wanted us to fast and pray before the exorcism. No wonder he told me not to envy Aidan, but to pity him. I doona think sunset can get here fast enough for all of us. Sis, were ya aware of this?"

"I had no idea the spirit was violent."

Colin said, "Which spirit? I thought Aidan was overwhelmed with a spirit of fear."

Caitlin said, "He doesn't know I know. Aidan doesn't know he has talked in his sleep. We all know about his dreams of Quazel, but it hasn't been her name or mine he has spoken sensuously in his dreams."

Mary Kate gasped, "Me?"

Caitlin nodded. Colin laughed angrily. "Peradventure, Aidan's more afraid of me than the spirit."

Caitlin's eyes widened, but Colin precluded her comment. "Doona worry, Sis. I am not going to hurt Aidan. Tonoight all this will be over. I think the four of us should stay together and pray. We need one another's strength."

The day dragged for the seven people who would assist the reverend in freeing their loved ones from the clutches of evil. At noon Duncan summoned everyone to his house for a consultation. The governor of Draconis paced as he talked.

"Draco is taking the children to his cave. He and Esmeralda are tending them tonight for as long as it takes. Also, the rest of the family has asked to be present tonight. They sent Rennin earlier today to plead their case. The reverend has agreed that they can form an outer circle of prayer, but they will not have any hands-on involvement except for Drake whom Reverend Devereaux has asked to be present in case either Aidan or Ricardo or one of us should need medical attention. By the way, Caitlin, what happened to you? Have you seen your father?"

Caitlin whispered, "I encountered one of Aidan's spirits. I'm afraid it won't go quietly."

Duncan exclaimed, "Aidan did that to you?"

"Not Aidan. One of his spirits," Caitlin corrected. "Nothing's broken. I'm a little sore, but I'll be fine."

Duncan kissed the top of Caitlin's head. "Alas, dear." Then, he addressed the group. "We leave in one hour. Reverend Devereaux wants to anoint *The Privileged Character* with oil and holy water before nightfall. We'll stay together and pray the rest of the afternoon.

"If you're afraid, 'tis perfectly natural. I don't mind telling you I'm scared to death. We'll need to draw strength from one another and lend strength to the two men we love. Danielle, I want you especially to know you're not alone in your love for Ricardo. I've grown to care for him very much. Indeed, I count him as a dear friend."

"As do I," confirmed Diggory.

Elizabeth said, "He's my family, Danielle."

Colin took Danielle's hand. "Ricardo is a good man. We aire going to support him just as strongly as we support Aidan. Know this, too: We love *ya* dearly."

Danielle smiled at her friends. "Many thanks."

Duncan gave one final instruction. "Be sure to wear your talismans. Reverend Devereaux says we should drink water, but eat nothing. Meet in one hour in the clearing."

Looking around, Colin said, "Where is the reverend?"

Duncan said, "He spent the night on *The Privileged Character*."

Aidan and Ricardo had prayed until the sun streaked the sky. From sheer exhaustion both men slept. Near sundown, Char entered the cave to find them still asleep. Gently, he roused them. As they prepared to leave, Aidan hesitated.

"Ricardo, find some rope and bind me."

Ricardo started to refuse, but Aidan insisted. "I pray you. I fear it could be necessary."

Rather than rope, Ricardo pulled his silk handkerchief from his pocket. "Aidan, this is strong. It will not be easily broken, but neither will it cut your wrists."

Ricardo smiled wryly and joked to relieve the tension of the moment. "I suppose this piece of cloth is appropriate to bind lust. I often used it to tie women's wrists who wanted me to bind them without injury. Ironic, is it not?"

Aidan himself chuckled at the thought. "I suppose 'tis."

Aidan made another request. "Char, will you stay on the beach? I'll be able to feel your strength and devotion should I need to draw from it."

Char replied, "You need not ask. I wouldn't leave you even if you told me to."

With Aidan's hands securely bound, the two men left with the hope of having their minds cleansed of the unwanted voices and images and desires.

60
The Appointed Hour

Aidan and Ricardo arrived at the appointed hour to find the entire family waiting for them. Caitlin had told Reverend Devereaux about her encounter with the demon, and when he saw Aidan had voluntarily bound himself, he was pleased. He addressed Aidan kindly. "Don't think me cruel, but I don't want you on deck while we deal with Ricardo, and considering the severity of your spirit, I want to attempt you last."

The reverend then addressed Aidan's sons. "Kieran and Rennin, take your father into the hold. Don't let him out or bring him out until I tell you."

Aidan asked, "Reverend, I don't remember anything from last night from the time I went to sleep until I awoke with Ricardo in the mountains. Did I do something awful? You all seem to be keeping something from me. Caitlin?"

Until that moment Caitlin had avoided her husband. Knowing the heartbreak Aidan would feel, she said with her back to him, "Mayhap 'tis better you never remember."

"Caitlin," was Aidan's only plea.

Knowing, too, she could not lie to her husband, Caitlin slowly turned to face him. The suffering hero released a compunctious grunt. "Noooo." He reached his bound hands out to the battered face.

Caitlin let him touch her and she kissed him softly as she whispered, "Put it from your mind. Now, go with Rennin and Kieran so we can put this behind us quickly. I love you."

Aidan deliberately went below with one son on each side, his heart rent to pieces.

Meanwhile as Danielle held Ricardo's hand, neither of them speaking, but feeling the one-mindedness, Miranda approached her father and took his free hand. "Da, I hope you don't mind I came. I had to be here."

Ricardo smiled. "I am glad you came. Many great thankings."

Miranda slipped her arms around his neck, and Ricardo held his daughter in their first real embrace. She kissed his cheek and returned to stand with Morgan. The two girls clasped hands, and Priscilla, Alexander, Drake, and Declan joined them.

Devereaux said, "That is as good a place as any for you to pray while we work. Keep your prayers focused on the task at hand."

He turned to Ricardo. "Are you ready?"

Ricardo answered, "I am beyond ready."

The reverend cautioned Ricardo, "Some of these spirits might flee easily; others could put up a fight. I want you to be prepared for anything."

"I understand," assured Ricardo.

The reverend smiled and patted the tormented man's shoulder. "You think you do." He steered Ricardo into the circle of friends and said, "Will you kneel here?"

Shakily, Ricardo did as he was requested. The spirit of confusion had already descended upon him.

Reverend Devereaux spoke to the seven and asked, "Will each of you lay a hand on Ricardo? Pray specifically about the spirit I name. I've already told you the Latin term for each spirit."

Each member of the group put a hand on Ricardo. He clutched Danielle's hand, drawing strength from her love. Reverend Devereaux anointed his head with oil. "We'll start with the one that has plagued you most."

The old man shivered as the air around the ship cooled dramatically.

He dipped his finger in the holy water and made the sign of the cross on Ricardo's forehead. *"Confusio Turbatio, iubeo vobis nomine tenus Patris et nomine tenus*

Redemptor Filius et nomine tenus Sanctus Spiritus, relinquo hic homo hominis, Ricardo Manuel Morales-Mendez. Adstringo vobis et repeto vobis fovea Damno oriundus numquam." ("Confusion, I command you in the Name of the Father and of the Son and of the Holy Ghost to leave this man, Ricardo Manuel Morales-Mendez. I bind you and vanquish you to the pit of Hell, never to return.")

A voice, which was not Ricardo's taunted the reverend, "I'm having too much fun to leave this man."

At the sound of a strange voice, several members of the party of seven gasped.

Francois commanded, *"Derelinquamus!"* ("Leave now!")

Ricardo shuddered and the voice screamed, but said no more.

The reverend repeated the sign of the cross and said, *"Avaritia, iubeo vobis nomine tenus Patris et nomine tenus Redemptor Filius et nomine tenus Sanctus Spiritus, relinquo hic homo hominis. Adstringo vobis et repeto vobis fovea Damno oriundus numquam."* ("Greed, I command you in the Name of the Father and of the Son and of the Holy Ghost to leave this man. I bind you and vanquish you to the pit of Hell, never to return.")

Another voice said, "Why did you choose me? I'm not so bad, but you don't have to tell me twice. I'm going."

Once again Ricardo shuddered, and again the reverend repeated the sign of the cross.

"Subiungo, iubeo vobis nomine tenus Patris et nomine tenus Redemptor Filius et nomine tenus Sanctus Spiritus, relinquo hic homo hominis. Adstringo vobis et repeto vobis fovea Damno oriundus numquam." ("Oppression, I command you in the Name of the Father and of the Son and of the Holy Ghost to leave this man. I bind you and vanquish you to the pit of Hell, never to return.")

Not a sound was made. The only evidence the spirit had heard was another deep shudder by Ricardo.

Again Reverend Devereaux made the sign of the cross and gave the command. *"Contemno, iubeo vobis nomine tenus Patris et nomine tenus Redemptor Filius et nomine tenus Sanctus Spiritus, relinquo hic homo hominis. Adstringo vobis et repeto vobis fovea Damno oriundus numquam."* ("Hate, I command you in the Name of the Father and of the Son and of the Holy Ghost to leave this man. I bind you and vanquish you to the pit of Hell, never to return.")

A growling voice said, "What man? Do you mean this bit of human refuse? Until you call him what he is, I'm here to stay."

Devereaux shouted, *"Ne effor! Relinquo, adhuc! Iubeo vobis nomine tenus Patris et nomine tenus Redemptor Filius et nominee tenus Sanctus Spiritus!"* ("Be quiet! Leave now! I command you in the Name of the Father and of the Son and of the Holy Ghost!")

As the voice faded away it screamed, "I don't want to go!" However, the anticipated shudder was present.

One last time, François Devereaux put the sign of the cross on Ricardo's forehead and commanded, *"Cruor, iubeo vobis nomine tenus Patris et nomine tenus Redemptor Filius et nomine tenus Sanctus Spiritus, relinquo hic homo hominis. Adstringo vobis repeto vobis fovea Damno oriundus numquam."* ("Murder, I command you in the Name of the Father and of the Son and of the Holy Ghost to leave this man. I bind you and vanquish you to the pit of Hell, never to return.")

A cruel and vicious laugh came from Ricardo. It sounded much like the laugh he had uttered years ago as captain of a pirate ship. "You command *me*? Oh, I think not. I'm not as weak as my comrades. Think again, old fool."

Devereaux commanded, *"Ne effor!"* ("Be quiet!")

The voice countered, "Be quiet yourself. I shall say whatever I damned well please!"

The reverend spoke again, *"Ne loquor! Adstringo tui lingua nomine tenus Patris et nomine tenus Redemptor Filius et nomine tenus Sanctus Spiritus. Relinquo adhuc!"* ("Do not speak. I bind your tongue in the name of the Father and of the Son and of the Holy Ghost. Leave now!")

The voice, now hoarse as someone with laryngitis, spat, "If I go, I'll take him with me!"

Ricardo fell backward and his eyes rolled to the back of his head. Only the whites were visible. His body convulsed and he shook as one having an epileptic seizure. Devereaux shouted, "Drake, we need you!"

In an instant the doctor had placed a wooden spoon in Ricardo's mouth. Everyone had released hold on Ricardo except Danielle. She still clutched his hand. Drake worked frantically, but none of his medicines seemed to quell the seizure.

Simultaneously Devereaux commanded, *"Cruor, iubeo vobis denique relinquo hic viri!"* In English he spoke, "Murder, I command you in the name of the Father and of the Son and of the Holy Ghost, leave this man!"

Danielle gathered Ricardo in her arms and cried, "Oh, God, I beg You help my husband. I beg You take this from him."

Instantly, Ricardo lay still as death. As Danielle held Ricardo tightly, Drake Fitzpatrick examined him closely. He triumphantly announced, "He lives. He breathes, barely, but he breathes."

Ricardo's body stiffened, shuddered, and relaxed in Danielle's arms. Danielle mumbled, "Thanks be to God."

Devereaux asked, "Colin, will you and Declan take Ricardo to one of the cabins to rest? Miranda, sit with your father in case he wakes. Danielle, we need you to stay for Aidan."

Danielle nodded. "Let me walk with them. I shall return with Colin."

"Very well, dear. I think we need a short break before we attempt anything with Aidan. At least there are only two to vanquish, but they're very strong," said the reverend, and he gusted a breath.

Aidan, Kieran, and Rennin had been in the hold only a few minutes when Aidan asked, "Kieran, an' it please you, untie my wrists? They are bound so tightly my circulation is being impeded."

Kieran took Aidan's hands, but Rennin said, "No, Kieran. We can't."

"Fie me," said Aidan. "The harlot's little spoiled brat would defy his father."

Kieran dropped Aidan's hands. "Da, what did you just call Mam?"

Slowly Aidan's voice changed and the room became frosty. "I thought I had strangled that wench. How did she survive? Zounds! Cats have nine lives. She has used three now. Thanks to the two of you, she lost one of them. Bad boys! You killed your mummy."

The twins realized quickly they were not dealing with their father, but with something sinister. The voice kept taunting Kieran and Rennin.

"Kieran, was it fun *taking* Miranda? I think she liked it though she pretended to be hurt. Was that feeling of power coursing through your veins exhilarating? Did you enjoy my little visit to you?

"What?" Kieran asked, his own voice husky.

"Of course 'twas me. You're not man enough to control a woman so forcibly."

Kieran clenched his jaw and fisted his hand.

And evil laugh from Aidan's throat preceded, "I wonder how she would like the feel of an older man?"

Kieran lunged for his father and Rennin restrained him. "Kieran, stop. 'Tis not Daddy talking."

"I know that, Rennin, but that thing is talking about my wife, the mother of my child." He heaved great breaths. "Whatever it is just admitted it made me rape her."

"Kieran, soon it will be gone."

The voice laughed sadistically. "Trow you, I thought verily I wanted Mary Kate." Bound hands rubbed across Aidan's groin, causing an instant erection to strain against his pants. "But on second thought I think Morgan would be much better. Am I right, Rennin?" He licked his lips and breathed as if smelling a flower. "Of course, Aidan is very familiar with those soft caressing hands. Think of all that time they spent alone. Rennin, have you ever wondered just how cozy that relationship was under Quazel's tutelage? Your little whore learned from the best. Mayhap the reason she lost the baby was punishment. 'Twas not yours!"

Rennin looked at his brother. "Kieran, forget what I said. I shall help you beat the hell out of it."

Kieran smiled broadly. "I have an idea." Kieran ripped apart an old sheet from Aidan's voyage to Draconis. "Hold him, Rennin."

Rennin grabbed his father from behind in a vice-like grip, pressing Aidan's arms tight against his body. Still, Aidan thrashed.

As Rennin held their father, Kieran gagged him. When he knelt to bind his feet, Aidan kicked him. Kieran pressed the other man's feet together under his arm and managed to coil the cloth around and around. "Da, if you can hear me, know we both love you, but enough is enough. We can't abide any more words from this demon."

They shoved the immobile man onto the floor in the room.

The wait seemed interminable for Kieran and Rennin. The twins tried to combat their anger by praying together for their father. The demon became angrier, making Aidan scream and writhe on the floor. Finally, Duncan came for his son.

As the boys hauled him up, Duncan said, "What is this?"

Rennin defended their actions. "Trust me, Granddaddy. 'Twas necessary."

Duncan nodded his understanding.

When Revernd Devereaux saw Aidan bound hand and foot and gagged, he knew this leg of his endeavor would be more difficult than the last. He requested a chair be brought and had Aidan tied to the chair for he knew the spirit manifesting itself would never kneel.

Caitlin trembled as she laid her hand on her husband's head. Aidan craned his neck and glared at her. Despite her fear she whispered, "You fight. Hear me and know I love you."

Kieran and Rennin joined the small group of prayer support. "Where is Miranda?" asked Kieran.

Morgan said, "She's sitting with Ricardo."

"How is Ricardo?"

"Exhausted."

The conversation ceased when Reverend Devereaux rose to begin the ritual. The group laid hands on Aidan. Each person's fingernails turned purple from the extreme cold that descended on the ship. Devereaux anointed Aidan's head with oil and made the sign of the cross and began the process again. *"Metus, iubeo vobis nomine tenus Patris et nomine tenus Redemptor Filius et nomine tenus Sanctus Spiritus, relinquo hic homo hominis, Aidan Duncan O'Rourke. Adstringo vobis et repeto vobis fovea Damno oriundus numquam."* ("Fear, I command you in the Name of the Father and of the Son and of the Holy Ghost to leave this man, Aidan Duncan O'Rourke. I bind you and vanquish you to the pit of Hell, never to return.")

Aidan jerked his head back and forth and dark eyes flashed at the reverend. A quivering voice tried to speak around the gag in Aidan's mouth.

"Ne effor," Devereaux commanded. *"Relinquo hic homo hominis adhuc!"* ("Be quiet. Leave this man now!")

Again, Aidan thrashed. Briefly his eyes returned to their vivid green and he frantically searched for Caitlin. The reverend said, "Caitlin, speak to Aidan. Let him know you're here."

Caitlin pulled Aidan's head against her chest and whispered, "Honey, I'm right here."

Aidan relaxed momentarily and then thrashed again. The twitching ended in a violent shudder and a distant scream.

When the reverend attempted to make the sign of the cross again, Aidan yanked his head from side to side. Caitlin held his head firmly in her hands so that Reverend Devereaux could make the sign. Even before the reverend spoke, the spirit screamed semi-distinguishable obscenities around the gag.

Undaunted, Devereaux spoke authoritatively. *"Cupiditas, iubeo vobis nomine tenus Patris et nomine tenus Redemptor Filius et nomine tenus Sanctus Spiritus, relinquo hic homo hominis. Adstringo vobis et repeto vobis Damno oriundus numquam."* ("Lust, I command you in the Name of the Father and of the Son and of the Holy Ghost to leave this man. I bind you and vanquish you to the pit of Hell, never to return.")

Aidan spasmed violently, so hard the chair fell over onto the deck. Somehow in the fall the gag loosened and the demon issued a stream of profanities.

"I'm much stronger than the pansies you've been dealing with. I won't be subdued so easily, you old fool."

"Ne effor! Relinquo nomine tenus Patris et nomine tenus Redemptor Filius et nomine tenus Sanctus Spiritus." ("Be quiet! Leave in the Name of the Father and of the Son and of the Holy Ghost.")

"Drop dead, old man!"

"Ne loquor!" ("Do not speak!")

An evil laugh reverberated throughout the ship, and with a burst of strength, Aidan broke the knot that held his wrists. His hands flew to his ankles and he was free. With the strength of several men, Aidan pushed aside those who held him.

The reverend fell hard and lay dazed. Caitlin jumped on Aidan's back, but he flung her to the deck. Aidan's eyes were black, and he leered at Mary Kate.

The already fridgid air around the ship became almost intolerably cold.

Aidan grabbed the petite woman and threw her to the deck. Mary Kate screamed. The voice that was not Aidan's said, "I will have what I want."

Colin pulled Aidan from Mary Kate and the two men struggled. Aidan hit Colin with a blow that sent him sprawling. Duncan and Diggory reached for Aidan, but he swept them aside as if they were no more than lint. Elizabeth placed a hand on his arm, and he chortled, pushing her aside. Danielle stepped toward him and a frosty breath from his mouth blew her over.

From the shore, Char, his chin pointing skyward, blasted an arc of fire over the ship. The great black beast shook violently in the sub-freezing temperatures. His roar caused the island to tremble.

Again, Aidan grabbed Mary Kate, ripping her bodice from her. In the struggle, Aidan's hand touched the opal talisman, and the demon shrieked with pain as the jewel seared the man's flesh. He slammed Mary Kate against the deck, but she did not scream. Instead, she enfolded Aidan in her arms. For an instant, the demon was taken off guard.

Aidan's body relaxed. Mary Kate spoke forcefully, *"Cupiditas, iubeo vobis nomine tenus Patris et nomine tenus Redemptor et nomine tenus Sanctus Spiritus, relinquo hic homo hominis. Adstringo vobis et repeto vobis Damno oriundus numquam."* ("Lust, I command you in the Name of the Father and of the Son and of the Holy Ghost to leave this man. I bind you and vanquish you to the pit of Hell, never to return.")

Aidan pushed himself from the woman, and the voice screamed agonizingly, "Nooooo!" Aidan's body hit the deck with a loud thud. He shuddered and lay perfectly still.

Drake Fitzpatrick bent over his son-in-law. "He breathes." He also examined the reverend and pronounced that other than a headache, he would be fine. No one else appeared seriously injured, only shaken.

Caitlin held Aidan in her arms. As she caressed his hair and kissed his forehead, Aidan opened his eyes. They were sparkling green even if ringed in dark circles. Aidan reached up and touched Caitlin's black eye. A sob died in his throat. "I remember everything. Oh, God, how could I?"

Caitlin smiled through her tears. "'Twas not you, my love. Think no more of it. I'm rejoicing to have you back. Don't ever leave me again."

"I promise. Heart of my heart, life of my life, you are my reason for breathing, and I will love you until the day I die. How long has it been since I said those words?"

"Too long."

61
Free at Last

Char flew a weary group to their homes. He insisted the babies stay in the mountains except for baby Martha who needed her mother's milk. As the families stumbled home Rennin announced, "I'm starving."

Everyone realized how hungry they were. Mary Kate said, "I have a turkey already prepared." Calls came from all the ladies who had something to add to the fowl for a meal. Once again, the families dined together under the stars. This meal was marked by laughter and a prevailing sense of peace. A calm breeze rustled the palm fronds that dotted the dirt lane where the homes of King Satin's Realm sat.

Ricardo whispered to Danielle, "I shall be right back. I have a surprise I have not shared with anyone here, not even Alexander. I hope you like it."

Danielle listened as weird sounds came from her house. A few minutes later Ricardo returned with a strange shaped piece of wood and a long skinny thing with horsetail hairs on it. Danielle asked honestly, "What is it?"

Ricardo laughed softly. "I can see one of my jobs will be to bring some culture to this island. This is a musical instrument called a violin."

Danielle's eye grew wide. "It makes music?"

"Let me show you. It has been a long time since I last played. I hope I am not too out of practice." Ricardo pulled the bow across the strings and sweet melancholy sounds rang out clearly. The whole company sat, enthralled by the haunting tune.

When he finished, he asked, "Well, Danielle, what did you think?"

"'Twas beautiful, but it sounded so sad."

Ricardo laughed. "Then, I shall make it sound happy for you. Miranda, Morgan, get those young lads to dance." Ricardo played a lively tune. It seemed the whole company came to life, dancing and laughing.

When the music stopped, the cheers went up for another and Mary Kate remarked, "Marry, I do miss my harpsichord."

Colin said, "Ricardo, ya aire a skilled carpenter. Perchance ya can help me make me wife a new harpsichord."

"I can build the cabinet if you can figure out the strings, hammers, and keys."

After several dances, weariness caught up with the crowd, and they began to retire for the evening. Caitlin was about to invite the reverend to stay with them, but Alexander insisted Deveraux and he should keep each other company.

Mary Kate took Colin's hand and whispered, "Let's go. I've found myself lusting after a certain man at this gathering."

Colin teased his wife. "Is it anyone I know?"

"Mayhap. He's tall and has red hair. I've been told his name is Colin. Alas, I fear he's a married man with an anniversary tomorrow."

"Aye. I know the chap well. I would love to introduce the two of ya."

The two disappeared without warning, and Colin and Mary Kate raced upstairs, leaving a trail of clothes in their wake.

A while later Danielle and Ricardo meandered toward home. When they passed their door, Danielle asked, "Where are we going?"

Ricardo chuckled, "I do not know. I feel so free. I want to breathe the air and watch the stars and feel the grass. I want to appreciate the majesty of this place. Danielle, I do not know how to explain how wonderful I feel. There are no voices screaming at me. I am not worried about what will happen next. I feel like a boy again with only anticipation for the future and zest for life. I want to say good-bye to the cares of life forever."

"Aren't you the least bit tired after the day we had?"

"I was earlier, but I feel refreshed. Danielle, the brook is only a few yards from here. Let us go for a swim."

Pretending to object, she said, "Ricardo, 'tis midnight."

"And Char told us to sleep until noon tomorrow. I know you can swim."

"Aye, like a dolphin," Danielle said lightheartedly with a twinkle in her eyes.

Ricardo pulled her to him and said, "Were you being impish? Do you know what I do to imps?"

"No, what?"

He poked Danielle in the ribs, and she squirmed and giggled. Then he took off running toward the brook, casting over his shoulder, "I race them to the brook, and the winner gets to choose the next activity."

Danielle lifted the ends of her skirt and ran after him, laughing like a child, "'Tis cheating, Ricardo!"

"'Tis the remaining pirate in me!" he joked as he disappeared over the hill.

The bright white full moon lit the way better than lanterns. A hundred feet from the bank Danielle followed a trail of clothes and stopped at the water's edge.

"Come on," said Ricardo. "'Tis not cold."

Danielle looked at the clothes on the bank. "Ricardo?"

"Danielle, everyone else is asleep unless they are implementing their own plans. I am your husband. Do not be a prude."

Haughtily she asked, "Did you call me a prude? You know better."

"Prove it," he teased.

Danielle smirked and mumbled, "I shall show you prude." The petite redhead slowly and deliberately removed one article of clothing at a time, beginning with her shoes, then her stockings. Next she let her skirt fall to the ground.

Ricardo said impatiently, "Danielle, hurry and get in here with me."

She continued her calculated pace, but said alluringly, "I think an element of anticipation is in order here." At long last she appeared ready to enter the water, yet she took the time to remove the combs from her hair. Then she slowly waded into the stream until she had to swim. When she reached Ricardo, she wrapped her arms around his neck as he started to speak, but she kissed him in the middle of his first word, a deep, long sensuous kiss.

He gasped, "Anticipation? You were driving me mad."

Danielle breathed, "'Twas the prude's intention. Now, what's the winner's next activity?"

"Let me show you."

Aidan and Caitlin sat on their porch serenely holding hands. "This is nice," sighed Caitlin.

Aidan whispered, "Is it midnight yet?"

"A little after I would say by the position of the moon. Why?"

Aidan brushed Caitlin's hair from her face. "Do you realize what the date is?"

Caitlin shook her head. "With all that has occurred during the last two years, I've practically lost track of the days."

"'Tis our anniversary. Today marks twenty years together. Do you realize we have been together longer than we were apart?"

Caitlin's demeanor changed. She said excitedly, "'Tis our anniversary. I must make you a special supper tonight."

Aidan laughed. "Ginny will be home tonight. Why not make it a special breakfast? Do you have any strawberries and whipping cream?"

Caitlin laughed nervously, stood, and walked to the end of the porch. Aidan stood behind her with his hands on her shoulders. As he kissed her hair, he felt a tear plop onto his hand. "What's the matter, my love?"

Caitlin took a deep breath. "You don't know how much I'd love to have that kind of breakfast with you, but I don't know if I can."

"Why?"

She pivoted to face her husband. He kept his arms around her. "I hurt, Aidan. I mean I physically hurt. I have bruises in unspeakable places."

"Show me."

"Oh, Aidan, I shouldn't. You've suffered enough."

"Caitlin, I have to burn the bridges behind me. I want to be completely free. The spirits that attacked Ricardo sought only to hurt him. On the other hand, one of mine wanted to hurt everybody I love, from you to my sons, to my dearest friends. On the morrow I shall apologize to each one individually, but tonight I want to help heal your wounds, especially the ones I can't see. Show me what I did to you."

Caitlin argued, "'Twas not you."

"'Twas not my spirit, but 'twas my physical presence. Caitlin, this will help me forget, too."

Caitlin took Aidan's hand. "An' it please you, but I think 'twill hurt you more."

"Initially, but in the end, I think it will free me."

Aidan lit the lantern from the table inside the front door, and they climbed the stairs without conversation. In the bedroom, Aidan lit another lantern. Caitlin unlaced her blouse with trembling hands.

She stammered, "I can't do this, Aidan. You'll have to help me."

Gently as a mother would undress a baby, Aidan removed his wife's clothes. With one look at her abused body, the man was overwhelmed with emotion. "Caitlin, how can you bear to be in the same room with me? How can you still love me?"

Caitlin put her finger to her husband's lips. "'Twas not you. You're my life." She kissed him and ran her fingers through his still golden curls. The only place the man she loved showed any age was fine lines around his emerald eyes. "You're the same boy I fell in love with twenty years ago. Nothing will ever take my love from you. Never forget that."

Aidan held his wife gingerly, not wanting to hurt her in any way. Tenderly he laid her on the bed and starting with her eye, he kissed every bruise on her body.

"What are you doing?" Caitlin asked.

As if speaking to a child, Aidan answered, "Making your booboos all better."

Caitlin giggled. "All of them?"

"Every one."

"You'll have a hard time reaching some of them," she teased.

"I shall try anyway." He did.

She giggled again. "Aidan, that tickles. Stop."

"Does it still hurt?"

"Aye."

"Then, I can't stop."

"'Tis feeling much better."

"How much?"

"Would you like me to show you?"

"Aye, an' it please you."

Ricardo awoke to the smell of fresh-baked bread. He scampered down the stairs, still in his night clothes. "Good morrow, beautiful. What are you making?" Ricardo kissed the back of Danielle's neck.

"I recall someone saying he had never tasted anything better than my fresh-baked bread. If he was lying, when he eats this with raspberry jam, he will break out in hives." Danielle laughed and kissed Ricardo.

Ricardo burned his fingers cutting a slice of bread. "Hot!"

"Mr. Impatience, let it cool a few minutes."

"Then, the butter does not melt."

Danielle fried some sausages and scrambled some eggs to go with the bread, and the couple sat down to breakfast. Ricardo spoke seriously. "Danielle, I want to ask you something. We are not getting any younger, but I was wondering something."

She pointed her fork at Ricardo and joked, "Are you going to remind me I'm a year older than you?"

Ricardo laughed. "No, but 'tis something rather selfish."

"What? I doubt 'tis selfish."

"I want to have another baby. I enjoy being a father so much I would have a dozen, but I will not ask that of you."

Danielle's eyes danced. "Do you, now?"

"Aye, but mayhap we can have a little girl with auburn hair."

Danielle lifted one eyebrow. "What's wrong with a little boy with black hair? Is it that you want a little girl to name Charlotte?"

"Danielle, are you jealous?"

"Aye. I admit it." She started to clear the table. Ricardo pulled his wife onto his lap.

"How would you feel about naming her Leila? 'Twas my mother's name. She died in childbirth when I was five."

Danielle put her arms around Ricardo's neck. "I like Leila much better. What if 'tis a boy?"

"Does that mean you agree? We can work on making another baby?"

"No. That means we can practice for the third one."

"The third one?"

She kissed her husband. "And the fourth and the fifth. The second one is already on the way——I think; and I want to name him Richard."

"Danielle! When were you going to tell me?"

"I just told you. I still need to visit Elizabeth or Drake to be sure, but I'm pretty sure. Are you truly glad?"

"Overjoyed."

A knock at the door interrupted the couple's private celebration. Ricardo was mildly irritated. "Who could that be?" He shouted, "Go away! We are busy!"

Danielle hit him playfully. "Ricardo Morales, 'tis rude." Danielle answered the door.

Rennin grinned sheepishly. "I can come back another time. I've only been married a few weeks longer than you, and I have a child the same age as yours. I know how valuable a few moments alone are. 'Twas not thinking clearly when I knocked."

"Don't be silly, Rennin. Come in."

Rennin entered and asked, "Where's Ricardo?"

"'Twas not yet dressed. He'll be back in a moment."

Ricardo threw on his pants and a shirt and came back down the stairs. Rennin was having coffee with Danielle. Ricardo greeted their guest jovially. "Good morrow! Glorious morning, is it not?" Ricardo clasped Rennin's hand firmly.

It dawned on the young man he had never seen Ricardo so absolutely happy. "Have you looked at the sky this morning? 'Tis going to rain buckets before long."

Ricardo glanced out the window. "Sí, absolutely spectacular shades of blue and gray. Look how the sun breaks through, giving the rays a stage-light effect. Positively marvelous."

"I have never seen stage lights, but the colors are remarkable."

Ricardo smiled. He looked years younger. "They use looking glasses to reflect the candles in numerous directions. Sometimes they place candles behind bottles of red wine, ale, or some other liquid of color to cast colored shadows."

"I would in truth like to talk to you sometime about the things you've seen and the places you've been. I would love to hear more about the distant lands and the scientific discoveries, as well as the music and the literature, but 'tis not why I barged in on you. Kieran, Declan, Morgan, and I are throwing a huge surprise party for our folks in Seanathair's cave tonight. 'Tis their twentieth wedding anniversaries. We wanted to make sure you would be coming."

Ricardo answered lightly. "We would not miss it. What can we do to help make it a success? However, I do have one question. Why did not my son-in-law come to invite us?"

"Honestly? I asked to come to you because I want to get to know you better. I want you to teach me and tell me about things beyond Draconis. Daddy taught Kieran and me to read and to cipher. We read history and studied geography, but you've experienced so much. I read all of Seanathair's books. I want to learn all I can. There must be more to life than this island."

Ricardo looked grave. "Rennin, do you want to leave Draconis?"

"I can't answer that yet. I've always longed to see other places and have grand adventures, but I also have a family to protect." The young O'Rourke gave a slight shrug. "I don't know."

"Very well. We shall talk, but another day. 'Tis your parents' anniversary. Tell us how we can help."

"Danielle, would you prithee make a great big chocolate cake? You make the best chocolate cake I ever tasted, but don't tell Mam I said that." Rennin practically bubbled his request.

"Will one be enough? How many people are you expecting?"

"Around a hundred."

"All right, Rennin, I shall take care of your cake."

"Gramercy. Smoke will come and get you about an hour before sunset. Now I need to make sure Granddaddy is going to get Mam and Daddy and Uncle Colin and Aunt Mary Kate to the cave without their being suspicious. Whatever you do, don't even let on as if you know what day 'tis."

As Rennin walked jauntily to his grandfather's house, Ricardo remarked, "Two years. 'Tis how long I give Rennin before he leaves this place forever. He has the wanderlust."

"What about you?" asked Danielle.

Ricardo put his arm around his wife. "No, Señora. He encontrado mi rincón pequeño del mundo." ("No, Madame. I have found my little corner of the world.")

Mid-afternoon Duncan barged into Aidan's house without knocking. "Aidan, Caitlin, we have an urgent situation. I need you to come with me. Leave Ginny with Danielle. I need Colin and Mary Kate, too. Meet Draco in the clearing."

Duncan ran across to Colin's house and delivered the same message. They all met in the clearing, and Draco flew them to Isla Linda.

Upon arrival and a brief inspection, Aidan said, "Daddy, I don't see anything here that could be classified as a crisis."

Duncan shook his head. "I don't understand. I was told that there was a catastrophe here and to bring you with me. 'Tis not a funny shenanigan. After all we've been through, the word urgent throws me into panic. I'm getting too old for this sort of thing." Duncan feigned indignation.

"Daddy, who told you there was an urgent situation?"

"Nobody. 'Twas a note on my mantle."

Aidan sighed deeply. "If he was not a grown man with a child of his own, I would swear this had Rennin's hand all over it."

Duncan snorted, "Why would Rennin do something like this to his aging grandfather? Shame on you, Aidan. Give the boy the benefit of a doubt. He has turned into a fine young man, even if he does have a wild streak. I like him. He reminds me of me, except he talks a lot."

Colin asked calmly, "Uncle Duncan, could ya have misunderstood the note?"

"Mayhap. Oh, let's go home. I feel foolish."

As prearranged, Draco flew more slowly going home. As they neared the beach on Draconis, Duncan asked, "Would you mind if I stopped and picked up a book I told Father I would get for him a few days ago?"

"Of course not," all answered in unison.

The five people walked behind Draco down the passage to Alexander's Cavern. Caitlin said, "This reminds me of the first time we walked behind Draco."

"Aye," said Mary Kate. "Draco is still beautiful, but much larger. Draco, when do dragons stop growing?"

"I don't know," said the white beast. "Alexander thinks we grow until we die, and that's a long, long time. He says some of the dragons before were hundreds of years old." Draco stopped in his tracks. "Duncan, how long do humans live?"

"Back in Ireland, fifty was old. Here"—Duncan shrugged—"I don't know."

"Alexander is much older than fifty."

"Aye, Draco. He's very healthy, and he's a wizard. Wizards tend to live longer, mayhap, even a hundred years."

"Duncan, you aren't a wizard. You're over fifty. Are you going to die soon?"

Duncan laughed. "I hope I live many more years."

Draco was truly worried. His brow ridge hooded his eyes. "Duncan, what will I do for a human when you die? I'll live much longer."

"Methinks you can take on one of my grandchildren."

"Rennin already has Smoke. Kieran doesn't seem interested in having a bonded dragon. I think I shall take Ginny. She has spunk, but I do hope she doesn't plan to jump from the cliffs the way Rennin did."

"Draco, I shall put the arrangement in my last will and testament this eve, just in case I die in my sleep."

The massive dragon looked over his shoulder. "Duncan, do not say such things."

"All right, Draco. Get moving. We have things to do."

Draco walked into the golden chamber and stepped aside. The room resounded with the word, "Surprise!"

Aidan said, "I knew it had Rennin's hand all over it, but I had no idea my father was a co-conspirator."

Rennin and Kieran hugged their parents, as did Declan and Morgan and Miranda. "Happy anniversary. We thought twenty years together deserved something special," Rennin said.

Many friends shared the day with the two couples. Jean and Isabella Noir were there, no longer horses and now married. Eunice, the last unicorn, came. Lars Willoughby, Connor Donohue, Patrick O'Leary, Leslie Malone, and Jackson O'Hara made an appearance. Even Rory Smythe and Carl Covington came to the celebration. Of course, the families from King Satin's Realm and the dragon families attended.

The center of the food table held Danielle's three-tiered chocolate cake. Caitlin spoke to her fellow redhead. "Danielle, I can cook all kinds of food, but I can't bake a decent cake. How do you make such wonderful cakes?"

"I read the recipe. I'll give you my recipe if you'll teach me to make a pot roast 'twill melt in your mouth. Ricardo loves your pot roast."

"You have a deal. What's going on with you?"

"What do you mean, Caitlin?"

"You're positively glowing."

Danielle linked her arm with Caitlin's. "I am dying to tell someone. Ricardo and I are having another baby."

Caitlin hugged her friend. "'Tis wonderful. Is Ricardo excited?"

"Very. He wants a little girl, but I feel 'tis another boy. I want to name him Richard. Do you think Aidan would mind if we named the baby after him, Richard Aidan?"

"I think he would be honored. I know I would."

"What's your middle name?"

"Leanne."

"I promise to name one of our children after you. Without you, I might not be having Ricardo's child."

Aidan sneaked up behind the two murmuring women. "What's the big secret?" he whispered.

Danielle laughed. "There is no secret, but I'm sure I shall be big again."

Aidan grinned. "Big? Does that mean there's another little Morales on the way?"

Danielle nodded. Aidan hugged her. "Congratulations."

Aidan found Ricardo and gave him a bear hug.

All in all the evening was a huge success. The revelers went home to sleep and dream wonderful happy dreams.

62
C'est la Vie

A few weeks passed and the church was finally finished. The members of the community had decided Reverend Devereaux should pastor the small congregation.

As Caitlin started down the stairs to go to the first service in the new church, she held tightly to the banister and called, "Aidan!"

Aidan came to the bottom of the stairs holding Ginny. Caitlin sat on the top stair. Putting Ginny down, Aidan ran up the staircase and sat beside his wife. "Honey, what's the matter?"

Caitlin laid her head on Aidan's shoulder. "'Tis a boy. It has to be a boy. Ginny didn't do this to me. The boys did."

"What are you babbling about? Do you think you're with child?"

"Aye."

Aidan laughed. "Mayhap we'll need a bigger house." He kissed his wife.

Caitlin held Aidan's arm as they walked to church. Colin and Mary Kate joined them in their walk. Mary Kate slipped her arm around Caitlin's. "Walk with me for a minute. I have to tell you something."

Aidan looked apprehensively at Caitlin. "I shall be fine," she assured him.

Mary Kate questioned, "What's wrong, Caitlin?"

"I'm expecting again. I'm having dizzy spells this time, but you'll hold me up, won't you, my sister?"

Mary Kate smiled. "You know I will. Caitlin, I'm so happy for you."

"Are you truly, Mary Kate? I know how much you and Colin have wanted more children. Sometimes I feel badly for being blessed."

"Don't be silly. I do have to tell you something. Daddy Fitzpatrick confirmed it last night. I'm with child. 'Tis a miracle, but 'tis true. I thought mayhap I had started the change early, but Colin and I are going to have another baby. Both Daddy Fitzpatrick and Momma are going to be with me just in case I have trouble again. Momma says she has never had a woman have another child after the procedure she performed on me. Caitlin, 'tis truly a miracle."

Caitlin hugged Mary Kate. "Aye, 'tis. I'm thrilled. You know Danielle is expecting, too. What fun we can all have together."

After the service, Caitlin took the cleric aside and spoke to him privately. "Reverend, I'm expecting a child. If this child was conceived the night the demon attacked me, how might that affect my baby?"

"Don't concern yourself about that. The demon is gone. Each human is responsible for his own soul. Nothing that happened to Aidan can determine anything about your child's soul. You do want this child, don't you, Caitlin?"

Guiltily, Caitlin answered, "I was afraid this might be that demon's child. As long as 'tis my husband's baby, I'm overjoyed to have it."

"Then be joyous, dear. Demons are spirits. They cannot father children."

"'God is a spirit and hath not a body like man.' Mary conceived His Son." Her blue eyes stretched wide.

"That was God Almighty, not some cast-down spirit. This baby came from a union between you and Aidan, even if it was conceived the night he was under the influence of that thing. Have you not been with him since then?"

"Oh, aye. It was just the timing."

"I understand. Be happy, dear. Rejoice in the gift."

Caitlin stooped and kissed the shrunken old man on the cheek. "Gramercy. With whom are you having Sunday dinner?"

"Kieran and Miranda. Miranda wants to ask me about baptizing the babies. I think we should baptize them all next week. How does that suit you?"

"'Tis an excellent idea. You know, Kieran, Rennin, Declan, and Morgan were never baptized. They were born at sea before we came here."

"That, too, can be remedied. I shall see you next week, dear."

Caitlin took Aidan's arm. He asked, "What took so long?"

"I needed to get something clear in my head and my heart."

"About the baby?"

"Am I that see-through?"

"No, but I can count weeks, too. What did Reverend Devereaux tell you?"

"To rejoice in the gift. He said no matter when this child was conceived it was from you and the spirit had nothing to do with its soul."

"Does that mean I can announce the news?"

"Aye. By the way, did Colin tell you their news?"

"Of course. I think 'tis marvelous."

Not only were the older wiser women with child, but so were Morgan and Miranda. Duncan joked and asked Priscilla if she had been drinking the same water as the other women. She answered, "Aye, but, alas, I'm not Sarah, and you aren't Abraham."

Life settled into an easy routine. The next Sunday, Reverend Devereaux performed multiple baptisms, including the four adults. In the weeks that followed, the other communities built their own churches, following the example of King Satin's Realm. Then, they were faced with the dilemma of finding someone who could pastor the churches. Reverend Devereaux agreed to teach theology classes and to share what knowledge and wisdom he had acquired. Each township sent a young man to prepare for the ministry.

François Devereaux visited each of the young men in King Satin's Realm and asked them to join the classes. Declan refused, saying he had enough to study with the medical books from his grandfather. Rennin agreed to attend the classes because he wanted to learn, but laughed at the idea of ever replacing the old man. Kieran asked, "What's wrong with being the preacher, Rennin? The man is well-respected, and he's responsible for leading the hearts and minds of the people."

Rennin defended himself. "I never said 'twas anything wrong with it. 'Tis an honorable profession, but 'tis not what I want to do. You'd be better suited for that job, brother."

"I plan to attend the classes," stated Kieran. Thus, the reverend taught the classes two nights each week because all the young men had many other responsibilities as well.

Ricardo spent his days at Alexander's side, learning with Elizabeth all Alexander could teach them. The two often competed to see which one could master a spell or an herb mixture or potion first.

The late afternoons Ricardo often spent with Rennin, who proved to be an apt pupil. He quickly learned the scientific theories and studied all the maps Ricardo had at his disposal. He also learned to speak Spanish, which thrilled Ricardo because he could converse in his native tongue with someone. Rennin then learned French with the help of the reverend and Ricardo, since Ricardo also spoke French and Latin besides English and his native Spanish. Often Rennin took Morgan on the sloop and spent hours, even days sailing the waters of his home. He flew on Smoke less and less, and sailed in increasing hours.

Smoke commented on one of his and Rennin's excursions, "I'm losing you to the sea. I fear one day 'twill take you forever. What will I do without you, Rennin O'Rourke? You're my dearest friend."

Rennin rubbed the dragon's head. "Don't worry yourself, Smoke. No matter where I should roam, you'll always be in my heart, and I in yours."

Duncan and Aidan surveyed the growing community. Aidan commented, "Daddy, before long we'll need a school for all the children. We'll need a teacher, but whom would you ask to teach all these little ones?"

"I think Miranda would be perfect. She's even-tempered, intelligent, and gifted. I've watched her with the little ones. They seem drawn to her. I think we should start teaching right away."

"The children aren't old enough for formal education, Daddy."

"No, but there are other young ladies and gentlemen from the other towns who need to learn so they can in turn teach the children in their towns."

With great excitement, Miranda began to teach a number of other women about her age and two young men to read, write, and cipher. She declared she had never had so much fun. Kieran teased her, "Never?"

Refusing to be subdued, she countered, "At least not in a large group."

One of the young ladies that came to learn was a tall brunette with soft sable eyes and an olive complexion, the sixteen-year-old only daughter of Lars Willoughby. Jocelyn Brianne Willoughby was bright, articulate, and eager to learn. She often stayed later than the other students on the pretext that she had not finished her reading; when, in actuality, she usually finished far ahead of the rest. Realizing her small deception, Miranda confronted her. "Why do you pretend to be slow? You're by far the brightest pupil I have."

Jocelyn blushed all the way to the roots of her hair. "If I stay late, I can usually get young Dr. Fitzpatrick to take me home."

"I see. Jocelyn, if you're interested in Declan, don't pretend to be dumb. He'd much rather have a woman with a brain. He has had a lot of fun since all the young women have been restored, but he has found many of them insipid and tedious. He has confided in me he's looking for someone who's smart, emotionally strong, genuine, and even-tempered to counter his sometimes hotheadedness."

"How can I get his attention if I'm not here?"

"You're henceforth invited to supper tomorrow evening. I shall invite Declan, and the two of you can get to know each other without the games."

The supper was a delightful success. Jocelyn surprised Declan when he talked about the constellations and she found the ones he named. He walked slowly to the clearing to grab the dragon of the day to take Jocelyn home and did not return from Sierra Bluff until very late.

At midnight, Declan banged on Miranda's door. He was in a dither. "Why have you been hiding that girl?"

"What?" Miranda asked in a state of confusion. "You've taken her home several times."

"I've escorted someone home who looked like her, but that was a different girl, no woman. She's wonderful. I'm going to marry her. I spoke to Mr. Willoughby tonight."

"Declan, 'tis it not a little soon? Your rendezvous this evening was set up for the sole purpose of your getting to know the real Jocelyn. She and I planned it."

"Many good thankings. You're the best sister! We shan't marry tomorrow. I've agreed to court her for six months. She'll be seventeen then, and we'll marry." He hugged Miranda, "Good night."

Diggory and Colin spent their waking hours tending the fields for the whole township. The system of economy for Draconis was primarily a barter system since there was no form of currency. Diggory and Colin traded their melons, squash, and other fruits and vegetables for the corn, wheat, cotton, and slaughtered animals of Prairieville or the fish and other seafood from Waterford. Likewise they traded for the wool from the sheep and the beef and hides and meat from Sierra Bluff and nuts and other fruits and lumber from Wildwood. Isla Linda bartered with granite for building stronger structures.

Thus, the life on Draconis went day in and day out until the month that came to be known as the "Month of Delivery." Drake Fitzpatrick, the new Doctor Declan Fitzpatrick, Elizabeth Danaher, and Connor Donohue jaunted all over the two neighboring islands as babies were born left and right. Never again in Draconian history were there ever so many babies born so close together. Once again, Elizabeth rejoiced that three doctors had learned all she could teach them about the workings of a woman's body. Though powerful in magic, she had not learned to split herself.

Danielle started the month in King Satin's Realm. Remembering how long it had taken for the petite redhead to deliver Seamus, Drake sent Declan for his first solo delivery with explicit instructions to send for help if his patient had any complications. Drake flew to Sierra Bluff where two other women were delivering, and Elizabeth was in Waterford. Connor Donohue had taken residence on Isla Linda. Drake expected to have plenty of time to get back to Danielle, considering her history. History does not always repeat itself.

As with Seamus, Ricardo stayed by his wife's side. However, Danielle did not wait twenty-four hours to deliver the new infant. It took her only five hours before

Declan delivered his first baby, Richard Aidan Morales. Danielle gloated, "I told you 'twas a boy."

Over the next three years, Danielle gave Declan a great deal of practice delivering babies as she gave birth to two daughters, Leila Catherine Morales and Charlotte Leanne Morales. Over her jealousy, Danielle insisted the last baby be named after Charlotte Montgomery and her best friend, Caitlin.

A couple of weeks afterward, in the middle of lessons, Miranda dismissed her class. Jocelyn stayed to find whichever doctor was available. To Jocelyn's great joy, Declan was the only one in the village. Jocelyn stayed to assist her beau. Miranda did not have so easy a time as before. After twelve hours, Declan realized he was dealing with a complicated birth, but neither Elizabeth nor Drake had returned to the village.

With a great deal of trepidation, Declan told his adopted sister, "Miranda, this baby is breech. I need to turn him, but I have never done this before. I have seen Papaw do it only twice."

Unlike herself in the least, Miranda screamed at Declan, "Just do it! Turn the stubborn little devil and get him out!"

Kieran's jaw dropped and he winced as Miranda squeezed his hand. "Prithee turn the baby before you have to amputate my hand."

Miranda rolled her eyes at Kieran and screamed, "Shut up you selfish jackass before I truly break every bone in your hand."

Declan chuckled, "I hope Jocelyn will not be like this."

"I hope she's worse," grunted Miranda. "Now think about me instead of her."

Declan did what he had to do just as Drake walked in. Fifteen minutes later, Declan handed Miranda a little boy. "Here's your stubborn devil."

Miranda narrowed her eyes to slits at her doctor. "Don't ever call my son a devil, and his name is Alistair Sean O'Rourke."

Declan laughed loudly. "Papaw, take over here before I strangle Miranda. Are all women in labor this bad?"

Drake's eyes twinkled. "Before I got here, I delivered very few babies. It was unseemly for a man, so midwives did the work. Since I began more and more deliveries, I have discovered some aire worse; but, Declan, this is the best job ya will ever do as a physician. It brings joy and happiness." Drake laughed. "As a matter of fact, I only delivered two babies before I came to Draconis. When I told Lizzie the circumstances, ya would have thought I was the Devil himself."

Declan dipped an eyebrow. "What were those circumstances?"

"Yes, well." Drake cleared his throat. "The first, my professor paid a woman of ill repute to allow his students to attend and watch."

"A whore?" Declan shook his head in disbelief. "And the other?"

"I just happened to be the nearest person with any kind of training." Drake shrugged. "Draconis is a different world."

The two doctors had not washed their hands before Rennin knocked at the door. Drake said, "How close aire the pains and when did they start?"

Rennin smiled. "Morgan has been in labor all night. The contractions are very close. She's brave."

Drake laughed, "Declan, aire ya up for a calm delivery? Morgan barely even screams in pain, although she might break Rennin's hand."

"Good now, Papaw. Let's go"

When the men walked in, Morgan gripped the headboard and let out her controlled scream. Drake examined Morgan, "Well, little girl, start pushing. I wish all me deliveries were as easy as yers, but that might render me obsolete."

Three pushes and stifled screams brought forth Cameron David O'Rourke. Laughingly, Drake said, "I really do need some sleep now." He patted Declan on the shoulder. "If anyone else starts this tonight, ya aire on yer own, unless 'tis Mary Kate."

Before dawn streaked the sky, a harried Declan knocked at his grandfather's door. "'Tis Momma. Nana is with her already, but she's very worried. Papaw, so am I. Momma's already weak. The last two weeks she has had no energy, and she has hardly eaten a thing. Papaw, I'm afraid she could die."

Drake hugged his grandson. "We will do whatever it takes to keep yer mother with us. Next to yer sister, she is the bravest woman I have ever met. It must be an inherited trait that gets stronger with each generation."

Drake examined Mary Kate and consulted with Elizabeth. "What do ya think, Lizzie?"

"Drake, she's too weak to deliver a baby. Frankly, I'm surprised she has carried this child to term. I think we have no choice."

"All roight. Ya prepare the deadening herbs. I am going to give her a strong sedative. I think she should sleep through this."

With Mary Kate in a deep stupor, Drake performed the procedure he had watched Elizabeth do three times in the past month. Declan stayed to learn. Uneventfully Drake delivered Colin and Mary Kate a second set of twins. He chuckled, "What is it with this little woman and twins?" After the delivery he looked at Elizabeth. "Lizzie, do ya see the condition of Mary Kate's womb?" He whispered, "I have only seen wombs of dead women for I had an instructor who paid for cadavers."

Elizabeth stretched her eyes wide. "And I thought you would see this practice as barbaric."

Drake shook his head. "These babies aire truly miracles. She should never have been able to carry a child. Colin, if Mary Kate ever tries to have another baby, they will both die. I need yer permission to see to it that she never gets pregnant again."

"What aire ya gonna do, Da?"

"I am going to remove her womb. 'Tis too damaged to carry another baby." He grimaced. "I have never attempted this surgery."

"Do what must be done, but she will be very disappointed."

"She will deal with it just as she has dealt with all the other hard things in her life, with grace and dignity."

Colin sat with Mary Kate while she slept. He tried to think of the words to tell her part of her was missing and there would be no more miracles in their lives. Then he looked at his two little ones and knew his father was right. Mary Kate would accept her fate with dignity and grace. He kissed her gently and whispered, "I love ya, Mary Kate. Ya alone aire me miracle."

Mary Kate stirred at Colin's touch. Slowly, she opened her eyes. "Colin?"

"Good morrow, love. Did ya sleep well?"

"Wonderfully. Tell me about my baby."

"Well, love, ya did it again. Ya had twins, one of each."

Mary Kate laughed. "Oh, it hurts to laugh. Why does it hurt so much this time?"

Colin took Mary Kate's hand. "Honey, Da had to do more extensive surgery this time. He had to take yer womb. Ya know Lizzie thought ya would never be able to have another baby because of the damage from the procedure she did. After having it done twice, there was too much damage to risk yer trying to carry another child."

Mary Kate was quiet. She pressed the heels of her hands to her eyes to keep from crying. "I see. Colin, we have four of our own, plus Miranda. Are you satisfied with that?"

"Mary Kate, I was satisfied with two. I am overjoyed with our new miracles, but as long as I have ya, I am happy. Lady, ya aire me miracle." Colin kissed Mary Kate's fingers.

"Then you don't see me as less than whole?"

Colin laughed. "Ya aire the same sweet, unspoiled, compassionate, loving woman I fell in love with. Mary Kate I love the person ya aire, not yer parts. The fact that ya aire absolutely beautiful is icing on me cake."

Mary Kate squeezed Colin's hand. "Will I be able to nurse the babies?"

"Aye, but ya must stay in bed for the first two weeks. Elizabeth and I will be here to help."

"Colin, we need names. I want to name them for Momma and Papa."

"'Tis fine with me. Diggory and Elizabeth aire downstairs. Would ya loike me to ask them to come up for the official naming?"

"I would love that, and a glass of water."

As he started out the door, Colin said, "Water, aye, but Da said only soup for a few days."

Diggory and Elizabeth tiptoed into the bedroom as Colin brought Mary Kate chicken broth and tea.

Mary Kate cheerily said, "Come in." She tried to pull herself up. "Papa, help me." Diggory pulled Mary Kate to a half sitting position and propped pillows behind her back.

"Momma, I want my babies."

When Elizabeth disturbed the little ones, they proved their lungs were healthy. Mary Kate nursed the fussy babies, and they hushed their crying. The gentle mother spoke softly. "Momma and Papa, I want to name these two after you, Diggory Logan Fitzpatrick and Elizabeth Diana

Fitzpatrick. Now I would like to rest for a while. Papa, will you sit with me? Colin needs to rest somewhere else for a few days, and I need you to stay with me for a while."

Everyone left Mary Kate to rest except her father. "Baby, what is wrong?"

"Papa,"—Mary Kate's voice caught—"Papa, they took a part of me without asking. I understand the medical reasons, but they should've asked me. They should've at least prepared me for the possibility." Diggory sat beside Mary Kate and let her cry out her anger onto his shoulder.

"Do ya feel better now, baby?"

"Aye. Papa, promise me you won't leave me for a long time."

"I shall go when ya tell me."

"'Tis not what I mean. Don't die anytime soon."

"Baby, I will stay until God calls me home. I canna promise ya even tomorrow."

"I know, Papa, but will you promise to spend more time with me?"

"*That* I promise. I love ya, baby."

"I love you, too, Papa."

In her usual style, Caitlin made a grand entrance when, after being two weeks late delivering, her Water broke in the middle of church. Aidan carried his embarrassed wife home. Drake followed closely behind with Declan in tow.

Aidan asked, "Is this one going to come as fast as Ginny?"

Drake told Declan to go to work and that he would observe. "After all, soon ya will be taking over me practice completely."

Caitlin said, "What will you do, Da?"

Drake chuckled. "I am retiring to become a fulltime grandfather."

Declan declared, "Aunt Caitlin, I don't think this one is in as big a hurry as Ginny was."

Caitlin joked, "Because 'tis a boy."

After another three hours, Caitlin stopped joking and went into serious labor. "Aidan, I have never called you ugly names when delivering, unlike some women I know, but I swear if you ever do this to me again, I'm sending you to live somewhere else."

Taking Caitlin in stride, Aidan said, "You don't mean that. You love me too much."

"Cocksure, today, are you?" Caitlin retaliated.

"Aye, ma'am. We fight too well and make up even better to be apart."

Declan laughed loudly. "Are you two always like this?"

"You had better believe it," laughed Aidan. "Our life is never boring. Caitlin, you're breaking my fingers."

"'Tis not what I'd like to break right now."

"Then we could not make up, darling."

"I do like the making up part, but, Declan, can you do something to Aidan like they do to horses so I don't have to do this part again?"

Declan laughed hard. "Aunt Caitlin, Uncle Aidan isn't a horse."

"I refuse to be a talking animal," quipped Aidan as he kissed Caitlin's forehead.

Caitlin kissed Aidan fully on the mouth. "We shall make up in a few weeks."

"'Tis an appointment I shall be glad to keep."

Declan grew more serious. "Aunt Caitlin, have you ever delivered one arse first?"

"No."

"Well, this one is coming arse first, and 'tis definitely a boy."

"Well, turn him around."

"'Tis too late. Push!"

With Declan doing a little maneuvering, Shannon Michael O'Rourke actually came out feet first, and Caitlin always told him he came out with his feet moving to his own drummer.

With a slew of new babies and only a few women in the early stages of pregnancy, Declan and Jocelyn planned their wedding. It was a gala affair and the first wedding Reverend Devereaux performed in the little church of King Satin's Realm.

The bride wore a dress with flounces and flounces of ruffles and lace, and the ceremony was decorous with no surprises or deviations, save that Declan dipped Jocelyn when he kissed her. At the reception that followed, Lars Willoughby took his new son-in-law to the side and reminded him, "I don't care whose son you are; you had best remember I was once a wolf, as was Jocelyn. I can be extremely vicious. If you do anything to hurt, harm, or make my only daughter unhappy, you'll discover how vicious. I do believe, however, you'll do everything in your power to make her happy because I think you do love her. I know she adores you."

Declan sidled up beside his own father. "Da, why are fathers so protective of their daughters. Do sons not matter?"

Colin glanced at his son. "Lars threatened ya with bodily harm, did he?"

Declan nodded. "I would never deliberately hurt Jocelyn, but even you and Mam have had disagreements over the years."

"Lars was not talking aboot arguing. He meant things such as hitting her or infidelity. When ya have a little girl, ya will understand, but, aye, sons matter. Ya aire me pride and joy." Colin hugged his son. "I love ya Declan. Ya aire a fine man."

After a time of celebrating, once again Draco flew another newlywed couple to the honeymoon suite. The difference with this couple was both were completely innocent. Their wedding night was new, exciting and frightening at the same time, and well worth the wait.

Not all life was happy on Draconis. As is true in all of life there was sadness and loss. Reverend Devereaux lived only a year after his first wedding. When on Sunday morning he did not come to the church, Aidan went back to Alexander's house to find the old man sitting at his desk with his Bible and his notes for the day's message spread in front of him. He had simply stopped breathing.

Kieran filled the pastor's shoes admirably. He told Rennin, "I love this. Knowing even after the evil things I've done I've been forgiven, makes me want everyone to know the same thing."

"I feel wonderful about the fact, too, but I don't think I could be responsible for all the other people. I'm happy you've found something you love."

"Rennin, what do you want to do?"

"Kieran, I want to see the world."

"You want to leave Draconis?"

"Kieran, don't say anything to Mam and Daddy. I haven't decided exactly what I'm going to do. I'm afraid of leaving the security I have here, too, but there's this voice that calls me to come see the world."

"How does Morgan feel about it?"

"Morgan says she will follow me to the end of the world. I know 'twould be hard for her. Kieran, I just don't know yet." He sighed. "I have to think and pray some more."

Elizabeth was pruning her roses when her daughter walked up the path. Mary Kate and Diggory had spent several hours together every day since little Diggory and Elizabeth had been born. Some days she brought the babies. Others, she came alone. This day she was alone. Mary Kate greeted her mother with a hug and a kiss. "Momma, the roses are gorgeous. They smell so good. Where's Papa?"

"He came from the field a little early and said he wanted to take a short nap before you came today. He got a glass of lemonade and lay on the davenport. I have two bushes to go. Go on inside and pour us some lemonade. I shall be there shortly."

Mary Kate scampered into the living room where she saw her father lying on the couch. "Papa, is the lemonade sweet or sour?"

Diggory did not answer. "Papa?" As Mary Kate walked around the couch she saw the glass on the floor in a puddle of lemonade. Diggory's hand hung limply over the spilled glass. Mary Kate touched the gentle loving hand. "Papa?"

Sitting on the floor beside her father, she cried softly. "Papa, you can't leave me this soon. I need you."

Elizabeth came humming through the door with a bunch of fresh clipped roses to brighten her table. She saw Mary Kate sitting on the floor with her head on her knees. "Mary Kate, what's wrong?"

Through strangled tears, she said, "He's dead, Momma."

Elizabeth dropped her roses. "No, he's not. He sleeps."

Mary Kate shook her head. "No, Momma. He has gone Home. He said he was tired yesterday when Aidan was here. We didn't realize how tired he was."

Elizabeth collapsed into a weeping heap. She sobbed, "Mary Kate, pray and bring him back."

The daughter put her arms around her mother. "No, Momma. Papa would not want that. He would say, 'Sometimes ya have to let people go, no matter how much ya love them.' Momma, go lie down. I'm going to get Aidan. He's the only man home right now."

"Mary Kate, what will I do without my love?"

"We'll get through this together."

Elizabeth walked slowly up her stairs as Mary Kate went to Aidan's house. Aidan opened the door. "Why are you back so soon? Have you decided to take the children?"

The tears fell unbidden. "Aidan, 'tis Papa."

Aidan shook his head. "No. Not Diggory. Mary Kate, we have to find Declan or Drake."

"'Tis too late, Aidan."

"No!" Aidan ran all the way to the house down the lane without notice of other white-washed houses or stone cottages or attention to fragrant flowers or chirping birds or chattering squirrels.

Caitlin came to the door from the other room. "Mary Kate, what's the matter?"

"Papa's dead, Caitlin."

Caitlin gathered her friend into her arms and let her cry while Aidan held the man who had loved him like a son and sobbed in sorrow at his loss.

63
Good-bye Is Forever

All Draconis mourned the loss of the man who had brought the Promised One to their shores. He had been a legend in his own right, and he would be greatly missed. After the funeral service, all the families of King Satin's Realm gathered to remember their friend and loved one's life. They laughed and cried as they shared stories of the man they had all loved. Duncan shared stories of Diggory and the sea. Aidan remembered how Diggory had taken him in and loved him. Priscilla retold her version of the story of finding the "three biggest rats ye done ever seen."

Aidan ended by raising a glass of Diggory's hidden Irish whiskey in a toast. "With this never well-hidden whiskey, I salute my dear friend and mentor. In this case, good-bye will not be forever, for we shall meet again. Diggory, we love you."

Four years after Rennin began his lessons with Ricardo, he was still on Draconis. Ricardo remarked, "I was wrong about you, Rennin. I thought you would be leaving us."

"I am. I couldn't bring myself to leave right after Diggory died. Daddy and Aunt Mary Kate were heartbroken enough at the time. Besides, if I'd left then, I wouldn't have been able to see your brood. Sorry, Ricardo. You didn't get a single auburn-haired little girl."

"Alas. Mayhap they will not have their mother's temper either."

"Don't count on it." Rennin smirked. "I've been told not all redheads have tempers and that Spaniards are hot-tempered."

Ricardo laughed. "You said you are leaving. When?"

"I need to get the sloop ready for a long voyage. I'd thought about taking *The Privileged Character*, but since no one else seems to want to go, the smaller vessel would be more practical. Besides, I suppose *The Privileged Character* is home. The magical dry dock and other enchantments will protect her forever."

"Have you talked to your father yet?"

"No. I must admit I'm reluctant to speak to him. He'll not want me to go."

"No, he will not, but he will let you follow your heart."

Rennin knocked on Aidan's door. Ginny let him in. Rennin asked, "Where's Daddy, pee mite?"

"At Uncle Colin's. They're finishing the cradle for Jocelyn. Her baby will be here soon."

"I know. Where's my hug? Have I done something to anger you?"

"No, but I'm getting to be a big girl. I'm five years old."

"I never thought the day would come when you'd be too old to give your big brother a hug." Rennin shrugged. "Alas. Mayhap I shall have to find some other little girl to give me hugs. Peradventure Martha or Elizabeth will not be too big."

"I'm not that big yet." Ginny hugged her brother tightly. Rennin held her a moment longer than usual. He sighed, "I'll miss your hugs."

"Why?"

"I shall tell you another time. Right now I need to talk to Daddy."

Rennin walked across the way to his uncle's house where he found the two men admiring their handiwork. "It looks great." The younger man made his presence known.

"Uncle Colin, are you ready to feel even older with another grandchild?"

"Aire ya trying to tell me something?" asked Colin.

"No. I was talking about Declan and Jocelyn this time. Forsooth, I came to steal Daddy for a while."

"What's on your mind, son?"

"How about going out on the sloop with me?"

Aidan looked at Colin who grimaced. Aidan sighed, "I suppose the hammer's about to fall."

Rennin and Aidan climbed aboard Char and flew to the harbor. They did not talk until the small ship was sailing along smoothly. Finally, Aidan said, "When are you planning to leave?"

Astonished, Rennin said, "How did you know?"

"You've always had the wanderlust. I'm surprised it's taken you this long."

"The time was not right. I thought you'd try to convince me to stay."

"Rennin, I don't want you to go. I'm afraid I'll never see you again, but I know you must follow your heart, just as I did when I came here. I don't know how I can ever let you leave. You'll take a piece of my heart with you, a piece that can never be replaced even if your mother and I have a dozen children. You're my daredevil, my wild child. You're my Rennin. I love you with all my heart."

"I love you, too, Daddy, but you'll always be in my heart, no matter how far I roam."

"Your mother may not be so understanding." He adjusted a rope. "Have you considered your aunt and uncle?"

"Aye, but Morgan's my wife. We're a family. My family goes with me. I shan't go alone, Daddy."

"Of course not. A part of me would like to load *The Privileged Character* and go with you."

"So do it."

"I can't, Rennin. I've had my adventures. Now I have my responsibilities. What about your brother?"

"No, Daddy, Kieran's happy with his life. So is Declan." He rolled his lips together. "'Tis not I'm unhappy. I just want more."

Aidan stared a long moment at the aqua-marine waves. He watched schools of fish dart just beneath the sea's surface. "I understand." He put his hand on his son's shoulder. "For me, Draconis was more. You're just like your grandfather and me. You have the need to explore, to do and see all you can."

"'Tis what Granddaddy told me years ago. He said I would conquer new worlds. I didn't understand then. Now, I do."

"When do you plan to leave?"

"When we can get everything ready. We plan to take the sloop. It'll be big enough for us to handle. Morgan wants to wait until Declan's baby's born."

"You should wait at least six months so you can avoid the storm season. The storms can be rough."

"I shall take all the advice I can get."

"I shall give you the maps we made."

"Many good thanks, Daddy."

Caitlin was livid at Rennin for weeks. He came to visit her to smooth the wrinkles in their relationship. "Momma, you must understand. You followed Daddy."

"Rennin, you're my baby. Do you know what a hard thing you ask of me?"

"No more than you demanded of Memaw and Papaw when you sneaked away. At least I'm giving you the opportunity to say 'good-bye.'"

"I will never say good-bye. Good-bye is forever."

"Momma."

"'Tis 'Momma' when you want to butter me up, but 'Mam' when you get your way."

Rennin sat on the floor by his mother's chair and laid his head on her lap the way he had always wanted to do when he had been a naughty little boy, but Caitlin had been a tigress. "Momma, you'll always be my momma, and I'll always be your little boy. It doesn't matter where we live or how far apart we are. We'll see each other again, too, whether 'tis here or in Heaven. I promise to come back someday."

Caitlin caressed her son's head the way she had so wanted to do when he was a child. "When you were little you would lie beside me, and I would lick your head. I wager you'll not meet anyone out there who had a tigress for a mother."

"You've been the best mother I ever could've wanted with the exception of the time I thought you were going to kill me."

"Rennin Drake O'Rourke, you're just plain bad. You know I never would've killed you. I love you too much."

"I love you too, Mam."

"See. You got your way. Now 'tis 'Mam.'"

Aidan spent his days helping Rennin get the sloop ready for a long voyage. Every barnacle scraped broke his heart.

Colin helped some days, but he also spent many hours helping Morgan gather the stores they would need. Colin had been almost as angry as Caitlin. Mary Kate took the situation in stride. It seemed to her Morgan had never been her child. She had always been with somebody else. She had had her less than two years before Quazel took her and then only a few months before Rennin married her.

Mary Kate and Colin also had an exciting event to fill the days. Declan and Jocelyn blessed the island with Quentin Colin Fitzpatrick. Miranda laughed when she heard Jocelyn had let loose a string of profanities and obscenities aimed toward her husband while she was in labor and had questioned Declan's parentage during the delivery. "I told you she would be worse than I was."

The whole community prepared for Rennin and Morgan to leave, sadly, but staunchly. Smoke wailed he would not have a human. Rennin decided to cure that ailment. "Smoke, when I leave, I want you to take care of Kieran. Remember he's my twin brother. 'Tis very special. Papaw says when two people are identical twins, that means they were once one that divided into two. So, Kieran's really a part of me and I, a part of him. If you take care of him, you'll still be taking care of me."

Smoke and Kieran agreed to the arrangement.

As the day for Rennin's departure neared, Ricardo took him to Alexander's Cavern. "I have something I want to give you. Kieran and Miranda will never leave here, so, as my son-in-law's brother, I want you to have these things. I would have destroyed them, but Danielle said they might come in handy one day. She had tremendous foresight."

Ricardo opened the chest. "I have decided to give a jewel to each dragon, but the rest are yours. You can sell them if you need money. I also am signing over my ownership of these business ventures to you. If you discover they have failed, destroy the papers and let the thieves who took them from me suffer the loss. However, if they are successful, claim them as your own. These documents prove my ownership, and I give them to you. If you have them, then I will be vindicated and some justice for my mistreatment will have been served."

"Ricardo, what about your other children?"

"There will come a time when Draconis will no longer be visible to ordinary men, mayhap to a few exceptional men, but not ordinary men. Rennin, when you leave, you might not be able to return, though I think you are an exceptional man. Methinks my children are destined to be a part of this mystical land always. Prithee accept my gift."

"Many thanks. Verily, you have made me a wealthy man."

"Rennin, in the world where you are going, wealth is power. I want you to be self-sufficient out there, depending on no man. Be wary out there. Many men have dark hearts. There are those with good hearts, too, but be discerning. Pray about *everything*. God will give you discernment."

"Gramercy, Ricardo, for everything. I'm proud to call you 'friend.'"

"As I am proud to call you 'friend.' Because you are my friend, I also will ask you to deliver a letter to my father. I would like him to know I am safe and happy. Will you do this thing for me?"

"You know I will." Ricardo handed Rennin a thick, folded bundle of papers.

The day of departure arrived. The weather was perfect for sailing. Family and friends gathered on the beach to say good-bye. Hugs and kisses abounded. Colin and Mary Kate smothered their daughter and their grandchildren with hugs. Colin embraced Rennin, "Take care of my little girl."

"With my life, Uncle Colin."

Kieran held on to Rennin longer than the little brother and sister had. "I feel as if a part of me is dying."

"No, Kieran. Our lives will always be bound together. I'll know if something happens to you, as you'll know if something happens to me. I love you."

"I love you, too."

"Remember, to take care of Smoke."

Kieran nodded and Smoke wailed, great dragon tears streaming from his eyes, sending hisses and steam as they fell to the ground. Rennin kissed the huge beast on the nose. "You take care of my brother."

Smoke sniffled, "I pledge it unto you."

Caitlin clung to her son. She could not speak for fear of losing control of her emotions. Duncan held Rennin and Morgan together. "Go and conquer your worlds. I love you."

Aidan kissed his two grandsons and held Morgan tightly. "My angel, remember your promise to God."

"I shall, Uncle Aidan. I love you so. 'Tis hard to leave."

"Go."

Morgan took the boys on board.

Rennin held onto his father. "Oh, Daddy. I shall to miss you so much. Am I a fool?"

"No," sobbed Aidan. "You're an adventurer, but, oh, how can I let you go?"

"Our hearts will always be bound together."

Aidan held Rennin again. "I'm so proud of you. Heart of my heart, life of my life, blood of my blood, I love this man with all of my being. I will love you until the day I die."

"I love you, too, Daddy, with all my heart."

Rennin boarded the sloop and cast off. His friends and family waved until the ship was far out to sea. Then, they slowly started home except for Caitlin and Aidan. They watched until the ship disappeared over the horizon. Aidan murmured, "Heart of my heart, I will love you until the day I die." He put his arm around Caitlin as they started home to the rest of their family, and they lived to a ripe old age. But hearing a slight chuckle, Aidan turned back to see a shadow following the ship. "It can't be," he muttered. And then, the sloop was gone.

Rennin and Morgan sailed away into a new life. They had promises to keep and worlds to conquer, but that is another story.

THE O'ROURKE FAMILY TREE

{Quazel Morales-Rodriguez}--Alexander O'Rourke---Genevieve Brady

Diggory Danaher---Elizabeth Gilhooley   Duncan Sean O'Rourke----Priscilla Cecelia Callahan

Colin Fitzpatrick---Mary Kate Murphy   Aidan Duncan O'Rourke---Caitlin Leann Fitzpatrick

Jocelyn Brianne Willoughby---Declan Quentin Fitzpatrick   Kieran Sean O'Rourke---Miranda Montgomery

Quentin Colin Fitzpatrick   Martha Nadine O'Rourke / Alistair Sean O'Rourke

Rennin Drake O'Rourke---Morgan Celeste Fitzpatrick   Rennin Drake O'Rourke---Morgan Celeste Fitzpatrick

Donovan Alexander O'Rourke / Cameron David O'Rourke   Donovan Alexander O'Rourke / Cameron David O'Rourke

Diggory Logan Fitzpatrick / Elizabeth Diana Fitzpatrick   Genevieve Marie O'Rourke / Shannon Michael O'Rourke

{Charlotte Montgomery}--Ricardo Manuel Morales-Mendez---Danielle Martin--{Seamus O'Donnell}

Miranda Montgomery---Kieran Sean O'Rourke   Seamus Manuel Morales

Richard Aidan Morales / Leila Catherine Morales / Charlotte Leanne Morales

August 12, 2000

Epilogue
(About two hundred fifty years later)

The young man with the dark brown hair and lively green eyes arranged flowers on the two graves, one of which had been there quite some time and one with freshly turned earth. He removed his hat and spoke to the departed.

"Father, I'm going now. I shall never forget the things you taught me. The girls will all still be here to see to matters. I shall probably come back someday, but I must go. It's as you said. I have the wanderlust."

Outside the cemetery gate six ladies waited for the young man. They took turns hugging him. The eldest, a tall red-haired woman spoke a warning. "Rennin, you be careful with those two men. I have my doubts about that Bart, and I don't trust that Pierre at all. Sleep with one eye open. That one would slit your throat in your sleep. I wish you would wait and find better traveling companions."

The young man laughed lightheartedly. "You worry too much, big sister. Seriously, Caitlin, keep me in your prayers, but I must go now. The gold in California won't be there forever."

Caitlin argued, "It's not as if you need the money. We have plenty."

"No," said Rennin. "I want the adventure. I just know there's something wonderful waiting for me out there."

"If you live to find it."

"I will," Rennin assured his sister, "and I shall bring it home for you to see. Who knows? Perhaps it's that special lady you keep trying to find me."

Rennin hugged his big sisters once again and climbed on his horse. He and his two traveling companions rode west.

Janet Taylor-Perry , B.S., M.A.T.
Author, Editor, Educator

Like many of her characters, Janet is a history buff and loves anything of historical significance from old cars to old cemeteries. Get to know Janet and you'll see why she's been critically acclaimed at the Faulkner Wisdom Competition and why her writing continues to receive 4 and 5-star reviews, as well as placing in the top 10 Mississippi reads—It could be that readers see so much of her in her characters: mother, educator, author, editor, and a person who has overcome great obstacles and still holds on to her faith.

http://www.janettaylorperry.com/
http://janettaylor-perry.blogspot.com/
https://authorcentral.amazon.com/gp/profile
https://www.facebook.com/Author-Janet-Taylor-Perry-299698950061301/
janettaylorperry@gmail.com

Spirits' Desire

The Legend of Draconis

Draconis Calls the Heart in

Book II

The lust for adventure leads Rennin O'Rourke to read the memoirs of his ancestor and namesake as he shares parallel exploits. His quest brings him to his wife, the California gold fields, close encounters with death, a murder charge, The War Between the States, and ultimately back to a mythical land where only exceptional people may go.

Rennin meets Rebekah Sinclair, and the two of them embark on a lifetime of love and adventure as both are constantly compelled to return to a mythical place they have only read about. Draconis calls them home.

Made in the USA
San Bernardino, CA
17 April 2016